There was a lot of terrified screaming and bawling from those around Jerry, but he felt Ingrid against him, took courage from her presence, and opened his stinging eyes as the exploding, swirling light contracted and dimmed, shrinking down to the height of the average man, and eventually formed a faintly glowing cocoon of ectoplasm in which two apparently human figures were slowly, magically materializing.

That glowing ectoplasm illuminated the sarcophagus – and there, on either side of the empty stone coffin, shimmering in an unreal manner with faint stars showing through them, were the silvery-haired gentleman, Saint-Germain, and his mysterious partner.

They were both wearing snow-white *galabiyehs* and staring, with faintly sinister but oddly seductive smiles, directly at Jerry and Ingrid.

'You cannot have the Lodestone,' Saint-Germain said, his voice ethereal and unreal in the glowing darkness. 'To pursue it will damn you . . .'

THE LODESTONE

Allen Harbinson

SPHERE BOOKS LIMITED

SPHERE BOOKS LTD

Published by the Penguin Group
27 Wrights Lane, London W8 5TZ, England
Viking Penguin Inc., 40 West 23rd Street, New York, New York 10010, USA
Penguin Books Australia Ltd, Ringwood, Victoria, Australia
Penguin Books Canada Ltd, 2801 John Street, Markham, Ontario, Canada L3R 1B4
Penguin Books (NZ) Ltd, 182–190 Wairau Road, Auckland 10, New Zealand

Penguin Books Ltd, Registered Offices: Harmondsworth, Middlesex, England

First published in Great Britain by Sphere Books Ltd 1989
Copyright © Allen Harbinson 1989

Made and printed in Great Britain by
Richard Clay Ltd, Bungay, Suffolk
Filmset in Monophoto Ehrhardt

For Art and Anne
Who have been there and back

CONTENTS

PROLOGUE

Escaping the February freeze of Park Avenue, New York, and entering the brightly lit, warm splendour of the Waldorf Astoria, the man travelling under the name of Christian Grabbe, which was but one of his many pseudonyms, felt instantly at home – and certainly looked it. Wearing an immaculately tailored Savile Row grey suit, with a Harvie and Hudson design striped shirt and matching tie, and hand-made shoes from John Lobb of St James's Street, London, the man was slim, elegant and powerfully attractive in a very odd manner.

Standing momentarily beneath the glittering chandeliers, and glancing quickly around the great lobby with his wintry-grey, almost silvery eyes, he was not unaware of the fact that more than one of the ladies seated beside the high pillars and under the potted plants had, while subconsciously adjusting their Arnold Scaasi evening dresses and Tiffany jewellery, turned their heads to stare at him with a combination of instinctive fear and helpless longing.

He stared back at some of them, offering a dangerously seductive smile which, combined with his oddly mesmeric gaze, caused most of the ladies to breathe far too deeply, before blushing and lowering their eyes again.

Having thus amused himself, and seeing no potential threat in the Waldorf's busy lobby, the pseudonymous Mr Grabbe checked his Rolex wristwatch, noted that he was on time, then purposefully crossed the lobby and took the elevator up, his presence in that enclosed space making the other passengers uneasy, some actually heaving a sigh of relief, without quite knowing why, when he stepped out at the twenty-fourth floor.

He checked the corridor automatically, very quickly, missing nothing, then walked to the door that had the number he had been given over the telephone.

His silvery-grey eyes were calm, his stance languid, as he rang on the bell.

The man who opened the door (very promptly, as Grabbe noted) was tall, broad, obviously not too bright, and wearing a black leather jacket, fawn trousers, check shirt with no tie, and rather tasteless brown suede shoes. He had a pugilist's scarred features, cold green eyes and lips too thin to smile properly.

'Grabbe?'

'Yes.'

'Come in,' the man said.

Grabbe stepped inside, heard the door close behind him, then saw two other men at the far side of the suite, near the window above Park Avenue, framing the skyline of New York, beside a table on which rested a small silver box which, Grabbe assumed, contained a hypodermic, some needles and a dose of the truth serum, Pentothal.

Grabbe glanced behind him. The big dummy who had let him in was resting with his back against the locked door, his right hand in a pocket which, by the look of it, contained some kind of small pistol. Grabbe smiled and turned back to the front.

'I'm Grabbe,' he announced.

One of the men was a fairly precise replica of the muscle-bound Neanderthal who had let Mr Grabbe into the suite — but this one with curling golden locks instead of the auburn head-stubble of the heavily breathing ape now guarding the door — and the other was a male creature as wide as he was tall, which was not very tall at all, with his potbelly bursting his waistcoat and threatening to burst his pinstripe suit, and with thyroid eyes blinking repeatedly behind rimless glasses which, as he continuously wiped sweat from his pale face with a handkerchief, kept slipping down his stubby nose.

'So,' this little man said, as if talking through his nostrils, 'you came.'

'Obviously,' Grabbe replied testily. 'You called, did you not?'

The little fat man blinked behind his rimless spectacles, wiped more sweat from his face with the already damp handkerchief, glanced once across the skyline in the direction of the Hudson River, then coughed into his free hand and managed to get his words out.

'So,' he asked, 'you have brought the Tuaoi Stone with you?'

'Perhaps,' Grabbe replied. 'Perhaps not. Do you wish to forcibly search me?'

The Neanderthal man quivered, opening and closing his brutish fists, but the little man simply wiped his face again and took another deep breath.

'Please,' he said. 'I cannot go back without it. And you *did* say you had it.'

'I was informed that you were looking for it,' Grabbe replied. 'That is why I am here.'

'You sound German,' the little man said.

'So do you, Mr Kleist. And the man who sent you here, that mysterious billionaire, is, I believe, also German.'

Mr Kleist, obviously startled, wiped yet more sweat from his moon-shaped pale face.

'How did you –?'

'One of the world's most mysterious and richest men,' Grabbe said, smiling icily. 'But known to you and I as Wilhelm Zweig . . . And he wants the Tuaoi

Stone. No doubt for no other reason than to add it to his collection of other masterpieces stolen from far and wide.'

The very small Mr Kleist, appearing to grow smaller, licked his lips and croaked fearfully, 'You should not know –'

'I do.'

'How?'

'That is not your concern. Just take it that I know how badly he wants the Tuaoi Stone – and that I've heard he'll do anything to get it.'

'Yes,' Mr Kleist stuttered, studying his soaked handkerchief and then, perhaps disgusted by his own nervous sweating, returning his gaze to the disturbingly attractive Mr Grabbe.

'So,' he said. 'You know how badly my superior wants it. And so . . . do you *have* it?'

'Perhaps. Perhaps not.'

'It is a lodestone. Basically a crystal. It is a very small pyramid. There can be no mistaking this object – and if you have it, you know it. So . . . *do* you have it?'

'And you will *pay* anything – or *do* anything – to obtain it?'

'Yes,' the roly-poly, sweating German said. 'Any-thing. *I cannot go back without it!*'

'In that case,' Grabbe said, smiling chillingly. 'I can give you nothing . . . Nothing but this.'

He raised his right hand and spread his fingers in the air just as the heavyweight behind him jerked a pistol from his pocket, the other thug moved towards him and the little man with the sweating face and stutter reached for the silver box on the table.

Ignoring the latter pair, Grabbe turned towards the man behind him, his hand still upraised, then closed his eyes and quivered visibly, as if jolted by a bolt of elec-tricity.

4

Even as the heavyweight by the door was raising his pistol to aim at Grabbe, a hot bright light filled the room – so bright it was almost blinding – and the man with the pistol cried out in panic, let his pistol fall to the floor, then was picked up and slammed backwards into the door as if hurled there by an invisible assailant.

He bounced off the door and was falling to the floor as the plaster began exploding from the wall around him to fill the air with fine powder.

'What?' Kleist shrieked. '*What –?*'

Jagged cracks were shooting out in all directions from the exploding plaster of the wall above the unconscious man as Grabbe, hearing Kleist's quavering words of fear, turned back to face him, his bright gaze terrifying.

'*Mein Gott!*' Kleist shrieked. '*Kill him!*'

Yet even as the panic-stricken little man was giving this command, the walls cracked and spat plaster, light bulbs burst and ornaments exploded, then the windows were blown inward by a sudden, fierce wind which immediately filled the room with flying glass and a hurricane's howling.

Grabbe was still standing in the middle of that maelstrom, his body silhouetted by the quickly fading light, the debris from the exploding walls whirling around him while Kleist and the thug beside him, both slashed by flying glass, bled profusely and screamed in pain, doubling over for protection, then were picked up, hurled against the wall, and fell to the floor.

At that moment, the wall around the shattered window exploded, as if blown apart by a hand grenade, and the roaring wind rushed back out, sucking Kleist and his thug through the large, jagged hole, to fall screaming to the pavement of Park Avenue, many storeys below.

A few minutes later, when the manager of the hotel

and some assistants burst into the room, they found nothing but one dead hoodlum in the drifting dust and debris of complete, inexplicable devastation.

They didn't find Christian Grabbe.

PART ONE

THE PURE AT HEART

CHAPTER ONE

In his large, untidy bedroom, the walls of which were plastered with photographs of UFOs, ghosts, poltergeist occurrences and other unusual phenomena, Jerry was completing the packing of the large suitcase resting on a bed littered with computer diskettes, cassette tapes, CDs of classical and rock music, and a daunting pile of heavy hardcover books, most of which he had wanted to take with him for light reading but simply couldn't fit into his suitcase.

The true squalor of the room could not be seen since the curtains had been pulled across and the lights dimmed to enable Jerry to watch more clearly, as he packed, the TV screen's blurred image of a great gaping hole on the twenty-fourth floor wall of the Waldorf Astoria Hotel on Park Avenue, while a voiceover explained that a very bad explosion, the causes of which were unknown, had devastated a suite on that floor, killing the three male residents, one of whom had died in the actual explosion, the other two being blown out of the suite and crashing to their deaths on the pavement of Park Avenue.

'Oh, boy!' Jerry exclaimed.

When the grainy image of the large jagged hole in the wall of the great hotel had faded from the screen and the newscaster had reappeared to explain that so far there was no 'logical explanation' for the explosion, Jerry switched the TV off and spent a few minutes tormenting himself with the realization that he would simply have to leave behind most of his truly heavyweight tomes and settle for his paperback editions of *In Search of Schrodinger's Cat: Quantum Physics and Reality*, Koestler's *The Ghost in the Machine*, Fodor's *Egypt* and Charles Fort's *The Book of the Damned*.

Feeling intellectually deprived, he closed the almost bursting suitcase, lifted it off the bed with difficulty, then opened the door of his room, took a deep breath and walked out.

What he walked into was the stunning main lounge of his very wealthy mother's luxurious suite on Central Park West, the panoramic windows overlooking the frozen lake in the park and the buildings of the East Side. The leaden sky's grey light was falling obliquely on white walls and rare paintings, and his mother was sitting in her favourite French Louis XV armchair, dressed in a sublimely understated Zoran pyjama-pants outfit in mottled grey, matching cashmere sweater and stylish evening slippers. She had a small glass of dry sherry on the Chippendale table by her side and was reading the collected works of Robert Frost, from which she was only distracted when Jerry dropped his heavy suitcase on the floor and lowered his shoulder bag.

'Did you see it?' he asked, and then, before waiting for an answer: 'No, you didn't. You were reading that book.'

That made her look up, thin face framed by silvery hair, pencilled eyebrows lifting sardonically over steady grey eyes.

'If *you* read books like this,' she said, 'instead of your awful rubbish, you might cease your adolescent behaviour and become a mature man.'

'Mature men are bores,' he replied. 'They don't see the real world.'

'Oh, God,' his mother said, 'not *that* again! Not that ridiculous Charles Fort theme.'

He wasn't about to fall for that old turkey, having heard it too often. Charles Fort was the eccentric author of one of the books he had just packed – *The Book of the Damned* – a notorious work on bizarre phenomena for which there is no logical explanation; and while it was true that Jerry had a fondness for Fort's work, he was in fact more interested in the serious study of UFOs, the paranormal, the occult and, especially, the realities behind the myths of antiquity.

'I'm *not* a Charles Fort freak,' he insisted to his mother, feeling that he was wasting his breath but compelled to try anyway. 'He's merely one of my many interests. I'm into unexplained phenomena in general, and that includes the occult and antiquities – which is, as you damned well know, why I'm going to Egypt.'

His mother offered a very familiar sigh of histrionic despair.

'At least you managed to carry on your father's interest in antiquities, even if distorting, with your infantile reasoning, everything you were taught.'

That one was below the belt. His father, Martin Sydney Remick, had been the Professor of Archeological Studies in the Antiquities Department of Harvard University; and Jerry, while not following in his footsteps, had certainly not distorted his teachings. He *had* sidetracked a little, but not all that much, and he knew that his father, a good-humoured man, would not really have minded.

'Just because I was thrown out of –'

'You were such a nice boy, once. So clean and well-dressed. I thought I would have a priest for a son, and then . . . I can't speak of it.'

She shuddered melodramatically, making it clear that what she could not discuss (but would) was the fact that since his father's death two years ago – a death that had shocked and hurt him much more than he could admit – he had changed from a shy kid with an obsessive interest in religious matters into a rebellious bright spark who had been expelled from his father's famed university for outrageous behaviour.

Clearly his mother had hoped that the dramatic change in him would pass away with time, but unfortunately such had not been the case. Formerly an intense young academic, he had become, instead, an oddball – odd at least in the sight of his mother, who even now was looking him up and down as if valuing merchandise.

'Can't you at least wear a suit,' she asked laconically, 'instead of those awful denims?'

'I *like* denims,' he replied, aware that he was shuffling his feet on the carpet like a nervous schoolboy. 'And besides, I'm not travelling first class. I want to meet the *real* people.'

'The riffraff, you mean. Like that trash you meet in SoHo. Living in overpriced lofts and admiring themselves. I don't know how you manage it.'

In fact, he didn't associate with the upwardly mobile in SoHo, but with the much more colourful denizens of Times Square and 42nd Street, having decided, with the death of his father, that wealth meant nothing to him.

While he was honest enough to accept that he had justifiably been dismissed from Harvard for what they had accurately described as 'habitual drunkenness, the possession of marijuana, and general behavioural patterns unacceptable to this fraternity', he was not about to forget that he was still pretty bright and not prepared to take crap from anyone.

'You once showed such promise,' his mother said wearily, as, picking up her glass of sherry, she stared balefully at him. '*Now* look at the state of you. Your father would turn in his grave if he could see what's become of you.'

Standing beside his suitcase, wondering how he could take his leave, he automatically gazed down at his own tatty denims and loafers, trying to figure out what made them so offensive. However, even as he did this, he realized that what his mother was talking about was *not* his appearance, but the manner in which his education was, in her opinion, being squandered.

'Mom,' he said, trying to sound determined, 'I've got to go now.'

'Of course, dear,' she replied. 'If you must, you must. I just wish you were going to research the pyramids properly, rather than this unsavoury pursuit of nonsensical theories.' She sighed, sipped her sherry, put the glass down again. 'Why can't you decide on a career and put your intelligence to some good use? I simply can't bear to see you go such a long way in pursuit of these ghosts of yours.'

'I'm *not* pursuing ghosts, Mom. I'm simply studying the more mysterious aspects of the Great Pyramid. It's reported to have certain magical properties, and I want to find out if that's true or not.'

'I say no more,' his mother replied. 'Every man to his hobby. I just wish you would concentrate for once on what to do with your future. I mean, what's all this *for*?'

'You want me to get married and settle down,' he offered by way of reply.

'Well, you *could* do with settling down a *little*.'

'I won't surrender my individuality to a *bourgeoise* living death.'

'Don't you like it here, dear?'

'I'm still here, aren't I, Mom?'

'I *do* wish you would call me "Mother",' she replied. 'I don't go well with apple pie.'

'Anyway,' he said stubbornly, 'before I leave I just want you to know that while you were reading that obsolete poetry, the news on TV was revealing that an inexplicable explosion – repeat: *inexplicable* – blew out the front wall of one of the suites in the Waldorf Astoria hotel *and* two of the three people sharing the suite. Those two fell to their deaths, many storeys below.'

'And the third one?' his mother asked in her practical manner.

He snapped his fingers at her. 'Also killed,' he said. 'They found him lying in the rubble of the room, which looked, as one observer put it, as if it had been torn apart by a tornado.'

'How unpleasant,' his mother said. 'But what's the point of this story?'

Jerry sighed with exasperation. 'The point, *Mother*, is that the explosion wasn't caused by a gas leak, by electrical malfunction, or by any kind of bomb or incendiary. In short, the explosion is completely inexplicable – and, even more mysterious, it didn't affect either of the adjoining rooms. So, whatever wrecked that room, it wasn't anything known to rational science.'

'I'm *sure* there is a rational explanation for it, dear. Almost certainly a gas leak. You know how antiquated the plumbing and wiring in some of these old hotels are – and how reluctant the management would be to admit it was their fault. The truth will be revealed in time, I'm certain, and my bet is a gas leak.'

'An explosion caused by a gas leak or electrical fault would *at least* have affected the adjoining rooms – and probably lots more. No, *Mother*, you can't wriggle out of this one: that explosion was as unnatural as anything found in the works of Charles Fort. I only wish I could stay to investigate it, but I've got to be going now.'

'I think that's best, dear. The air of Egypt should do

14

you good. It might even clear your head of all this nonsense, which would be a blessing. So, come and give me a goodbye kiss.'

Rolling his eyes, he crossed the room, leaned over and kissed her on the cheek.

'Okay,' he said, straightening up. 'I'll see you in four weeks. Look after yourself.'

'*You* look after yourself. Watch out for thieves and beggars. And *do* be careful of involvement with those foreign ladies. I believe they are not really –'

'Yes, Mother, I hear you.'

'And you have your passport and money?'

'Yes, Mother.'

'And you're certain you've packed everything you need?'

He sighed again, loving her, wanting to strangle her.

'Yes, Mother,' he said.

'Well, you *know* what you're like,' she said. 'All brains and no commonsense – hopeless at human relationships and life's little chores, such as dressing decently, conversing pleasantly, looking after your money . . . and packing a suitcase. You don't belong in the real world.'

'I'm not as inexperienced as you think,' he insisted. 'I can look after myself.'

'Oh, yes,' she said. '*Naturally.*'

At that moment the doorbell rang, and when Jerry raised his eyebrows enquiringly, his mother stood up and said, 'Well, *naturally*, darling, I arranged for the porter to carry your suitcase down.'

'Mom, it's only one suitcase!'

'That's what porters are for, dear. And what's he going to think if he sees my son carrying his own luggage? So don't be silly. Let him take your suitcase down and find you a cab.'

'God, Mom, you're such a *snob*!'

'We all have our place in life, dear, and you have yet to learn yours.'

Shaking his head in disgust, and wanting even more to get out of this *bourgeoise* mausoleum, he just stood there, brimming over with frustration, while his mother walked regally to the door of the apartment, opened it and pointed silently at the suitcase on the carpet.

The porter nodded and walked in, grinning as usual. He picked up the suitcase and said, 'On your way at last, are you, sir? You must be pretty excited.'

This sly reference to the fact that he had never before left the United States did not amuse Jerry, who simply glared at his mother while the porter picked up the suitcase and walked back out of the room. Jerry was about to follow him, but reluctantly turned back to his mother and let her kiss *him* on the cheek.

'I can *really* look after myself –' he began to say, but was cut off in mid-sentence when his mother, smiling brightly, said, 'I know, dear, but certain standards must be kept. Now have a good time, send me a card, and I'll see you in four weeks.'

Then, still smiling brightly, she closed the door in his face.

'The elevator's here, sir,' the porter said, sounding faintly amused.

Jerry took a deep breath, glanced along the corridor, then let his breath out in a loud sigh and walked up to the porter where he stood by the open door of the elevator. Ignoring him, Jerry walked into the lift, turned around to the front, and kept his face expressionless as the porter carried his suitcase in, then pressed the button to close the door and let them descend.

'So,' the porter said, leering sideways, 'your Mom tells me you're off to Egypt to see the pyramids. That's some trip to be making.'

'My mother talks too much,' Jerry responded as

frigidly as he could manage. 'But, yes, that's where I'm going – for research, of course.'

'Some research,' the porter replied, winking lewdly. 'I bet those Egyptian broads know how to shake it – and you'll be researching *them*, right?'

Jerry felt like shoving the porter's head through the meshed steel bars of the elevator and then shutting the door on it, but contented himself with the thought that the creep was a traitor to his own working class and should, instead of wearing that pansy uniform and tipping his cap to rich people, be out in the streets, encouraging the overthrow of capitalism by robbing banks and mugging Fifth Avenue shoppers.

Relieving his tension with this radical thought, he was even more relieved when the elevator glided to a stop, the door opened and he was able to follow the porter into the hallway of the ground floor, then through the swinging doors, onto the pavement of Central Park West where the porter, after considerable effort, managed to wave down a cab.

'Well, sir,' he said, opening the door for Jerry, 'have the time of your life.'

'I will, thank you very much.'

Suddenly ashamed of the manner in which, when angry, he would quickly adopt his mother's Anglified, glacial, very superior manner of speaking, he took a few coins from his jacket pocket and pressed them into the porter's sweaty palm. Then, before the bastard could count them and sneer, he slid into the cab, slammed the door and told the driver to take off.

Settling back into the seat, sighing with pleasure at the thought of what was to come, and contemplating the possibility of asking the driver to stop by the Waldorf Astoria to enable him to check the latest info on what had occurred there, he suddenly remembered that the coins he had pressed into the porter's hand had in fact been the last of his loose change. Immediately, without thinking, he leaned forward in his seat, tapped the window separating himself from the driver, and asked:

'Hey, Mac, do you take the American Express Gold Card?'

There was an instant squealing of brakes and the cab jerked to a sudden halt, throwing Jerry forward as the cab driver's face, monolithic and unsmiling, turned very menacingly in his direction.

Jerry immediately offered his most charming grin and spread his hands in a mock gesture of defence.

'Okay, pal,' he said. 'Just a joke! Now take me to Kennedy.'

The cab driver stared at him, lips pursed, eyes like stones, then took a deep breath, sort of *rolled* his broad shoulders, then turned back to the front, accelerated and raced along Central Park West, while Jerry, instead of thinking about the great adventure to come, wondered if the brute would accept his wristwatch in lieu of dollars and cents.

CHAPTER TWO

As she did much too often, Ingrid dreamed about brutal sex, about the violation of the female body, saw her father with his many women leering at her as he pawed them openly, then felt a great weight falling upon her as his laughter rang in her ears. She became a child again, retreating into warmer memories, saw her mother's glowing smile, then her tears, then her face in a coffin. Ingrid wept and was reprimanded, was beaten black and blue by her father, then turned back into a woman and was still being beaten and heard her own screams from far away, as if coming from someone else. She screamed again and then stopped, sobbed instead, started groaning, then dropped down through her pain into a well of despair – and was whimpering when she opened her eyes and escaped from the dream . . .

The morning light filled her room, beaming in through the window, falling obliquely on pine wardrobes, the grey carpet on varnished boards, the romantic novels piled on the low cupboard beside the bed, reflected off the mirror on the dressing table facing the window, back onto the crumpled white sheet over her body, where she lay gazing upward. She was thinking of her dream, one of many similar dreams, and silently saying her thanks that she hadn't cried out loud enough to be heard.

It was morning. Late morning. She had overslept on her last day. She yawned and sat upright, rubbed her eyes and blinked, then stared through the window at the placid, transparent, deep blue surface of Lake

Geneva, with the majestic snow-capped mountains to the south, the lush vineyards and pastures to the north, all under a white-clouded blue sky, turning silvery with sunlight.

She was tempted to make her way down to the shores of the lake, then board a boat and sail away; but she knew that her father's helicopter would come for her this morning, and that such an escape was therefore impossible. The thought of seeing him frightened her, but this sanatorium was worse, so she gritted her teeth, shook her head and slid out of the bed.

Still shaken by the realization that her screaming, if heard, could have had her incarcerated here again, she hurriedly disrobed and stepped into the shower, letting the icy water slap her awake. Refreshed, she stepped out, dried herself, then went to the mirror.

There were no bruises on her body, which was slim and well formed, but the woman staring at her was the one she had seen in her dream, being ravished and punished.

In her worst dreams, she always was.

Hearing her own sigh like a breeze from far away, she sat at the dressing table and examined her still naked body, not pleased with what she saw. She had been in this particular sanatorium for six months, and every time she looked in the mirror she was shocked by herself.

She was hazel-eyed, auburn-haired and quite pretty, but irremediably marred by melancholy and fear.

Closing her eyes, she recalled her latest nightmare, chilled by her understanding of what it meant, but not able to cure herself.

She thought of her rich and powerful father, a bull of a man at sixty-two, and burned with shame at recalling his behaviour with his various women. Ever since she could remember he had used those women to taunt her, deliberately pawing them and talking obscenely in her presence in order to shame and humiliate her. He had done it out of contempt for the memory of her mother, and in doing so had succeeded in breaking her like a twig in his huge hands.

Now, at thirty-one, still a virgin and extremely timid, after five years of being in and out of various sanatoriums, she knew exactly what she had become ... a woman defeated.

The nightmares, she knew, represented her fear of sex, as well as releasing the revulsion she felt for her father, since what she *suspected* he had done to her mother was worse, infinitely worse, than his crimes against her.

Opening her eyes again, she saw herself – a ghost in the mirror. She wanted to escape, to flee from this place *and* her father, but knew it was too late for that now, that she hadn't the will.

She was trapped by her fear of him.

Shivering, she proceeded to get dressed, then applied the minimum of make-up to her pale, frightened face. When she had done this, she carefully arranged her long auburn hair on her head, pinned it into place, put on her flat-heeled shoes, then glanced distractedly around her.

Apart from her many romantic novels, which she was leaving for the next patient, she had cleaned the room out completely in preparation for her departure; and her suitcase, packed tight but still open, was resting on the low wooden rack. Satisfied that she had done everything necessary, she removed the last of her things from the dressing table, divided them between a small zip bag and her leather shoulder bag, placed the zip bag in the suitcase, locked it, and then walked out.

This Swiss sanatorium was for only rich patients, and this particular wing, with private rooms and total freedom, was for those who were deemed to be recovered and preparing to leave. The rooms were comfortable, the corridors bright and covered in carpet, and as she walked in the direction of the manager's office, she glanced out through the panoramic, metal-framed windows and saw the boats cruising on a shimmering Lake Geneva, minute in the vast expanse of mountain and vineyard and pasture.

The very beauty of the place was a mockery to her sense of oppression.

Arriving at the closed door of the office of Madame Boullard, and thinking ruefully of how only a sanatorium for the very rich could blandly call its supervisor a *manager* (as if this clinic for the mentally disturbed was actually a hotel), she pressed the bell beside the door and then heard a female voice telling her to enter. She did so, closing the door behind her and walking across the broad expanse of luxurious carpet to where Madame Boullard was sitting behind her large desk, the panoramic window behind her again framing the lake and mountains, as well as overlooking the expansive lawns and, further back, the landing space where the richest of the very rich patients were usually brought in by private helicopter, well away from the public gaze.

Indeed, even as she stopped in front of the desk and glanced past the stern face of Madame Boullard at the green lawns and blue lake, she saw the sun reflecting off a helicopter which, though in the distance, was obviously heading straight for the sanatorium to take her on the first leg of her long journey back to her father – the thought of which merely deepened her fear and foreboding.

'*Bonjour*, Madame Boullard,' she said, turning her attention to the heavy-set, neatly dressed, grey-haired Frenchwoman who, with hands folded on the desk, was staring up sternly.

'*Bonjour*, Fräulein Zweig. I trust you slept well last night and are prepared for your journey?'

'*Oui, Madame*. I feel fine.'

Madame Boullard did not invite her to sit, but merely unfolded her fat hands, leaned back in her chair, and stared at her with a well-furrowed brow and pursed, disapproving lips.

'So,' she said, 'the time has come for your departure. I hope I am not making a mistake in recommending release.'

'*Non, Madame*, you are not.'

'You have been here for six months. Your behaviour has not been excellent. Nonetheless, with proper treatment and God's help, you have shown much improvement.'

'*Oui, Madame. Merci.*'

She felt awful saying it, despising her own cowardice, hating and fearing this woman as much as she did her father, recalling the tortures and punishments that the bitch had put her through, taking pleasure from the agony she bestowed in the name of a cure. In fact, when she looked directly at Madame Boullard's face, she almost choked with nausea.

'Your father is a rich and powerful man,' Madame Boullard said, 'and expects to get what he has paid for – which, in your case, I think he has. When you first came here, you were sick, a kleptomaniac, always weeping, the first being your immature plea for attention, the latter a manifestation of your refusal to accept the adult world. I think you now know better. You have accepted the inevitable. The anger and fear that motivated you, the frequent nightmares you suffered, were all caused by resentment at the very privileges which your father could give you. That anger and fear has been removed, thus dispelling your nightmares and, in learning to respect your father, you have hopefully also learned to respect yourself. I hope you are grateful, Fräulein Zweig –'

'*Oui.*'

'– and will not disappoint your father or myself by abusing your freedom.'

'*Non, Madame.* I will not.'

Aware of how close she had come to giving away the fact that her nightmares were still tormenting her, but pleased that she had been able to hide that fact for so long, she glanced out the window, watched the helicopter approaching, and was only distracted from it when Madame Boullard stood up, looked back over her own shoulder, then walked around the desk.

'So,' she said, 'the helicopter has arrived. You have packed your things?'

'*Oui, Madame.*'

'Excellent. I will have the porter sent to your room to collect your suitcase. When he collects it, please follow him to the helipad – and leave your room unlocked.'

'*Oui, Madame* – and thank you.'

She was just about to hurry out of the office when Madame Boullard's voice, softly malicious and precise, made her stop on the spot.

'It is strange, is it not, that your father has not visited you once during the whole of your six months in this establishment?'

Ingrid bowed her head to hide her burning cheeks and humiliation.

'He is a very busy man, *Madame.*'

'Apparently so,' the old bitch replied. 'He certainly has an extraordinary reputation – controversial, in fact.'

'Controversial, *Madame?*'

'Is it not true that he has been described as one of the richest and most mysterious men in the world?'

'I wouldn't know. I rarely read the papers.'

'And that he engages in international dealings of a dubious nature, including –'

'I really can't say, *Madame*.'

Ingrid kept her gaze focused firmly on her own feet, feeling the rise of nervous tension, her cheeks still burning brightly. Madame Boullard was silent for some time, obviously studying her, torturing her, then she sighed, as if weary of her presence, and spoke softly again.

'So,' she said, 'the great man was too busy to come and visit you during all this time. He must be busy *indeed*.'

'*Oui, Madame*.'

'Are you now looking forward to seeing him?'

'*Oui, Madame*.'

'I don't think so, my dear.'

Madame Boullard sighed again, then reached out with one hand, pressed her fingers under Ingrid's chin and forced her head up, making Ingrid look at her. She studied Ingrid for some time, smiled in a mocking manner, then eventually removed her fat fingers and stepped back a little.

'So,' she said. '*Au revoir*.'

'*Merci, Madame. Au revoir*.'

Madame Boullard responded with a glacial smile and a self-satisfied nod of her head, then held out her hand. Ingrid shook it, aware of its sweaty warmth, then let go, gave a little curtsey and gratefully hurried out of the hated office.

Returning to her room, she took a deep breath, glanced at the lake and mountains, then sat on the edge of the bed and waited in a trance of growing dread for the porter's arrival. He came soon enough, a familiar face, a kindly man, and when he picked up her suitcase and had walked to the door, she stopped him, pressed some francs into his hand and then pushed him away.

'Please go on ahead of me,' she said. 'I'll be there in a minute.'

'I'm supposed to escort you out, Fräulein Zweig.'

'It's all right. I won't be long.'

The old man smiled and nodded, then walked off along the corridor, and Ingrid, turning back into the room, stood on tiptoe, reached up to the top of a wardrobe, and pulled down a packet of cigarettes and box of matches.

It was forbidden to smoke in the sanatorium and for that very reason, although she didn't normally smoke, she had made it a point to do so secretly at least once or twice a week. So she lit a cigarette, threw the pack into the wicker basket at her feet; then, inhaling deeply, walked to the window and exhaled as she surveyed the stunning lake and the scenery around it.

Suggesting freedom, it was her prison, incarcerating her hopes, and, unable to look longer, she removed her troubled gaze, studied the lawns of the sanatorium, focused on the helicopter that was roaring beyond the green grass, then blew another thin cloud of smoke and turned away from the window.

Glancing around the small, comfortable room, she thought of how she had come here six months ago, weeping hysterically, crying out for her dead mother, cursing the father who was paying for her treatment, and shredding her own clothes the first night before they rushed in to strap her down.

She had not been here before, but she had been to others, and each, though for the rich, masking human pain in luxury, had had its own particular brand of horror to add to her own ... Gleaming hypodermic needles; Valium washed down with water; nights spent in delirium or nightmare, then awakening to punishment. Nurses, male and female, some brutal, some kind, others simply indifferent in the face of the

traumas of the wealthy with their strident demands ...
It hadn't mattered much to her – it was a very familiar
nightmare – and she knew that the torments she was
enduring were all she might ever have.

So, she had suffered, and recovered (at least temporarily); and between her nightmares about brutish men,
sexual fear and humiliation, dreamed in vain of that
rare man of absolute goodness who would, with his
platonic love, renew the faith destroyed by her father
and raise her on high.

She almost laughed at this thought, knowing how
foolish it was, then just as quickly had to choke back
tears at what she had lost.

Lowering her gaze, she saw the bulging wicker
basket, recently filled with the torn sheets of the many
love letters she had written to some imagined lover
during her worst days ... Six months of letters. Six
months of self-delusion ... She thought of the father
who had driven her to that state, and of Madame
Boullard who had conspired to torment her in this
awful place ... Six months of self-delusion and torture
in this luxurious hell on earth.

Almost sweating with terror, yet unable to stop
herself, she inhaled on her cigarette, exhaled a cloud of
smoke, then deliberately dropped the glowing cigarette
into the wicker basket, waited until it was clear that the
papers were catching fire, then walked casually out of
the room, feeling better already.

A few minutes later, strapped into the helicopter as it
ascended towards the clouds, she looked down at the
sanatorium, watched it shrinking into the expanding
earth, and then saw the black smoke billowing up and
streaming across the green lawns like ink staining a
blotter.

'Jesus Christ!' exclaimed the pilot sitting beside her.
'The sanatorium's on fire!'

'Really?' she heard herself replying dreamily. 'Oh, dear, how dreadful!'

Amused, she put her head back, closed her eyes and took a deep breath, then let the helicopter give her wings and fly her away on the first leg of a journey around the globe to rejoin her father.

CHAPTER THREE

Standing on the deck of his 180-foot luxury cruiser, the *Landsberg II*, feeling much younger than his sixty-two years, and gazing with pleasure at his fleet of thirty smaller high-powered boats, Zweig took deep breaths of the fresh air, stretched himself, and gazed up at the sky.

At first briefly dazzled, he soon managed to adjust to the bright light and saw his courier's helicopter in the distance, taking shape and growing larger as, en route from Recife, it approached his large fleet of heavily armed boats. He studied the helicopter for a moment, impatient for its arrival, then snapped his fingers at the white-jacketed steward near the cabinet outside the saloon, took a glass of bubbling Dom Perignon from the proffered tray, and waved the steward back to his position by the door.

'Ah,' he murmured, sipping the champagne. '*Sehr gut!* Really excellent.'

Enjoying his drink, he gazed again with pride at the boats of his private fleet which, at anchor just outside the territorial waters of Brazil, formed a protective ring around him and were crewed by his most fanatically loyal or fearful men.

His own enormous boat, the pride of the fleet, had a white-domed structure that housed satellite communications equipment, a swimming pool at the fore-end of the deck, a helipad on the stern deck just above the ramped garage for his custom-built Range Rover and amphibian; and a lavishly equipped interior containing many priceless paintings and antiques, most of which had been gained by dubious means.

Stretching himself, he shaded his eyes with his free hand as the helicopter, now hovering above him, whipped the wind around him before passing on to settle on the helipad with a final stuttered roaring.

Finishing his champagne, he gave the empty glass back to the Filipino steward, walked to the railing of the upper deck and gazed down at the helipad, where the crewmen in coveralls were clamping the machine to the steel floor.

The sea was a rippling blue and green sheet, its low waves capped with white foam.

His personal assistant, Hans Mayer, wearing a plain grey suit with black patent-leather shoes and carrying a briefcase in one hand, climbed out, then turned back to help down a lady who, even from this distance, was clearly in her early thirties, moved self-consciously and gracelessly, had her auburn hair piled primly on top of her head, and wore thick-rimmed spectacles.

Zweig felt a twinge of disgust at the sight of his daughter, Ingrid, and watched coldly as she and Hans disappeared just below, en route up through the various levels of the boat to report directly to him.

He studied the fleet of boats spread across the sunlit, glittering sea and thought of how far he had come from his days as a Nazi Wolfcub. First a frightened boy fighter, then an eighteen-year-old soldier who had suffered terribly at the hands of Soviet troops during the fall of Berlin, he had learned to fight for survival after the war, and had gone on to great success as a mercenary in Argentina and Paraguay before broadening his criminal activities to take in the whole world.

Yes, he was powerful now, but it brought him little joy; he was growing old too fast, awakening each day to fear.

He could not face the future.

Sighing, he turned around to greet Hans and Ingrid as they arrived on the deck.

Hans was blond, blue-eyed, and nervous, but at least more attractive than Ingrid. A forlorn creature, truly, completely inhibited and none too bright. He took note of her lowered head, that visible air of defeat, and wondered that even the best finishing schools had failed to give her some dignity.

'*Guten Tag*, Herr Zweig,' Hans said. 'I am sorry I'm late, but –'

'No matter,' Zweig interjected. 'Please expand on your ambiguous telex. What happened in New York?'

'Hello, father,' Ingrid began timidly. 'It's so –'

'*Ja! Ja!*' Zweig said impatiently, keeping his gaze focused on Hans, to whom he said, '*So?*'

Hans started to tell him about what had occurred in the Waldorf Astoria hotel in New York, but Zweig, feeling even more impatient, cut him short with: 'Yes, yes, I already know all that! What *else* did you find out?'

'Well,' Hans said nervously while Ingrid blushed with humiliation, 'they obviously know that the men in the Waldorf Astoria were working for you, since someone calling himself Grabbe – *Christian* Grabbe – rang them at the hotel and asked them for whom they were working; and, when they refused to tell him, he apparently just chuckled over the phone and said that he knew they were employed by someone reported to be one of the most mysterious and richest men in the world.'

'So this man, this Christian Grabbe, made an appointment to see them, saying that *his* superior, someone unknown, was actually in possession of the Tuaoi Stone?'

'Yes, Herr Zweig. One of the three men rang me,

31

where I was then staying in Florida, to inform me that this man, the so-called Christian Grabbe, was coming to see them at the hotel, and that they hoped to purchase the Tuaoi Stone off him. Those men died when Grabbe should have been there with them – but there was no sign of him, dead or alive, in that wrecked room. Nor was he with the other two who died on the pavement below the room.'

'So he never turned up,' Zweig surmised. 'Instead, he planted some kind of bomb.'

'No, Herr Zweig. No bomb was used. Nor was the explosion caused by leaking gas or electrical malfunction. That explosion has already been described as a total mystery, in the sense that no reason can be found for it. In fact, it seems that it could *not* have been an explosion – since the other rooms were not affected – though the devastation was caused by some kind of inexplicable, powerful force.'

'We just don't know *what* kind.'

'Exactly, Herr Zweig.'

'Come. Let's go inside.'

Deliberately ignoring Ingrid, but pleased by her wounded look, Zweig led her and Hans through the luxurious saloon, down two flights of steps, and into a suite-sized cabin containing a surgical bed, spa bath, steam bath and one of the boat's two Jacuzzis.

Lying on a couch under a window with a sea view was his secretary and mistress, Elena. Blonde-haired, blue-eyed, wearing a skin-tight *cheongsam*, she was propped up against some cushions, filing her fingernails, and occasionally moving her exposed left leg in a sensual manner.

'My daughter has arrived from the sanatorium,' Zweig informed her.

'Terrific,' she responded, glancing up with eyes constantly nervous. 'Hi, kid. Nice to see you.'

As she automatically waved the hand that was holding the nail file, Zweig said, 'I'm delighted to see you, Ingrid, but please wait outside. I must discuss business first.'

Blushing, Ingrid backed towards the door, bumped into it, opened it, and hurried out as if desperate for fresh air.

Glad to see the back of her, Zweig sighed.

'Fetch the doctor,' he said.

Hans picked up the intercom and asked for the doctor as Zweig undressed, not ashamed of his nakedness, then lay face down on the surgical bed, turning his face towards Hans.

'So,' he said, 'what else can you tell me?'

'Well, Herr Zweig,' Hans replied, 'we *do* know, from the phone call made to that suite in the Waldorf Astoria before it was destroyed, that the so-called Christian Grabbe, whether or not he was in *possession* of the Tuaoi Stone, or Lodestone, at least knew exactly what it was, since, when asked by one of our men to describe it, he did so with complete accuracy. He also knew that you wanted to purchase it – and stated that you wanted it because of its famed magical properties.'

'And he confirmed that it had such properties?'

'On the telephone – yes. In fact, we think that the destruction of that hotel room was a demonstration of the powers of the Tuaoi Stone – a demonstration and warning.'

'That I'm not to pursue this matter further?'

'I'm afraid so, Herr Zweig.'

The door to the cabin opened and his hawk-faced, white-jacketed doctor entered, wheeling a steel trolley on which were resting numerous silver bowls filled with various health foods, drinks and tablets, as well as a tray of gleaming hypodermic syringes. Adjusting his glasses, he nervously commenced to aid Zweig in his daily battle against disease and old age by giving him five subcutaneous rejuvenating injections in his rump – the injections containing, as he knew, the lyophilized cells from the different organs of unborn lambs; foetal thymus to help in fighting infection, plus liver, hypothalmus and vertebrae bone marrow cells, aimed at improving general back tension; as well as a sixth injection of Bogomoletz serum, obtained from the tissues of the brain, placenta and heart of young car accident victims which in turn had been injected into rabbits – a serum once used by the Soviets, as Zweig never failed to remind himself, to keep Stalin alive.

When the doctor had finished and left the cabin, Zweig drank a pint of his favourite protein drink – consisting of two tablespoons of powdered protein, one tablespoon of granula lecithin, a banana, raw egg and two cups of skimmed milk, all whipped together in a blender for thirty seconds – and finally, while talking, had a selection of the exotic health snacks in the silver bowls, including fertilized chicken eggs from the Bahamas, fertilized turtle eggs from the South Pacific; walnuts and honey from the Caucasus regions of Russia; dried apricots from the remote village of Hunza, in the Himalayas; guavas, mangoes, loquats and the white root, yuka, from Vilcabamba, Ecuador's so-called Valley of Eternal Youth; and the root of Eleutheron Ginseng, from the desolate mountain villages of Siberia.

'Who *are* these people?' he asked between mouthfuls. 'That's what we must find out. They knew I wanted the Lodestone, and they got in touch with me by phone, then they managed to kill my men in that room in New York – and they did it in some inexplicable manner. So who *are* they?'

'There *is* one clue,' Hans said. 'One of our men in New York, before his untimely death, informed me that prior to the arrangement to meet Grabbe in the

Waldorf Astoria, the meeting was supposed to be with Grabbe's superior aboard a lecture cruise boat that is due to journey along the Nile from Aswan to Cairo just a few days from now. So, the man we were *originally* supposed to have met – the one claiming to either possess or know the whereabouts of the Tuaoi Stone – might still be making that journey.'

'You think so?'

'Why not? He was going to meet our men on that boat, then changed his mind and had them killed instead – so there's no reason to suppose that he's not still making that journey. I think that man, whoever he is, will be on that boat.'

Having sated his appetite, Zweig had his daily dose of revitalization drugs in tablet form, including some HCG capsules, which are hormone extracts from the urine of pregnant women. He washed all these down with another pint of his protein drink, then stared grimly at Hans.

'Yes,' he said, 'I think you're right. I think that man will be on the boat. And, if that bastard will be aboard, so too will we. Book passage immediately for the four of us and two personal stewards.'

'What if the boat's fully booked?' Hans asked.

'No problem,' Zweig replied, glancing sideways at Elena who, though experienced in the ways of men, was clearly terrified of him. 'If the boat's fully booked, simply purchase the whole tour company outright, cancel the reservations of those scheduled to utilize the cabins we need, then book our entourage into them instead.'

'What if the man we want is one of those whose trip is cancelled because of our requirements?'

'He won't be. If he's the man we want, he won't let himself be pushed off that boat. He'll have money – and arrogance. Anything else?'

'I haven't had anything to eat or drink since —'

'Yes, yes,' Zweig said impatiently, having no time for trivialities. 'I understand, but you can do all that later. You must book the boat or buy the company immediately — so get straight to the telex. Report back when you've done it.'

When Hans had left to do as he had been bid, Zweig turned to Elena.

'My muscles need toning up,' he said. 'Come here and do what you're paid for.'

She swung her long legs off the sofa and sauntered over to him, every movement of her body accentuated by the shiny *cheongsam*, the curves of her legs emphasized by stiletto-heeled shoes. Her peroxide blonde hair was spilling over full breasts, her brightly painted lips pouting when she stopped in front of him.

Zweig lay back on the surgical bed and sucked in his belly.

'You want the oil?' Elena asked, her gaze roaming.

'Yes,' Zweig replied. 'And please bring in my daughter.'

'*Now?*'

'Yes,' he said. 'Now.'

She nodded and pressed the intercom, asked someone to send Ingrid in, then picked up a bottle and leaned down across him. Licking her scarlet lips, breathing sensuously in his face, she poured warm oil from the bottle onto his belly, then started rubbing it into his skin with the palms of her hands.

'Cover me up before my daughter arrives.'

'You're real considerate, Zweig.'

Nevertheless, she draped a white towel over his stiffening member and continued rubbing the oil into the pores of his skin.

'What's this Tuaoi Stone?' she asked to fill the silence. 'Why the big deal? Is it some kind of diamond?'

'No,' Zweig replied. 'It is much more than a diamond. It is perhaps the most valuable, least known antique in the world – much discussed but very rarely seen. It is a pyramidal stone – possibly the peak of the Great Pyramid of Cheops in Egypt – and is reported to possess magical properties and extraordinary powers. In fact, it is said that the man who holds the Tuaoi Stone will own the whole world. Certainly it is the world's most sought-after object – and, if that's true, it obviously belongs in my collection.'

'It's probably just a diamond,' Elena said. 'You know? A girl's best friend.'

'Yes, dear,' he replied, stifling his impatience, not amused by her feeble wit. 'You're probably right.'

Ingrid entered like a wraith, her gaze wandering nervously. Her shoulders appeared to be stooped by the weight of her piled up hair; and her face, which had a delicate, restrained beauty, was filled with the kind of trepidation that made breathing difficult.

Studying her, he despaired, wondering what would become of her, but also taking pride in the fact that she was his handiwork.

He had terrified her from the day she was born and now saw the results of it.

'Ingrid,' he said, enjoying his little sport. 'Come here! It's been *such* a long time. Say hello to Elena.'

'Hello, Elena,' Ingrid whispered, lowering her gaze. 'It's nice to see you again.'

'Yeah, kid. That's for sure.'

Elena's practised hands had very thoroughly smeared the oil all over his body, and her fingers, long and thin, the nails like razors, were kneading the oil into his skin and exciting him greatly. He almost groaned with pleasure, but instead sighed discreetly, smiling up at his disconcerted daughter, aware of how this was wounding her.

'Would *you* like a massage?' he asked her. 'I'm sure Elena would –'

'No thank you, Father,' she replied.

'Of course not,' Zweig said. 'You would have to take your clothes off, after all – and that isn't you, is it?'

Ingrid didn't reply, but simply studied the floor. She was slender and fragile in her shapeless cotton dress, which perfectly matched her hazel eyes and colourless pallor.

Zweig knew that she was trying to avoid the towel over his loins, since, given its shape and quivering movement, it called attention to everything she feared, which could only amuse him.

'Since you are back here for six weeks,' he said, 'and since you clearly have no friend to look after you, I have decided to bring you with me on a voyage along the Nile. This trip, if not exciting – since nothing, I fear, could truly excite *you* – will at least keep you occupied. Is that acceptable, *mein Fräulein*?'

'Yes, Father.'

'You didn't have any other plans, did you?'

'No, Father.'

'Well, that's settled, then.'

He was just about to tease her about her mother – or, even better, her non-existent love-life – when Hans returned to inform h<u>i</u>m that he had been compelled to purchase the Egyptian tour company outright, that the deal should be completed by midnight, and that he had therefore booked the master suite for Zweig and Elena, one single cabin each for himself and Ingrid, and a double cabin for the two stewards who would accompany them.

'And when do we leave?' Zweig asked.

'We'll have to fly out from Recife tomorrow,' Hans replied.

'Excellent. You've done well. I trust you'll now attend to all the details, such as luggage and so forth. Please start right away on that.'

'Yes, Herr Zweig. Thank you, sir.'

Hans made a small bow, glanced sympathetically at Ingrid, then left the cabin, closing the door behind him.

'Ah, nice,' Zweig said. '*Nice*.'

Elena's expert hands, the nails painted blood-red, fine fingers oil-slicked, were kneading his flabby flesh, squeezing here, pressing there, sliding down under the towel, which, he noted, was still raised on high and visibly quivering. He sighed, almost groaned, remembered his daughter and stared at her. She was keeping her shamed gaze on the floor, but could not hide her burning cheeks.

He stared at her, amused, then started losing his senses, so eventually waved his right hand in the air and said: 'Yes, child, you may go now.'

She glanced at him once, her hazel eyes filled with reproach, then threw another glance at the grinning Elena before turning on the heel of her foot and rushing out of the cabin.

The door slammed shut. Elena chuckled softly. Zweig smiled and closed his eyes, giving in to his glowing flesh, transported by Elena's fingers, sliding along him, turning him into a pyramid, his phallus supporting the whole edifice, his burning loins setting fire to the temples of his mind and exposing him to memories of flame and destruction – the bloody fall of Berlin; his early days as a common criminal; torture, murder, the odd rape here and there; then his days as a mercenary in Argentina and Paraguay, setting the Indian villages to the torch, murdering those who opposed him – then to fancies about the Tuaoi Stone and the power it would give him.

He saw it, almost touched it, then came as he thought about it; crying out in guttural ecstasy as the towel fell off him, and his essence, a pure Aryan seed, found a home in Elena's hand.

'*Mein Gott!*' he groaned. '*Christ!*'

Each orgasm destroyed him more.

CHAPTER FOUR

'Now remember,' Zweig said, sitting opposite Ingrid and Hans in the *felucca* that was taking them the short distance from Elephantine Island to the corniche, wiping sweat from his sunscorched forehead, adjusting his heavy legs and stroking Elena's knee with his free hand, 'we must remain as anonymous as possible once aboard and not draw too much attention to ourselves until we find who we're looking for.'

Ingrid didn't know how her father, with his icily autocratic nature and large entourage, including two servants, could possibly imagine that a low profile was in order, but she didn't attempt to raise that delicate question and instead, simply to make conversation, asked, 'Who *are* you looking for, Father?'

'Never mind,' he replied. 'It's not your concern. What *you* can do, *mein Fräulein*, is appreciate the exotic squalor of Egypt and be a good little girl.'

Ingrid stared between her father and Elena at the receding Elephantine Island, where the dirty-brown, ruin-like walls of the Nubian villages were surrounded by a paradisal profusion of tall shrubs and palm trees.

Aware that Elena was smiling sardonically at her, she deliberately turned her attention to the black granite islets and many *felucca* on the silt-laden waters of the first cataract of the river, just beyond the corniche.

She should have felt intoxicated, overwhelmed by Egypt's strangeness, but instead was feeling claustrophobic and very depressed.

Since leaving the sanatorium on Lake Geneva she

had not been able to sleep at nights because, after her initial exhilaration at setting fire to that hated building, she had succumbed to guilt, shame and fear. Frightened of her father at the best of times, she had been even more frightened to think that someone at the sanatorium, realizing that the fire had started in her room, might have contacted him with that information. In the event, such had not happened – and was now unlikely to – but she still suffered deep shame and horror over what she had done and was shivering even in the scorching heat of the Egyptian noon.

'God,' Elena said with a sigh, adjusting the sunglasses on her nose and glancing wearily around her, 'I'll be glad to get on the *real* boat. This bathtub's making my stomach turn.'

Ingrid studied the Arab boatsmen, observed the gently splashing water, glanced up at the billowing, breeze-blown sails of the *felucca* and then sideways at the silent, watchful Hans.

Wearing white shirt, shorts, matching shoes and knee-length socks, and framed by the village of Aswan and the exquisite Egyptian sky beyond it, he looked very attractive in an oddly bland, perpetually tense manner.

After being told by her father that he would have no time for her until he had settled comfortably into his suite aboard the Nile cruiser, Ingrid had been placed in the care of Hans for the duration of the journey from her father's fleet in the South Atlantic to Aswan; and she appreciated the fact that while escorting her through the mandatory sights en route, he had also been the only one in her father's entourage to display the slightest recognition that, apart from being her father's daughter, she was a human being with the need for communication.

Hans had always baffled Ingrid. He was not yet

thirty, classically handsome and intelligent, yet she had never known him to be involved with a woman and thought of him as extraordinarily passive, virtually her father's slave. Originally hired as her father's accountant, he had shown himself to be exceptional at general administration and soon became her father's personal assistant, factotum, dogsbody. His passivity, Ingrid assumed, sprang from a combination of healthy fear of her tyrannical father – a fear common to all those who knew him – as well as his childhood in an orphanage in Bremen and subsequent adoption by two fiercely puritanical German Protestants who had, according to what Hans had told her, often punished him severely for the slightest infraction. He was, she suspected, a deeply inhibited personality who would, sooner or later, break free from the many constraints that bound him – but not, she suspected, until he had broken free from her father.

She realized he was very much like herself – and possibly even more oppressed.

Grateful to him for easing her own burden, she heard the whipping sails, returned to the present, stared past the white-robed Nubian standing at the prow of the *felucca* and saw the shoreline of the right bank approaching, with the large cruiser anchored against the corniche, framed by azure sky and shivering palm leaves. There were tourists massed near the boat, by dusty buses and taxis, and some were struggling up the ramp, between Arab porters.

'Now we join the tourist scum,' her father said. '*Scheisse*, how I suffer!'

The *felucca* ground gently against the side of the corniche and the Arab boatmen jumped out to secure the craft to the bank and help the passengers out.

Ingrid and Hans disembarked first, to be followed by Zweig's two Filipino stewards and Elena, then finally by Ingrid's father who, when he stood upright in the *felucca*, made it rock dangerously.

'The luggage!' he snapped at his hapless stewards. 'Get the luggage on board!'

As the Filipinos hurried to do as they were bid, Hans took hold of Ingrid's elbow and hurried her along the corniche towards the boat's gangplank.

'God,' she said to Hans, 'he gets in such *terrible* tempers!'

'Increasingly so,' Hans replied. 'He wasn't always this bad. He's changed over the past few months.'

'What do you think it is?'

'Old age. What else could it be?'

She looked at him and saw him grinning, which was something he rarely managed. 'Well, whatever it is,' she said, 'it's awful. I don't know how you can bear to work for him. It must be like hell on earth.'

'I didn't know what he was like when I became his accountant. And unfortunately, once one becomes involved with your father, it isn't that easy to break away. In fact, it's downright impossible.'

'You mean, you'd leave if you could?'

'Don't quote me on that.'

He grinned even more broadly, briefly looking much livelier, but put on his impassive mask again when they arrived at the gangplank.

The large blue and white boat held over eighty passengers, the last of whom were now making their way up the gangplank.

'He's in a foul mood,' Elena said, managing to catch up with them. 'He can't stand getting in and out of small boats. It makes him feel real embarrassed.'

'*Embarrassed?*' Ingrid asked. 'My father?'

'Yeah,' Elena said, 'your father. Just because he doesn't spoil you rotten, doesn't mean he's unfeeling. I mean, he cries like a baby.'

44

Ingrid shuddered at that thought and then slipped in behind the last person moving up the swaying, creaking gangplank. Glancing to her left, she saw the two Filipino stewards pushing a trolley laden with luggage along the edge of the dock, with black water, green palm trees and blue sky behind them, and her huge, bloated father shouting at them.

Mortified by that sight, she continued up the gangplank, stepped into the reception area of 'C' deck, received smiling greetings from the French captain and some stewards, then turned back towards the gangplank and looked down the quay as a battered cab, churning up clouds of dust, screeched to a halt.

The rear door of the cab opened and a man who looked to be about twenty-five, wearing a crumpled blue denim jacket and jeans, with a camera bouncing off his open-necked check shirt and his brown hair flopping untidily over the forehead of an unshaven, pleasant face, emerged from the vehicle, slammed the door shut, then retrieved his suitcase and paid the Arab driver.

'Now give me a bite of *that*,' Elena said admiringly as she looked down at the dishevelled Caucasian on the quay. 'Most of the people on these boats are geriatrics – so what a sight for sore eyes *he* is! Uh, uh, looks like trouble . . .'

Obviously convinced that he had almost missed the boat, the Sight For Sore Eyes picked up his single suitcase and hurried to the foot of the gangplank just as the first of the two Filipino stewards was about to step onto it with a heavy suitcase in each hand. The two men collided and were struggling to disentangle themselves when Ingrid's father stepped forward, grabbed the white man by the shoulder, threw him away from the gangplank, and bawled, 'How *dare* you come this late! The crew should have been on board

45

hours ago. You're dismissed! On your way, you *Schwein!*'

The young man dropped his suitcase and stared disbelievingly at Zweig. 'Swine . . .? Dismissed . . .? *Crew* . . . What the hell do you mean? *I'm* not a member of the goddamned crew! I'm a tourist! A passenger!'

'You're a *passenger*?' Zweig rejoindered, obviously not believing his own ears. 'You look like you belong in the engine room. What kind of boat *is* this?'

'Hey, hold *on* a minute,' the younger man said, speaking in what was now clearly an American accent and melodramatically holding up his right hand with the fingers outspread. 'Just who do —?'

'The name is Zweig! *Wilhelm* Zweig! And I have no time for small talk. So step aside and let me board this boat – which I happen to own.'

'Oh, great,' the American replied. 'Big deal! I'm *impressed*! The owner of the boat no less. Well, just remember that I've paid for this trip. I'm *supporting* you, buddy!'

Elena gave a low whistle of admiration at hearing that one, but Ingrid, when she noticed her father straightening his spine, held her breath and felt an unexpected rush of concern for the brash young American.

'Who *are* you?' her father growled. 'What's your name? *I want to know who you are!*'

'Remick,' the American replied, staring fearlessly at Zweig. 'The name's Remick. *Jerry* Remick. From New York City. And don't *you* forget *that*!'

Ingrid couldn't resist feeling admiration for the American as he grabbed his suitcase and walked up the gangplank, ignoring Zweig who fiercely observed his every move, opening and closing his ham fists.

Stumbling into the gloomy reception area, the young man – named Jerry Remick, as Ingrid reminded herself – dropped his suitcase again, checked in at the booking office, then glanced back over his shoulder to where Zweig, at the bottom of the gangplank, was suddenly galvanized back into action and hissed at his stewards, 'So what are you staring at, you imbeciles? *Get that luggage on board!*'

The stewards rushed to obey as the American grinned mischievously, then shook his head from side to side in a rueful manner.

'You people are on this boat as well?' he said. 'Oh, boy, I'm in *heaven*!'

He reached out with his right hand and said with childish pleasure, 'The name's Jerry. Jerry —'

'Remick,' Elena said, undulating like a scenic railway as she moved forward to take hold of his outstretched hand. 'We heard it all from up here. I'm Elena, a friend to Mr Zweig; this is Hans, Mr Zweig's personal assistant; and this is his daughter, Ingrid. We're all *delighted* to meet you.'

'Whoops,' Jerry said. 'I'm sorry. I mean, I didn't know that Kraut, the old goat, was related to —'

'Don't worry,' Elena said, chewing gum, smiling flirtatiously. 'We understand perfectly. Are you going all the way downriver, to Cairo?'

'Right.'

'That's terrific,' Elena said, taking a deep breath. 'Let's get together *real soon.*'

The attractively dishevelled American opened his mouth to reply, but before he could do so Elena had brushed past him and posed herself at the top of the gangplank, spreading her hands in a theatrical gesture of welcome to Zweig.

'And you?' Jerry said, staring directly at Ingrid in a way that made her feel pleasantly strange. 'You're that guy's . . . *daughter*?'

Ingrid shrank helplessly into herself. 'Yes,' she whispered, 'I am.'

'Don't worry about it. We can't pick our own parents. I mean, I'm not holding you responsible for him. It's the way of the world, right?'

When he grinned, she felt warm all over and slightly unreal. She tried to meet his gaze, to stay calm, but just blushed even more.

'Yes,' she said. 'I suppose so.'

'You have really lovely eyes behind those specs. And your shy smile's a winner.'

'Please stop that. You're embarrassing me.'

'Yeah, I can see that. Well, Ingrid, it's nice to have you aboard. I hope we meet again soon.' He glanced back over his shoulder and saw her father stepping onto the deck. 'Jesus,' he said, 'I better get out of here. Your old man's bigger than I am.'

He nodded at her, then picked up his suitcase and quickly departed, disappearing through the nearest door to go in search of his cabin.

Sighing, feeling almost bereaved at his departure, Ingrid turned reluctantly towards her father and his tarty Elena.

'Herr Zweig?' the ship's captain asked, stepping forward. 'I am Captain Malraux. Please let me welcome you aboard the –'

'Yes, yes,' Zweig responded in an irritable manner, contemptuously slapping aside the captain's extended hand. 'I am already sick to death of this filthy ship. Where are our cabins?'

'*Excusez-moi*,' the captain managed to respond, his voice breaking fearfully. 'This way, Herr Zweig.'

He escorted them along a corridor, then up to 'A' deck and on to their cabins.

'This, Herr Zweig,' the captain began at the first open door they came to, 'is your master cabin, which as you can see, is –'

'*Oui, Monsieur*,' Zweig replied. 'I know what it is. I

am not a halfwit, after all. So please go up on deck and get this boat on the move before any more American tourist scum can crawl aboard with the rats. *Au revoir, mon Capitaine.*'

The captain inched backwards, bowing repeatedly, then disappeared gratefully up the stairs while the Filipino stewards sorted out the luggage, placing the bulk of it in Zweig's master suite and the others in their respective cabins.

Ingrid had been hoping that her father would invite her into his cabin for a discussion on her six-month period in the sanatorium, but alas, such was not to be the case. Even as she thought to confess to having set the sanatorium on fire – feeling that his anger could not be worse than his indifference – he opened his mouth, yawned loudly and said, 'Thank God we are here at last. Now I must have my sleep. I will see you this evening, my child, when dinner is served. *Elena, where are you?*'

Ingrid did not need to be told that Elena was already in the master suite, stretching out on the double bed, preparing to earn her keep; so, shuddering, she whispered agreement and hurried away along the narrow corridor and entered her much smaller cabin, closing the door carefully behind her and sitting on the edge of the narrow bed, where she sighed with relief.

Recovering from her hurt feelings, she was almost amused by the idea of her father imagining he could remain incognito on this boat; but then, when she thought of the young American she had met, her growing amusement gave way to a longing to see him again.

Young? Not really. He was obviously in his late twenties. But he *looked* young, in the manner of a brilliant naif, and that touched her oddly. She thought of his blue eyes, his innocent fearlessness, and wondered if he would even recognize her the next time they met.

Sighing again, she was about to lie down on the bed when the muffled growling of the boat's engines made her twitch. Relaxing, she lit a cigarette, thought of the blazing sanatorium, then gazed out of her cabin window as the boat pulled away from the corniche. She saw the village of Aswan, white walls and green palm trees, receding and then slipping smoothly past, to give way to the desert.

Egypt, she thought. *I am in Egypt . . . And I don't give a damn*.

Sweaty and exhausted, feeling lonely and unreal, she wondered whether to unpack, couldn't find the energy for it, so lay on the narrow bed, closed her eyes and let herself drift away . . .

She visualized her dream lover, a darkly handsome, kind man; imagined him, then *felt* him pressing upon her to obliterate pain and fear. He would touch her very gently – as she was touching herself right now – and in so doing transport her through rapture, away from the real world.

She saw him, almost felt him, was reaching out to him – and then he suddenly disappeared, melting magically back into darkness, and was replaced by the image of her smirking father, who seemed to loom over her.

Even as she thought of him, she actually heard him – yes, in the adjoining cabin – and was brought back to reality by the sound of his head banging against the dividing wall as he took his disgusting pleasures from Elena and groaned his instructions.

'That's it! Take it easy. Yes, yes, that's the way! Yes, Elena! *Sehr gut!*'

His head banged the wall again, a loud noise that

shocked her, and she jerked upright, fighting to control her racing heart and stop her cheeks burning.

Planting her feet firmly on the floor, she stared through the porthole, watched the shimmering haze of the Egyptian afternoon turn into a crimson dusk. Her father's moans and groans faded away into silence, and she thought of being trapped with him on this boat for another five days.

It was a terrible thought.

However, just as she was about to plunge into a deep depression, she thought of Jerry Remick, that brash young American, remembered that he had flirted in a mischievous manner with her, and felt a warm rush of affection for him.

Startled by her feelings, unable to shake him from her mind, feeling better each minute that she sat there thinking about him, she finally decided that she had to get out of the cabin and go up to the open deck.

He might be up there, after all. In fact, he was almost certain to be there. He would want to watch the boat leaving Aswan and heading along the great river.

Yes, of course he would. He wouldn't remain in his cabin. He was bound to be up there on the deck, watching Egypt slip past the boat. He would be there at the railing, looking out, when she walked up behind him . . . .

She realized, then, how badly she wanted to see him, so stood up, put on her shoes and hurried out of the cabin, heading with all haste for the open deck.

She did not see Jerry immediately. Instead, she saw — leaning against the railing of the upper deck with a few other passengers, but turning his head to stare very steadily at her, as if, indeed, he had been expecting her arrival — a man who seemed to be about sixty but was exceptionally handsome, silver-haired and suntanned, his face remarkably unlined, his grey eyes extremely bright and penetrating even from that distance.

His smile was not malicious, but seemed gently mocking, and the intensity of his gaze was such that it almost made her swoon in an unnatural, disturbing manner before releasing her by simply moving elsewhere.

At that moment she was convinced that the strange man at the boat's railing was deliberately redirecting her own hypnotized gaze – which, in obedience to him, came to rest in the opposite direction, where the American, Jerry Remick, still dishevelled but appealing, was leaning on the boat's railing, staring into the crimson sunset, his blue eyes reflecting palm tree, sand dune and darkening sky, before turning in her direction, staring at her, focusing upon her, to give life to the thin line of his lips and encourage a melting smile.

'Gee,' he said to her in the cloudily pock-marked Egyptian twilight. 'It's the girl with the rainbow eyes and shy smile. Can I buy you a drink?'

Consumed with emotion just to see him, she nodded agreement.

CHAPTER FIVE

Dusk over the desert was intoxicating. It was just such a mood that encouraged Jerry to stand at the ship's railing during his first evening aboard and, gazing out over the darkening, whispering river, quietly curse the fact that he hadn't been able to bring along his fatter books on ancient Egypt. Realizing that thinking about this too much was going to frustrate him greatly, he decided to return to his cabin and relax with a beer and dip into his book on quantum physics.

It didn't work out that way.

Turning his back to the railing, he saw Wilhelm Zweig's shy daughter, Ingrid, staring at him from across the deck, the light reflecting off her spectacles and making her look very odd. She stepped towards him, then stopped, hesitating, glancing around her, and he realized she wanted to speak to him but couldn't quite manage it.

Normally awkward with people, he felt surprisingly at ease with her, and said, 'Gee! It's the girl with the rainbow eyes and shy smile. Can I buy you a drink?'

She just stood there, surprised, then stepped out of the violet twilight, nervously rubbed her eyes with a finger stuck up under her spectacles, and eventually managed to nod as if in assent.

'Does that mean yes?' he asked her.

She nodded again.

'You're a real fancy talker,' he said, surprised by his instant ease with her. 'This conversation is red hot.'

That at least got a smile out of her. She moved a

little closer, looking at him with her sombre eyes magnified behind her spectacles. He didn't think she would come any closer, but that didn't bother him. He hadn't had a good sex life (he was too involved with his mind) and after all the groping and groaning, after all his romantic debacles, he was happy to be in the company of someone worse off than he was.

'You don't *mind* coming with me for a drink, do you? I mean, I don't want to *force* you.'

'No!' she exclaimed in a soft, breathless burst that did his heart good. 'Of course not! I wouldn't say I wanted to come if I didn't mean it. I wouldn't do that at all.'

She seemed so intense he almost laughed, but something stopped him from doing so. It was something about her, a fragility, a naïve, helpless honesty . . . He wasn't too sure *what* it was, but he sensed she'd bleed easily.

'Your first trip along the Nile, is it?' he asked, feeling stupid, but not knowing what else to say.

'Yes,' she replied.

'Looking forward to it?'

'Yes,' she said again, thus reminding him that conversation with her might not be too easy, and that a drink of the alcoholic variety might loosen her tongue.

'Well,' he said, very aware of his own histrionic sigh. 'I suppose we're wasting time standing here talking, so let's go find the bar.'

'Yes,' she said. 'If you want to.'

He knew she was shy, but started thinking her strange when she finally stepped close to him and asked, in a melodramatic whisper, 'Do you know that man standing further along? On your right. The one with silvery hair.'

When he looked, no such person was in sight.

'*What* man?' he asked her.

She stared along the deck, furrowed her brow in consternation, her eyes blinking behind the thick-rimmed spectacles and displaying bewilderment.

'He was there,' she said. 'I swear it. A handsome man with silvery hair. He looked at me when I came out on deck . . . and then looked at you.'

'I promise you, I didn't arrange that. I had nothing to do with it.'

'You're sure?'

'Yeah, I'm sure.'

Visibly shivering, and again blinking as if dazed, she studied the people wandering to and fro in the humid air of the Egyptian evening, then returned her gaze to him, staring up with an air of confusion and rising embarrassment.

'You won't believe me,' she said. 'It sounds silly, I know . . . but that man was definitely there, leaning on the railing, and when he stared at me, with very intense, grey eyes, I almost swooned on the spot. No,' she hastened to add, obviously sensing his scepticism, 'I don't mean it was like a fainting spell . . . it was more like some kind of brief trance . . . a sort of wide-awake dream in which he controlled me. And then he smiled – a strange smile, as if he didn't quite know how to – and turned his gaze on you – and I swear that by simply doing that, he made me look at you as well.'

'Really?'

'Yes, really.'

Instantly attracted to her, and intrigued by the possibility of having a mesmerist on board, he gave her an encouraging smile, then tried to look serious.

'Gee, that's real strange. I mean, it's pretty far out. But maybe you just had a little turn caused by the heat – which after all, you're not used to – and that silvery-haired guy probably had nothing to do with it and has doubtless just disappeared into the bar or back to his cabin. So if we go, as we agreed, for that drink, he might be in the bar.'

'Yes,' she replied, almost fearfully. 'I suppose that's a good idea.'

He thought it was a *terrific* idea and couldn't wait to get there, so he took hold of her elbow and guided her along the deck, past where the mystery man had stood, and then down a single flight of steps to the boat's only bar. She was plain, but he found her sexy, a bit vulnerable, sort of helpless, and he was conscious, *very* conscious, of her warmth and suppressed femininity.

'He's not here,' she said, her face falling as she glanced into the bar and saw only the normal folk.

'Oh, really?' Jerry replied. 'Well, don't worry. He's probably just gone back to his cabin to read a good book.'

'It's the first night aboard ship,' she insisted. 'You'd think he'd want to explore it.'

'He's not as young as you and me. I mean, you *did* say he had silver hair so he must be well past it.'

'Yes,' she murmured, but with no great sign of confidence. 'I suppose that's the answer.'

'Anyway, stop worrying about it,' he said after ordering a brandy for her, a Stella beer for himself, and indicating the nearest vacant seats. 'You probably just imagined it. You're in a new country – a very strange and *different* country – and that can be very disorientating and play tricks with the mind. I mean, the guy probably just smiled at you in a friendly manner – sort of welcoming you aboard – and you probably imagined all the rest. Don't you think so?'

'Well . . . maybe . . .'

Wondering what had *really* disturbed her, finding himself increasingly sympathetic to her chronically shy nature, and realizing that had it not been for her

56

pinned-up hair, thick-framed spectacles and un-imaginative clothing, she would be pretty attractive, he decided diplomatically to change the subject.

'Well,' he started, 'at least we've left Aswan. Now the sky will be visible.'

Although this was true, the boat had only travelled a short way along the river where it was to spend the night before embarking on its two-day journey to Luxor first thing in the morning; so facing Ingrid over a low table in the small bar – which was now filled with mildly drunken, mostly geriatric fellow-travellers – he tried to distract her from her neurotic concerns by pointing through the panoramic window at the sand dunes silhouetted by the starlit splendour of the Egyptian night and showing her the different constellations in the sky.

'I know the sky like the palm of my hand,' he said. 'And that's not *all* I know. I mean, I study a lot, you know?'

'You go to university?'

'I did,' he replied. 'But they threw me out. I was studying divinity at Harvard, but got sidetracked into related subjects, such as unexplained phenomena and the occult.'

'Unexplained phenomena?'

'*You* know – flying saucers, things falling out of the sky, haunted houses, the magical properties of pyramids and so on.'

'Oh,' she said meekly. 'How interesting.'

'It is, Ingrid. Believe me.'

'You must be really bright.'

'Yeah,' he agreed, suddenly feeling really dim. 'Which just means I talk a lot.'

He had always been socially inadequate, emotionally distant, distracted, and he still hadn't learned to speak to women as if they were human. He was trying right this minute – he really was – but kept saying the wrong things.

'It's nice to meet an intelligent woman,' he said, 'instead of a dumb blonde. Now let's have another drink.'

Covering his confusion and regaining his confidence with a second round of drinks, he soon found himself telling her all about his life in New York and, after that elaborated on his fascination with ancient Egypt and its possible relationship to inexplicable phenomena, including the reported magical properties of certain of the pyramids, most notably the Great Pyramid at Giza, to where they were headed.

'And so,' he finished, 'that's why I came to Egypt – to solve all these historical mysteries and then write about them.'

'You're going to write a *book*?'

'Nothing to it. I'm a writer to the manner born. The problem with most writers is that they write impressively about nothing. But me, I've got a fairly high I.Q., and that means I can think straight. So I've come here for research before writing a great book.'

'I think that's really admirable,' Ingrid said.

'So do I, Ingrid.'

Having explained himself, and not wanting to hog the whole conversation, he asked her if *she* believed in inexplicable phenomena. She coughed into her right fist, finished her drink, looked distinctly uncomfortable, then muttered, 'I don't really know what to say. I mean, I've never *personally* taken an interest in such things . . . but my father, strangely enough, does. He is, I believe, making this trip for that very reason.'

'Really? No kidding! Well, I never would have guessed it. I mean, your old man doesn't seem the sort to have such interests. In fact, he seems like a materialistic, very powerful guy who scares the hell out of everyone around him. He even seems to scare *you*.'

'Yes,' she agreed sadly. 'He does.'

'I hate to say it, since he's your old man, but I nearly punched him down on that jetty. It was just his age stopped me.'

'I'm glad you didn't try it, Jerry. I mean, he's really very *strong* for his age.'

'He's all blubber and hot air . . . Christ, I'm sorry. I didn't mean that. I —'

'It's all right,' she said. 'Could you get me another drink?'

'Sure, Ingrid. Right.'

Grateful for an escape from his *faux pas*, he bought two more drinks — not without dwelling upon the fact that the timid Ingrid Zweig was drinking neat brandies — and then returned just as gratefully to the table, surprised at how much he wanted to see her after a two-minute absence.

She certainly was plain, sitting there at the low table, framed by the splendid Egyptian night (which was itself framed by the window), with her shoulders hunched in a pitifully self-effacing manner. But when he gave her the fresh brandy, she licked surprisingly sensual lips, rubbed her flushed cheeks, confessed that she didn't normally drink, then sniffed back some tears.

'Oh, shit,' he blurted out, thinking it was his fault. 'I'm real sorry. I didn't mean to —'

'No, no,' she insisted to his great relief. 'It's not you. It's just . . .'

'Your old man?'

'Yes.'

'He mistreats you?'

'Yes . . . Yes, he does.'

He realized, then, that every minute in her presence was making him feel even more masculine and in command. That pleasant feeling was only enhanced when she glanced distractedly around her, as if seeking escape, then wiped tears from her cheeks, readjusted her spectacles, and eventually, as if releasing a great deal of anxiety, blurted out, 'I hate him! I *despise* him . . . and I'm frightened to death of him.'

Having got it off her chest, she sank back into her chair, folded her hands in her lap, turned them this way and that, examining them, trying to hide from his gaze. Touched by that sight, unexpectedly concerned for her, he reached across the table, laid his hand on her shoulder and said, 'It's okay. There's no need to be embarrassed. Why not tell me about it?'

Clearly disturbed, she looked left and right, studied her hands again, then said, almost whispering, 'My father was a Nazi Wolfcub and soldier during World War Two –'

'That's nothing to be ashamed of,' he interjected helpfully. 'I mean, you can't be responsible for your parents, so you mustn't worry about that.'

'No,' she said, shaking her head, 'that's not the problem. I only mention it because it has a bearing on everything else. According to what relatives told me, he was trained as a Nazi Wolfcub to bait the Jews, had actually killed by the time he was sixteen, then, during the fall of Berlin in 1945, when he was eighteen, he was caught and sexually abused by Soviet troops. Initially traumatized by this experience, he seems to have defeated the trauma shortly after the war by scavenging for survival in the ruins of Berlin, becoming a black marketeer, then pimping for Allied troops, and eventually moving on to full-scale crime, including extortion and murder. In other words, he had become totally ruthless – and, according to some reports, sadistic – and he *was* sadistic, which was what led to the rest of it . . .'

'Okay, Ingrid, go on.'

She sighed, turned her hands this way and that, keeping her eyes fixed upon them.

'By 1948, when he was twenty-one, he was quite well off financially and had learned to handle himself socially, with fine clothes and good manners. Because of this, he managed to marry the wealthy daughter of an aristocratic Berlin couple, thus ensuring himself some very useful connections during the post-war boom. Then, in 1950, his wife *and* her parents were killed instantly when they were involved in a hit-and-run crash. However, according to certain relatives, the police later located the driver of the truck involved in the crash, and he swore that he had been paid by an unknown person to arrange that crash. That unknown person was never found – but the leading suspect was Zweig.'

'You mean he killed his own wife and in-laws?'

'Yes, Jerry. Exactly.'

Her sigh was like a light breeze through tall grass – a sad and lonesome refrain.

'Go on,' he prodded her gently.

'Shortly after that so-called accident,' she continued, studying her ragged fingernails and not pleased by the sight of them, 'my father fled from the Law in Berlin, taking with him the wealth he had inherited from his dead wife and in-laws, as well as a great collection of the art treasures he had purchased from those Nazis who had stolen them from the Jews. Eventually finding his way to Argentina, he married another woman, my mother, the daughter of Protestant Germans who had left Germany many years before.'

'What in hell could she have seen in *Zweig*?' he asked her – none too subtly, as he instantly realized.

She just shrugged forlornly. 'I don't know. Maybe he just overwhelmed her. Certainly, having heard

61

certain stories about my father's past activities, my grandparents tried to prevent his marriage to her; however, they *also* died in mysterious circumstances – and not long after, possibly when still in shock, my mother married my father.'

'The shock,' he said. 'That would certainly explain it. You don't marry a monster like that unless you're out on a limb.'

He saw the hurt in her eyes and knew he'd said the wrong thing again, but covered up for it by again reaching across the table and taking hold of her shoulder, shaking it gently.

'Hey, I'm sorry,' he said. 'I shouldn't have said that. I mean, he's still your old man, after all . . . Sometimes I could cut my tongue out. I mean, I –'

'It's all right, Jerry. It doesn't matter. I know what you mean.'

'What about your mother?' he asked to change the subject. 'Do you even remember her?'

'Just. My father became some kind of mercenary, involved in a lot of very dirty work for the dictators of Argentina and Paraguay – the extermination of the Indians, the murder of political opponents and so forth. My mother despised him for it – and her contempt encouraged him to abuse her terribly. She committed suicide in a hospital in Cologne – where she had been admitted for severe depression – apparently by taking an overdose of the drugs she was then being treated with . . . though there were certain doubts about that as well.'

'Doubts? What doubts?'

She shrugged again. 'I don't know. I don't think about it. It's not something I want to think about. It's all in the past now.'

Her voice trailed off into a lengthy, pained silence. Now he wanted to protect her, to make amends for all her suffering, and found himself squeezing her shaking hands and drawing one of them to him.

'You might as well tell me the rest,' he said. 'You might as well let it out.'

'Yes,' she said. 'Yes, I think so . . .' She stuck a finger under her spectacles, rubbed her tears away, sniffed and looked down at the table, then said softly, 'By the time of my mother's suicide, my father had already been very successful at using his inherited money and stolen works of art as the basis for ever-expanding wealth and power; and with the passing of my mother, whose inheritance he also claimed, he just doubled his energies in that direction.'

'Of *course*!' Jerry exclaimed when realization finally dawned on him. 'You mean *that* Wilhelm Zweig! And you're *that* bastard's daughter?'

'Yes,' she said shamefully. 'Unfortunately I am. And I've been in and out of mental institutions for that very reason.'

Shocked by this confession, deeply pained by its necessity, he squeezed the hand he was holding and said, 'That's okay. Don't worry.'

She nodded, offered a grateful smile and sniffed back more threatening tears. 'My father seemed to hate me as much as he had my mother, so sent me to a series of different private schools rather than have me around him. The most I ever saw him was once or twice a year; and during those visits he would only make my life more miserable by humiliating me – usually when with one of his mistresses or whores – and then laughing at my misery or, if I annoyed him, beating me and locking me in my room.'

'The bastard! The shit!'

But this time *she* squeezed *his* hand, as if pacifying him.

'Naturally,' she continued quietly, 'I soon came to

dread my visits to him – even more than I suffered because of his neglect – with the result that I did very badly at school and was, by adolescence, failing exams, shoplifting, breaking windows, and generally misbehaving in some very odd ways. In short, by the time I was an adolescent I had a lot of neuroses – all of which were caused by my mother's suicide and, even more, by my father's obvious contempt for me.'

At that moment Jerry could have happily killed Zweig, but he didn't mention that fact. He simply nodded, hardly knowing what to say, feeling a deep ache inside when her voice stripped him naked.

'More than that,' she continued. 'Since he's become a power unto himself – wheeling and dealing internationally in finance, art, property speculation and, particularly, the sale of armaments to all and sundry – he's also grown increasingly megalomaniacal, and now seems to be dreaming of the day when he'll personally resurrect his eternal Third Reich – as envisaged, so he told me, by the only man he's ever revered above himself . . . namely, his beloved Führer, Adolf Hitler.' She paused, took a deep breath, then said in a sorrowful voice, 'So . . . that's my father.'

After watching her slip her thick-framed spectacles down the bridge of her nose, wipe more tears from her hazel eyes, then push the spectacles back into position, Jerry said: 'Jesus Christ, what a story! What a *bastard* your father is!'

He could hardly believe the extent of his outrage; was shaken by the depth of his feeling for her, his swiftly growing desire to hold her and breathe new life into her. He knew the pain he had felt when his father had died, vividly recalled the horror, grief and anger it had brought him; but the passing of her mother must have been even worse, since it was likely that the suicide had been murder – and that her father had done it. Yes, she had lost her mother just as he had lost his father, but in her case the haunting was more acute because of what remained unresolved.

When he thought of that, his heart went out to her, taking part of him with it.

He didn't want to believe it, was frightened to feel it happen, and was denying it to himself in the turmoil of his thoughts when the blond young German, Hans, to whom he had been introduced, offered a welcome distraction by walking into the bar. He was wearing a white shirt and trousers and looked very handsome.

'I'm sorry to interrupt,' he said, in what sounded like a genuinely apologetic tone of voice, 'but your father sent me to remind you that dinner is served and to escort you, if you're agreeable, to his cabin.'

'Oh,' Ingrid said meekly, 'I forgot.'

'After that he wishes you to go to bed. He is concerned,' Hans explained, 'that lack of sleep, combined with the heat, will spoil the trip for you. He only thinks of your own good.'

It was clear to Jerry that the façade of concern camouflaged a command – and Ingrid, blushing as if embarrassed that he should witness her subtle subjugation, yet clearly unable to resist the thinly veiled order, thanked him for the drinks and obediently started following Hans out of the bar, much to Jerry's disgust.

'Are you sure you don't want another drink?' he asked her.

She stopped walking, glanced at him, then lowered her eyes demurely. 'Thank you,' she murmured, 'but no.'

He stared directly at her, trying to will her to stay and have dinner with him, but she merely smiled wanly at him.

'If I happen to see that guy tomorrow, I'll check him out for you.'

Hans glanced at Ingrid, his brow furrowed anxiously. 'A . . . *man?*' he asked.

'It was no one,' Ingrid replied too quickly. 'It was just one of the other passengers, on the deck . . . a nice man . . . he smiled at me.'

'I hope you didn't smile back.'

'No, I didn't. I promise.'

Hans nodded, relieved. 'Good night, Mr Remick.'

'Oh, sure,' Jerry replied, trying to sound laconic. '*Guten nacht.*'

Hans flushed, turned away, held Ingrid's elbow and led her out, leaving Jerry not only with a virulent detestation of Wilhelm Zweig, but with an uncomfortable dose of jealousy at the suspicion that there might be something between Ingrid and that handsome, oddly impassive young German who had taken her from him.

Finishing his drink, he got up and left the bar, stood by the railing of the deck outside, and studied the great umbrella of stars that glittered gloriously above the dark desert and whispering black Nile. He was filled with protective love, with the urge to be a knight errant, and although he knew the reason for this, he couldn't really believe it.

Was he in love? Of course not! That wouldn't make any sense. He had simply responded to a kindred soul, to a form of suffering he recognized, to the fact that she, just like him, had lost the parent she most loved. His heart had gone out to her – certainly, that was natural – because of the singular nature of her suffering and the doubt she must live with. That's what it was all about: her tale had stirred his emotions. He was filled with pity because of what she had told him, and now felt protective.

Love? He couldn't love her if he tried. That was just for the birds . . .

Yet later that night, sleeping alone in his narrow

bunk bed, he dreamed about the rather drab and timid Ingrid Zweig ... though the Ingrid of his dream was neither of those, but completely, exquisitely naked ... and passionately carnal.

He awoke at dawn, wanting her.

CHAPTER SIX

The first leg of the two-day journey was the cruise from the magnificent rock amphitheatre of Aswan, past darkening granite and sweeping vistas of yellow desert, to the *wadi* of Kom Ombo. There, where the ancient ruins of the Roman-Grecian Temple, perched about thirty feet above a bend in the river, rose against a flawless azure sky from yellow sand dunes, green grass and trees, Jerry found himself standing at the boat's railing with Ingrid, aware that he wanted her there – real close, within arm's reach.

'Fantastic, isn't it?' he said.

'Yes, Jerry, it is.'

'This is what we came to Egypt to see, right?'

'Right, Jerry.'

'It was dedicated to two deities. The falcon god Haroeris and the crocodile god Sobek. When we get up there, you'll see the columns of the hyostyle hall, and lots of reliefs and carved inscriptions.'

'You remembered that information from your guide book?'

'Sure, I did. So what? I tend to remember everything I read. And I'm a *freak* for guide books!'

He quoted a lot from his guide books because it filled the silence brought on by his fear that he might say something too sentimental. He hadn't been himself all day, and now he felt pleasantly flustered in her presence, his mind filled with soft thoughts. He wanted to say nice things to her, catch her smile, let it warm him, but he didn't know how to go about it, was too embarrassed to try it. He wasn't used to feeling this way, couldn't really believe it, and found himself skirting around his own emotions like a beginner on ice skates.

'Anyway,' he said, covering up for his confusion and wishing he could sort out his emotions, 'this sure is a sight to see. That's why I'm surprised that your old man, if he's so interested, hasn't left his damned cabin.'

'He's probably seen all this before. He's been everywhere, after all.'

'Then why did he come in the first place?'

'It's something to do with antiques, I think. He was hoping to meet someone aboard ship, but I don't think he has.'

'How can he, if he doesn't leave his cabin?'

'He doesn't *have* to leave his cabin,' she replied with a touch of weariness. 'He gets Hans to do that for him. I know that Hans, apart from keeping his eye on me, is trying to identify the man they're looking for.'

'They *don't know* who they're looking for?'

'No. I think they've reason to believe he's on board this boat, but don't know who it is. They were probably tipped off about him by someone – another dealer in antiques.'

'Yeah – *if* it's antiques. And the man they're looking for *could* have been the man who was watching you last night. Except, of course, that he almost hypnotized you, which might make him *too* odd.'

She smiled at that, adjusted the spectacles on her nose; then suddenly shivered, looking very confused, and glanced over his shoulder along the deck, her eyes widening gradually.

'Oh, dear,' she murmured.

Jerry turned around and scanned the crowded open deck to see what she was looking at. He saw a silvery-haired man, very handsome and distinguished, gazing at the spectacular ruins above the Nile, his eyes protected by sunglasses.

'That's him,' Ingrid said.

Jerry studied the man carefully, hoping to see something unusual, but saw only a tall, athletically slim, silvery-haired male who had the air of a born aristocrat and wore clothing to match.

However, even as he was making this assessment, the man, as if knowing he was being watched, turned his head quite deliberately to stare first at Ingrid, then, after removing his sunglasses, directly at Jerry, his gaze steady and, even from this distance, clearly intense.

For a moment – a very *strange* moment – Jerry felt that he was going to faint – or, more precisely, was falling into a trance – but the feeling passed away as quickly as it had come, leaving him normal once more, if a little confused.

Getting a grip on himself, he shook his head and looked up again, but the man simply smiled pleasantly at him, almost as if he knew him, then turned away and glanced beyond the quay below to where the rust-red, crumbling columns of the ancient temple dominated a brilliant sky.

Determined to speak to the man, and assuming that he was about to join the other passengers on the sightseeing trip, Jerry stuck close to Ingrid when they disembarked and made the short walk along the corniche, past dilapidated tenement buildings, ramshackle stalls and Arab vendors to the magnificent columns of the ancient temple – but as they mingled with the other sweating tourists in the fierce heat, it soon became obvious that their quarry wasn't among them.

'He must still be on the boat,' Ingrid said, her brow furrowed with thought as they stood together near the reliefs in the outer passage of the temple.

'Right, Ingrid. Obviously.'

Yet he wasn't so sure. He was feeling very odd vibrations. Some of these were for Ingrid, who was turning him upside down, but the rest had to do with the way she had introduced herself to him. She had looked like a woman coming out of a trance; and her first words had been about a geriatric with silvery hair and hypnotic eyes.

Maybe he *had* hypnotized her. He had certainly made *him* feel strange. He felt a bit nervous, then. If not for himself, at least for Ingrid. That man had certainly been watching them – him and Ingrid – yet so far he had only been seen on the boat's upper deck, not anywhere else. That made Jerry even more uneasy, and he determined to speak to the mysterious man the next time he saw him.

'The way he smiled at us,' he said to Ingrid. 'That was a tease – a sort of come-on. I don't know what he's playing at.'

'He scares me,' she replied.

'Why?'

'I don't know.'

'I'm going to speak to him the next time we see him. I'll just ask him what's cooking. We might be imagining this whole thing, so let's at least have it out.'

'That seems sensible, Jerry.'

She didn't sound like she meant it, but he knew she was just nervous, and that made him even more determined to speak to the man. However, he was frustrated again when, during the subsequent afternoon journey to Idfu, past cultivated fields, earth-brown shore, Arab women doing their laundry, and donkeys and cattle drinking from the river, the man was not to be seen anywhere on the boat – nor at the noisy Egyptian-style *galabiyeh* party given that evening, to the delight of the many other silvery-haired passengers, most of whom seemed to have more stamina than Jerry and Ingrid.

'He's vanished again,' Jerry said in frustration. 'He must sleep an awful lot.'

'You think so?'

'Yeah. I mean, what else could it be?'

'He might not even be one of the passengers. He might be a ghost.'

'You believe in ghosts, Ingrid?'

She smiled. 'I don't know.'

'If you ever see a ghost, let me know – I mean, I'm into that subject. In the meantime, I just want a chance to talk to that guy.'

He thought his chance might come the following morning, when he saw the man leaning once more on the railing, observing the hungover passengers moving wearily down the gangplank, en route to an exploration of the great temple of Horus, at Idfu – but before he could get to him, the man turned away and disappeared through a doorway – and later, when Jerry looked for him among the many other passengers, as, sweating profusely and rendered featureless in the heat haze, they swarmed around the massive, pharaonic walls, pylons and colonnades of the temple, the man was nowhere in sight.

'I can't imagine why he's on this boat,' Ingrid said, squeezing Jerry's hand affectionately as they stood together by the inside wall of the base of the immense pylon, studying the inscribed scene of the marriage celebrations of Horus and Hathor. 'He hasn't been on a single trip yet. He hasn't once left the boat.'

'Neither has your old man,' Jerry responded, leading her up onto the sun roof where the ceremony of the Union with the Solar Disc was celebrated. '*He* hasn't been seen since he boarded – so why not our mystery man?'

'My father's a different kettle of fish. He wouldn't be seen dead with what he deems to be the common riffraff – the paying passengers – and on top of that, he hates coloured people, particularly Arabs.'

'Your father hates me and I'm white. I mean, that bastard hates *everyone*!'

'Yes,' she agreed, dabbing beads of sweat from her nose, her slim body distorted in heat waves, a light breeze beating at her. 'That's true enough.'

'At least he's got a sexy blonde mistress. She must make him feel young again.'

'You think Elena's attractive?'

'Yeah. *No!* I mean, she's not really attractive. She's just . . . *sexy* in a sort of . . . Oh, God, I've said the wrong thing.'

'It's all right,' she said, obviously hurt and trying unsuccessfully to hide it. 'I'm sure most men would respond the same way. She has that effect on them.'

'Not on me,' he said as they left the great hypostyle hall, stepped into scorching sunlight, and walked across the dust-blown colonnaded forecourt past the other tourists and Arab guides. 'I didn't mean it that way. I mean, she's sexy in a sort of whorish way. Not my type at all.'

'Oh? And what's your type?'

'The quiet type. The modest type. I like my girls to be modest in speech and dress, as well as slim, just like you.'

'Is that some kind of compliment?'

'I only deal in facts. But why am *I* being grilled? What about that blond beauty, Hans? The ski instructor who fancies you?'

'He's not a ski instructor and doesn't fancy me, Jerry. He's simply my father's personal assistant and has to keep his eye on me.'

'Why?'

'Because my father is concerned about who I talk to – which is why Hans is watching us right now.'

Jerry *was* aware of the fact that everywhere he and Ingrid had been together, Hans had been as well, keeping a discreet distance away but rarely losing sight of them – and now, when he glanced past the soaring colonnades of the great temple, he saw that same handsome German, his blond hair windblown, turning away to gaze with studied attention at the river flowing thirty feet below them, past fields of green sugar cane and parched, dusty earth.

'Sonofabitch!'

'Pardon?' Ingrid said.

'I'm beginning to feel that we're being watched by *everyone*!'

'You look funny when you're angry.'

'I'm not angry. I'm just annoyed. And I really want to talk to that mystery man before he gets on my nerves.'

In the event, the man *did* materialize again, early that evening, shortly after they had stopped at the riverbank farming village of Isna and were passing through the lock prior to cruising downstream to Luxor.

Jerry was leaning beside Ingrid on the railing of the open deck, looking down on the palm-fringed village with its peeling, red-rust walls, its many camels and heaps of sugar cane, when again he felt as if he was about to faint, or perhaps go into a trance.

Recovering quickly, but impelled by an inexplicable conviction, he glanced back over his shoulder, through the panoramic window of the bar ... and saw the mystery man sitting at one of the tables inside, his sunglasses resting on the table beside him, his intense gaze and enigmatic smile disturbingly clear.

Startled that he had so strongly sensed the man staring at him, Jerry took a deep breath, squeezed

Ingrid's hand, and said, 'To hell with the lock. Let's go and speak to that guy.'

'I don't want to,' Ingrid replied.

'You have to,' he insisted then, lying deliberately, added, 'At least to reassure yourself that he's perfectly normal.'

He wasn't too sure if the man was normal. Nevertheless, he dragged a reluctant Ingrid into the bar, where he bought both of them a drink – the Nubian *Karkade* for her, a Stella beer for himself – then after a rather theatrical study of the area, which was otherwise empty, nodded casually at the man and said, 'Hi. Do you mind if we join you? You seem all alone there.'

'One is never alone in Egypt,' the man replied in velvety tones. 'The whole of human history is here . . . But, yes, please do join me.'

Sitting at the low table, directly opposite his quarry and with an uneasy Ingrid between them, Jerry was relieved to note that up close the man – handsome, suntanned, and wearing immaculate white shirt, trousers and shoes – seemed perfectly normal . . . other than having a youthfulness belied by his silvery hair and possessing an unusually steady grey gaze.

The man placed his gin and tonic back on the table, then offered his right hand.

'Saint-Germain,' he said softly. '*Count* Saint-Germain.'

The quiet pomposity of the introduction, as well as the anachronistic nature of the title, took Jerry by surprise. He was also confused, as he repeated the name in his head, by his conviction that he had heard of it before, though didn't know where or when.

'A *count*?' he said, taking hold of that outstretched hand and observing that there were no rings on its fine fingers. 'I'm common Jerry Remick, from New York City – and my friend here is Ingrid Zweig.'

'You are German, of course,' the Count said, holding Ingrid's hand lightly in his own, as if weighing it. 'I myself am of German descent – my family originated in Freiburg – but of course I haven't resided there for many years.'

'Where *do* you live?' Ingrid asked him.

'Here, there and everywhere,' the Count said, releasing her hand and indicating the world beyond the window. 'I have travelled much in my lifetime.'

'For work,' Jerry asked, 'or pleasure?'

'A little of both,' the Count replied, without being more specific, then studied Ingrid with a rather odd intensity. Eventually, as if the silence had made him realize what he was doing, he offered a wintry smile.

'You are travelling together?' he asked.

'No,' Jerry said. 'We just met here on the boat. I'm travelling alone, but Ingrid's with her father and some other friends.'

'Ah, yes, Herr Zweig. I think I saw him when you were all coming aboard, but have not seen him since.'

'He's like you. He doesn't leave his cabin much.'

Saint-Germain feigned surprise, raising one fine eyebrow. 'Me?' he said. 'But I am hardly *ever* in my cabin. I love the scenery so much.'

'Oh, yeah?' Jerry rejoined, trying to sound conversational. 'Well, I've seen you on deck a couple of times – though not on any sight-seeing trips.'

'Yes, I suppose you're right. But then I've come on this trip so many times, and now the sight-seeing exhausts me. So I'm happy just to wander around the boat and watch history drift by me.'

The boat had left the village of Isna well behind and was heading downstream, towards Luxor, as the sun began sinking over the sand and crags of Gebelein, with the palm trees shading into silhouette, as still and solemn as monks in prayer.

Saint-Germain smiled and pointed, indicating the world outside, then had another sip of his drink and put the glass down.

'So,' he said, smiling with icy charm at Ingrid, 'I am happy to remain on board the boat and watch the ancient world drift past – just like Herr Zweig.'

Ingrid twitched at the mere mention of her father's name; then blushed and lowered her eyes.

'I doubt that he's even doing that,' she said. 'He just likes his privacy.'

'Ah, yes,' Saint-Germain replied, 'that is understandable. I have read about him in the newspapers. He is a man of great power and many responsibilities, so doubtless needs to have his solitude. However, why come on a trip such as this just to hide in a cabin?'

Ingrid shrugged. 'I don't know.'

Saint-Germain, Jerry noted, was staring at Ingrid with veiled intensity, as if willing her to raise her eyes and look at him – which, to his amazement, she soon did.

'I have read that your father is a collector of precious antiques,' the Count said in a measured manner, 'so perhaps he has come on this journey in search of some more.'

'Yes,' Ingrid replied. 'Maybe. In fact, I think so. I mean, I think he was meant to meet someone on board, though I'm not too sure why. What you say could explain it.'

Saint-Germain looked sceptical. 'We have an *antique* dealer on board?'

'I don't know,' Ingrid replied. 'I don't even know if such a meeting was arranged. I only know that he was *hoping* to find someone on this boat – though I haven't a clue who it is, nor why my father wants to find him.'

'And you, Jerry?' Saint-Germain said. 'What brings *you* on this cruise? Study or pleasure?'

He had a smoothly modulated, slightly theatrical voice that could certainly have suited a mesmerist – and that, plus the fact that his gaze was *too* steady, was starting to make Jerry think that there *was* something distinctly odd about him.

'A bit of both,' he found himself replying, not wishing to be as enthusiastic as he was sounding, but strangely unable to help himself. 'I have an interest in mythology, unexplained phenomena and, in particular, the reported magical properties of the Great Pyramid of Cheops, so the main purpose of this trip is to go there.'

'And you *really* think the Great Pyramid has magical properties?'

'I think it might have. I'm particularly interested in the fact that the Great Pyramid, widely reported as a flawless structure, *isn't* a perfect pyramid, since its tip, the *real* tip, is actually missing.'

'Missing?' the Count asked, his eyebrows raised.

'Well,' Jerry said, helplessly warming to his favourite subject, 'it has been reported by various travellers over the past couple of thousand years that the final stone courses below the summit of the pyramid are not, in fact, there.'

'And you believe this?'

'Sure. And I'm not alone in believing that the original apex of the pyramid was once in place, but was of a very different material from the rest of the pyramid – a material so rare and valuable that it was removed, way back in the past, before the original marble facing on the lower pyramid was stripped to provide stone for Cairo.'

'And what size was this rumoured missing tip?'

'About five inches from base to apex.'

'Very good, Jerry,' the Count said. '*Very* good.' He then leaned further over the table and stared steadily at

Jerry, making him feel drained and unreal. 'And what else do you know about the Great Pyramid?' he asked.

Gazing directly into Saint-Germain's mesmeric eyes, Jerry realized that he didn't want to speak to him any more, but for some reason or other could not resist him. He felt wide awake, fully conscious and alert, but something had been paralysed inside him, leaving him helpless. The Count wanted him to talk, and he knew that he *would* talk, irrespective of his own wishes – and even as he fully grasped this frightening fact, he heard himself speaking.

'I know,' he said, 'that the sides of the Great Pyramid are orientated precisely to face the four points of the compass, which suggests that it's an instrument of astrology; that geographically speaking it stands at the centre of Egypt, at a place which has also been accepted widely as the centre of the terrestrial world; and that its dimensions, when analysed, have convinced many that it is not *just* a tomb or pharaonic toy, but something possibly constructed as a link between Earth and the cosmos. And I believe that the missing tip of the Great Pyramid – the smaller, flawless pyramid – is possibly the magical key to the Great Pyramid's nature.'

Having completed what he wanted to say, he found himself slumping back into his chair, unnaturally exhausted. He also noticed, before managing to turn his heavy eyes back on the mysterious Count Saint-Germain, that Ingrid, sitting beside him, was looking distinctly dazed.

There was a slightly mocking smile on the ageless face of Saint-Germain; then Jerry felt those hypnotic eyes starting to release him as that mellow, seductive voice resounded with an eerily unreal resonance.

'You may be right,' the Count said, pushing his chair back and standing up. 'But *why* is the tip of the pyramid missing? Who took it? To where? These, my friend, are some of the age's great mysteries . . . and only a few know the answers.'

He waved his right hand slightly, almost across Jerry's face, and as he did so Jerry felt himself emerging from what had seemed like a dream.

Blinking repeatedly, licking lips that were too dry, he just about managed to get his willpower back as Saint-Germain's voice, as mesmeric as a swinging pendulum, crooned, 'Good night, my young friends.'

He was about to walk out of the bar when Jerry, on an impulse and feeling normal again, said, 'I appreciate that you could read about Ingrid's father in the papers – but how did you know it was him when he boarded the boat?'

Saint-Germain stopped walking, turned back, stared down coolly, then, as if having second thoughts, offered a slight, chilly smile.

'One recognizes power when one sees it,' he said. 'And Herr Zweig, without any shadow of doubt, exudes that kind of power. One recognizes one's own kind, my young friend. Now good night . . . and *auf wiedersehen.*'

So saying, he smiled again then spun on one heel and walked out of the bar, leaving Jerry drained and exhausted, not too sure of his sanity.

Taking a deep breath, trying to control his racing heart, he glanced through the window at the starlit sky outside, the great moon above Egypt, the palm trees silhouetted where the desert met the Nile – then he focused on Ingrid.

She rubbed her cheek with her hand, turned dazed eyes upon him, then said with a sigh of bewilderment, 'What was all that about?'

'Don't insist on an answer,' he replied. 'I wouldn't know what to say. Come on, let's get out of here.'

Without giving her time to disagree, he took hold of

her hand, tugged her to her feet, then led her out of the bar and into the fresh air. The sky was lustrous with stars, the desert gilded by moonlight, and the silence of the night had its own resonance, a magical quivering. He breathed deeply of the cold air, looked down at the black river, faced Ingrid and felt a great fear rising up from his depths.

She was staring sombrely at him, as if trying to read his mind, and he saw in the plain lines of her face the beauty waiting to spring out. He wanted to encourage that, to release her from the past, but he felt too confused by the present.

Who was Saint-Germain? And what did he really want? Was his interest in Ingrid or Zweig? Was it friendly or dangerous?

Such questions had no answers, but they shook him leaf and bough, making him step closer to Ingrid, his hands reaching out to her. He touched her, stroked her shoulders, explored her spine and pulled her to him; he saw her eyes close, felt the sweetness of her lips and was flooded with love.

He felt that he was tumbling down through himself, into waves of pure feeling.

It didn't last long. She was too shy to linger. She kissed him once, pressed against him, let him feel her beating heart, then turned and raced away along the deck, disappearing indoors. He watched her go, saying nothing, in a trance of delight and trepidation; then took hold of the railing and raised his face to the wind, his eyes and ears closed to the streaming night, his body turned to pure flame.

He stood there for a very long time, aware of nothing but Ingrid's face.

CHAPTER SEVEN

He had trouble sleeping that night. Torn between sleep and waking, between sensual visions of Ingrid and nightmarish thoughts of Saint-Germain, wondering if he had been hypnotized, if he had hallucinated the whole thing, he tossed and turned for hours, hearing the humming air conditioner, his thoughts in a state of chaos, then eventually groaned aloud and got out of bed to stare through the window.

It was just before dawn and a thin blade of crimson fire was spreading along the dark horizon as the boat started heading for the East Bank of the Nile, the water reflecting faint stars and a pale, undulating moon.

Arousing himself from his sleepless stupor, dressing quickly and carelessly, he left his cabin and went out to observe the sun rising over the desert.

He emerged onto the deck and was slapped by a chill breeze, which made him feel instantly more awake, then walked to the railing and looked out to where the Nile met the desert. The blade of crimson light was brightening, turning purple, then faintly golden, spreading out through the sky to dissolve the stars as the rim of the sun appeared.

He was surprised to find himself alone on deck at this time, the only one to view this spectacle; but then, when he thought of his restless night in his narrow bed, of his shifting through dream and memory and intangible fears, he also remembered that he had been strangely reluctant to open his eyes – and had indeed, at one point, just before finally rising, been convinced that an ominous, bass humming sound – not the boat's engine or the air conditioning – had seemed to *physically* press him back down.

Now released from that odd sensation and feeling more normal, he watched the rising sun, a pulsating gold and purple crescent, taking shape as it ascended, and thought of his conversation the previous evening with the very strange Count Saint-Germain, who had made him and Ingrid feel dazed. Then, just as the sun was breaking away from the horizon to resemble boiling lava being poured over the desert sands, he heard the bass humming sound again, felt something pressing him from behind – an indefinable, pulsating pressure against the back of his legs and spine – and very slowly turned away from the rising sun to see what was happening.

The second he turned around, the invisible pressure disappeared, but he saw at the other end of the boat, just above the tops of the superstructure containing the cabins, a pulsating white light that flared up with a soft whooshing sound, then shrank abruptly and disappeared into the east.

Momentarily stunned, then feeling wildly excited, he padded softly along the deck and saw the mysterious Saint-Germain standing silently at the railing and looking intently towards the east, before waving one hand, as if in languid farewell, and then walking away to disappear into a passageway between rows of cabins.

Jerry glanced to the east, saw only the brightening empty sky, then quietly hurried around the deck, between the cabins and swimming pool, hoping to see Saint-Germain but failing to do so.

'Jesus Christ,' he whispered to himself.

Determined to find the Count, he prowled the boat restlessly as the sun rose majestically over the golden sands of the desert, as the other passengers crept from their beds and the boat anchored against the East Bank, as breakfast was served and Ingrid entered the restaurant – and her smile, as lovely as that of a bashful child, made him glow with strange pride.

'I've looked all over the boat,' he confided to Ingrid, 'but that bastard's just vanished.'

'I hope he vanishes for ever,' she replied. 'He gave me the shivers.'

'He hypnotized you,' Jerry said.

'And what about you?'

'I'm not easily hypnotized,' he lied shamelessly. 'I've got a lot of willpower.'

She put two spoonfuls of sugar into her white coffee and stirred it in a desultory manner while looking out through the rectangular window at the palm trees on the high banks of this narrow part of the Nile, their webbed leaves hanging down over parched earth and the muddy-brown river.

'You shouldn't do that,' he said.

'What?' she asked.

'You shouldn't put that sugar in your coffee,' he explained. 'In fact, you shouldn't take sugar at all, let alone put milk in your coffee, let alone drink coffee in the first place. Coffee, milk and sugar are bad for you – that's why you don't look so good.'

'Oh,' she responded, looking down at her cup of coffee, then taking the spoon out and laying it on the saucer. 'I didn't know that. I see.'

'Oh, *shit*!' he said, knowing he'd done it again. 'Christ, I didn't mean *that*! I mean, you look real good, real attractive – but your colour's a bit off. It's not your *appearance* – you're just not *healthy* – you don't look after yourself. Here, have a fresh orange.'

Feeling really tactless, he peeled the orange for her, broke it into slices, then placed the slices neatly on a plate and handed it to her. She accepted with a wan smile, slipped a slice into her mouth, chewed it with no sign of appreciation, then looked sad again.

'What do you most want at this very moment?' she finally asked him.

'I want to find that bastard Saint-Germain,' he replied, 'and have a good talk with him.'

'And that's all?'

'That's all.'

'Well,' Ingrid said, looking so crestfallen that he instantly realized he should have said it was *her* he most wanted at this very moment, 'you better find him fairly quickly, because we only have a few days left on the boat – then we'll all be in Cairo to go our separate ways. Not everyone on this boat is booked into the hotel in Cairo – and your Saint-Germain may not remain with the group any longer than that.'

'Yeah,' Jerry said, 'I know. I mean, thanks for the thought. It's just that I'll go crazy if he disappears.'

'Why not go and see the purser?' Ingrid suggested helpfully. 'He'll have the list of everyone on this tour.'

'What a bright girl you are,' Jerry said. 'Come on, let's get going.'

Excited again, and pleased because she was so bright, he rushed with her to the purser's office to check the passenger list ... but no one was listed under that name.

While this could have meant that Saint-Germain was travelling under a pseudonym, neither the purser nor any of the stewards could confirm from his description whether or not they knew the silvery-haired man, as distinct from the many other geriatrics on board.

'That name of his – or that pseudonym – rings a bell,' Jerry said. 'I just can't place it at the moment. But I know it. I'm *sure* I do.'

'It's a town just outside Paris,' Ingrid said.

'Yes, but apart from that,' he insisted. 'The name definitely rings a bell in my head, and it's driving me nuts. Saint-Germain, Saint-Germain, Saint-Germain . . . It'll come to me. It's *got* to come to me. Goddamnit, where *is* he?'

Already disorientated by his swiftly growing love for Ingrid, he was further excited and confused by his one encounter with Count Saint-Germain – which he was increasingly convinced had been an hypnotic experience – as well as by the eerie experience on the deck in the chill light of dawn.

'Anyway,' Ingrid said, sounding marginally less timid, 'I don't know why you're making such a fuss about that man. Even if he *was* some kind of hypnotist – so what? He's probably in show business, or something. There's nothing *strange* about hypnotists.'

'There's something strange about *this* one. And when I tell you what I witnessed this morning, you just might believe me.'

However, when he recounted what he had seen on the deck of the boat that morning, Ingrid merely removed her sunglasses, stared at him, smiled and said: '*So?* The man was out for a morning stroll. What's so strange about that?'

'Didn't you hear me?' he said, outraged that she was doubting him. 'There was a very weird light – there were strange noises as well – then whatever that thing was, it rushed away to the east – and when I got there, Saint-Germain was *waving goodbye*!'

'He was probably just waving at a bird.'

'Jesus Christ, Ingrid! *Really!*'

Yet he knew that her reaction was a perfectly natural one; and that what he had seen, if not an hallucination, was something so out of the ordinary that it defied rational thought.

He tried to apply rational thought, became confused

and frightened, then gave in to a mounting excitement and deep curiosity which, while setting fire to his imagination, made him fearful for Ingrid.

If anything, his intoxication and bewilderment over what had occurred were only strengthening his emotional bonds to her; and he kept her close by him, perhaps also out of fear, throughout the rest of the day, pleased that Zweig had remained in his cabin with his blonde whore, Elena.

'What does your old man *do* all day?' he asked Ingrid as they prepared to disembark and take another bus through the hellish noonday sunlight, choking dust and hordes of babbling Arab touts. 'I mean, even that Elena can't ... Well, you know! Not *all day*, they can't!'

Ingrid actually managed a giggle, leaning against him on the gangplank. 'Why not?' she replied. 'All things are possible. Some things are more gross than others, but they're not quite *impossible*.'

He helped her off the gangplank, wiped dust from her pale face. 'You're really pretty attractive,' he said. 'I mean, I like you a lot.'

She lowered her eyes demurely. 'That's nice,' she whispered. 'I like you a lot, as well, Jerry. You've made me feel much better.'

'Let's get the bus,' he said.

'Yes, of course.'

'I'm real good-looking as well,' he said, 'but you don't have to mention that.'

He helped her up into the bus and sat beside her near the back, squeezing her hand now and then as the battered vehicle coughed into life and bumped and rattled its way towards more of the glorious ruins of ancient Egypt.

However, Saint-Germain was haunting him and wouldn't let him go; and thus, during this particularly hectic day on the Nile, as he was rushed with the other passengers through his sight-seeing, he did not give Luxor and Karnak the attention he had thought he would, since one half of him was drowning in a sea of emotion over Ingrid while the rest of him, instead of focusing on the glories of the Valley of Kings and Queens, or the fabulous Temple of Karnak, was agog only with the expectation of once more seeing that elusive gentleman.

In the tomb of Tutankhamen, in the great temples of Karnak – walking past the rams' heads of the Avenue of Sphinxes; surrounded by the colossal statues and Osiride pillars of the temple of Rameses III; overwhelmed by the hypostyle hall with its forest of soaring, time-warped columns; standing in the haunting silence of the ruined houses of the Sacred Lake – in all of those wondrous places, which for years he had wanted to see, he saw only the wounded eyes of Ingrid Zweig and felt the *presence* of Saint-Germain.

'It's as if he's watching us,' he said to Ingrid as, close together, they studied the carved head of Hathor, the goddess of music, love, fertility and dancing, above the entrance to Queen Hatshepsut's temple in the Valley of Queens. 'I can't see the bastard anywhere, but I feel that he's watching us.'

'He's not,' Ingrid replied, taking his hand and leading him to the chapel dedicated to the underworld god, Anubis. 'Now it's *you* who's imagining things. We were never hypnotized – we were just tired – and all the rest you've invented.'

'I didn't invent what I saw on the deck of the boat this morning.'

'And what did you actually see?' she asked as they left the protective shadows of the colonnade, felt the blazing heat of the sun and squinted up through their sunglasses at the awesome cliffs of Deir-el-Bahri. 'You

saw a flash of light – which could have been anything –
and a perfectly normal human being taking his morning
stroll.'

'That light was some kind of UFO!'

Ingrid smiled. 'Maybe so. But then you didn't really
see too much at all – it was gone before you could
blink.'

'Pull your hat down,' he said, outraged, changing the
subject. 'You're going to get your nose burnt. You
should always put cream on your nose – and on your
face and arms, too. You've got delicate skin. It's not
used to the heat. You should learn to look after yourself
better, particularly when travelling.'

He knew what he had seen, and was excited and
frightened by it – excited by its magical nature;
frightened of what it could imply; wondering why
Saint-German was so interested in Ingrid's father;
concerned that Ingrid might be endangered because of
it – and so, pressed pleasantly close to her in the
milling throng of fellow tourists, blinded by the
shimmering white light of midday, drained by the blue-
lighted humidity of the afternoon, he was totally
disorientated by physical exhaustion and his burgeoning
love.

'I hardly know where I am,' he said to Ingrid. 'I
might as well be in bed.'

'I'm glad you're not,' she replied. 'I wouldn't have
enjoyed any of this without you. I'd probably have
stayed in my cabin.'

'Really?'

'Yes, really.'

She blushed and then sighed, carefully avoiding his
eyes, and he felt his spirit turning in the breeze to fall
protectively over her.

'You're real cute,' he managed to say when they
returned to the town of Luxor and were wandering,

hand in hand, through the crowded bazaar in the deepening violet light of the early evening. 'I mean, you *could* do something about your appearance – but apart from that, you're really pretty attractive. I mean, more than you know – you know?'

It may not have been a compliment, but *he* thought it was; and later that evening, when the violet glow had turned into starlit darkness, when the *son et lumière* spectacle brought Karnak to magical life, when the light and sound washed over him, taking him back to ancient Egypt, to the heart of the mysteries that so enthralled him, he turned Ingrid in towards him, tugged her close, held her tightly, saw himself reflected dimly in her upturned, thick-rimmed spectacles, and said, 'What about when we get to Cairo?'

'It's all right,' she replied, her tears magnified by the spectacles, her eyes blinking repeatedly in love's sweet confusion. 'Don't worry about my father or Hans. We'll be in the same hotel, so no matter what they say, I'll see you there. I promise! *I swear it!*'

He wanted to kiss her trembling lips, to loosen her pinned-up hair, to remove her thick-rimmed spectacles and clothes and make tender love to her – but he could only squeeze her hand, feeling foolish, almost childish, and parted from her on the boat's upper deck, under the starlit sky.

He walked to the stern, his soul filling up with feeling, with the mystery and magic of this singular time and place, and stood there a long time, until midnight, until the deck was deserted and only the pale moon moved ... and then suddenly he went cold, sensing something, *feeling* something; and eventually heard that sound – the faintly familiar, bass humming noise – and then saw the same pulsating white light beyond the last of the cabins.

Feeling a hot flush of excitement, but also the chill of

fear, he took a deep breath, muttered, 'Jesus, here goes!' then padded as quietly as possible along the empty deck and turned left, between two blocks of cabins.

Reaching the other side, he stayed hidden by the cabin walls, hearing the bass humming noise, feeling an odd, unnatural pressure, and staring out at the pulsating white light that fell over the starboard deck.

The unnatural pressure kept tugging at him, the bass humming sound continued . . . then he heard the soft murmur of two voices farther along the deck, obviously coming from roughly the same area as the strange light and noise.

With his heart racing fearfully, but unable to control himself, he inched along the cabin wall, took a deep breath and then carefully peered out.

At first he was almost blinded by the fierce, striated light; but then his eyes adjusted quickly and he saw two human males silhouetted in a white haze that seemed to emanate from the disc-shaped light source hovering magically beyond them.

He stared, hypnotized, not understanding what he was seeing, his senses being upturned by that relentless, bass humming sound, while the disc-shaped white light, very brilliant, pulsating rhythmically, threatened to draw him out from where he was hiding and suck him towards it.

Resisting that force, releasing his breath and rubbing his eyes, he looked out again as the talking men moved a little, as the light around them dimmed and seemed to move further back, and the men, both wearing normal suits, became recognizable.

One of them was the silvery-haired gentleman who called himself Saint-Germain.

For a moment, Jerry couldn't quite see the other man, but then he nodded at Saint-Germain, stepped out of the distorting haze, and walked away – straight into that hovering, disc-shaped light source, where he turned back to face Saint-Germain.

The man raised his right hand in a gesture of farewell – and at that precise moment, as the light flared up around him with a sudden whooshing sound, briefly illuminating his features, Jerry saw with stunning clarity, even from that distance, a pair of wintry-grey, almost silvery eyes and a dangerously seductive smile which, with that slightly inhuman, mesmeric gaze, made the man appear strangely ageless and slightly unreal.

Stunned and shocked, caught in a sudden seizure of unnatural, overwhelming desire for that distant man, Jerry was about to step out from the protection of the bulwark when the light flared up even more, beat and swirled around that haunting prince of darkness, then seemed to dissolve him where he stood in a prismatic brilliance.

Abruptly, with another soft whooshing sound, the light raced off at startling speed into the distance, until it was no more than a pinprick of light, another star in the heavenly vaults, which, after flaring up one last time, winked out completely . . . leaving nothing but the majestic, star-filled sky and its vast umbrella of silence.

Jerry was sweating and shaking, felt dazed and unreal. He took another deep breath, let it out slowly, then glanced around the bulwark, to where the two men had been, and saw Saint-Germain, all alone in the moonlight, walking casually along the deck and turning the corner at the far end, for all the world like a perfectly normal passenger out for a midnight stroll.

Jerry didn't attempt to follow him. He knew that he wouldn't find him. Instead, he tried to control his breathing, to still his helpless shaking; then slid down the cabin wall until his backside touched the deck; and just sat there, trembling, holding his head in his sweaty hands, staring across the black ribbon of the Nile to ancient Egypt's eternal night.

CHAPTER EIGHT

When Ingrid entered her father's cabin suite, Zweig was propped up on the bed, supported by a lot of pillows, his flushed, humourless face framed by the pillows and windows on either side, both of which showed the spires and minarets of Cairo as the boat slowly approached its docking bay alongside the corniche.

Her father was naked, his pendulous breasts hanging down, but a badly rumpled white sheet was covering his loins and thighs, and was itself covered in the newspapers of many different countries. Balanced precariously on his lap was a tray on which stood the emptied pint glass for his health drink and the numerous small bottles containing his vitamin, rejuvenation and other tablets.

'Good morning,' he said without warmth as she entered. 'I'm sorry I haven't been able to see you over the past couple of days, but as you can see –' and here he indicated the newspapers – 'I have been very busy. A man's work is never done.'

Elena, hearing that one, chuckled falsely and winked at Ingrid. 'He puts his heart and soul into his labours,' she said, 'and I can say that without doubt.'

Ingrid blushed and lowered her eyes, but not before noting that while her father was still naked in his very rumpled bed, Elena had already prepared herself for disembarkation and, as she adjusted her body-hugging jeans and shirt, which clearly were too tight for her, she gazed balefully at the Filipino steward who was packing the suitcases.

'I can't wait to get to the hotel,' she said. 'I'm sick to death of this creaking crate.'

'You should have taken advantage of the sun-deck and swimming pool,' Zweig reprimanded her, 'instead of staying cooped up here with me.'

'I had to keep you warm in bed,' Elena replied. 'I'm a *masseuse*, after all.'

Ingrid lowered her eyes again when her father offered a mocking smile; she looked up when her secret friend, Hans, immaculate and handsome in white shirt, shorts and socks, stepped forward to remove the tray from her father's lap and hand him his dressing gown.

'We'll be docking any minute,' he said. 'You better have your shower now, sir.'

'I don't *need* a shower,' Zweig replied. 'I will therefore have my little chat with my daughter before dressing myself. So, Ingrid,' he continued while taking the dressing gown from Hans, but forgetting to put it on, 'I note that you have a pleasantly sunburnt face. You have obviously been out and about.'

'Yes, Father,' she replied, trying not to be so humble in front of him, wishing Jerry was here.

'So?'

'Pardon, Father?'

'*Where* have you been, you stupid child? And *what* have you been up to?'

'I've just been on a few sight-seeing trips, Father.'

'Were you alone on those trips?'

'They were all organized trips, Father. I went on buses with a lot of the other passengers.'

'You weary me, my child. Why do you lie so shamelessly?'

'Lie? I don't –'

'You were not *just* with the other passengers. You made most of those trips with a particular individual.'

She knew there was little point in denying Jerry's existence, since Hans had, after all, followed them on most of their trips together. Still, she was filled with woe because her father had raised the subject, knowing only too well the kind of mockery that would soon come her way.

'Well, yes,' she began, almost stuttering, 'it *is* true that a certain person –'

'Hans informs me,' her father interjected, 'that you've been seeing the young American with whom I had a nasty encounter when boarding this boat.'

'He didn't mean to be offensive, Father. He just has a kind of American brashness of the kind we're not used to.'

'Another member of the great unwashed,' her father said. 'So why is he being so friendly with *you*?'

'I think he just . . . *likes* me.'

'Are you suggesting a romantic interest?'

'No, Father, I –'

'I should hope not, my child, since it is clear that such a worldly young man would find little of interest in you – romantically, sexually or otherwise.'

She tried very hard not to show her humiliation, but couldn't stop the burning of her cheeks.

'I take it that you and the American have *not* yet . . .?'

'No, Father! Of course not!'

'Good,' Zweig responded. 'Since, after all, you and he can have little in common.'

She didn't respond, but felt a hint of anger. She had previously felt only fear in her father's presence, so the anger surprised her.

Staring steadily at her, his gelid gaze unrelenting, her father held the dressing gown in Elena's direction, indicating that he wanted her, his slave, to help put it on.

'I would normally be embarrassed to stand naked in front of my daughter,' he said as Elena removed the gown from his large hands, 'but since she has finally become *involved* with a member of the opposite sex, I can assume that nothing she will see will shock her. Is that not so, Ingrid?'

Aware that she was being mocked, Ingrid couldn't hide her blushing ... but she also felt the rise of unfamiliar resentment and that new, simmering rage. Surprised by the growth of these more positive feelings, and understanding that they were caused by her father's contempt for her and Jerry, she willed herself not to cry, to keep her gaze as steady as possible, and loosened the fists clenched by her sides, letting the air cool her sweating hands.

If she could not prevent him from being so crass in her presence, she could at least deprive him of the satisfaction of seeing her pain.

'I really don't know what you're talking about,' she said, 'but please don't mind that.'

He raised his bushy eyebrows, obviously taken aback by her tone, gave a slight, icy smile, then deliberately flipped the sweaty sheet off his wrinkled white body.

'Good,' he said. '*Very* good!'

She tried not to see too much when he swung his legs off the bed, stood upright with some difficulty, then stretched his arms out to let Elena drape the dressing gown over him. When she had done so, he tied the belt and turned back to Ingrid.

'So,' he said, 'what did you talk about?'

'Pardon?'

'The *American*,' he emphasized with ill-concealed impatience. 'If you and he have nothing in common, what did you talk about?'

97

'*Talk* about?' she replied, trying to avoid the issue. 'I don't know what you mean.'

'I know you're not the most vocal of creatures, *mein Fräulein*, but even *you* must have talked about *something* with your dishevelled young man. And whatever it was, it could be important – so please tell me about it.'

'*Important? To you?*'

'You sound like a tape recording,' he sneered. 'Repeating my words. Please don't do that – it grates on my nerves . . . and you know what that means.'

Indeed, she did – and Hans' warning glance confirmed it – her father's annoyance could lead to swinging fists and the blue sheen of bruised flesh, most notably, in a case such as this, that of Hans or herself.

'Nothing much,' she said cagily. 'I mean, nothing in particular. His hobby is ancient Egypt, so he talked about that. He knows an awful lot about the pyramids and the country in general.'

'That doesn't explain his interest in *you*,' her father said, obviously still convinced that no member of the opposite sex could possibly like her for her own sake. 'I mean, what did he *want*?'

'I don't think he wanted anything, Father – other than company.'

'*Your* company?'

'Yes. I suppose so.'

He sighed again, snapped his fingers at Hans, said, 'Get me a glass of champagne. I can't stand this without it.'

While Hans rushed to do as he had been bidden, Zweig placed his hand on Elena's backside, gave it a squeeze, then took a deep breath, stretched his arms and stared at Ingrid again.

'The young gentleman wanted your company – and you thought this was *normal*?'

'Well, I –'

'I do *not* think it was normal. It simply doesn't make sense. I have observed you very carefully, from your adolescence onward, and I cannot think of one occasion when a male wanted *you*, rather than an introduction to *me* and the help I could give him –'

'I think –'

'– so I'm sure that this young man, the American, had a reason for treating you so kindly . . . Did he talk about *me*?'

'No, Father. When I mentioned your name, he obviously knew who you were – but apart from that, he didn't talk about you.'

He actually looked disappointed. 'So what was his interest in Egypt?'

Ingrid shrugged. 'Most of Egypt, really. I think he was particularly interested in the pyramids – especially the Great Pyramid of Cheops – the one he said he was taking me to see tomorrow.'

Her father changed when she said that: his cold eyes went out of focus. He glanced blindly about him, as if he had received some surprise, but he recovered as Hans walked back into the cabin carrying a glass of champagne.

'Oh, yes?' Zweig said casually, taking the glass from Hans and having a sip. 'And why his interest in that?'

'It's just one of his hobbies, Father. He's interested in all sorts of strange theories – including flying saucers and poltergeists and the reported magical properties of pyramids – and he has a theory about the missing tip of the Great Pyramid.'

'The missing *tip*?' her father asked, sipping some more champagne, his gaze steady upon her. 'I'd like to hear about *that*.'

Still thinking it a nonsense, not believing it could be harmful, she repeated what Jerry had told Saint-Germain about the missing tip of the Great Pyramid of Cheops – the one adjacent to the Sphinx at Giza – to where they would go tomorrow. When she had finished, her father gargled with his champagne, spat it back into his glass, handed the glass to Hans, then stared at her as if seeing her afresh.

'In other words,' he said, 'your long-haired American believes that the tip of the Great Pyramid, being a smaller, more perfect pyramid, contains magical properties and was stolen many thousands of years ago?'

'Yes. He thinks the missing tip of the Great Pyramid of Cheops is potentially the most rare and valuable artefact on the Earth – and he's come here to try and prove that theory and, if he does, write a book about it.'

Her father's response to this was to untie his belt, let the dressing gown fall to the floor and say to Elena: 'We are obviously heading in the right direction. Now please dress me, my dear.'

He was not unhelpful – raising an arm here, bending a knee there, while the gum-chewing Elena worked his clothes over his white, quivering flesh.

'There has to be a reason for everything,' he said to Hans as Elena dressed him, 'even the most ridiculous things – and now we know why the insolent American finds my daughter attractive. According to the so-called Christian Grabbe, our quarry could be on this boat – the man who knows about the Tuaoi Stone – and since the stone, as we know, is shaped like a small pyramid and possesses magical properties, it is clear who the man we want is. It's obviously Ingrid's boyfriend, Jerry Remick. This odious creature, this Philistine American, will lead us to the Lodestone.'

'I don't think –'

'You *can't* think,' her father told her brutally. 'I knew that from the day you were born – since you came from your mother's womb. Now be quiet. Listen. Please don't bore me with your sentiments. You are going together to the Great Pyramid?'

'Yes, but –'

'*Very good!* Hans, Elena and I will come along for the ride. You will be nice, but quiet, mentioning nothing about our talk. Your young man, whom you think is fond of you, is obviously the man we've been searching for. He knows about the missing pyramid. That small pyramid is the magical Lodestone. I will not rest until I possess it – and your young man may well lead me to it. So don't say a word to him. Simply go where he leads and we will follow. Is that understood?'

'*Really*, Father,' she said, starting to worry about Jerry's welfare, 'I don't think Jerry is the man you're looking for. I think –'

'Thank you, dear, for your advice,' he interjected sarcastically, 'but you do not, as your American friend would put it, know shite from shinola. So please do as I say. In other words, be nice to him. What happens to him after that does not concern you.'

He stared at her, his face like a block of stone, making her feel very concerned indeed about what he might do to Jerry. It wasn't Jerry he actually needed – it was almost certainly Saint-Germain – but when she thought of telling her father that that strange man was on board, she suddenly saw Saint-Germain's eyes floating in front of her – and couldn't open her mouth.

She took a deep breath, avoided her father's gaze, tried to shake Saint-Germain from her mind and think of Jerry instead; but that only made her dwell on what her father was planning – and a tremor of fear rippled through her like cold air on a raw nerve.

'Of course, Father,' she murmured obediently, feeling sick to her soul. 'I understand perfectly.'

'Very good, Ingrid. *Excellent!*'

At that moment the boat bounced lightly against its

docking bay, making everyone in the cabin rock a little before steadying themselves. Ingrid stared through the windows, saw the white glare of the noon sun, and longed to be out there, away from her father. She thought of the mysterious Saint-Germain, then of what her father had told her, and her love for Jerry, swelling up to fill her heart, made her yearn to protect him.

'I don't think that Jerry –' she managed to say.

'You *don't* think,' Zweig corrected her. 'You simply stick with your young man, who has appealed to your childish vanity, and leave all other concerns to us. Is that understood?'

'Yes, Father. Of course.'

'Gee,' Elena said, 'what a sweet kid. She's so goddamned obedient.'

'Just like you and Hans,' Zweig retorted without mirth as Ingrid hastily left the cabin, desperately needing to get out in the open and breathe the fresh air.

CHAPTER NINE

Jerry had to admit it to himself: even though he had often professed his contempt for his mother's luxury, he was delighted to be off that Nile cruiser and having breakfast alone on the balcony of his air-conditioned room in the modern wing of the historic Mena House Oberoi Hotel, surrounded by forty acres of lush gardens and with the pyramids of Giza, only half a mile away, appearing to virtually tower over him, dominating the brilliant azure sky.

Sighing with pleasure, he finished off another glass of orange juice, wiped his lips with a napkin and stood up. He glanced down at the already busy swimming pool beyond the palm trees, smooth green lawns and Egyptian-styled white walls of the rest of the modern wing, then went back into his room to prepare for what he fully expected to be the most exciting day of his trip, namely a visit with Ingrid to the Sphinx and three of Egypt's oldest pyramids.

If anything, his fascination with the pyramids, particularly the Great Pyramid of Cheops, which he could clearly see from his window, had only been heightened by his conversation with the mysterious Saint-Germain, as well as by what he had subsequently witnessed on the deck of the boat. He therefore dressed with some urgency, hardly able to contain his excitement, donning a short-sleeved shirt, long white trousers and sensible shoes, then left his room and walked through the gardens to the reception lobby of the main hotel, which, according to his guide book, had once been a hunting lodge, furnished by the *khedive* Ismael for the sole purpose of receiving Empress Eugenie at the opening of the Suez Canal in 1869.

Such small details were of endless fascination to him; and so, as he entered the luxury hotel, he breathed deeply in the belief that he was actually breathing in history.

His enthusiasm was dimmed a little when he entered the pleasant chill of the air-conditioned, exotic lobby and saw that while Ingrid was indeed waiting for him – wearing a nondescript loose grey dress and flat shoes, with dark lenses on her thick-rimmed spectacles and her hair piled untidily on her head – she was with her father, Wilhelm Zweig, his whorish mistress, Elena, his handsome assistant, Hans, and a turbaned, *galabiyeh*-draped Egyptian, whom Jerry assumed was a cab driver.

His spirits sinking, he froze where he stood, intent on making a discreet retreat; but Ingrid, when she saw him, smiled shyly and waved him on with her right hand, while her father, also seeing him, actually *smiled* and nodded in a friendly manner.

Chilled to the bone by Zweig's smile of welcome, he walked forward and, when he reached the group, was even more surprised to note that Herr Zweig was holding out his large hand.

'Mr *Remick*,' he said with feigned enthusiasm. 'Good morning! Please let me introduce myself. You and I did, of course, have our little difference the day we boarded the boat at Aswan, but let's put it down to traveller's fatigue and the heat of the noonday sun. I am Wilhelm Zweig, Ingrid's father' – and here he shook Jerry's hand – 'and I believe you've met the rest of my little group.'

'Hello,' Hans said.

'Hi,' Elena added.

'Good morning, Jerry,' Ingrid whispered.

'I know Hans,' Jerry said, determined not to be too friendly, 'since he seems to have followed Ingrid and me everywhere – on your instructions, no doubt.'

'Please don't be offended,' Zweig replied. 'A father *has* his concerns.' He then placed an arm around Jerry's shoulder and walked him out of earshot of the rest of the group. 'Please understand,' he said, 'that it wasn't *you* I was worried about. It was Ingrid I was keeping my eye upon – since, as you may have noticed, she is not the most mature of adults, and has indeed been in and out of various mental institutions for –'

'I know. She told me.'

'She *did*?' Zweig responded. 'How surprising that is! She must trust you a lot.'

'I hope so, Mr Zweig.'

'Anyway,' Zweig continued, ignoring Jerry's sarcasm, 'you can understand why Ingrid, though thirty-one, has to be protected like a much younger woman – from her own immaturity, as it were – and having Hans keep a concerned eye on her was simply my way of doing that. And I must say, Mr Remick, that your behaviour has been at all times exemplary. I am very impressed.'

'Okay,' Jerry said. 'No sweat.'

Zweig patted his shoulder, then led him back to the group, where Hans remained blank-faced, Elena was chewing gum, and Ingrid, her head lowered, the living picture of humility, looked at him over the top of her darkened spectacles.

'And so,' Zweig said, still holding him by one shoulder and, taking Ingrid by the elbow, tugging her towards him, 'you can come with us in the cab – or, if you prefer, take the bus.'

'The bus,' Jerry said.

'Of course,' Zweig agreed. 'Understood. Shall we go?'

He nodded at the turbaned Arab, who bowed and led them all out of the hotel, to where the coach and a lot of dusty cabs were waiting, the former already almost filled with passengers, those not with the tour haggling ferociously with the drivers of the latter.

Although it was a good half mile to the pyramids, their sheer enormity made them seem a lot closer than that; and Jerry found himself staring at them in a state of disbelief, finally understanding why no photograph could quite capture their gigantic, eerily alien symmetry.

'Oh, boy!' he murmured.

'So,' Zweig said, offering a fleeting, unnatural smile, 'our car is waiting behind your coach – and the coach is, I note, already almost full. You two best get going.'

Hardly able to look at him, Jerry took Ingrid by the elbow and hurried her towards the coach, pushing her up into it before she could say goodbye. He followed her in, sat beside her in the rear seat, glanced down through the window and saw Zweig in a gleaming limousine, sitting beside the Arab driver, the two shadowy forms behind him obviously being Hans and Elena.

Zweig caught Jerry's glance and waved at him, but Jerry looked away and moved closer to Ingrid, taking hold of her hand.

'What did I do to deserve your father's friendship?' he asked her. 'I mean, why is God punishing me?'

She smiled. 'I'm not supposed to tell you,' she said, 'but I certainly will.'

At that moment, their English-speaking Arab guide boarded the coach, introduced himself, explained what they would be doing on their short trip, then closed the door. The coach coughed into life, lurched forward, settled down, then rolled out of the shade of the hotel entrance and into the baking heat of the plain of Giza, with the pyramids disappearing momentarily before coming back into view, seeming to float magically in the air beyond the red earth of the plain and the shimmering heat waves.

'I can't wait to see inside that pyramid,' Jerry said. 'So, Ingrid, what about your father? Why the welcoming treatment?'

'You're not going to believe this.'

'Go on – try me.'

'Well, you know that my father had been hoping to meet someone on the boat, but didn't actually know who that someone was?'

'Right.'

'Well, he seems to think that someone is *you*.'

'*Me*? Why *me*?'

She squeezed his hand, as if to reassure him, but only succeeded in making him feel even more concerned.

'As you already know,' she continued, 'my father has one of the world's greatest collections of very rare art treasures –'

'Right.'

'– and is fanatical about getting his hands on more.'

'I believe it,' he said as the coach bounced and rattled along the road to the pyramids and the sunlight, beaming in from the plain of Giza, dazzled his vision.

'Well, apparently,' she continued, 'the thing he most wants in all the world is something called the Lodestone, which is said to be a tiny, pyramid-shaped object, made of an unknown substance, and possessing extraordinary magical powers.'

'The missing tip of the Great Pyramid. It can't be anything else. That tip, a pyramid five inches high, was removed centuries ago by a person or persons unknown, and hasn't been seen since – though there have been countless *rumours* about its whereabouts.'

'I see,' Ingrid said solemnly. 'Anyway, it seems my father's been after that object for many years, and that recently, in New York, information picked up by some of his men before they were killed in mysterious circumstances, indicated that someone who would be travelling on the boat we were on, at the same time as us, knew of its whereabouts – which is exactly why my father made the trip. Then, when I innocently told him your theory about the missing tip of the Great Pyramid, he put two and two together and assumed that you were the man he was looking for – the one who was going to lead him to the Lodestone.'

Jerry stared at her, not believing his own ears.

The coach hit a pothole, almost throwing him off the seat, and he grabbed Ingrid and then glanced out the rear window. Zweig's limo was out there, not too far behind, obscured by the sand being churned up by the wheels of the coach. Jerry turned back to Ingrid.

'*Saint-Germain!*' he exclaimed, snapping his fingers with glee. 'He knew about the missing tip of the Great Pyramid – and seemed very interested in my theories. In fact, he only questioned me to find out what I knew – he *already* knew all that – so the Lodestone probably *is* the missing tip of the Great Pyramid, and Saint-Germain is the one who knows of its whereabouts. It's not *me* your old man should be following – it's our mysterious Count Saint-Germain!'

Straining to see down the aisle, between the shoulders and heads of the other passengers and through the distant front window of the coach to the approaching pyramids, he could hardly contain his excitement.

'Unfortunately,' Ingrid said, tugging his elbow to regain his attention and then dampening his ardour, 'Saint-Germain was not seen to either board or leave that boat, was not registered with the purser, and appears to have disappeared into thin air after you saw him with that other mystery man under very peculiar circumstances. In a real sense, he doesn't exist – and that, as far as my father is concerned, leaves only you.'

'You didn't tell him about Saint-Germain?' he asked her.

'No,' she replied. 'There was no point. He wouldn't have believed me. I tried to tell him you knew nothing about the so-called Lodestone, but he didn't believe that either. So he's being friendly to you because he thinks you're here for a purpose. In short, he thinks that if you don't actually lead him to the Lodestone, you'll at least give him a clue as to where it is.'

'And if I don't?'

'You're in trouble.'

Her eyes were hidden by dark lenses, but her face showed her concern; and being no stranger to trouble, he saw it coming straight at him.

'Terrific,' he said.

The coach did not take the left fork to the Sphinx, but instead drove straight on to the three great pyramids and stopped where the tickets to the site were sold, letting the passengers out into the dazzling light and draining heat, in the midst of babbling Arab salesmen with their souvenirs, camels and donkeys.

Jerry enjoyed the touts, being amused by their relentless hustling, but was even more amused when, as the tour guide led his group towards the pyramid of Cheops, he saw them swarming eagerly around Zweig who, waving angrily at them, was like a man in a swarm of bees.

After being besieged by Arabs trying to inveigle them into purchasing souvenirs or rides on donkeys and camels, the tourists from the coach were led by the tour guide straight to the pyramid of Cheops, the Great

Pyramid, prior to their tour of the whole site, including the Sphinx.

Surrounded by smaller funerary temples and flat-topped *mastaba*, the three large pyramids soared up from the desert sands in awesome, geometric splendour, with the Great Pyramid dominating all, its truncated peak seeming to pierce the immaculate azure sky, and its grand stairway, constructed in irregular tiers of stone, leading up to the boundless blue of the cosmos.

Dwarfed by the immensity of those eroded, sloping walls, but exhilarated by the magic and mystery of their history, Jerry wanted to climb the steps and stand at the very top – just below the missing apex – to look across the barren wastes of the shimmering desert. However, that wasn't permitted (the pyramid walls were too dangerous) and so, as some of the other tourists settled for walking around the ruins, he stuck to his original plan of venturing with Ingrid into the Great Pyramid and making the reportedly strenuous journey to the king's burial chamber, hidden deep in the heart of the towering edifice.

As he and Ingrid were checking the torches they had brought with them for this occasion, Zweig hurried up to them, accompanied by an already weary Elena and a clearly anxious Hans, trailing a stream of Arab urchins and touts, and hissing through clenched teeth: '*Scheisse!* How I detest this Islamic scum!'

'Oh, God,' Elena said, wiping sand from her face and arms, 'let's get the hell out of here. Let's go back to the hotel and have a drink and then jump under the shower.'

'Stop complaining!' Zweig snapped. 'These babbling Arabs are enough! I'm getting a headache just listening to them, and your moaning won't help.'

Stopping breathlessly in front of Jerry and Ingrid, he

wiped more sweat from his flushed face and offered a waxen smile.

'So, Jerry,' he said. 'I note that you and Ingrid are holding torches. Do you intend going inside?'

'Yeah,' Jerry said. 'Right.'

'Elena, my dear, would *you* like to go inside?'

'I most certainly would *not*,' Elena responded indignantly. 'I'm already filthy enough as it is. I want a cool drink and a hot shower.'

'I myself would like to see the King's Chamber,' Zweig said, obviously lying, 'but unfortunately tend to suffer from occasional claustrophobia and therefore couldn't take the narrow tunnels. However, *Hans* would like to see inside the Great Pyramid – *wouldn't* you, Hans?'

'Yes, sir,' Hans replied without enthusiasm. 'Naturally, I would.'

'Well, take that torch out of your pocket and join Jerry and Ingrid. I think that's sensible, don't you?'

'Yes, sir,' Hans said.

Removing the torch from his pocket, he reluctantly joined Jerry and Ingrid where they were standing with the Arab guide and three other tourists – two men and a woman – preparing to enter the Great Pyramid.

'I will wait for you out here,' Zweig said. '*Au revoir.* And enjoy it.'

Jerry switched on his torch, watched Ingrid do the same, then took hold of her free hand and moved in directly behind the Arab guide as he led them up the steps in the base of the Great Pyramid to the entrance. The heat was fierce, burning down on his head and shoulders, the light seeming to beat back from the sloping wall to dazzle his vision. Then he stepped inside the pyramid, felt a chill, smelt stale air, and saw a short passage straight ahead, leading to a flight of stone steps in the gloom farther on. They climbed up those steps, into a deeper gloom, and found themselves at the bottom of a steeply ascending tunnel, most of which receded into darkness.

'Damn!' Hans whispered behind them.

The passage was low-ceilinged and dramatically shadowed, climbing steeply into increasing darkness; and the beams of the torches, moving up and down nervously, illuminated smooth blocks of stone with handrails on the walls. The air became warmer, the darkness more frightening, and soon Jerry could hear the amplified echo of his own breathing, the tortuous scraping of his shoes on the dusty wood underfoot. Eventually, still clambering uphill, covered in sweat and breathing harshly, he found himself leaning forward as the ceiling dropped lower.

'God!' Hans muttered. 'I hate this!'

Jerry had to let Ingrid go and clamber up the gallery ramp just behind her. He glanced back over his shoulder and saw only pitch darkness; looked ahead and saw only the round lights of the torches sliding along and over the smooth, finely joined stones as the roof of the tunnel dropped progressively lower and the passage became uncomfortably narrow – to the degree, eventually, where the ceiling was only about three feet high and the walls not much wider apart, thus forcing them to stoop over even more until they were almost bent double.

'Are you okay?' he asked.

'Yes,' she replied, her voice breathless and echoing around him like a ghost's shifting whisper.

The journey seemed longer than it actually was, taking them into a deeper darkness, into a silence that resounded only with their cramped, heavy breathing and scuffling footsteps. Jerry sensed Ingrid's tension and understood it. He also understood why many tourists couldn't take this particular journey and turned back before they reached the burial chamber deep in the pyramid.

'Shit!' Hans whispered behind him in perfect English. 'I can't breathe! I don't like this!'

Mercifully, at that moment, they reached the top of the gallery ramp, clambered through another short, low-ceilinged tunnel, then entered an empty, pyramidal chamber which, soaring nearly thirty feet above their heads, allowed them to breathe more freely, even though its actual base, hemmed in by side ramps, was no wider than the height of the low passage out of which they had stumbled.

Jerry just had time to glance above him at the high, narrow roof of the pyramidal gallery before the guide was disappearing into another passage, thus forcing them all onward again.

When this other, more humid darkness fell about him, causing him to sweat and blink, he found himself struggling awkwardly across dangerously sloping polished stones, then through another claustrophobically low chamber, and finally – as the female tourist made a whimpering sound of protest or fear – stumbled into the relative spaciousness of the burial chamber, which was also in darkness.

'Thank God!' Hans murmured behind him, sounding breathless and hoarse.

In the dim light of their torches Jerry was able to see the empty sarcophagus, the structural perfection of the walls and the great roof, formed by nine granite slabs weighing over 440 tons – and in those few seconds of complete, heart-stopping silence, hardly even aware of Ingrid, Hans or the presence of his fellow tourists, he felt the presence of the Pharaoh's *ka*, or spiritual double, and was filled with the mystery of the ages covered up by the desert sands.

The silence was ethereal, other-worldly, almost palpable, and he sensed it pressing in around him, as if trying to steal his soul. Then Ingrid took his hand, squeezed it tenderly, tugged him to her, letting him know that she was sharing his feeling of unreality and awe.

He acknowledged her presence, pressing against her, smiling at her, not believing he had finally made it here and was standing beside her. They were at the centre of the earth's landmass, in the very heart of Man's universe, and he felt himself shaking with that knowledge, his senses draining away from him.

Then he felt a hand falling upon his shoulder and gripping it painfully.

'What do you *really* want here?' Hans asked quietly. 'Is this the home of the Lodestone?'

At that instant all the torches blinked out – abruptly plunging the burial chamber into complete, terrifying, pitch darkness.

'Oh, my God!' the woman cried out, her voice echoing horribly. 'Oh, my God, what's happening? The torches! *Oh, dear God, I can't see!*'

In her panic, she dropped her torch and let out a high, piercing scream which, reverberating shockingly around the stone chamber, was soon joined by the equally terrified babbling of the Arab guide and the hoarse, panic-stricken voices of the two men – all of which blended into a ghastly, purgatorial cacophony that ricocheted around the chamber in a darkness so complete that Jerry felt he had lost his mind and was spinning into vertiginous depths beyond hope of escape.

He was only rescued from this fate – which he realized was his panic – by the feel of Ingrid's body against his own as he tried in vain to get his torch to work.

'Christ!' he exclaimed in frustration. 'What's happening?'

'I can't see! I can't see!' the woman wailed. '*Oh, dear God, we'll be trapped in here!*'

There was the sound of rushing feet as the woman tried to escape, then a dull thud as she ran into a wall and slid down it, sobbing.

'Oh, no!' Hans said softly behind Jerry. 'What the hell . . .?'

And even as the whispered question trailed off into silence, and as Ingrid shivered softly in Jerry's embrace, he looked straight ahead into that immaculate, pitch-black darkness and saw, where he assumed the wall and sarcophagus had been, what appeared to be a pinprick of light.

A pinprick of light that was gradually growing bigger – as if someone was drilling a hole in the wall to admit the outside world.

'It's not possible!' Hans whispered.

'What's *that*?' a man bawled hoarsely as the Arab guide, after a couple of seconds of stunned silence, also saw the expanding light and let out another demented wail.

'No!' the woman shouted. 'I don't believe . . . *No!*'

It was a cry of protest against the unbelievable – but at that moment, as the pinprick of light grew into a distant, pulsating glowing, the impenetrable sheet of darkness where the wall of the chamber should have been, filled up with a faint glowing, took on a pale blue sheen, then brightened until it became a vast, alien sky, filled with glistening stars and great moons – an overwhelming cosmos.

'No!' the woman screamed. '*No!*'

Her final cry of protest trailed off into a demented sobbing which, blending in with the babbled prayers of the Islamic guide, filled Jerry's head as, transfixed and with Ingrid's heart beating against his breast, he watched as that pulsating white light raced out of the star-flecked distance – out of dizzying depths of space in which there was no north or south, no east or west – and expanded as it approached, becoming a fiery globe, then a flaring white disc that grew bigger and brighter, racing towards him at incredible speed, paralysing him as it flared up and obliterated the stars, then suddenly exploded into the dark chamber, temporarily blinding him.

There was a lot of terrified screaming and bawling from those around him, but he felt Ingrid against him, took courage from her presence, and opened his stinging eyes as the exploding, swirling light contracted and dimmed, shrinking down to the height of the average man, and eventually formed a faintly glowing cocoon of ectoplasm in which two apparently human figures were slowly, magically materializing.

That glowing ectoplasm illuminated the sarcophagus – and there, on either side of the empty stone coffin, shimmering in an unreal manner with faint stars showing through them, were the silvery-haired gentleman, Saint-Germain, and his mysterious partner.

They were both looking younger than Jerry remembered them, both wearing snow-white *galabiyehs*, and staring, with faintly sinister yet oddly seductive smiles, straight past him at whom he assumed could only be Hans.

'You cannot have the Tuaoi Stone,' Saint-Germain said, his voice ethereal and unreal in the glowing darkness. 'To pursue it will damn you.' He then stared directly at Jerry, his glance brilliant, terrifying, and said: 'You must know that the first number is "one". Now depart from this sacred place.'

'Shit!' Hans shouted. '*Christ!*'

Jerked out of his terror by the sound of that outcry, Jerry glanced back over his shoulder.

Illuminated in the faint glowing of the ectoplasmic light, Hans was drawing a small pistol from his pocket. Yet even as he did so, the light around him dimmed, making him glance up in surprise and then, with his jaw hanging open, freeze where he stood.

A gasp from Ingrid made Jerry look to the front where, still standing on either side of the sarcophagus, the two figures in *galabiyehs* were becoming more transparent, the stars shining more brightly through them, before the globe of glowing matter flared up brilliantly again, obliterating those inside it, then filled the chamber with a blinding radiance, a roaring whirl-pool of light, which then seemed to burn through the chamber wall just above the sarcophagus to race away at incredible speed towards the distant stars, until it was only a pinprick of light . . . then nothing at all.

The chamber was plunged abruptly back into pitch darkness, making the woman scream again — but immediately, simultaneously, all the torches blinked back on — some lying on the floor, others still in their owners' hands — to illuminate the stone walls and floor.

The praying Arab jumped to his feet, shone his torch at the chamber's exit, and was heading urgently towards it as the screaming of the woman broke down into hysterical sobbing. A bulky man rushed over to her, helped her onto her feet, put his arm around her waist and practically dragged her, still sobbing, out of the funeral chamber and into the exit passage, where they fell in behind the fleeing guide.

Jerry glanced at Ingrid as she wiped tears from her cheeks; he smiled reassuringly at her and then glanced at Hans who, with the pistol dangling limply from his right hand, was still staring in utter disbelief at the very smooth, solid stone wall above the sarco-phagus.

'Let's get the hell out of here,' Jerry said. 'And that means you as well, Hans.'

The Arab guide's terrified praying resounded with the weeping of the hysterical woman all the way back down through the low chambers and dark passages of the pyramid – and didn't stop when they finally made their escape back into blinding daylight; where the woman, still sobbing hysterically, sank to her knees in the sand and the Arab guide raced up to his friends, gesticulating frantically as he tried to explain what had occurred.

As his eyes were adjusting to the sudden fierce light, Jerry saw Zweig clamber out of the rear of the limousine, rush up to Hans, grab him by the collar of his sand-covered white shirt and shake him violently while demanding to know what had caused all the fuss. When Hans told him, Zweig just glared at him, not believing what he had heard, then jabbed his index finger at Jerry and hissed, 'So what about *him*?'

'No!' Hans exclaimed, his eyes far too bright. 'It was the person *in there*!' He jabbed his thumb back towards the Great Pyramid. '*It had to be Saint-Germain!*'

As if slapped in the face by the very sound of that name, Zweig took a step backwards, glanced blindly at Jerry, then said icily to Hans, 'Don't just stand there with your tongue hanging out! Get in the car, you fool!'

Hans hurried to join Elena in the rear of the limousine as Zweig, sweating profusely, his face flushed with rage, marched towards Jerry, kicking up small clouds of sand, and eventually stopped in front of him and Ingrid, glaring at both of them.

'I should have known!' he said to Jerry. 'You're nothing but worthless scum! Don't ever approach my daughter again – if you do, I'll destroy you. Now come here, Ingrid! *Here!*'

Before Jerry could fully regain his senses, Zweig grabbed Ingrid by the wrist and dragged her to the limousine, pushed her in the back, clambered into the front seat and then slammed his door.

The limousine roared into life and raced off along the road, churning up sand, leaving Jerry standing alone, the sand settling around him, the sobbing of the hysterical woman filling the stunned silence behind him, his back turned to one of the sloping walls of the Great Pyramid, his gaze focused, first dazedly, then with more thought, on the distant Sphinx, that lion with the human head, which had silently surveyed the Egyptian desert for centuries, and might still be doing so when he and the rest of human life had disappeared from the earth.

He stood there a long time.

CHAPTER TEN

The following morning, knowing that Jerry was due to fly to London, Ingrid awakened very early in her luxurious single bed, quickly showered and dressed, then left the room, closing the door quietly behind her, and walked through the lovely gardens in the morning's fading pink light, planning to bid Jerry farewell before he departed.

She had assumed he would be in the main reception area by now, but was surprised to see him standing alone by the swimming pool, staring beyond the arched doorways and flat roofs of the modern wing at the three great pyramids which dominated the skyline half a mile way with their symmetrical perfection.

Still shaken by her experience of the previous day, but swelling up with love for Jerry and heartbroken that he was leaving, she walked down to the swimming pool, stopped beside him and, standing on tiptoe, pressed her lips to his cheek.

Surprised, he jerked his head around, stared at her, then smiled.

'Well,' he said, 'this is a *very* pleasant surprise. I didn't expect to see *you* again.'

'You thought I'd let you leave without saying good-bye?'

'I thought your old man might lock you in your room. He sure seems the type.'

'He is . . . but I'm here.'

She wanted him to hold her and kiss her properly, on

the lips, but instead he just shuffled his feet, shyly avoiding her gaze.

'So,' she said, 'you're going.'

'Yeah,' he said. 'In twenty minutes.'

'We won't see each other again after that.'

'No . . . I suppose not.'

She sank into her pain, but tried not show it; instead, she just sighed and gazed down, with very little interest, at the crystal-clear, rippling blue water in the very smart swimming pool.

'Have you recovered from yesterday?' she asked him.

'Yeah,' he said. 'At least I think so. I've been lying awake all night thinking about it – but, yes, I've recovered.'

She had wanted him to say that he had stayed awake thinking of her, but since the pyramids were obviously more important to him, she decided to stick with that subject.

'Did it really happen?' she asked.

'Yes, Ingrid, it really happened. Saint-Germain materialized with his very strange friend, warned Hans – therefore your father – to stop pursuing the Tuaoi Stone – note, the *Tuaoi* Stone; *not* the Lodestone – then informed *me* that the first number was "*one*" – whatever that means. Yes, Ingrid, it happened.'

'It frightens me terribly,' she told him. 'I'll be glad to get out of here.'

'*Everything* frightens you,' he replied. 'That's one of your problems.'

Shocked, feeling as if he had slapped her face, she raised her eyes from the swimming pool and studied him, searching for malice. She saw none, just a distant, wounded look, then he turned away from her, until he was facing the pyramids, a slight slump to his shoulders.

'So your father wants the Lodestone,' he said, 'which obviously is also called the Tuaoi Stone. He thought someone on that boat knew where the Lodestone was, and that I, because of my interest in the missing tip of the Great Pyramid, was the guy he was looking for . . . But I wasn't. Saint-Germain was . . . and we don't know who *he* is.'

She didn't reply. She just wanted to flee this country. She couldn't bear to be this close to Jerry and not be in his arms.

As if sensing this, he sighed and turned back to face her, his blue eyes slightly misty.

'Why does your father want it?' he asked her. 'Apart from the fact that it's the world's most rare, priceless treasure?'

'You *know* why. You've recently been told. The Lodestone is reported to possess awesome magical properties – and it's rumoured that he who owns the stone can own the world if he chooses.'

'And right now,' Jerry said, 'that's most likely to be Saint-Germain . . . or his mysterious partner.'

'Yes. And if my father could have that power – the power we witnessed yesterday – he would certainly use it to threaten the whole world and thus bring about the dominion of his own, even more terrible version of the Third Reich – a magical order based on his power, with all subservient to him. My father, dear Jerry, is a psychopath and megalomaniac – and he certainly wouldn't consider using the stone to do *good* for mankind.'

'I'm going to stop him,' Jerry said. 'I'm going to find out all I can about the Tuaoi Stone and Saint-Germain; and then, whether it turns out that Saint-Germain is good or evil, I'll ensure that the Tuaoi Stone isn't allowed to fall into the hands of Zweig or anyone like him. I'm going to do that for myself, but I'm also doing it for you – because I can't stand the way your father treats you, nor what he's done to you, and I'll get my revenge by depriving him of what he most wants. I'm determined. I'll do it.'

She felt herself melting in the warmth of her love; her skin was burning with an ethereal heat – but she still couldn't say much.

'What did you mean when you said everything frightens me? Why did you say that?'

'Your father frightens you,' Jerry replied. 'He has you completely terrified. You're so frightened of him, you can't make a move without him – and he knows that and uses that. He has your life in his pocket.'

'That's not true,' she said.

'Yes, it is, Ingrid.'

'I can do anything I damned well please.'

'Then come with me,' he said.

She was shocked, rendered speechless, at once delighted and ashamed; swelling with pride because she knew he was expressing his love for her, but sinking simultaneously into humiliation because she could not find the courage to prove him wrong.

'No,' she said. 'I can't do that.'

'Why?'

'He'd just follow us relentlessly wherever we went; and then, when he found us, he'd destroy you – just to hurt me.'

'And that's why you won't come? For my sake?'

'That's right.'

'That's a lie.'

He turned away from her again and spoke with a quiet, suppressed fury, a smouldering passion.

'I love you, Ingrid. I've never been in love before. But I love you and know you love me – and yet you're giving me up. You're doing it out of fear, out of cowardice, and I simply can't stomach that.'

'I'm sorry,' she said, ashamed that she couldn't conquer the fear that was holding her prisoner.

'And that's it?' he said. 'You're sorry?'

'I don't know what else to say, Jerry. I can't go with you. *I can't!*'

'Damnit, Ingrid, you *have* to. For your own sake, as well as mine. If you don't leave with me, you won't leave with anyone. You'll be stuck with that monster for the rest of your life, living a life filled with regrets and enduring a slow death. So come with me . . . *please!*'

She knew that what he said was true, that giving him up would destroy her; yet even as she felt the pain surging up from her centre, even as her heart broke and shame overwhelmed her, she couldn't find the courage to break free and take what he offered her.

'I'm sorry,' she whispered.

Jerry lowered his head. His back was still turned towards her. He was framed by the Great Pyramid, where their love had defeated fear, but even when she saw his body trembling she could not fight her oldest fear.

'I love you, Ingrid,' he said. 'But clearly that isn't enough. Don't touch me. I can't bear to have you touch me. I love you too much. Oh, God, Ingrid . . . *goodbye!*'

To leave, he had to pass her, his elbow brushing her breasts, and she saw a hint of tears in his blue eyes as he hurried away. She watched him departing, resisting the urge to call him back; desperately wanting to do so, but dreading the humiliation, knowing that even if he came, she still would not leave with him.

He waved once as he crossed the gardens, but he didn't look back; she saw him disappearing around a white-arched doorway, between the rooms of the modern wing, some large palm leaves shivering briefly over his head, as if in mournful farewell.

Then he was gone.

Ingrid was destroyed. Her cheeks burned as her heart raced. She felt her eyes fill up with tears, let them roll down her cheeks, then wandered slowly back through the gardens, weeping silently, ashamed of her cowardice, grieving for the loss of her first love and wanting to die.

She returned to her lonely room, lay back on the bed, cried even harder, then stopped and stared up at the ceiling. She felt drained, depleted, immune to all but pain – and was starting to slip into quiet hysteria when her father arrived.

He knocked and then entered, not waiting to be invited, offering a rare smile and with Elena right behind him, her grin also suggesting a private joke as she leaned in the doorway.

'Good morning, my child,' he said, his eyes untouched by his smile. 'I note that you're already up and dressed – but with moist, swollen eyes. Now why would that be, my pet?'

She tried not to be frightened of him – and was, for the first time, surprised to find the fear falling away from her, taking a weight from her shoulders. Emboldened, and realizing what pride meant, she returned his hard stare.

'It's nothing,' she said. 'My eyes are stinging from the water in the pool. I went for an early-morning swim.'

'Really?'

'Yes, really.'

'You wouldn't *lie* to me, would you?'

'No, Father,' she deliberately lied, feeling a warm flush of pleasure.

'Well,' her father said, 'I'm glad to hear *that*. I mean, I couldn't bear to witness *two* people crying before breakfast is served.'

She felt herself stiffening, wondering what was to

come; but she managed to keep the fear from her face and her eyes on her father.

'*Two* people crying?' she asked him. 'What do you mean?'

'That young American,' Zweig said, sighing with triumph. 'We just saw him leaving. Taking the bus to the airport. We tried to be pleasant – to say goodbye, as it were – but he couldn't see us through the tears in his eyes, and so went off without a word . . . *Very* strange. You think there's *someone else*? But then you wouldn't know, would you?'

Elena couldn't contain herself and started giggling into her hand, leaning forward to hide her face against Zweig's broad back, her arm snaking around him. Zweig guffawed and turned towards her, wrapping his thick arms around her, then together they staggered out of the room, convulsed by their sick joke.

Ingrid closed her eyes, bit her lip and took a deep breath; she held her breath for some time, letting her pain turn into rage, then opened her eyes again, let her breath out, and eventually climbed to her feet with the strength she had almost lost.

She went to her window, looked down upon the gardens, then thoughtfully studied the wondrous symmetry of the three dazzling pyramids beyond that mere half mile of desert. She thought of the Nile cruise, of her growing love for Jerry, of his accusation that she was ruled by her own cowardice – and of how, by letting him go, she had simply proved he was right.

She didn't cry again. There were no tears left to shed. Instead, she thought of the sanatorium, of the contempt she had mustered there, and of how she had thrown her cigarette into the wastepaper basket and later watched the smoke billowing up from the fire in her room.

Remembering that, and the satisfaction it had given

her, she smiled and shook her head in an affirmative manner.

'Yes, she said, speaking to herself, 'you need positive thinking.'

When she heard the maid opening the door across the hall, she left her own room, followed the girl into her father's room, and told her that she was going to wait there for her father. She watched the girl in silence, taking pleasure from her efficiency, then, when the girl had left, she glanced down at the neatly made double bed and said, '*Au revoir* – to you *and* your blonde whore.'

She rifled every drawer and took all the cash she found there, then returned to her own room, packed a shoulder bag, wandered leisurely out of the hotel, as if just off for a stroll, and caught a cab to Helipolos International Airport – determined, for the first time in her life, to brave the world on her own.

PART TWO

THE SEVEN STATIONS OF LEARNING

CHAPTER ELEVEN

Jerry was sick. Awakening in the stifling bedroom of his crummy rented flat in Notting Hill Gate, London, and hearing the amplified sounds of a Rasta Reggae band practising already at nine o'clock in the morning for the forthcoming evening's frolics, he was pouring sweat, felt as if his head was splitting, and also suffering his long dark night of the soul in very rare English sunshine. He was depressed, enervated, devoid of his normal zest, and as he dragged himself out of bed, feeling grey on this sunny day, he knew exactly what he was suffering from.

He was obviously lovesick.

Despising himself, telling himself to act his age, he ran the hot water then climbed into the bath, thinking distastefully of how squalid the English were, washing in their own filth. God, he wanted a shower. He wanted Ingrid naked in it. He wanted to be naked in it with Ingrid, soaping her soft skin. Instead, he was in this filthy English bath, thinking of drowning himself.

Disgusted to see the grime of London wash out of his hair and lap around his unprotected skin in the soap-sudded water, he hastily climbed out, pulled the plug, then dried himself. Refreshed, or at least relieved to escape the bath, he put on some clothes, not really caring what he wore, beyond mere mortal vanity.

Mere mortal vanity didn't prevent him having an orange juice and something to eat. What he had, in fact, was some atrocious English bread with really terrific

Cheddar cheese, followed by a cup of Italian black coffee, which he sipped by the window.

It was now ten in the morning and the street below was already busy; the West Indians and Rastas were taking in the sun while the tourists, walking past their pounding music, looked on agog. Jerry liked it in Notting Hill Gate. It reminded him of New York. His only problem was that he no longer slept well at nights, obsessed, as he was, not only with losing Ingrid, but with the mystery of Saint-Germain and what had occurred in Egypt.

Helpless over what had happened with Ingrid, he was at least able to start progress on his search for the legendary Tuaoi Stone and, incidentally, unravel the mystery of Saint-Germain; and to this end had already placed an advertisement in the *Guardian* newspaper, asking for an 'adventurous, open-minded, personal assistant with experience in historical research'. That ad had been printed in yesterday's newspaper, there had already been phone calls from aspirants, and Jerry was hoping to interview a couple of them tomorrow.

If nothing else, it would take his mind off Ingrid.

In fact, even though Ingrid had broken his heart by not showing more spirit and coming with him, Jerry understood what a lifetime's humiliation could do to someone and had therefore already forgiven her in his heart. The person he could not forgive was Wilhelm Zweig, that bloated arsehole who had turned a potentially beautiful young woman into a timid, emotionally distraught victim with no hope for the future.

No, he could not forgive that; and so, apart from his own insatiable need to find the legendary Tuaoi Stone, he was filled with delight at the very thought of depriving Zweig of the one thing he wanted most in all the world.

Unfortunately, his major problem was money. It was

one thing to embark on an epic voyage of discovery (which is how he liked to think of it) and quite another to do so without even the bread to pay for the assistance he so badly needed, not to mention his own everyday expenses. So, whether or not he liked it, he would have to call his mother in New York and lay the word on her.

Deciding that he might as well get this over with as soon as possible, he removed his keen gaze from the busy street below, drank the last of his coffee, then picked up the telephone, dialled the operator and asked her to ring his mother's number, reverse charges. He could actually hear his mother's phone ringing in New York, but she took a long time to answer it; then, when she did, sounded tired and irritable until told by the operator who was calling. At that, she yawned loudly, murmured, 'Oh, dear God,' then added impatiently: 'Yes, of course I'll accept the charges. Now please put him on.'

'Hello, caller?' the London operator said.

'Yes,' Jerry replied obediently.

'You're through to your number. You can speak now.'

'Terrific,' Jerry said. 'Mom? Is that you, Mom?'

'Yes, dear, it's –'

'I'm sorry I haven't called before, but I've been tied up with –'

'Do you know what *time* it is in New York, Jerry? It's five o'clock in the *morning*.'

'Aw, gee, Mom, I'm sorry. I didn't think. I mean, I was just sitting here thinking about you – and, you know, called on impulse. I'm real sorry if I've got you out of bed –'

'You have.'

'– and I'll call you back later.'

'No, dear, don't do that. You'll probably catch me in

the middle of my bridge party or having a bath. So, how did it go, dear? Your trip to Egypt, I mean!'

'Terrific,' he said. 'Absolutely fantastic. I won't forget it as long as I live. It was money well spent, Mom.'

'Please call me "Mother", dear. You *know* I hate "Mom"!'

'Sorry, Mother.'

'So, why aren't you *home* already, dear? You should have been back here two weeks ago.'

'Well, Mom – Mother – the thing is . . .'

'Why are you hesitating, Jerry? Are you in some kind of trouble? You must tell me *instantly* if you are. I knew it! I just *knew* it!'

'No, Mother, I'm not in trouble. I've just got a little problem that I think you can help me out with.'

'Of course, dear. Just get on the next airplane. We'll sort your problem out as soon as you get home. There's no need to worry, dear.'

'I'm *not* worried, Mother. I just need some money – some *cash* to live off for the next three or four months, using this place, London, as my base.'

His mother was silent for some time, obviously trying to take in what she had heard. Eventually, with an audible sigh, she said: 'You want to stay in *England* for another three or four months?'

'Yes, Mother, that's right.'

'Has this something to do with some . . . *female*?'

'No, Mother,' he said, feeling distinctly uncomfortable. 'I mean, not really. I mean, it *has* in a sort of way, but not *really* – you know?'

'No, dear, I do *not* know. Please elucidate.'

Hardly knowing where to begin, and aware, when he *did* begin, that what he was saying probably sounded like nonsense, he recounted the most important events of his trip, specifically those involving the bloated

Wilhelm Zweig, his heartbreakingly suppressed daughter, Ingrid, and the mysterious Count Saint-Germain and his unknown partner.

As he talked into the disbelieving silence at the other end of the transatlantic line, he became fully aware, for the first time, that he had spent the last fortnight like someone in a state of shock – only leaving his flat to purchase food and drink; usually only getting out of bed when forced to consume what he had purchased; sweating under the stale sheets, sleeping badly, if at all – an unprecedented condition that was obviously caused not only by the loss of the weirdly attractive Ingrid, but by his own enormous difficulty in accepting that what he remembered of Egypt had actually occurred.

His state of suspended animation, or chronic disbelief, had hardly been helped by the pain he was feeling over the loss of Ingrid – and even now, as he talked into the vacuum of his mother's growing incredulity, he was lacerated by that pain, remembering Ingrid's shy smile, her inhibition and fear, her hazel eyes magnified by the old-fashioned, thick-rimmed spectacles which, in conjunction with her piled-up auburn hair, had made her seem like a forlorn Victorian servant or the living personification of an equally forlorn, clichéd spinster.

When he thought of that pitiful creature, he felt completely heartbroken. Nevertheless, he kept talking, pouring his words into his mother's silence, reaching his climax with the extraordinary happening in the burial chamber of the Great Pyramid – vividly remembering, as he talked about it, that dizzying glimpse into the abyss of the infinite, with Saint-Germain and his mysterious partner materializing magically out of the ether. He then explained that he had to stay in Europe until he had solved the awesome riddle, at no matter the cost.

'And that's what I need the cash for,' he explained. 'I suspect that my investigations will take a lot of time and involve a lot of travelling, possibly even back to Egypt, and I'm going to use London as my base of operations. So, Mom – Mother – apart from my credit cards, I need some hard *cash*.'

As a former amateur actress of some standing, his mother was a dab hand at the double take and dramatic pause – and now her silence, which seemed to stretch out forever, also stretched his nerves to breaking point before, with another beautifully timed sigh, she released him.

'Oh, dear God,' she said. 'You haven't learned a thing, have you? Still ignoring the real world and inventing these ridiculous stories. I give up, dear. I really do.'

'Mom, it's true! It all happened!'

'Of course dear. I understand. Now put the young lady on the phone and let me talk to her.'

'*What* young lady?'

'The one you had all these great adventures with – and whom you doubtless need the money to support while you live there in sin. Please let me talk to her.'

Jerry was outraged and wanted to slam the phone down; but his need for his mother's money was greater than his need to be proud.

'I told you!' he almost screamed. 'We said goodbye in Cairo! I left her and came straight back to London and rented this place. I don't even know where she is, Mother! I'm on my own here! I promise!'

'Stop being so melodramatic,' she said, and then was silent again. 'I *do* hope you understand,' she said, after a great deal of thought, 'that I *would* like you to have a serious relationship with a member of the opposite sex – but not, dear God, with a *German*, let alone with the offspring of that Nazi, whom I've read all about.'

'She wasn't really German,' he felt obliged to explain. 'She was born in Argentina, then educated in England and Europe. Not that it makes any difference, since she's out of my life now.'

He felt real pain in saying it, but his mother, obviously not feeling the same, said, 'Well, I'm sure it's all for the best, dear. Water finds its own level.'

There was another long silence which seemed, to him, to be some kind of black hole into which he could hurl his grieving soul and lose it for ever.

'So,' she said eventually, sounding very suspicious, 'you intend staying in London, whether I like it or not.'

'Yes,' he said.

'And if I don't finance this latest lunacy?'

'I'll starve,' he said, 'but I'll *still* stay.'

'I don't seem to have much choice, do I, dear?'

'Well, if you *don't want* to help me,' he replied, sensing his moment, 'then you *don't have* to help me. On the other hand, I'm staying here anyway. It's just a matter of *how* I stay – comfortably or miserably.'

'And how much would you need to be comfortable, dear?'

Having planned to stay three or four months, he said, 'Six months. I need enough cash to last me at least that long – then, whether successful or not, I'll come home, I promise.'

'How very thoughtful,' his mother replied.

'So, are you going to send me some money?'

'Of course not,' she said firmly. 'I've never heard such nonsense in all my life. Flying saucers, ghosts, precious stones and mad Germans – you've obviously made all of this up for some reason or other.'

'I haven't!'

'*My* belief,' she went on, completely ignoring his cry of protest, 'is that you are involved in some way with the young woman you mentioned, and are staying in England in the hope of seeing her again.'

'I'm not!'

'Or, if that's not true, you've simply got this bee in your bonnet and are going to squander the money in pursuit of a highly nonsensical theory. So, dear, no, I won't be sending you the money – and my suggestion is that since you are presently devoid of cash, you simply use your American Express card to purchase an air ticket back home, when we can discuss all of this much more sensibly in decent surroundings.'

'I'm not coming home, Mom!'

'I'm your mother, not your mom, and I'm hanging up right now. I'll expect you home within a day or two. Goodbye, Jerry. Be sensible.'

The line went dead when she hung up, and he stared at his own phone, wanting to eat it or smash it, outraged that his mother didn't believe him and was leaving him in penury, doubtless hoping to pressure him into coming home.

'Well, you *won't*!' he snapped. 'Damn you!'

He slammed the phone back onto its receiver, then walked to the window and looked down, feeling defeated. Below him, on the sunny street, one of the colourful Rastas, his plaited hair decorated with beads, was strumming a guitar and singing while his friends clapped rhythmically and added vocal counterparts.

Their very happiness was a slap in the face to him, and as he stood there, looking down at them, he felt the tides of defeat creeping over him to drown his aspirations.

Without money from his mother he had no chance of staying on in this country, let alone hiring an assistant and pursuing, wherever it might lead him, the mystery of Saint-Germain and the Tuaoi Stone.

Dwelling on this harsh reality, and having difficulty

in accepting it, he muttered a soft oath to himself and then left the room.

Outraged and in despair, he determined to spend the last of his cash by getting drunk and letting tomorrow take care of itself. This he did, plunging into the noisy, smoky atmosphere of a typical London pub and drinking one pint of beer after another. Drunkenness came soon enough, illuminating his confused thoughts, increasing his more naïve tendencies and almost making him stupid.

Almost, but not quite, since, when he found himself engaged in drunken banter with a tattily dressed, peroxide blonde, and was invited back to her place, he was sensible enough to think of AIDS, herpes or syphilis, and also thought, with real pain, of what he owed to the memory of Ingrid, then resolutely stood up, waved the blonde goodbye, and unsteadily left the pub.

Returning to his modest flat, and realizing that he had just spent the last of his hard cash, he decided to telephone those who had answered his advertisement for a personal assistant and were due to be interviewed by him the following day. However, instead of doing so, he lay down on the bed for a brief rest and fell into a troubled sleep, during which he first dreamed of Ingrid naked in the bed beside him, then had another dream, a much less pleasant one, about his beloved Ingrid's awful father, the monstrous Wilhelm Zweig, getting his hands on the Tuaoi Stone and using its powers to set himself up as overlord of the whole world.

In his dream he saw smouldering cities, mass graves, desolation; he watched thousands enslaved in some future where Zweig had dominion. There was fear and suppression, a widespread despair, and Zweig's face took shape out of the dark clouds gathering overhead. First Zweig, then Saint-Germain, then his mysterious partner ... each emerged from the other, became the other, all as one, then merged back into the vast desolation of the abused and forsaken.

Yes, he dreamt of a new world, one of masters and slaves, then saw lightning strike a wall, burning the number "one" into it; was hypnotized by that number, started dissolving into it . . . and was jerked from his dream – or, more accurately, from his nightmare – by the shrill and incessant ringing of his telephone, which seemed to drill through his brain.

First groaning, then cursing, he sat upright, shook his head, then swung his legs off the bed and walked to the telephone. He was unwashed and unshaven, his clothes shabby and dishevelled, and he ran his fingers through his uncombed hair and picked up the receiver.

'Yeah,?' he said.

'Jerry? Is that you?'

'Yeah,' he said, unable to believe who he was hearing, his heart starting to race.

'It's me, Jerry. It's Ingrid. I'm ringing up for that job you advertised. I'm in London, Jerry.'

He heard the singing of birds.

CHAPTER TWELVE

With the helicopter roaring all around him and the wind beating through his thinning hair, Zweig glanced down through sunlit haze at his fleet of thirty high-powered boats – which formed a large circle with a dot (his own boat) in the centre, about halfway between the Brazilian Basin and the Mid-Atlantic Ridge.

He felt pride, but little else. Not even pleasure. Certainly not after the hell he had recently been through – first, all those filthy Arabs along the Nile and in Cairo; then the flight of his daughter, Ingrid; finally, the awfulness of arriving in Recife at the height of another of their damned carnivals, with the already narrow streets rendered impassable by cheering crowds, noisy bands, and the customary dance performance of the *caboclinhos* in their ridiculous Indian garb, who had merely added to the already atrocious bedlam by beating rhythmically with their bows and arrows while leaping and spinning like whirling dervishes, making way for the procession of king, queen and chanting *tirador de loas*.

He had been greatly relieved when his limousine had managed to break through the primitive madness and carry him to what had once been the relative tranquillity of his lavish villa in the southern suburb of Boa Viagem – but even there, when he attempted to go for his evening stroll along the palm-fringed promenade, he had found himself hemmed in by horrible tourists and madly jogging Brazilians of a pedigree that could not have afforded the area just a few years ago.

Nauseated, he had retired early to his bed in the villa, and there, with the sound of the Atlantic in his ears, had slept an uneasy sleep, filled with dreams of his daughter, the American and Saint-Germain; and had felt relieved again when, the next morning, his helicopter had taken off from Guararapes Airport and carried him through the pure morning air to the relative peace of his floating empire near Ascension Island, not too far from the island of St Helena, where another of his heroes, Napoleon Bonaparte, had spent his days of despair and humiliation.

Shuddering at the thought of what could happen to the world's finest, he settled back into his seat and sucked on a tablet as the helicopter dropped towards the fleet and made his ears pop. Having sent Hans and Elena on ahead, in order to allow himself an evening's privacy in his villa, he was eager to get back to business, particularly his pursuit of the legendary Tuaoi Stone, starting with a constructive business chat with Hans.

The helicopter dropped lower, almost directly over his own boat, whipping up the waves in surging arcs of white and blue as it hovered briefly over the swaying helipad, then began its final descent. It soon touched down, bouncing lightly on the deck, then came to a rest.

Zweig unclipped his safety belt and let himself be helped out of the helicopter even before the rotor blades had stopped turning. Hurrying away from the still-whining machine, he stopped just outside the area of turbulence caused by the slowing rotor blades and stared around him with pride at the many other high-powered boats that were forming a protective cordon around him in the choppy green-blue waves of the South Atlantic.

He took a deep breath, nodded curtly at those saluting him, then saw that Hans had been waiting for him by the doorway which led into the upper saloon, or lounge.

'So,' he said, 'it is good to be back, *ja?*'

'Yes, sir,' Hans replied.

Zweig nodded and glanced around again at his watery domain, then let Hans lead him through the saloon and down to the lower deck, into the master cabin containing his surgical bed, spa bath, steam bath and Jacuzzi.

Elena was in the Jacuzzi, enjoying the swirling water, her blonde hair protected by a plastic cap that emphasized her large eyes. As he entered, she turned those eyes upon him, not without trepidation.

'Hi,' she said. 'Welcome back.'

Zweig leaned forward, kissed her on the forehead, then stood up again.

'Thank you,' he said. 'I have to discuss business with Hans, but once that's done I'll join you. Perhaps a drink in the meantime?'

'Champagne?'

'You have developed expensive tastes.'

He pressed a buzzer to call the steward in, gave the Filipino his order and waved him out again. He then snapped his fingers, pointed to the nearest chair, and said, 'So, Hans, sit down. I want to hear what you've been doing since you returned. Not sleeping, I hope.'

'No, sir,' Hans replied, pulling a chair out, but waiting until Zweig had seated himself before also sitting down. 'I've been looking into our affairs in general, and also checking on your daughter's whereabouts. Regarding the latter, we have confirmation that Ingrid did indeed fly to Heathrow Airport, London.'

Zweig felt a flush of rage, but simply nodded acknowledgement.

'She has been staying for the past fortnight in a modest hotel in the Bloomsbury area, and to date has not contacted the American, presumably because she doesn't know where he is. However, a telex just received an hour ago from our offices in London states that someone placed an advertisement in the *Guardian* newspaper, asking for a personal assistant with historical research abilities. We can't yet confirm that this is Remick, but it's being checked out right now – and it's our belief that if it is, Ingrid might also see the advertisement and find the American through it. Should that be the case, we will, as you requested, abduct her before she gets to him and bring her back here.'

'Good. And if it *is* the American, as you suspect?'

Hans sighed sadly and lowered his long-lashed eyes. 'He will, as you requested, be terminated in a manner that makes his death look like a suicide. Ingrid will then be informed of his death, and there the matter will rest.'

'Very good,' Zweig said. 'Excellent.'

At that moment, the door opened and the Filipino steward returned with a bottle of chilled champagne and two tall-stemmed glasses. When he had poured the drinks, he handed Zweig and Elena each a glass, then bowed his way back out of the cabin and closed the door quietly.

Ignoring the fact that Hans was dabbing sweat from his face and licking his thirsty lips, Zweig raised his glass to Elena and then had a sip.

'So,' he said, removing the glass from his lips. 'That takes care of my daughter and the American. Now what about business?'

Hans coughed nervously into his fist before replying. 'Alas, the situation is not good. In the past, as you know, we have been able to conduct most of our international business transactions with minimal legal restrictions by the simple expedient of operating from this fleet –'

'Yes, yes, I *know* that,' Zweig interjected, thinking with pride of the numerous corporations he headed anonymously in many countries, while ensuring that his own domicile was this fleet anchored outside territorial waters, thus beyond the reach of international law.

'So,' Hans continued with maddening solemnity, 'we have been able to amass a considerable fortune, along with political and fiscal influence, from our extensive international trading in armaments, gold bullion, various pharmaceutical products, and the purchase of valuable works of art.'

'You mean the *theft* of valuable works of art,' Elena corrected him.

'Be quiet,' Zweig said, starting to feel nervous. 'This is no time for frivolous remarks. This is *serious*, Elena.'

'Unfortunately,' Hans continued, again coughing nervously into his right fist, as if frightened by what he had to say, 'there has, over the past year or so, been a noticeable increase in press exposés of our so-called manipulation of international laws to suit our own ends –'

'Bastards!' Zweig whispered.

'– and as a consequence, the major Western powers can no longer feign ignorance of our activities – which in the past they had done for their own benefit.'

'Naturally,' Zweig said. 'We are offering the hypocrites a service they could not do without.'

Hans shrugged. 'They may still want the services we provide,' he said, 'particularly in the area of armaments and other potentially embarrassing requirements; but the unprecedented build-up of adverse media publicity about our activities has forced them to agree publicly that action must be taken to curtail our unlicensed operations.'

'And how do they intend doing that?'

'By the application of sanctions,' Hans replied. 'The

countries involved in this, mainly the United States and Europe, have started applying sanctions against those countries dealing with us – particularly Soviet-backed Third World countries – and those sanctions, along with other legal restraints, are gradually crushing the life out of us, most commonly by attacking our holdings in their respective territories.'

'Bastards!' Zweig said again, this time much louder.

'For the past six months or so,' Hans continued remorselessly, 'we have found it increasingly difficult to either purchase or sell armaments; our income in that area is therefore down approximately seventy per cent. Even worse is that the Inland Revenue departments of the United States and the European Economic Community are investigating our financial affairs and have already prevented the transfer of our most recent assets to off-shore tax havens. The only revenue still out of their reach is that being held in Switzerland and a few other off-shore tax havens; but even that is dwindling rapidly because of our general lack of trading and inability to shift cash on the open market. In short, we can no longer trade with, or within, the United States, the British Commonwealth or Europe.'

Zweig took a deep breath, opened and closed his restless hands, then let his breath out again and collected his thoughts.

'And the Soviets?' he asked.

'The Soviets have refused to cooperate with any of the aforementioned powers,' Hans said, 'and have therefore become, willy-nilly, our sole source of future revenue and our one remaining area of influence.'

'Damn!' Zweig exclaimed – then, before he could stop himself, he had swung his fist over the table to send the champagne bottle and glasses flying across the room. They exploded against the far wall, just above the Jacuzzi, with shards of glass spraying out and raining down on the floor, not too far from the shocked Elena who let out a frightened shriek.

'*Damn!*' he heard himself screaming – then he picked the table up and threw it across the room, this time in the opposite direction, well away from Elena. It was still bouncing noisily off the wall, one of its legs already broken and spinning towards the floor, when, exhausted by his outburst and feeling a bit embarrassed, he dropped back onto the divan and found himself staring in a vague, distracted manner, first at Elena, clearly frightened, in the Jacuzzi, then at Hans, who was still sitting, rigid with tension, where the table had been.

'It's all right,' he said to Hans, feeling the need to make amends and waving his hand in a gesture of dismissal. 'It's not your fault. Nor *mine*. These are circumstances beyond our control, and that's all there is to it. Nonetheless, something has to be done – or we'll be doomed. *We'll be doomed!*'

The sound of his own voice shocked him (that unfamiliar, shrill hysteria), but he managed to gain control of himself while wiping sweat from his brow.

'Elena,' he said, 'get out of that Jacuzzi. You've been in it long enough for one day.'

'I *like* the Jacuzzi,' she replied on a nervous impulse.

'You'll like the back of my hand if you receive it – now get out and get dressed.'

Shrugging, she stood up, stark naked, in front of Hans, and reluctantly started putting on her dressing gown, which, being soaked by the water, clung to her ripe body. Hans carefully lowered his eyes to avoid looking at her.

Zweig sighed. 'I will never forget my experiences at the hands of those Russian bastards when they raped Berlin in 1945 – and yet now I have to deal with the sub-human swine. Well, so be it. Time waits for no man. Hans, kindly arrange a meeting with that ill-mannered cretin, Colonel Andropov Kuragin – who has been wanting a larger contribution from our hoard of arms – and I will try to come to an agreement and make up for our losses. But in order to rescue us completely we need only one thing – the legendary Tuaoi Stone, or Lodestone.'

Elena tightened the belt of her expensive dressing gown, then started sauntering towards him, her hips swaying seductively. She stopped beside him, placed her hand on his shoulder, leaned softly against him.

'Yes,' he said, suddenly wanting to get rid of Hans, 'we will simply direct more of our attention towards those swinish Soviets and play them off against the Western powers. While not making up *completely* for our losses, this will at least buy us enough time to pursue the Tuaoi Stone – which we now know to be in the care of Count Saint-Germain. So once I have met our good friend, Colonel Andropov Kuragin, and arranged increased trade with the Soviets, I will give my full attention to the finding of the mysterious Count Saint-Germain – and, through him, the Lodestone. Now please go and fix up the meeting. Elena, come closer!'

Unable to come much closer, she pressed her belly against him as Hans retreated hastily from the cabin, his face a bright red. When Hans had gone, Elena smiled and knelt between Zweig's outstretched legs. Her large eyes, which pretended to be admiring, were admirably cautious.

'Do you want me badly?' he asked her. 'Do you *need* what I have?'

'Oh, yes!' she said softly.

He had to smile at that, but then closed his eyes; remembering Egypt, the cruise along the River Nile; his treacherous daughter, Ingrid, and that crude American, Jerry Remick; recalled how they had, with Hans, rushed out of the Great Pyramid, all of them obviously stunned by their experience inside it.

Count Saint-Germain, he thought. *That scoundrel – or magical genius. Certainly history's most mysterious man . . . and possibly still alive . . .*

He shook his head, feeling bewildered, disbelieving his own thoughts, then tried to accept that it was actually possible . . . that the Tuaoi Stone, the legendary Lodestone, truly existed.

'Oh, you're *big*,' Elena said, breathing upon him, exciting him. 'You're so big, so strong, so *hard* – who could possibly resist you?'

He felt her warm breath, her pliant lips, her tongue's sensual lapping. Then he briefly thought of Ingrid, Jerry Remick, their flight to freedom; felt the rage boiling up to give him back his strength while Elena's lips and tongue, as soft and smooth as worms dipped in honey, worked their wonders upon him.

'You have the best,' she murmured. 'I've never seen another like it. I want it night and day, every way, and I need it right now. It's so powerful, so ruthless, so *unbending* – there's no way to resist it. Oh, I want it . . . *right now*!'

The lying bitch was irresistible. She knew just what she was doing. He heard her, felt her, surrendered willingly to her, pushing up to let her drink of his outpouring maleness, accepting her sly deceit as he cried out in ecstasy, despising himself even as he shuddered and gasped with relief – losing himself all too briefly.

'I want my daughter,' he groaned.

CHAPTER THIRTEEN

'So I flew directly to London,' Ingrid continued, sitting close beside Jerry on the settee in his bric-a-brac flat in Notting Hill Gate, feeling that she had wings, had flown towards the sun, and was glowing with a soft, febrile warmth, 'and booked into a hotel in Bloomsbury, not knowing how to find you, convinced that I probably wouldn't, but determined that no matter what happened I wouldn't return to my father. Then, yesterday, when I saw that advertisement in the newspaper, I knew it could only have been placed by you – and so, after thinking about it all night, worked up the courage to call you.'

Her hand was resting in his, and she saw his unusually bright blue eyes registering surprise, perhaps hurt or confusion.

'You had to work up the *courage*?' he asked her. 'Why? You *know* what I feel about you, what I told you. You should have called straight away.'

She felt herself blushing and had to lower her eyes. 'I know what you told me,' she said, 'but couldn't be sure if you meant it. After all, I'm not all that attractive –'

'You are!'

'– and as you said to me, regarding another matter, when you're in a new country, a very strange and different country – as we both were in Egypt – it can play tricks on the mind.'

'And that's what you think my feelings for you are? A mere trick of the mind?'

'Well, I *hope* not. It's just that . . . *you* know . . .'

Feeling hot and confused, bereft of further words, she was relieved when he squeezed her hand again and pulled it into his lap.

'Damnit,' he said, 'I love you. I know it. And you must know it, too. Come here,' he said. 'Close your eyes.'

She felt his lips pressing upon her own, and she trembled, dissolving, concentrating on his lips, shaken by their softness, by their tenderness and warmth, automatically opening her own and responding inexpertly. She had wings and was flying, soaring away from doubt and fear, and only returned to earth with great reluctance when he pulled away from her.

'You've got to learn to kiss better than that,' he said, 'but don't worry. I'll teach you.'

She saw only his blue eyes, very bright, oddly naïve, his face solemn and particularly attentive, as if pondering her nature.

'Oh, yes,' she responded, surprised by the throaty trembling of her own voice. 'You do that, Jerry. Do it *right now*.'

Unfortunately, he didn't. Instead, his brow wrinkled as if in confusion, then he scratched distractedly at his nose.

'Right *now*?' he said. 'Right now, we've got to work out what to do.'

'Well,' she said, 'here I am. I am at your disposal. You don't need to hire an assistant. *I'll* be your assistant.'

He stood up and started pacing the shabby room, his unshaven face thoughtful.

'Well, I don't know –' he began.

'I'm perfectly capable, Jerry. I speak four languages fluently, have a BA in history, can type, take dictation and use a word processor, if necessary. Also, I've already travelled a lot and have time on my hands. What more do you want?'

He stopped pacing the floor and stared at her with what she felt was slightly melodramatic grimness.

'It might be dangerous,' he said.

'I don't care,' she replied, meaning it. 'I've run away from my father for good, I'll never go back voluntarily, and since coming to London, during those two long, empty weeks in my hotel, I've spent a great deal of time thinking about my past, about how my father abused my mother and then tortured me; and decided that not only would I never return to him, but that I'd avenge myself on him by frustrating his search for the Lodestone, which is what he most wants in all the world. My father is evil, Jerry. I've finally managed to accept that fully. And accepting it, I've determined to do something about it, no matter the cost. To hell with the danger. I don't care. I'm going to help you.'

It was the longest speech she had given in her life, and on completing it she felt breathless, very emotional, a bit embarrassed, but also exhilarated and free, no longer chained by self-doubt.

Jerry was staring at her, as solemn as an owl; he didn't speak for some time, as if surprise had rendered him speechless, but then he took a deep breath, shook his head from side to side, ran his fingers through his already ruffled hair and whispered, 'Oh, boy!'

He started pacing the room again, a genius in deep thought, but eventually stopped in front of her, wrinkled his brow, and nodded affirmatively.

God, he was sweet.

'Okay,' he said to her. 'Let's work it out logically. And the first thing is to recall what actually occurred in the burial chamber of the Great Pyramid. So, what *did* actually happen? First, that bizarrely dressed apparition who looked like Saint-Germain very specifically told Hans that he – meaning your father – couldn't have the Tuaoi Stone and would be doomed if he tried to pursue it – so he *knew* your father was trying to find it. Next, he stared right at me – no mistake about *that* – and told me that I had to know that the first number is "one". So what does that sound like?'

'Like he was warning my father off his search for the Tuaoi Stone, but encouraging *you* to try to find it.'

'Exactly . . . and the first clue we've got is the number "one" in some shape or form.'

'Which gets us nowhere.'

'Right. Because that number could mean anything. But it *does* mean that sooner or later we're going to have to remember that that number has a certain relevance – and in the meantime, the only thing we've got to go on is the identity of Saint-Germain himself. We need to know about Saint-Germain – who he is, *what* he is – and I'm certain I *already* know the name, though I still can't quite place it.'

'You think it's his real name?'

'Maybe, maybe not. It's possibly a pseudonym – but if it is, I think it's based on a real person, living or dead.'

'It's European,' she told him. 'Saint-Germain – France, Germany . . . or ancient Bavaria.'

'Right,' he replied. 'And we can check it out easily. Particularly if it's the name of a real person, which I think it is.'

'The British Museum Reading Room?'

'Right,' he said. 'That's a good place to start.'

'It's not that easy to get in there, Jerry.'

'Why?'

'You need a special pass card, which includes a photograph.'

'We're not talking about Fort Knox, Ingrid.'

'I mean it . . . that's what you need – and you're not even English.'

He grinned at her, filling her up with warmth and a languorous wanting.

'I'll get around that,' he said. 'What I can't get around is the fact that I'm broke and this investigation could take weeks, maybe months, and involve lots of travelling, meaning money. So! No money, no honey. We're stopped dead in our tracks, ducks.'

'Ducks? Did you say *ducks*?'

'That's an English expression, Ingrid. I pick up on these things pretty quickly. That's what makes me so smart.'

She knew he was smart, but she didn't care right now. She just wanted him to hold her, squeeze her tightly, press and stroke her; to kiss her and teach her to kiss and let her take wing again. *Oh, do it*, she thought. *Don't just stand there being bright* . . . But he just stood there, being bright, his brow furrowed, wanting to save the whole world.

'*I* have money,' she told him. 'I have a lot of money, actually. I've certainly got enough for what you need, so let's start straight away.'

'I don't think you have enough.'

'Yes, I have, Jerry. I have enough money to last us both for months – and perhaps even longer.'

'You have?'

'Yes, I have.'

When previously telling him about her flight from the hotel in Cairo, she had omitted the theft of her father's hard cash; now, she told him, taking pleasure from recounting how she had rifled all her father's drawers and clothes, informed him that the total amount stolen was about $20,000, and was taken aback to see his brilliant blue eyes widening in shock.

'You *stole* 20,000 bucks from your old man?' he asked incredulously.

'Yes,' she confirmed with pride.

He whistled softly. 'Wow!' he said. 'I can't believe my own ears. You're a girl of surprises.'

This time, when she felt the blush on her cheeks, she realized she was blushing with pleasure instead of her normal humiliation – and when Jerry grinned at her, with his admiration obvious, she glowed even more.

'This is beautiful,' he said. 'It's just too sweet to swallow. We not only keep that bastard from getting the Lodestone, but use his money to finance *our* search for it. What an irony. *Wonderful!*'

'Do you think the Lodestone really exists?' she asked him.

He shrugged. 'I don't know. But *Saint-Germain* certainly knows whether or not it actually exists – and if it *does* exist and we're to find it, we'll only do so through him.'

'Which gets us back to the British Museum Reading Room – for which we'll need passes with photographs.'

'No problem,' he responded, obviously enjoying himself. 'What are the rules?'

'You normally have to have a genuine purpose for being there – some kind of research – and it has to be for something pretty serious.'

'You mean I'd need a letter of authorization?'

'Yes. A letter of authorization from some well-known company.'

He didn't pause for a second. 'Okay,' he said. 'We both need passes. So let's go to one of those instant print shops and run off a set of letterhead paper with a well-known publisher's details printed on it. We'll obviously have to waste most of our print run, since we'll actually only need two sheets for two letters – one for you and one for me, both stating that the publisher has commissioned us to co-author a book on ...' He shrugged and grinned again. 'Let's say the French Revolution ... and then, with those letters and a couple of passport photos from a coin machine, we can pick up our Reading Room passes. You think that'll work?'

'Yes, Jerry, I do.'

'You're hired, Ingrid. *Definitely.*'

He grinned and moved towards her and she stood up automatically, only aware of her need to be close to him and give herself, body and soul, to him in order to find herself. She raised her head and closed her eyes, embarrassed by her inexperience, wanting him but stiffening with fear at the thought of what he might do to her. She felt his hands sliding around her, fingers pressing against her spine; he pulled her gently against him and his body seemed electric; but she stiffened even more when he kissed her and pressed her tight to him.

Then he must have sensed it – her involuntary, helpless fear – since his kiss, which had exalted her even in her fear, was too abruptly terminated when his hands, moving down from her shoulder blades and spine, came to rest lightly on her hips and then pushed her away from him.

Trembling, she opened her eyes and saw his puzzled gaze.

'What's the matter?' he asked her.

'Nothing,' she lied.

'You don't *like* me to kiss you?'

'Oh, I do!' She felt desperate. 'It's just that . . .' But she let her voice trail off, not knowing how to explain it, not even wanting to *think* about her years of humiliation, her father's sexual blasphemies; about the way he had abused her mother, often in front of her, the child, then later played about with his whores and mistresses while making her look on. She thought of her dreams in the sanatorium, those vivid fantasies of shame and revulsion, and wanted even less to tell Jerry what sex had come to mean to her: either power or submission, pain or shame, and always repulsively *physical* ... No, she couldn't tell him – at least not without losing him – and feeling torn between her love for him and her fear of letting him have her, she offered him a pained, concealing smile and hoped for the best.

He cupped her face tenderly in his hands, looking almost relieved.

'It's okay,' he said. 'That bastard. I understand. But it's okay, I can wait, give it time. You and I, we'll be all right. Let it take its own course. Right now, we've more important things to think about ... such as getting that letterhead paper run off and then applying for our British Reading Room passes. Let's do that tomorrow.'

'Yes, Jerry, of course.'

'And what about where you're living? You want to move in with me?'

'No, Jerry, I don't think so.'

'You don't have to ...'

'I know. It's not that. Well, it is. I mean, I'd *like* to, but I'm scared, so I'll stay in the hotel in the meantime. Also, it's located in Tavistock Square, which is near the museum, which makes it convenient.'

'Right,' he said. 'Fine.'

Did he look relieved as well? Or was she simply imagining that? Feeling flushed and pained, now confused by her own thoughts as well as by how he was reacting to her, she studied his face, brimmed over with love for him, felt tears springing to her eyes, and then leaned forward, stood on tiptoe and kissed him quickly, unsurely.

He reached out, pulled her to him, hugged her,

breathing heavily, then released her and let her walk to the door, feeling dizzy and weak with love.

'So,' she said, turning back to face him, 'I'll see you to-morrow.'

'Right, Ingrid. As early as possible. What about ten in the morning at your hotel, since that's near the British Museum?'

'Fine. Ten it is.'

He ran his fingers nervously through his hair, then glanced out the window.

'It's dark,' he said. 'I'll walk you to the station.'

'No,' she replied quickly, suddenly needing to get away; wanting him too much to be able to stand her own fear of sex, and feeling thoroughly ashamed of herself. 'I'll manage on my own, thanks.'

'I'd rather walk you there,' he insisted. 'It's not safe for a woman alone after dark, so let me at least take you that far.'

She smiled mainly to reassure him, but also out of amusement at his concern. 'This isn't New York, Jerry. It's London – and it's a very safe city.'

He studied her thoughtfully, then shrugged. 'Okay, then. If you insist.'

'I do.'

Wanting desperately to be held by him, but scared of what it could lead to, despising her own cowardice yet sensing an odd relief in him as well, she covered her confusion by opening the door, blowing him a kiss, then hurrying down the stairs of the gloomy Victorian house; and with a sigh of relief, of aching longing and frustration, left the building and stepped into the lamplit street, trying to sniff back her tears.

CHAPTER FOURTEEN

After Ingrid had gently closed the door in his face, Jerry stood there for a moment, just staring at the closed door, feeling like a fool, like the virgin he *almost* was, and wanting to rush down the stairs after her and confess all *his* fears.

Resisting this urge, he simply clenched his right fist and knocked it repeatedly against his lowered forehead, to punish himself. Having done so, he glanced around the small flat, wondered how he could survive in such a dump and then hurried over to the window to catch a last glimpse of Ingrid.

Just as he looked down, she stepped off the pavement and started across the dark, lamplit road, heading for the other side of the street. She was wearing a full-length summer coat that seemed more fashionable than her normal clothing, but her hair was still piled primly on her head, her shoes were flat-heeled and plain. Nevertheless, as she crossed the empty street, moving in and out of lamplight, he felt himself pouring out towards her on a wave of emotion. He wanted to call her back, take her clothes off and make passionate love to her ... but he just couldn't do it.

'You goddamned hypocrite,' he said softly to himself. 'You're just as frightened as she is.'

Well, it was true, wasn't it? As he stood there looking down, he thought of the few other times in his life when he had been involved with members of the opposite sex.

Very few, indeed, spread thinly over the years, beginning when he was a sophomore and fumbling awkwardly, frustratedly, in the back of an automobile; proceeding a few months later to seduction by an older woman, then a few well-spaced adventures in between. Nothing very permanent there, certainly nothing too successful, giving rise only to the conclusion that he was too *intelligent* for sex, that he really thought it a messy biological urge that was a lot more trouble than it was worth.

Well, that was *his* excuse.

Yet as Ingrid crossed the street, mounted the pavement at the far side and walked along it, moving in and out of shadow and yellow lamplight, he was swept by love for her, by the need to possess her. All his previous sexual relationships had been brief and unsuccessful – his own awkwardness had embarrassed him – and now, though he desperately wanted Ingrid, he didn't know where to start.

God, he thought, as he watched her moving along the sidewalk, a lonely figure in that empty street, *I wish you were Mata Hari, a man-eater . . . I wish* you *would take me*.

Feeling foolish, he sighed, trying to think of other things, but seeing only the eerie, lamplit darkness, thinking of all the dangers of a city in the dead of the night . . . Yet that was simply foolish. This was London, after all. As Ingrid had said, it was a very safe city and there was nothing to worry about . . .

Yet even as he was thinking this, an icy fear poured through him, as if injected into his veins. Temporarily frozen, only aware of his racing heart, he had a sudden, sharp vision of the face of Saint-Germain, blinked, glanced down again and saw Ingrid still on the pavement across the road.

A grey-suited man, very broad and tall, had climbed

out of an Audi car parked near the kerb and was hurrying after her.

'Oh, shit,' Jerry murmured.

On that instant, as his fear turned to immobilizing panic, he knew with certainty that the man in the grey suit was hurrying to catch up with Ingrid – and indeed, as the oblivious Ingrid kept walking, the man suddenly sprinted forward and reached out to grab her.

'Ingrid!' Jerry shouted out in vain, his hands pressed uselessly against the closed window of his apartment, as the man was just about to take hold of her.

Then, inexplicably, the man seemed to change his mind, abruptly stopping his forward rush, letting his hands fall to his sides, and glancing towards the alley to his right where, as the still oblivious Ingrid walked on, out of Jerry's range of vision, a pool of brightening light had formed.

Obviously dazzled by the light, perhaps knowing what it was, the man on the pavement took a frightened step backwards as another man, silhouetted in the increasingly brilliant light, emerged from the alley and walked towards him.

The man on the pavement flung one hand protectively over his face and was just about to turn away and flee when the silhouetted figure grabbed his shoulder. At that, the man on the pavement quivered like a bow-string, was surrounded by an unearthly phosphorescent light, went into what looked like an epileptic fit and then collapsed to the ground.

Jerry didn't wait to see any more. He turned away from the window, opened the door, rushed down the stairs and out into the street. Hardly able to think straight, oblivious to danger, he hurried across the road as that unearthly light in the alley flared up into a brief, blinding radiance, then abruptly winked out.

Temporarily blinded, Jerry stopped on the opposite

pavement, rubbed his stinging eyes, then looked down at the man lying near his feet. The man's jaw was slack, his wide eyes reflecting the lamplight, and his body was frozen in the contortions of his final moment of agony. The skin on his face and hands was scorched, and he was obviously dead.

'Shit,' Jerry said. 'Jesus!'

There was no sign of Ingrid.

Almost sobbing, he raced forward to the alley on his right, looked in and saw nothing but the darkness. Perplexed, but even more concerned for Ingrid, he raced on along the street, hoping to catch up with her. He didn't. She was nowhere to be seen along the route to Notting Hill Gate underground station, and by the time he reached there, he had decided that either she had been abducted or she had simply caught her train home.

He hurried back through the dark, empty streets until he reached the pavement opposite his building.

The body that had been there had disappeared – as had the Audi car parked farther along the kerb.

Aware that his heart was still racing, and finding it increasingly difficult to keep a hold on his sense of reality, he went back into his flat, poured himself a stiff whisky, drank it while he gave Ingrid enough time to get to her hotel, then, so filled with tension that he was hardly able to breathe, picked up the telephone and dialled the number.

The operator put him through to her room immediately.

'Yes?' Ingrid said.

He let his breath out in a long sigh of relief, then said, 'It's me . . . Jerry.'

'That's nice,' she replied.

'You got back okay, then?'

'Yes, of course.'

'Good,' he said. 'I just wanted to be certain. Now make sure your door's locked.'

'Oh, Jerry!' she exclaimed, obviously amused by his concern.

'Just double check, Ingrid,' he insisted. 'I love you. Good night.'

He dropped the phone quickly, too choked up to say more, then had another drink, trying to knock himself out, and lay back on the bed fully dressed, taking deep, even breaths before turning the light out.

Was he sleeping? Was he dreaming? He would never know for sure. Later he only knew that he had spent a long, troubled night, haunted by what had happened, trying to work it out, realizing that the man who had tried to grab Ingrid had obviously been one of her father's men; and convinced that the other man, who had emerged from the light-filled alleyway, had been the same man he had first seen, in a similar unearthly light, on the deck of the cruiser going along the Nile.

Either sleeping or awake, hardly knowing where he was, but chillingly aware that the people he was trying to find were actually following him and Ingrid, he tossed and turned more restlessly, sweated a lot, then either in a dream or in reality felt his body encased in heat, compressed by fierce pressure, and opened his eyes to see that same unearthly light filling his bedroom and heard an almost palpable bass humming noise that made the stifling air vibrate.

And there, in that shimmering light, stood Saint-Germain and his diabolically handsome partner, both of them staring directly at him, their lips forming half smiles.

There was nothing he could do. He was paralysed by the sight of them. He just lay there on the bed, pouring sweat, his heart racing, his thoughts blanked out by that relentless humming, his muscles tightening into knots as the unnatural pressure squeezed the breath out of him.

He thought he was going mad. He also thought he was going to die. He tried to scream, but failed, opening and closing his mouth in vain, struck dumb by the blankness in his mind and the breadth of his terror.

Saint-Germain was still smiling at him. The other man was hypnotizing him. He tried to break free, to resist, to make a noise or thresh his limbs, but felt his senses draining away into a deep well of terror.

Defeated, he closed his eyes and held his breath . . . and was instantly set free.

The heat and pressure disappeared, the humming noise receded, and he opened his eyes again to see a swirling white light shrinking until it was only a spark burning through the room door. Then that also disappeared, returning the room to normal darkness, and he let his breath out in a sigh that filled up the silence.

He lay there a long time, still too terrified to move, looking left and right, up and down, all around him, and only closing his eyes with great reluctance, still too frightened to face sleep.

Was he sleeping or awake? He must have fallen asleep *sometime*. When he awakened the next morning the room was normal, but his body was aching.

The fear was there to be fought.

CHAPTER FIFTEEN

Feeling ten years younger after his two-week Fountain of Youth rejuvenation treatment course in the Flora Cure Hotel in Bucharest, Zweig felt up to the task of meeting the despicable sub-human, KGB colonel Andropov Kuragin. Indeed, he took particular pleasure in doing it without the aid of a limousine, and instead walked all the way from Boulevard Poligrafei, past Piata Scinteii, along the wide, elegant Soseaua Kiseleff, with its many terraced restaurants and brasseries, to the webbed pathways and lakes of the city's playground, Herastrau Park.

There, in the restaurant Miorita, he was to have his very important meeting.

Having already convinced himself that Kuragin would try that third-rate psychological ploy of turning up late, and preparing himself for it, he was first pleasantly surprised, then very suspicious, to find the ruddy-cheeked, potbellied Russian, dressed in a surprisingly decent grey suit, shirt and tie, already seated at his table in the expensive restaurant overlooking one of the park's many lakes.

'*Guten tag*,' Zweig said, feeling grumpy and refusing to speak Russian. 'So you got here before me.'

'*Ja*,' Kuragin replied cheerfully, standing up and stretching out his hand. '*Buna seara*,' he said in fluent Romanian, obviously trying to make Zweig feel inferior. 'It is good to see you, my old friend.'

'*Multumesc*,' Zweig replied, determined not to be put down, then shook Kuragin's hand, squeezing it tighter than necessary, and sat down before Kuragin could do so, after which, having regained the upper hand, he waved his right hand in an impatient manner and said, 'Please, Kuragin, be seated.'

'Thank *you*,' Kuragin responded, taking his seat. 'So, here we are again. Can I get you a *tuica*?'

'I do not drink brandy even when made from fruit. A mineral water will do, thanks.'

'Of course,' Kuragin said. 'Naturally.'

He called a waiter and ordered the drink, then offered a Russian peasant's artificial smile.

'So, Wilhelm,' he said, 'you would like to eat?'

'I believe that was the general idea,' Zweig replied. 'And you said you were paying.'

'But naturally, Wilhelm.'

Glancing occasionally at Kuragin over the top of his menu, Zweig was not unaware of the fact that the Russian's moon-shaped, ruddy-cheeked, good-humoured face, with its son-of-the-soil attractiveness, was the pleasant mask hiding the death's head of a dedicated communist who had been elbow deep in blood many times. A survivor of Stalingrad, Kuragin secretly loathed all Germans and had put quite a few of them to death, often hideously, before the end of the war deprived him of the pleasure. Since then, he had clawed his way up the slippery, blood-slicked ladder of Soviet politics, surviving one purge after another, and was now one of the KGB's most valuable operatives. He would deal with Zweig if he had to – but his cheerful countenance, Zweig knew, concealed a detestation equalling that which Zweig held for him.

'You are ready to order, Wilhelm?'

'Yes, Andropov,' Zweig replied, deciding to cost him as much as possible. 'I'll start with the *oua umplute cu pire de spanac* and, perhaps, a hearty soup – shall we make it the *ciorba de perisoare*?'

'A filling combination,' Kuragin replied, not blanching at all, 'but an excellent choice. And the main course?'

'I think the *muschi poiana* might do,' Zweig said, 'with perhaps a little *mamaliga* on the side, and some stuffed potatoes, such as *cartofi Bucovinei*.'

'You're obviously making up for your deprivations in the health clinic,' Kuragin said, trying to make the comment sound like a joke but not quite succeeding. 'However, I'm sure you can manage it.'

'Oh, I'm *sure* I can,' Zweig replied, hardly able to conceal his pleasure. 'And I'll follow it up with a combination of *baclava* and cheese pie – the *placinta cu brinza* – with a couple of bottles of Murfatlar riesling to wash it down. That should set us up nicely, *ja?*'

Kuragin's smile wavered, but just managed to survive. 'Yes,' he said, 'it should set *you* up nicely. My own appetite, however, is more modest, but please don't mind me.'

For himself, he ordered only a small portion of skinless sausages, the *mititei*, a main course of *musaka* and dessert of apple pie, his peasant's gaze taking note of the prices before the waiter departed.

'So,' he said, sinking back into his chair and trying to hide his outrage. 'How are things with you, Wilhelm?'

'I am having my problems,' Zweig replied, 'but I'm sure I can sort them out.'

At that moment, one of the waiters returned with Zweig's glass of mineral water. He drank it in one gulp, put the glass back on the table, wiped his lips with the back of his hand and glanced idly around him.

'God,' he said, 'how I detest these Romanians. Is that why you meet me here?'

'I don't know why you detest them, Wilhelm. After

all, they entered World War Two on Germany's side.'

'And when the tide had unfortunately turned against us, they joined the Allies.'

'Of all people,' Kuragin said, '*you* should surely understand political expediency.'

'I do not change my allegiances,' Zweig replied. 'I still stand by my Führer.'

'Yes,' Kuragin said. 'Quite.'

The use of the word 'quite', so English and effete, made Zweig's blood boil, but he diplomatically kept his peace and made a lot of mindless small talk with the disgusting Soviet while the meal was served and devoured. Aware that what he was eating would not aid his longevity – and would, indeed, set back all the good work done during the past two weeks in the Flora Cure Hotel – but unable to resist the chance to feed off the despised Russian's expense account, he enthusiastically demolished his egg stuffed with spinach, lapped up his sour cream soup with meat balls, then tucked with relish into his main course of beef stuffed with mushrooms, bacon, pepper and paprika in a rich sauce of veal stock, tomato and vegetable purée, with corn mush and stuffed potatoes on the side.

'So,' Kuragin said, trying to make conversation while he picked at his *musaka*, 'you are having some problems. What might those be, my friend?'

'Problems?' Zweig said, stuffing his mouth with *mamaliga*. 'Not really *problems*. Merely a few aggravations.'

'Oh?' Kuragin said diplomatically, still picking at his food like an old woman minus her teeth. 'And they have bearing on us?'

'Alas,' Zweig said, 'yes.'

He was mindful of the need to tread with extreme

delicacy when dealing with the cheerful, barbaric Russian, but equally aware of his need to repair the damage done in recent months. So, treading carefully, offering what was necessary but no more than that, he told Kuragin of his current plight, with particular emphasis on how the Americans and the European Community were applying sanctions against his numerous interests as well as curtailing all trade with him. When he had finished, he had a long drink of the riesling and carefully studied the Russian.

'Ah,' Kuragin said, dabbing delicately at his lips with his napkin in order to try to hide his growing pleasure. 'I see. This doesn't sound too good at all, Wilhelm. At least not for you.'

'A temporary setback,' Zweig replied, wanting to strangle the Soviet slug. 'The solution is already at hand – and could benefit you.'

'Oh?'

'Yes, Kuragin. You have, after all, been complaining for some time that I have been trading *too much* with the West while ignoring your own more pressing needs. Well, that can now be reversed. The Soviet Union will become my prime customer.'

Kuragin's triumphant smile was enough to make Zweig feel like puking.

'So,' the Soviet swine said. 'You refuse our demands for years and only now, when rejected by your allies, do you grant us this favour.'

'Of all people,' Zweig said, throwing Kuragin's words back at him, '*you* should surely understand political expediency.'

Kuragin's smile wavered, but did not disappear. 'Quite,' he said. 'However, much as I appreciate your kind offer, I should point out to you that it will only be accepted on the strictest of terms – by which I mean *our* terms.'

'You think *I* would accept that, Kuragin?'

'I don't think you have much choice. With Europe and America turning against you, we're all you have left – so our terms it will be.'

'I would not be so foolish as to come here to beg on hands and knees,' Zweig replied. 'I have not come here to ask you a favour – I've come to offer a trade.'

'What can you offer now offer but your desperation?'

'Power,' Zweig said. '*Limitless* power.'

Enjoying his histrionics, he took even more pleasure from the way in which Kuragin actually stopped smiling and raised his right eyebrow.

'We have talked before of the legendary Tuaoi Stone, or Lodestone,' Zweig said.

'Yes,' Kuragin replied. 'Of course. We have discussed whether or not it actually exists – and, if it does, if it actually possesses the powers it is claimed to have. As you know, I believe it to be a myth – so why bring it up now?'

'Because recent events have convinced me that the Lodestone *does* exist, is possessed of magical powers, and can probably be located by myself.'

'Those are large claims,' Kuragin said.

'Allow me to convince you.'

Without naming names, and implying that he had *personally* witnessed the events described, he recounted what Hans, Ingrid and the American had experienced inside the Great Pyramid at Giza, tied those events to the death of his own men in the Waldorf Astoria hotel in New York, and finished by saying that he now knew the identity of the current protector of the Tuaoi Stone and could, therefore, given time and financial assistance, track him down and wrest the legendary stone from him.

Kuragin did not bite immediately, but Zweig knew he was going to.

'Let me get this straight,' Kuragin said. 'You had been pursuing the Tuaoi Stone for many years, and finally your aide received an anonymous phone call telling him that if you wanted the stone, it could be purchased from someone who would come to a certain room in the Waldorf Astoria. A man went there for that meeting, and your men died in that widely reported, apparently inexplicable explosion.'

'Correct,' Zweig said, feeling impatient.

'So whoever has the Tuaoi Stone, he certainly knows that you're trying to find it.'

'Also correct,' Zweig said, growing even more impatient.

'However, originally the men who died in the Waldorf Astoria were supposed to have made their contact on a cruiser going along the Nile – so after their untimely death, you took that same cruise and had reason to believe that the present owner of the Tuaoi Stone was aboard.'

'Yes,' Zweig said. 'And my encounter with him inside the Great Pyramid,' he continued, lying blandly, 'convinced me that he *did* possess the stone and had inherited its magical powers. Now, since I know who he is, I think I can find him – and, when I do, I will wrest the stone from him and then hand it over to the Soviets, to use as they see fit.'

'And what would you expect in return?'

'You will pay me handsomely,' Zweig said. 'Initially in material wealth; later, when you have the Tuaoi Stone and can thus threaten the whole world, in the handing over to me of a united East and West Germany, which I can then rule as *I* see fit.'

'Ah,' Kuragin said with soft sarcasm. 'The Fourth Reich.'

'Correct again,' Zweig said, wanting to crush the bastard. 'Once more there will be only one Germany –

a pure Germany – and I will ensure that it stays that way, under the umbrella of Soviet protection, since the Soviets will by then rule the world.'

He avoided Kuragin's thoughtful, peasant gaze by tucking into his combined dessert of *baclava* and cheese pie, swilled down with more riesling. However, he didn't miss the edge to Kuragin's voice when the Russian finally spoke again.

'Reportedly, he who owns the Lodestone can rule the whole world,' Kuragin reminded him. 'So why, if you find it, would you not want to keep it yourself?'

'It is too big for me,' Zweig lied. 'The *whole world* is too big for me. I do not want the Slavs and the Poles and the Romanians; I do not want all the other sub-humans or ignoble races. I only want my own New Order – a unified Germany purged of the impure and inferior; of all dissenters, Jews, homosexuals, mental defectives and radicals. I do not want the problems of the whole world to interfere with my country. I want East and West Germany united; the rest you can deal with.'

He knew exactly what the Russian was thinking. Kuragin was thinking that he, Zweig, wasn't thinking too straight; that he was so obsessed with his mad vision of a resurrected Third Reich, he had lost all his marbles and hadn't even considered that the Soviets, once in possession of the Tuaoi Stone, would simply renege on their promise and unite the divided Germany only to dominate it completely, as they would the whole world ... But he, Wilhelm Zweig, was no mad visionary, had not lost his marbles, and had no intention of handing over the Tuaoi Stone once he had found it. No, he would encourage the Soviets to finance his search for it, and then, having found it, use it to blackmail the whole world, including the Soviets, into submission.

The whole world was *not* too big for him. It was, in fact, all he desired and could not live without.

'So,' he said, finishing his gross dessert and washing it down with the last of the riesling, 'do we discuss the terms of our trade or not?'

The cheerful Kuragin was looking unusually sombre. He stared at Zweig for some time, his brow furrowed in thought, then eventually let his breath out in a sigh that sounded suspiciously like despair.

'Yes,' he said, 'let's discuss terms.'

An hour later, Kuragin had agreed to arrange for the shipment of a great deal of material wealth, including hard cash and invaluable art treasures (many of which, Zweig reminded himself with satisfaction, had been pillaged by the Soviets from the Germans at the end of the war) to him within the month, and to complete the rest of the deal when they were in possession of the Tuaoi Stone (which, Zweig thought with even more satisfaction, they never would be). Zweig then shook hands with the Soviet slug and headed back across the park, past green lawns and lakes and the many Romanians out for a stroll, safe in the knowledge that he was actually being followed at a discreet distance by Hans and two well-trained, armed guards.

The afternoon light was grey, making the park drab and gloomy, and he suddenly felt an odd melancholia that slightly dampened the ardour of his victory. Surprised by the feeling, wondering what had caused it, he tried to shake it off by reminding himself that he had won – that he had pulled off a coup and could now ignore the Americans and their allies – then wondered how to go about tracking down the mysterious Saint-Germain, whose name he had deliberately not mentioned to the Russian.

Thinking of Saint-Germain, he then thought of the

cruise along the Nile, of his daughter, Ingrid, and that American degenerate, Jerry Remick, and wondered if his men in London had managed to locate them yet.

That the American might already be dead was of some comfort to him; that Ingrid might soon be back and at his mercy made him feel even better.

She would suffer as her mother had suffered . . . only more so, the treacherous bitch.

Briefly lifted out of his gloom by the thought of retribution, he looked straight ahead, along the path bounding a still lake, and saw a man stepping out from under some trees and stopping to stare intensely at him.

He also stopped walking, frozen by the man's intensity, mesmerized by his darkly glittering, snake-like gaze and diabolical attractiveness.

The man said nothing to him, but he knew without doubt that that mesmeric gaze was directed at him; and even as he accepted it, trying to fathom its meaning – but felt his senses slipping into chaos and confusion, his every thought focused on that diabolically handsome, smiling face – he was, to his horror, consumed with an unnatural, overwhelming *desire* for the stranger – his libido inflamed, his emotions in turmoil, his every nerve singing in tune to what appeared to be the man's magically amplified heartbeat, his body straining to hurl itself upon him and either take or be taken.

Shocked, disbelieving, yet rapidly losing self-control, he was indeed just about to advance upon the man when his overwhelming desire changed abruptly to terror and he saw, in those seductive eyes, the portals of heaven or hell, the light-flecked darkness of the cosmos, and found himself taking a step backwards, as if for protection.

Jerking his head sideways, trying desperately to avoid that mesmeric gaze, he stared down at the still lake to his right – and was further assaulted.

The still water started swirling, then turned into a roaring whirlpool, the vortex of which became the eye of a tornado that sucked him through the vacuum of the ether, into the swirling stars and moons of an exploding galaxy. He fell, tumbling through the infinite, traversing time and space, and emerged to snow-capped mountains, glittering light on frozen peaks, a great hall hacked out of solid rock and filled with a faint mist.

Here another man, silvery-haired and ageless, was staring straight at him.

He knew it was Saint-Germain. It could be no one else. He knew by the strangely haunted brilliance of that gaze; by the agelessness of the face beneath the noble brow and silvery hair; by the calm, unfettered arrogance in his stance; by the steel in his gentle smile.

Zweig felt himself falling, his legs too weak to support him, his limbs burning with an ethereal heat that made him think he was melting. He collapsed into himself, body colliding into spirit, then returned to the earth, to solid ground, when he fell to the grass.

He heard noise – thrashing branches, running feet, his own men shouting – and looked up to see the foliage springing back into position where the diabolical stranger had just been standing.

Zweig was lying on the grass beside the placid, rippling lake. He was breathless, felt bruised and too hot, but otherwise was unharmed. He watched the branches settling down where the magical man had made his escape, then looked up as his bodyguards reached down to help him back to his feet.

'What happened?' Hans asked him, looking nervous. 'We saw you fall and thought you had been shot – but we didn't hear gunshots.'

'That man!' Zweig screamed, getting his breath back. 'Go and capture that man!'

Hans and the bodyguards looked at one another, all

obviously bewildered. 'What man?' Hans asked. 'We saw no one. Only you by this lake. Believe me, there was no one else.'

'And over there? By the trees?'

'We saw nobody. *Nobody!*' Hans shrugged and indicated the bodyguards. 'Shall I send them to look?'

Shocked and horrified – not only by his bizarre hallucination, or experience, but by the extent of his unnatural desire for that spectral stranger – Zweig walked resolutely to the bushes, each step taking him closer to the terror he had just shaken off, then pushed the bushes aside and, taking a deep breath for courage, looked beyond them.

He saw nothing but another stretch of park, some people wandering to and fro.

All perfectly normal.

Shaken, confused, still trying to accept what had happened, he was just about to turn back to Hans and the bodyguards when he noticed that his hand, brushing the branches aside, had become covered with a fine grey powder that smelt just like ash. Examining the leaves of the surrounding branches and bushes, he saw that they had been lightly charred to a height of about six feet above the ground, as if scorched by some invisible source of heat.

'*Mein Gott,*' he whispered to himself, remembering what Hans and Ingrid had told him of their experience inside the Great Pyramid. 'It must be true. *It was them!*'

He stood there, dumbfounded, exhilarated and terrified, realizing that what he wanted was within his grasp – and that all hell could be let loose.

Those he was trying to find were following him . . . and their powers were spectacular.

CHAPTER SIXTEEN

The five days Jerry spent with Ingrid in the British Library Reading Room were among the most enchanting he had known.

Enchanting because he could think of nothing to compare with the huge circular hall of the library, which could accommodate over four hundred readers, had a dome that could only be bettered by the Pantheon at Rome, and whose catalogue was the most extensive in the world. Enchanting, also, because he spent most of the time sitting at one of the desks beside Ingrid, poring over books with her, often holding her hand, stroking the back of her wrist, whispering as one whispered when in a library or in love, sometimes blushing at his own words and hiding his embarrassment by turning away from her to study the great hall.

The shelves curved around the room, the officials were raised high in the centre of the circle, the readers' desks forming spokes that radiated out from the numerous drawers of the General Catalogue and extended to the reference books and dictionaries, the encyclopedias and histories.

He could choke up just seeing it.

He felt awed and humbled when in the Reading Room, but he also felt bewilderment and the slow rise of fear as Ingrid, mostly solemn, but sometimes smiling shyly, filled out the application slips for books, questioned the murmuring clerks, waited patiently beside him for the books on order to come, then went through them with him as, together, they unravelled the mystery of the Comte de Saint-Germain, tracing his origins back into distant time, far beyond what seemed possible.

The revelations about Saint-Germain, coming one after the other, led Jerry from bewilderment to an excitement that was, much too often for comfort, not too different from fear.

That Saint-Germain had existed was beyond any doubt ... what Jerry found impossible to accept was the extent of his life.

The identity of the Saint-Germain on the Nile cruise remained a mystery; but historical records revealed that a Comte de Saint-Germain had actually existed – yet was a man whose life defied common sense and appeared to be magical.

'According to Eliphas Levi, the nineteenth-century occultist,' Ingrid summarized in a whisper from her notes during their last afternoon in the great library, 'the Comte de Saint-Germain was born in Lentmeritz in Bohemia, the bastard son of a leading Rosicrucian, sometime towards the end of the seventeenth century. Nothing was known about him until about 1740, when he began to appear in various historical records as a handsome man who appeared to be in his early thirties, moved in fashionable Viennese circles, and was renowned for his unusually sombre clothing, paradoxical fondness for spectacular diamonds, and penchant for telling extraordinary tales about his past life.'

As she read to him in a whisper, Jerry studied her closely, wanting to stroke her cheek, to loosen her hair and let it fall down.

'The Saint-Germain of those days,' Ingrid continued solemnly, 'was already widely spoken of as an enigmatic and remarkable figure who practised alchemy; was an expert jeweller; was known to speak five languages fluently – and possibly Chinese, Hindu and Persian as well; had a reputation as a "magical" healer, and was rumoured to be able to turn base metal into gold. He frequently described machines which bore remarkable similarities to locomotives and steamships – which hadn't even been invented at the time – and there were suggestions that he possessed the Alchemist's Stone, had drunk from the Fountain of Eternal Youth, and was approximately 4,000 years old.'

'This sounds like bullshit,' Jerry whispered. 'He was obviously a confidence trickster.'

At that point, a man at a nearby desk loudly admonished them to be quiet, and Jerry, just about to make an angry retort, caught Ingrid's warning glance, saw her nod towards the exit, realized the complaint was justified and stood up to leave with her.

Taking one last fond look at the great dome of the library, he also realized that the past five days he had spent here with Ingrid had been, in an odd sense, the most intimate of his life to date, bringing him very close to her without actually touching her. He touched her now, placing his hand on her shoulder, then followed her out of the museum.

'The Museum Tavern's just across the road,' Ingrid said, 'and it's a very nice pub. We can talk normally there.'

'Okay,' he agreed.

Once inside the pleasantly busy pub, Ingrid leaned towards him, over the table, and said, 'A *lot* of people thought Saint-Germain was a confidence trickster, but an awful lot more took him seriously – not least the governments of the major European countries. According to our notes,' she continued, looking down at the notes she had pieced together from their researches, 'the Count, already widely talked about as a remarkable man, also had the reputation of being someone involved rather shadily in politics. On the one hand accused by the French police of being a Prussian spy, he was, on the other, suspected by the Prussians of being a Russian agent. To complicate matters further, in November 1745, in a London obsessed with Jacobite plotters and their French sympathizers, he was arrested by the English authorities, accused of having pro-Stuart letters in his possession, claimed indignantly that the letters had been planted on him, and was eventually released.'

'Right,' Jerry said. 'And as I remember, your famous Hugh Walpole had something to say about that.'

'Yes. Commenting on the case in a letter to Sir Horace Mann, dated 9 December 1745, Walpole wrote the following odd description: "He [Saint-Germain] has been here these two years, and will not tell who he is or whence, but professes that he does not go by his right name." He then wrote that Saint-Germain "sings and plays on the violin wonderfully"; but added that he was, "mad and not very sensible".'

'An interesting interpretation,' Jerry offered, 'of the Count's refusal to discuss his true past or give his real name.'

'Perhaps,' Ingrid replied. 'Anyway, the more bewildering and legendary aspects of the original Saint-Germain began shortly after the Count had, according to the French Marshal de Belle Isle, cured him of a serious illness and was rewarded by being taken to Paris, where the grateful Marshal set him up with apartments and a laboratory for his alchemical experiments.'

'It was the age of patronage,' Jerry joked. 'I could do with that right now.'

'That's not important,' Ingrid said, obviously not hearing the joke. '*Here's* what's important . . . According to Touchard la Fosse, in his *Chroniques de l'Oeil de*

Bœuf, shortly after his arrival in Paris Saint-Germain attended a soirée given by the aged Countess von Georgy, wife of the deceased ambassador to Venice, who remembered meeting someone with the same name as, and similar appearance to, Saint-Germain in Venice in the 1670s. When the very youthful Saint-Germain confirmed to the ageing Countess that the man she had met all those years ago *had* been himself, she could scarcely believe it, since this would have made him nearly a hundred years old. However, Saint-Germain insisted that he was that same man, that he was in fact *very* old – but then, when the stunned Countess said he must be *a devil*, he trembled violently, told her not to use such names, and fled from the room.'

'He was also described as a charlatan,' Jerry said, 'and that could have been part of his act. Likewise for his claims that he had known the Holy Family intimately; been present at the marriage feast at Cana; been a good friend of Anne, the mother of the Virgin Mary; personally proposed her canonization at the Council of Nicaea in AD 325; and prophesied that Christ would come to a bad end.'

'There's no real proof that he ever said those things,' Ingrid corrected him. 'And if he *did*, there *may* have been something in what he said. However, please don't make me digress; let's get back to what he claimed to the ageing Countess at her soirée.'

'Okay, Ingrid, continue.'

She smiled at him and looked down at her notes, pushing her spectacles back up her fine nose with a delicate finger.

'A possible substantiation for Saint-Germain's claim that he was the man known to the much younger Countess von Georgy in the 1670s was recorded by Baron Charles Henry de Gleichen, a Danish diplomat, who in his published memoirs stated that the composer

Philippe Rameau and a relative of the French ambassador to Venice had both assured him that they had known Monsieur de Saint-Germain in the early 1700s when, according to them, he appeared to be a man of about fifty.

'Baron Gleichen also confirmed that Saint-Germain had a fondness for unusual diamonds when, in the same memoirs, he wrote: "He showed me some remarkable things – a great number of coloured brilliants and other stones of unusual size and perfection. I thought I was seeing the treasures of the fabled Cave of Jewels . . ."'

'Which could in fact have been more products of his alchemical experiments,' Jerry offered.

'That's certainly what was widely believed at the time – that Saint-Germain was an alchemist who could turn base metal into gold, or glass into diamonds, and whose alchemical experiments might also have led to his discovery of the elixir of life – which explained, for many people who remembered him from years previously, why he seemed relatively *ageless*. This latter aspect of his personality was heightened by his claims that he never ate – and certainly he was never *seen* eating or drinking in public.'

'That could have been a trick as well,' Jerry said.

'Yes,' Ingrid replied, 'it *could* have been . . .'

'But?'

'There's a lot more to come.'

'So sorry,' he said, impersonating an English gentleman. 'Please *do* continue!'

'In 1758,' she went on, 'while still in Paris, Saint-Germain was presented to Louis XV by Marshal de Belle Isle in the saloon of Louis' mistress, Madame de Pompadour. He charmed both of them, and two years later, in 1760, was sent by Louis XV to the Hague as his personal representative, to help settle the peace treaty between Prussia and Austria. While in Holland, he fell out with his former friend, Casanova, who then tried to discredit him – and this may have encouraged the enmity of Louis' Foreign Minister, the Duc de Choiseul, who convinced Louis that Saint-Germain had betrayed him and should be thrown in the Bastille. Subsequently, Saint-Germain fled to England.'

'We didn't find any confirmation for that,' Jerry said.

'Yes, we did,' Ingrid replied, pointing down at her neatly written notes. 'A *London Chronicle* article of 3 January 1760, which was mainly concerned with Saint-Germain's then widely reported "eternal youth", contained the comment: "No one now doubts it, although at first it was thought to be pure fantasy. In fact, everyone believes that, among other things, he knows of a panacea for all diseases and is able to overcome old age."'

As the frightening implications of Ingrid's summary gradually dawned on him, Jerry found himself glancing distractedly around the pleasant English pub – at the workers in their overalls, the gentlemen in pinstriped suits, the secretaries and Yuppies and tourists and casual staff – then started losing himself in the past, in recollections of the Nile cruise; recalling vividly the mysterious man he had encountered on the boat – his silvery hair, unlined skin, ageless face . . . and mesmeric gaze.

Another Saint-Germain? Someone simply using his name? Or was he truly the embodiment of something so remarkable that it went beyond the bounds of credibility and rendered normal reasoning prostrate?

He shook his head, hoping to clear it, trying to keep his senses together; but when he looked back at Ingrid and caught her solemn stare, he was forced to accept that her implications could not be avoided.

'You *do* realize what you're implying?'

'Yes,' Ingrid said. 'I do. We now know that he existed and was very odd indeed – a musician and composer; an astonishing linguist; an authority on world history; a magician and alchemist who claimed to be 4000 years old – and who, at least according to historical records, *did* live a remarkably long time.'

She trailed off in a hesitant manner, as if doubting her own words; and as fear crept coldly over Jerry, he welled up with concern for her.

'Okay,' he said, trying to keep his voice light and act unconcerned, 'what else do we have there?'

'From this point on,' she responded, staring down at her notes, 'the recorded facts make his life much more concrete. In 1762 he took part in the deposition of Peter III of Russia and in bringing Catherine the Great to the throne. A year later, he was known to be carrying out further alchemical experiments in his laboratory in the castle of Chambord, which Louis XV had put at his disposal in 1758. The following year he was living in Holland under the name of Count Surmount, where he established another laboratory in which he made paint and dyes, as well as continuing his alchemical experiments. Disappearing from Holland with about 100,000 guilders, he materialized in Belgium, this time calling himself the Marquis de Monferret, and there, in Tournai, set up another laboratory.'

'He obviously never stopped experimenting.'

'No,' she said. 'Never.'

'And so?'

She sighed. 'In 1768 he turned up in Russia in the court of Catherine the Great, whom he had previously helped bring to the throne; and according to Count Alexei Orlov, then head of the Russian Imperial Forces, he was an invaluable diplomat and palace advisor during the Russian–Turkish war of 1768–70. As a reward, he was made a high-ranking officer in the

Russian Army – which position he took under the ironic English alias of General Welldone – but instead of reaping the benefits of his prestigious position at the end of the war, he chose instead to leave Russia and go to Germany where, with his friend and pupil, Prince Charles of Hesse-Cassel, he carried out more alchemical experiments, as well as studying Freemasonry and Rosicrucianism . . .'

While her voice trailed off again and she shuffled some more papers, Jerry tried to accept what was being implied and realized that if it was true, it was something beyond belief.

It was also something frightening, without precedent, unparalleled; and as he looked at Ingrid's solemn face, which was filling up with excitement, he felt himself being submerged in a wave of guilt and fear at the thought of what he was leading her into by letting her share this.

'Now *this* is interesting,' Ingrid said, definitely sounding excited. 'Voltaire, on 15 April 1758, in one of his many letters to Frederick the Great, had described Saint-Germain as, quote, "a man who knows everything and never dies", and then added: "I think it quite probable that this man will visit you within the next fifty years."'

'Christ, yes – even Voltaire!'

'Yes, Jerry. And in 1779, the sister of Frederick the Great, Princess Amalie of Prussia, met Saint-Germain and became interested in him; however, when a letter from Saint-Germain to Frederick begging for patronage was ignored – possibly because of Frederick's embarrassment over widely circulated reports that Saint-Germain had worked for him as a double agent during his period in the French court – Saint-Germain went that same year to Eckernforde, in Schleswig, Germany, where he lived, and reportedly died, in the castle of Prince Charles of Hesse-Cassel.'

Jerry wanted to reach out and hold her, to protect her with his love; but remembering what had happened when she had left his apartment a week ago, remembering, also, the magical events of the Nile cruise, he was forced to accept, with shame and foreboding, that his love for her, as yet unconsummated, would not be enough to protect her if the wheel turned against them.

'The parish records in the Catholic church of Eckernforde,' she said, 'say that Saint-Germain died on 27 February 1784, and was buried locally. If this was true – and assuming that he *was* about fifty years old in 1701, it makes him – at a time when thirty-five was *old age* – over 130 years old when he died.'

'Except,' Jerry said softly, hardly recognizing his own voice, unable to accept what he was hearing and almost struck dumb by it, 'he may *not* have died . . .'

'Correct,' Ingrid said, smiling at him. 'He might still be alive.'

CHAPTER SEVENTEEN

Ingrid felt really proud of herself, in command, actually *doing* things. When Jerry nodded and stood up, she gathered the notes together, put them into her briefcase, then also stood up and followed him out of the busy pub into the sunlit street. When he took hold of her hand and smiled at her, she filled up with warmth at what she felt he had given her – the chance to prove that she existed and had worth, could love and be loved.

'Come on,' he said, 'it's time we got out of here. We have to pay someone a visit. I made the appointment last night.'

'You *did*?' she asked, surprised. 'An appointment with whom?'

'I'll tell you in a minute. Let's finish summing up first. We reached the conclusion that Saint-Germain may *not* have died, that he could be thousands of years old, but remarkably still alive. I want to get all this clear in my mind, so let's continue from there.'

'Right,' she said, opening the notes still in her hand and reading from them as she walked beside him along Great Russell Street, towards Tottenham Court Road. 'Although Saint-Germain's death is recorded in the records of the parish church in Eckernforde, a great deal of mystery surrounds his death. For a start, he was reported to have died when his good friend, Prince Charles, the Landgrave of Hesse-Cassel, was absent from home, and with only two nameless women servants in attendance. To deepen the mystery, Prince

Charles then burned all of Saint-Germain's supposedly invaluable papers – in his own words, "lest they be misinterpreted". Almost immediately, then, the rumours that Saint-Germain was still alive spread like wildfire.'

'That stuck in my mind,' Jerry said. 'The story that he *burned* all of Saint-Germain's papers. To me, that seems highly unlikely – especially when you consider that Prince Charles was Saint-Germain's devoted pupil. I don't think that anyone who'd worked as long or as intimately with Saint-Germain as Prince Charles did would have been capable of destroying the results of all that work. It's also very unlikely that Prince Charles would have been absent from the house when Saint-Germain died.'

'The implication being that Saint-Germain did *not* die at that time, but simply vanished, taking all of his papers with him, and leaving the devoted Prince Charles to cover up his trail.'

'Yeah,' Jerry said, 'that's right. And as I recall from our notes, there *are* grounds for thinking that the 130-year-old Count actually managed to grow even older.'

'You recall correctly,' she told him, moving closer to him as they entered the busy underground station, purchased two tickets to Holland Park, descended the lengthy escalator and eventually boarded the train. 'In 1785,' she said, as the train started moving, 'an important congress of Freemasons was held in Paris and attended by Rosicrucians, Kabbalists, Illuminati and members of other secret societies. According to the Masonic archives, the guests included the magician Cagliostro, the philosopher Louis Claude de St Martin, the renowned physician and hypnotist, Mesmer, and ... Saint-Germain, who is also recorded as having addressed the meeting. Mesmer later stated that it was Saint-Germain who explained the subconscious mind to him, thus paving the way for modern psychology and psychiatry.'

'Well,' Jerry said, 'whether alive or dead, our Count Saint-Germain certainly seems to have influenced a lot of very influential people.'

'Yes – and he continued to do so. It was recorded by the diarist Mademoiselle d'Adhemar that he visited her five times over a period of many years, beginning in 1789, when he also visited Sweden's King Gustavus III to warn him of danger, and ending in 1820, the night before the infamous murder of the Duc de Berri.'

'This is shivery,' Jerry responded, grinning at her. 'This is weird. Very *strange*.'

'Strange? It gets stranger. In her diaries, Marie Antoinette expressed her regret that she didn't take note of Saint-Germain's earlier warning about the forthcoming outbreak of the French Revolution. Reportedly, Saint-Germain also appeared to Madame du Barry on the scaffold, and to Marie Antoinette in prison, to warn her of the date and time of her execution.

'Nor does it end there . . . Twenty-eight years later, in 1821, the famed educationist, Madame de Genlis, mentioned in her memoirs a conversation she had had with Saint-Germain during the Vienna peace talks; and in the same year the French ambassador, the Count de Chalon, claimed to have spoken to him in St Mark's Square in Venice. By 1842, Saint-Germain's name was being mentioned in connection with Lord Lytton, whom he was said to have helped develop supernatural powers; in 1867 a meeting of the Grand Lodge of Freemasons in Milan, Italy, was attended by Saint-Germain; and in 1896 when, according to the evidence, he would have been approximately 245 years old, the famed theosophist, Annie Besant, wrote that she had recently met him.'

As the train pulled into Holland Park, Jerry, obviously intrigued and with his brain clearly working overtime, gazed out the window, stood up and exclaimed, 'I can't believe it! 245 years old so far! Come on, this is our stop.'

She followed him out of the train, then up the escalator and out onto another noisy main road.

'So,' she asked him, 'who are we going to see? You still haven't told me.'

Slipping in beside her, linking her arm with his and leading her along the road, he said, 'One of the most recent books I looked at in the British Library had a brief paragraph on a woman called Helena Barbanell, stating that she had been a leading member of the Theosophical Society, but had, a few years back, been expelled from the organization because of her public declaration that she was the *chela*, or disciple, of the legendary Comte de Saint-Germain, and that her renowned mediumistic powers were channelled through her from him. Apparently Miss Barbanell, now an old lady, is convinced that Saint-Germain still exists and operates through her. So, I just looked her up in the phone book, called her and made an appointment – and that's where we're going.'

'My,' Ingrid said, smiling at him, 'you're so efficient. I let that one slip past me.'

'No one's perfect,' he joked.

Looking up and checking the nameplate above the pavement, he led her along a broad, tree-lined street of elegant, early nineteenth-century houses, eventually stopping at one a short distance along. Like many of the houses in the area, this former family home had been converted into flats, and after climbing the steps to the front door and scanning the names on the numerous bells, he pressed the one belonging to Helena Barbanell. An electronically distorted female voice came out of the speaker above the bells, asking who was calling, and when Jerry had given both their names, a buzzing sound indicated that the front door could be opened. Jerry opened the door, let Ingrid walk in ahead of him, closed the door and led her across the hallway to the ground-floor flat of Helena Barbanell.

The woman who greeted them was old, grey-haired, heavily built, and supporting her arthritic limbs on a walking stick. However, Ingrid noted that her eyes shone with a deceptively youthful brilliance and her smile, as she ushered them inside, was welcoming and almost girlish.

Awkwardly seating herself and leaning her walking stick against a table, Miss Barbanell apologized for the state of her flat, blamed it on her arthritis, added that that was why she also couldn't make them tea, and asked if they would like a sherry instead. When Ingrid nodded, Miss Barbanell indicated the bottle sitting on the table, surrounded by antique glasses.

'I have a visiting home help for my three meals a day,' she said. 'Otherwise, I'm growing increasingly useless – so please help yourselves.'

'Would you like one as well?' Jerry asked her.

'Yes,' she replied. 'Why not? I'll be in my grave soon enough, so a sherry won't harm me.'

While Jerry poured the drinks, Ingrid glanced around the one-room flat and was saddened by the state and smell of it. The home help had not cleaned it well and the air had a musky smell. The furniture was old and darkly varnished, covered in dust; on the walls were photographs turning brown with age, while the tables and chairs were littered with old newspapers, magazines and books.

Helena Barbanell looked positively Victorian – and so did the room.

'You said on the telephone that you were working

on a book about the Comte de Saint-Germain,' she said to Jerry when he had passed her a glass of sherry.

'Yes,' Jerry lied. 'That's right.'

'Have you found out much about him?'

'Not enough for a book,' Jerry said.

Miss Barbanell smiled at him. 'No. I didn't think you would. The records on Saint-Germain are very scanty – and I can't tell you much more.'

'Well,' Jerry said, 'we've read of your expulsion from the Theosophical Society because of your stated belief in the existence of Saint-Germain. We also know that you believe him to be one of the immortals, and that in the course of history he's reappeared frequently, under various aliases, to interfere in the affairs of men.'

'That is correct, my dear. I am merely one of his many disciples, and my mediumistic powers come from him. It is the belief of the Theosophical Society that all mediumistic powers come from secret Mahatmas in a hidden colony in Tibet – the magical adepts who will one day regenerate the world – but they do not believe, as I do, that the Comte de Saint-Germain is such, and in fact believe him to be one of history's great impostors.'

'That's just what I was going to ask you about,' Ingrid said. 'There *is* a large body of opinion whch says that the supposed appearances of Saint-Germain throughout the centuries is some kind of elaborate hoax. What makes you so convinced that he exists?'

'Because he has appeared to me, spoken to me, and acts as my teacher. I am his *chela*, his disciple, and hope to join him when death comes.'

The bright eyes of the old woman were staring clearly and steadily at her, and Ingrid had to admire her calm conviction, whether rooted in fact or not.

'I naturally find that hard to believe, Miss Barbanell,' she said, feeling the blush on her cheeks.

'Naturally,' Miss Barbanell replied pleasantly. 'Since you have not had such an experience yourself, mine must be hard to believe.'

'Is there any way you can convince us,' Jerry said, 'that the known history of Saint-Germain isn't some kind of elaborate hoax?'

Miss Barbanell smiled, shrugged and shook her head in denial. 'It would be impossible for any individual, or organization for that matter, to extend such a hoax over such a long period of time, as well as keeping it alive in so many different countries and cultures. Besides, the historical records clearly reveal that most of the stories about Saint-Germain which gave rise to charges of charlatanism did not in fact originate with Saint-Germain, but indirectly from his arch enemy, the Duc de Choiseul who, in his hatred or jealousy of the Count, hired a look-alike named Gauve to mingle in society and exaggerate the Count's well-known claims as a means of discrediting him. This came to light through the extensive researches of Gustav Berthold Volz in the 1920s.'

'Given that Saint-Germain was supposed to have led such an extraordinary and active life, why are the historical records on him so thin?'

'The records *are* scanty,' Miss Barbanell agreed. 'but this was undoubtedly deliberate on Saint-Germain's part. For instance, Napoleon III was so intrigued by the stories about Saint-Germain that he set up a special commission to investigate him. However, the commission's findings were destroyed in a fire that consumed the Hotel de Ville in Paris in 1871 – and few were willing to ascribe that disaster to coincidence. Similar obstructions to the sources of information, and the mysterious destruction of discovered rare material evidence, have occurred throughout the years since Saint-Germain's final recorded materialization in 1820, when he last visited Mademoiselle d'Adhemar.'

'Such as the supposed burning of his papers, after his presumed death, by his devoted pupil, Prince Charles of Hesse-Cassel.'

'Precisely,' Miss Barbanell replied. 'The story that he died in Eckernforde in 1784 is nonsense. Saint-Germain evolved long ago from the physical plane into the non-physical plane of the magical adept – but he can take on the physical form at will. He did not die in 1784, but simply moved on – either in the flesh or in the spirit – and doubtless commanded Prince Charles, his disciple, to fake his death ... as it had been faked many times before.'

'*Before?*' Ingrid asked, surprised at her own lack of shyness.

'Of course,' Miss Barbanell said, having another sip of her sherry and pursing her lips. 'Saint-Germain knows the Hermetic secret which gives one immortality, and has thus reappeared many times throughout history under various aliases.'

'You really think that's possible?'

'It is possible for Saint-Germain, my dear. Through alchemy he discovered the elixir of life, and thus became an immortal, a spiritual adept, impervious to time and space.'

'I thought alchemy was a way of turning metal into gold,' Jerry said sceptically.

'That is a commonplace misconception,' Miss Barbanell said, her gaze calm and direct. 'Alchemy is, in fact, a means of purifying humanity, as well as Nature, and it can therefore be applied to material objects, the cosmos or man. The changing of metal into gold is only a small part of alchemy – a very unimportant part. The major purpose of the science is to find the ultimate purification – the panacea, the cure for all ailments, the elixir of life. It is no accident, my dear, that most of the great alchemists of history lived much longer than their fellow men of the time.'

'The Hermetic secret, then, is to be found in alchemy?'

'Yes, young man, it is.'

Ingrid caught Jerry's glance, took note of his raised left eyebrow, returned her gaze to the oddly youthful face of the arthritic old woman and didn't know what to think. She felt excited – yes, but also felt growing fear – and yearned to be held in Jerry's arms and lose herself in his warmth.

She finished her sherry, placed the glass back on the table, then spoke again to Miss Barbanell.

'Are you often in contact with Saint-Germain?' she asked.

'No,' Miss Barbanell said. '*I* am not in contact with *him*. *He* contacts *me* when it suits him, which is how it must be. For now, I am merely his disciple, his *chela*, but hopefully, with death, I will ascend to become one of the adepts.'

'Like Saint-Germain himself?'

'Not *quite* like Saint-Germain, but a spiritual adept on his plane. Saint-Germain is one of our hidden masters – one of the immortals whose vast, secret knowledge is available to adepts for the gradual enrichment of the world – along with such figures as Christ, Buddha, Merlin, Apollonius of Tyana and Roger Bacon.'

'And Christian Rosenkreuz?' Jerry asked out of the blue.

Miss Barbanell reacted as if slapped in the face. Visibly flushing, she stared at Jerry with her lined eyes glittering intensely, glanced at Ingrid as if betrayed, then blinked, had another sip of sherry and put the glass down.

'Christian Rosenkreuz?' she repeated, as if confused.

'Yes,' Jerry said. 'It's been suggested more than once that Saint-Germain was a member of the historically obscure Rosicrucian Society – and might even have been the original *founder* of the fraternity – or the son of the founder.'

Miss Barbanell appeared to tremble slightly, then regained control of herself. 'I *have* heard that theory,' she said, 'but cannot confirm or deny it. I only know that there is very little connection between the modern Rosicrucian believers and what you have rightly described as the historically obscure Rosicrucian Society – and that just as the origins of that society are obscured by history, so too is the identity of its founder. Whether or not Christian Rosenkreuz and Saint-Germain are one and the same – or even related – is something I can't say with certainty.'

'Can anyone?'

Miss Barbanell finished her sherry, set the glass back on the table beside her, played nervously with it, then sighed and looked directly at Jerry.

'I doubt that *anyone* can confirm it with certainty,' she said. 'However, there *is* someone who might be able to shed more light on the matter. A rather disgusting German sodomite and practising occultist who, before his descent into the quagmire of black magic, was a member of the reportedly still existing *original* Rosicrucian Society – the one whose origins are obscured in the mists of history. His name is Klaus Schiller.'

'And where might we find Mr Schiller?' Jerry asked.

'In Eckernforde, West Germany,' Miss Barbanell replied, suddenly looking disconsolate, shivering as if with shock, then taking a deep breath and blowing it out before looking up again. 'Klaus Schiller,' she continued in a less confident, trembling voice, 'is a degenerate descendant of Prince Charles of Hesse-

Cassel, and lives alone near the church in whose graveyard Saint-Germain was reportedly buried. I suggest you go see him.'

Ingrid was just about to ask her own questions when she saw the tears brimming in the old lady's eyes, then felt a hand on her shoulder. Twitching automatically, she glanced up at Jerry and saw him shaking his head in a negative gesture, warning her not to speak.

'Let's go,' he said softly.

When they left Helena Barbanell's flat, heard her door close quietly but firmly behind them, and stepped into the gloom of the hallway, Ingrid felt an even deeper gloom descending upon her, bringing fear and confusion.

Remembering the shock on Miss Barbanell's face when Jerry had mentioned Christian Rosenkreuz – as well as the old lady's sudden collapse into emotional desolation after confessing that the descendant of Saint-Germain's pupil, Prince Charles of Hesse-Cassel, was in her view a degenerate – she felt a touch of that desolation in herself.

The sun was still shining, but edging towards greyness as she walked beside Jerry down the steps of the building, unable to resist leaning against him, in need of his presence. She felt haunted by Saint-Germain, by his impossible history, and wondered if she was living a dream, or perhaps going mad.

Then she looked across the broad, handsome road and saw the men staring at her.

There were two men, wearing similar gaberdines, both on the opposite pavement, staring at her from behind a white Audi.

Seeing them, she stopped walking, briefly frozen with fear, convinced that the men were watching her, but not sure why she thought that. Then she noticed the white Audi and instantly understood her fear, believing that the men worked for her father and had come here to take her back.

Suddenly fearful, she reached out for Jerry's hand and felt his fingers curling around her own, returning her to her senses and giving her comfort and courage. Putting her fears down to imagination, she tried not to look back, but eventually, just before turning into the main road, had to glance over her shoulder, fully expecting to see the two men following her.

They were not doing so. They weren't even looking at her. Instead, they were walking casually across the broad road, heading in the general direction of the house she and Jerry had just left.

Wondering what was happening to her, she smiled up at Jerry, pressed herself against him once more and let him lead her away.

'Another shivery experience,' he said to her. 'So let's go to Germany.'

CHAPTER EIGHTEEN

Leaning heavily on her cane, Miss Barbanell looked down through her window as the young woman and her American boyfriend left the house and walked off along the pavement. The girl had been very sweet, but too strait-laced for her own good, while her young man, the American, had seemed bright but oddly innocent for his years, a naif, one of life's eternal optimists, a twentieth-century holy fool.

She watched them walking away, hand in hand, obviously in love, then sighed and turned away from the window to return to her chair.

They'll be back, she thought. In a day or two, a week or two. They had the look of two people obsessed . . . and their obsession was Saint-Germain.

Awkwardly, painfully, she hobbled back to her chair, slumped heavily into it, put the cane aside, then poured herself a more generous sherry. Sipping at it, appreciating its anaesthetizing qualities, she thought of the young American, her holy fool, and wondered if he'd been chosen. Perhaps, perhaps not. He had the boldness of innocence, the courage of the naïve; she had sensed that he was as pure as the driven snow – at least deep down inside himself, where it mattered the most.

If he knew what she was thinking about him, he would certainly laugh at her – since clearly he did not know himself, and thought of himself as a worldly man. Yet she sensed that he was not a worldly man, but a man of the spirit, his soul still undefiled.

She had another sip of sherry, trying to soothe her

sense of shame. Her own wavering faith had surfaced when she had told them of Klaus Schiller; and the young English-speaking German lady and her American boyfriend had obviously noticed her confusion at the very mention of Christian Rosenkreuz. They had witnessed the fissure in her faith and would surely return . . .

Sighing, she tried to forget the arthritic pains in her bones, could not stop herself from yearning for release from the body's betrayals, and then thought with a mixture of reverence and helpless suspicion about her venerable Master, Saint-Germain.

Most of her life, since adolescence, she had been visited by him, had observed his human form in its ectoplasmic radiance, had listened to his words and obeyed them, wanting only to follow in his footsteps and ascend to the summits.

She had thought him the essence of goodness, the embodiment of love, the supreme deity under God, but as old age and the body's failings attacked her, she had suffered from the first flickerings of doubt about his nature and motives. Too often, in recent years, his seductive, loving eyes had momentarily displayed an icy coldness or steely, suppressed rage. She had thought of him as strong, as aglow with inner peace and joy, but too often recently had she sensed despair and grief at his core.

Saint-Germain, her Master and hope, had more sides than a prism.

And what about Klaus Schiller? Why did *he* haunt her so? It was because he was the last of a long and noble line – the descendant of the blessed Prince Charles of Hesse-Cassel – and she couldn't understand how Saint-Germain, or the Order, could let that line degenerate so dramatically – and, even worse, let a corrupted former disciple remain so close to the hallowed ground from which the two adepts had ascended from Earth.

When she thought of Klaus Schiller, she thought of doubt – her own doubt and growing confusion . . . The young man and woman had seen it and would surely return.

She was thinking of that return when someone knocked on the door of her flat.

Convinced that it was the young lady and her American boyfriend returning already, she sighed, stood up heavily and made her way on her walking stick to the door, only managing to pull it open with some difficulty.

Two strange men, both wearing gaberdines, were standing in the hallway, smiling at her in a manner that instantly filled her with fear.

'Hi,' the smaller one said, his grin broadening maliciously. 'We're plainclothes policemen. We picked the lock on the front door and let ourselves in. We want to ask you a few questions about those people who just paid you a visit. May we come in?'

'Policemen?' she said. '*You're* not policemen! Just who on earth are –?'

The big man stepped forward, kicked her walking stick aside, and pushed her back into the room even as she was falling. She hit the floor on her back, was shocked by the pain, heard her own cry as if from far away as the two men entered the apartment and slammed the door shut.

'Put that bitch in the chair there!'

The voice was calm and unfeeling, filling her with dread; and as she tried to sit up, choking back the bile of terror, one of them grabbed her by the hair and dragged her in agony across the floor. Her heart raced dangerously. She gasped, choked, wept helplessly, heard her own groans, then felt herself being picked up and planted down on the chair. Her face was slapped and she opened her watery eyes and saw the men staring at her.

The bigger man, not smiling, which made him less frightening than the smaller man, held her walking stick up in front of him, then expertly broke it over his raised knee and threw the two pieces on the floor.

'This time it's just the walking stick,' he said with a guttural accent. 'The next time, if you don't answer our questions, it'll be your old woman's spine. Now stop snivelling and listen.'

She listened and answered automatically, stunned by pain, hearing her own voice repeating what she had said to the American and his young lady friend, understanding that her tormentors would follow them and most likely harm them.

'You spoke to the American pig and his girlfriend?'

'Yes!'

'About what?'

'Nothing. Just –'

She didn't know what they were doing. She only understood the pain. It shot up from her tortured fingers to her shoulders and made her shudder convulsively.

'Did they ask you about the Tuaoi Stone?'

'What?'

'Don't be boring. A masquerade of innocence won't help you – it will just make me hurt you more. Try this for size.'

Her normal world was blotted out. The pain became her one reality. Dissolving into the pain, she suddenly sensed that death was coming towards her, bringing chaos and terror.

'They *didn't* ask about the Tuaoi Stone?'

'No! I swear, *no*!'

'Then why did they come to see you, darling? And what's a fingernail worth these days?'

The worst torturer was herself. Her own screams drove her crazy. The pain had the bite of a reality she had not known before. Her shivering lips drank her own tears.

'Come on, darling, tell us some more. We're both hungry for gossip. What did they want to know, what did they learn, and where are they going? Why the tears? Am I *hurting* you?'

One of the men kept slapping her face. The other repeatedly stepped on her toes. When not doing this, they did things so obscene, so humiliating and painful, that she couldn't rise above the convulsions of her afflicted flesh, the pain's awesome dominion.

'Come *on*, darling, let's not be so coy. Let's have us some frankness. Is this nipple for sampling?'

They asked her what her visitors had wanted and what she had told them. It was a nightmare of terror, of pain expertly applied, and when she lied to them, or withheld information, they sensed it and applied some fresh torture until she gave in and told all.

'They're going to Eckernforde in West Germany,' were the penultimate words she uttered. 'They're going to visit Klaus Schiller. Oh, please don't! Not again . . .'

'Anything else?'

'No! Nothing! I swear it! Oh, please, not again . . .'

The chair was kicked from beneath her and she fell to the floor, was dragged by the hair from the lounge and into the bathroom.

She knew then that she was going to die – definitely, irrevocably – and as the taps were turned on, as the bath was filled with water, as they laughed and made jokes and occasionally kicked her pain-filled body, she travelled down through herself, to where the pain could not reach her, and took courage from the image of her Master, the revered Saint-Germain.

He materialized before her, a radiant presence in the darkness, watching calmly as they pushed her into the bath and held her under the water. She knew she was being murdered and that soon she would be dead, but also knew, when she saw Saint-Germain, that death would not have dominion.

In those few seconds before oblivion, with her chest about to burst, her faith, which had been wavering, was made whole by his light, and she felt her spirit rising out of doubt to remove her from terror.

'They will kill you,' Saint-Germain said, 'but they cannot finally harm you. What they do is done from hatred – but that hatred is a blessing; they are merely putting an end to your suffering and setting you free. Observe the light. Become part of it.'

Her chest and heart burst. She exploded into the light. Dying, she was resurrected on the instant, leaving life to the living. There was pain and then the radiance of immortality where the mountain peaks sheltered her.

'The fat cow's dead,' one of the men said. 'Let's get the hell out of here.'

Saint-Germain smiled in welcome.

CHAPTER NINETEEN

Hans was not feeling too good when he entered the Eforie Nord thermal treatment centre. In fact, he was exhausted, having just driven nearly 200 kilometres from Bucharest to Constanta, Romania's second largest and most ancient city, then south along the road between the sandy Black Sea shore and the freshwater lakes, not stopping until he reached Eforie Nord, close to Lake Techirghiol, famed for its health-giving sapropel mud.

What greeted him when he opened the door and tentatively entered the steaming mud-room was the sight of the gross Wilhelm Zweig, naked but for a pair of tight briefs, over which his bloated belly flopped in an ugly manner where he sat on the edge of a large, circular steel bath filled with warm sapropel mud, his feet in the bath, while two severe-faced white-overalled Ukrainian nurses spread the mud over his hairy legs and thighs.

'Ah,' Zweig said, staring directly at him, 'you got here at last.'

Having flown all the way from Bucharest to London and back again while Zweig rested in this expensive treatment centre, Hans did not take too kindly to the implied rebuke. However, he was frightened of Zweig, more so today than usual, and merely offered what he thought resembled a placating smile.

'Yes, sir,' he said.

'Did you stop in at the hotel in Bucharest on the way here?'

'Yes, I did.'

'And everything was all right there?'

'Yes. No problems.'

'And Elena was still there?'

'Yes, naturally,' he said, too frightened to tell Zweig that his beloved Elena, bored as usual, had made him join her on an early morning tour of the discos, cafés and brasseries of the city, and had then dragged him into her bed for some passionate sex.

He still could scarcely believe it.

Not a virgin, but with little time for romance, he had often secretly lusted after Elena, at once repelled and aroused by her sly teasing and sluttish behaviour. Yet he had never condemned her too much, thinking himself no better than she was, knowing too well how easy it was to give in, to surrender your will to the stronger will of another, as undoubtedly both of them had done with Zweig. So in one sense he had sympathized with her predicament – she had once been a professional whore and now was solely Zweig's kept woman, a virtual prisoner – and Hans, who felt increasingly that he was also a prisoner, had always felt that he and Elena had much in common, shared the same dirty cell.

So he had been drawn to her, lusting often in secret, and when she seduced him in that hotel in Bucharest he didn't need much encouragement.

He could still see her body, stark naked, voluptuous, could almost feel her limbs wrapped around him, drawing him in. The recollection was vivid, arousing him on the instant, but also resurrecting the fear that had been dogging him since leaving the hotel.

He was terrified of being found out, of Zweig seeing it in his face, and even more terrified that Elena would inadvertently tell Zweig about it. Yes, having had her that morning, having sampled her artful ways, he had to have her again (more so since she had told him that she also wanted him) but his lust could not dim his dread of what would happen should Zweig find out about them.

Zweig would certainly kill him.

Aware of this, he wanted to flee from the room, but forced himself to behave as if nothing had happened.

'Ah, God,' Zweig complained, as one of the women started rubbing the mud in between his fat thighs. 'These rheumatic pains of mine. I've tried everything, but only this works. You should try it sometime, Hans.'

'I don't have rheumatic pains,' Hans said, as usual embarrassed and appalled at the sight of his naked boss and trying hard not to look at him.

'That doesn't matter, Hans. This treatment would make you feel good, anyway. And you should think of the future, after all. You won't stay young for ever.'

'No, I suppose not.'

'So,' Zweig asked, 'what have you got to report? Did you bring back my daughter?'

'No, sir. We found her, but didn't bring her back — for what I feel are good reasons.'

'I can think of no good reason for not doing what you were told. I told you to terminate the American and bring back my daughter. I will accept no excuses.'

When Zweig stared at him with those gelid, inhuman eyes, Hans automatically removed his handkerchief from his pocket, wiped sweat from his forehead, and recalled with depressing clarity his childhood in Bremen, his hateful foster parents, all the times they had whipped him and locked him in the closet, caught him masturbating and whipped him again while threatening hell's fires. His childhood had been a nightmare, his adolescence worse; and then, as if being mocked further by God, he had taken employment with Zweig, not knowing what he was like, and had found out too late that he was working for a criminal and bully – possibly even a madman.

At first he had been excited by it, enraptured by the power it gave him, in thrall to the glamour of travelling the world to help coordinate the various offices and warehouses of Zweig's mighty empire, with its communications network of computers, telex and fax machines, satellite links, and numerous spies and informers in highly sensitive government, military and police institutions – but gradually, when it dawned on him just who he was working for, when he realized that his master was possibly a psychopath who was engaged in illicit activities on an international scale, he developed the desperate urge to escape, but just couldn't do it. He had learned of Zweig's tempers, of his homicidal tendencies, and understood that he would not be allowed to leave, now that he knew so much.

That's why he was still working for Zweig, no matter how much he hated it ... he was too frightened to leave without permission, too terrified of what might happen should he even mention the subject.

He was imprisoned by fear.

'I believe my reasons were sound,' he said, carefully avoiding Zweig's gaze. 'Please let me explain.'

'So explain,' Zweig replied, and then, when one of the women whispered something to him, swung his legs out of the bath and stood upright, looking even more awful, to let the women smear the mud over his body.

'We were right about the advertisement placed in the *Guardian* newspaper,' Hans said. 'It *had* been placed by the American and *did* bring Ingrid to him. Some men from our London office followed her to the American's flat in Notting Hill Gate, London ...'

'I know all this already,' Zweig interjected impatiently. 'We received the report in Bucharest. When one of our men tried to abduct the bitch, an unnatural light beamed out of a nearby alley and someone emerged from it, grabbed hold of our man, and somehow made him go into a fit and die. When the driver of our vehicle dragged the dead body into the Audi, he discovered that it had been slightly scorched all over by an unknown heat source.'

'Yes,' Hans said, blushing because he had forgotten that report, 'but a heat source very similar to the one that charred the bushes in the Herastrau Park in Bucharest, after *you* had had your very odd experience with a stranger.'

'Judging by your description,' Zweig replied, 'it was the same man *you* saw in the burial chamber of the Great Pyramid, when you were with Ingrid and the American.'

'Yes,' Hans said, recalling that terrifying experience, yet still finding it difficult to accept that it had actually happened, since it didn't seem possible. Indeed, repelled though he was by his own duties in Zweig's worldwide network of very materialistic, high-tech organizations, he still preferred them, or at least their reality, to the magical world they seemed to be grappling with.

Saint-Germain and the Tuaoi Stone were mysteries he could well do without.

'So?' Zweig said, now covered from neck to toe in the sapropel mud and looking like a gigantic chocolate bar. 'What has all this to do with the American and my bitch of a daughter?'

'Two days ago,' Hans explained, 'in a second attempt to capture Ingrid, I personally arranged for two of our best men to sit on her tail and attempt to grab her at the first available opportunity. Since our men also bugged both their rooms, there was little difficulty in finding out their movements. Ingrid had spent most of the previous five days with the American in the British Library Reading Room; and most evenings, after they had left the Reading Room, they had a meal together, then the American invariably walked Ingrid back to her hotel in Tavistock Square, not far from the museum.'

'So why didn't you abduct her from there?' Zweig asked, spreading his arms as requested by one of the nurses, to enable her to press more mud up under his armpits.

'Don't move,' the woman said softly in imperfect English. 'You must remain very still until the mud hardens.'

'*Sehr gut*,' Zweig said.

'We didn't try grabbing Ingrid in her hotel,' Hans said, secretly amused by the sight of Zweig standing between the two women, covered from neck to toe in hardening mud, 'because of the risk attached – I had thought it best to try to grab her off the pavement – but also because their repeated visits to the British Museum Library had convinced me that they were involved in some kind of research, and I was interested in finding out what that was.'

'Good thinking,' Zweig said, flicking his eyes in Hans' direction, but not daring to move even his head.

'Then,' Hans continued, wishing that the mud would constrict so tightly around Zweig that it would eventually crush the life out of him, 'when on the fifth day, the American and Ingrid did *not* go for a meal or return to her hotel, but instead left the library early and headed off in another direction, the men watching them followed them. When they entered the flat of one Helena Barbanell, in Holland Park, one of the men called me.'

'And you ordered the extermination of the American louse, yes?'

'I was going to,' Hans replied, feeling shockingly tired, but still intrigued by the sight of Zweig standing with his arms spread, as rigid as a rock, encased from head to toe in the *café-au-lait*-coloured sapropel mud. 'However, reasoning that the visit of Ingrid and the American to Miss Barbanell and their five days in the British Museum Reading Room were connected, I thought it best to let them go again and, instead, told our men to have words with Miss Barbanell and find out just what was going on.'

'Yes?' Zweig queried impatiently.

'Well, after a lengthy interrogation of the lady –'

'Under torture, I hope!'

'Yes.'

'She told the truth then.'

'I believe so,' Hans replied, feeling sick to think of what had probably ensued in that poor woman's room and deeply regretting that he was helplessly involved with it. 'Under interrogation,' he continued despairingly, 'the lady, Helena Barbanell – who had once been a leading theosophist but was thrown out of the society for publicly proclaiming her belief that Saint-Germain was her spiritual Master – imparted the information that Ingrid and the American had asked her about Saint-Germain in general, and wanted to know if she could prove his existence in particular.'

'And this woman actually believed that Saint-Germain was her spiritual Master?'

'Yes, Herr Zweig. She claimed that he visited her now and then, usually appearing out of an unnatural light – like the one I saw in the burial chamber of the Great Pyramid in Giza, and which was witnessed, also, by the driver of the car when our man was killed trying to abduct Ingrid in Notting Hill Gate.'

Zweig was growing excited by what he was hearing. His eyes darted left and right, obviously trying to catch the eyes of the women standing on either side of him, then he dropped his gaze as low as he could without moving his head, in an attempt to see if the sapropel mud had hardened.

'Take it off!' he snapped. '*Take the mud off!*'

'But it's too early, Herr Zweig,' one of the women protested. 'You will not get the full benefits of the treatment if you –'

'Damn you, *take the mud off*!'

Both of the women reacted as if they had been slapped, one of them turning very red, the other white – then one of them recovered and, using a small hammer and chisel, began chipping the hardened mud off Zweig's body.

'So, Hans, continue! Miss Barbanell!'

Distracted by the sight of the agitated woman first breaking and then peeling off the sapropel mud – like someone removing the chocolate coating from a giant Easter egg – Hans was jolted back to reality by the harsh imperative in Zweig's voice and said, 'Yes, of course, Herr Zweig!' With a rapidly drying throat he continued: 'So . . . Ingrid and the American wanted positive proof of the existence of Saint-Germain and were given, as a possible source of further information, the name of one Klaus Schiller, an excommunicated German Rosicrucian presently living in Eckernforde, West Germany – where Saint-Germain was reported to have died and been buried, before defying logic by reappearing many times in later years.'

'This is the same Saint-Germain so renowned in the eighteenth century?'

'Yes, Herr Zweig.'

'And he has reappeared frequently since, yes?'

'Reportedly, Herr Zweig.'

'And according to the Barbanell woman, he has appeared to her in an unearthly light?'

'So she seemed to think, Herr Zweig.'

'*Seemed* to think?'

'Yes, Herr Zweig, she is dead.'

'Good. *Very* good!'

The shell of mud was now being chipped off Zweig at a fairly fast rate, and for the moment he looked very odd indeed – a kind of jigsaw man, with large irregular patches of mottled white skin showing between equally irregular patches of mud. His flabby breasts with their hairy nipples were free, as were his waving arms.

'So!' he exclaimed excitedly. 'What you witnessed in the burial chamber of the Great Pyramid was not an illusion – nor was what I witnessed in the Herastrau Park. The legendary Saint-Germain actually exists – in one way or another – and is aware that we are trying to find him.'

'Yes. Just as Ingrid and the American are *also* trying to find him – which is why I didn't bring Ingrid back.'

Zweig's arms and upper body were now free of mud, and while one of the ladies wiped his bare skin with a hot cloth, the other got down on her knees to chip the rest of the mud off his legs.

Zweig glanced down distractedly at her – as if momentarily thinking of something more pleasurable – but then, perhaps regaining his senses, looked up again.

'Of course,' he said. 'Ingrid and the American have gone to Eckernforde in Germany . . . and our men are following them.'

'Yes, Herr Zweig,' Hans said, noticing, when the hardened mud fell off Zweig's loins, that beneath his trunks he had a slight erection. 'I've told them to follow Ingrid and the American, but not to go near them – at least not until they've led us to Klaus Schiller. I've told them to have a talk with Herr Schiller once Ingrid and the American have done so – then, as in the case of Miss Barbanell, we will silence Herr Schiller.'

'Excellent,' Zweig said.

The woman who had been kneeling in front of him

finally removed the last of the mud and stood up while the second woman, having wiped down his top half, now knelt on the floor to do likewise to his lower half. Zweig still had a slight erection beneath his pants, but the woman blandly ignored it.

'So,' Zweig summarized as the woman wiped him clean, 'the American is clearly in pursuit of Saint-Germain, no doubt in order to find the Tuaoi Stone. My first suspicions about him were therefore correct – he was on that Nile cruise in order to find the stone – and then he saw Saint-Germain, as you did.'

'Yes, Herr Zweig.'

'Yes, *indeed*, Hans. And now we must ensure that the American does *not* get killed – at least not until he has done our work for us and led us to the legendary Saint-Germain – and through him, to the Lodestone.'

Zweig looked down at the top of the head of the woman kneeling by his feet, which in fact she had just finished wiping. He spread the fingers of his right hand and was just about to lay them lightly on the woman's head, when, perhaps realizing what he was thinking, changed his mind, took a deep breath, and reluctantly watched her climb back to her feet.

Naked except for his briefs, he smiled at both women.

'Thank you,' he said. 'I'm sorry to have rushed you. Unfortunately, I have to rush you again and beg you to leave. Come back to clean this mess later on. *Multumesc. La revedere.*'

'*Cu placere,*' the women replied in unison, then curtsied and left, obviously very relieved.

Zweig waited until they had closed the door behind them, smiled at Hans with unusual warmth, then glanced down at his pitiful erection and walked to the window, waving his hand to indicate that Hans should join him.

Hans wiped sweat from his forehead with a handkerchief, then walked to the window and stood beside Zweig.

The Black Sea was stretched out before them, dark beneath a grey sky, the heavy clouds casting their shadows on the water's bleak surface.

'You have done well,' Zweig said.

'Thank you, Herr Zweig,' Hans replied, feeling even more nervous at the unexpected, unusual praise. 'I'm glad I took the right course of action.'

'You did,' Zweig said, glancing sideways at him. 'And to take the right course of action is important at all times.'

Not knowing what to say to that, Hans merely returned his gaze to the Black Sea and yearned for his freedom.

'Those women were very attractive,' Zweig said. 'Did you not think so, Hans?'

'Yes, Herr Zweig. I thought they were most attractive.'

Zweig sighed, almost as if disappointed. 'You know,' he said in a distant, rather melancholy manner, 'there was a time when I could not have controlled myself with such women, particularly under such ... *intimate* circumstances. However, now, in such circumstances, I find myself thinking, not really of the women, but of the days of the Third Reich, those final, tragic days, and of the fine young Wolfcubs who stood beside me when courage was needed.'

As if unaware of what he was doing, and still staring in a melancholy manner at the gloomily shadowed Black Sea, Zweig reached out and placed a hand on Hans' shoulder, then squeezed it affectionately.

Shocked by this intimacy, actually filling up with revulsion, and growing even more fearful in the presence of his master, Hans just stood there, staring at the grey-shrouded Black Sea while Zweig droned on, as if talking to himself, his voice histrionically emotional, each word pregnant with meaning.

'Yes,' he said, 'they were great days indeed – and now, in recalling them, I am filled with pride and love, and instead of feeling lust for common, peasant women, think of my Nazi comrades, those glorious young gods of war, and yearn for the purity of their blood and the steel of their spirit. We fought and frolicked together, ate and bathed together, and shared the knowledge of what was most important in life – which was, of course . . . *duty*.'

He turned to face Hans, now holding him by *both* shoulders, exhaled foul breath and offered a smile that chilled Hans to the bone. Hans wanted to run away, to be sick or hide his shame, but he did not, *could* not, move a muscle nor speak one word of protest.

'*Duty!*' Zweig repeated. 'The one word that gives life meaning. To obey, irrespective of personal feelings, is the sign of the *real* man. Do you not think so, Hans?'

'Yes, Herr Zweig,' Hans managed to croak through parched lips.

'*Duty!*' Zweig repeated, nodding emphatically, then pressed Hans onto his knees and placed his hands on his head. 'We must learn to obey. Do you understand, Hans?'

'Yes, Herr Zweig. I understand . . .'

And at that very moment, gripped by fear, sick with revulsion, Hans understood that he was a slave, that his fear of Zweig had paralysed him, and that the only future he could imagine was the hell of imprisonment. He closed his eyes and took a deep breath, willing himself to do his duty, then thought of Zweig's daughter, Ingrid – that oddly lovely, forlorn girl – and of the American and Saint-Germain and the Tuaoi Stone that Zweig wanted so badly. He let his breath out, hearing

Zweig's sigh above him, and only managed to retain his sanity by contemplating the possibility of some day, some way, turning the cards on his psychopathic master and setting himself free.

It was something to think about.

CHAPTER TWENTY

Jerry squeezed Ingrid's hand encouragingly as they stood side by side outside what was, according to the local telephone directory, the house of Klaus Schiller in the small, historic town of Eckernforde, in Schleswig-Holstein, in the Federal German Republic.

Not having been in Europe before, Jerry had been in a heightened state of curiosity for most of the journey – taking immense pleasure from Ingrid's learned dissertations on what they were seeing as they crossed the North Sea on the boat to Hamburg, spent the night in Hamburg like a pair of gauche tourists, then drove north in a rented car from there up to Kiel, and finally along the Jutland peninsula and the bleak Baltic coastline to this small, ancient town which had once belonged to Denmark – but now, standing outside the front door of Klaus Schiller, his tourist's enthusiasm was being replaced by a curiosity that was not without a certain latent fear.

'Well,' Ingrid said, 'you better ring the bell. Let's get it over with.'

It was a cold, wintry, late afternoon, and when he glanced at her through the deepening, rainswept gloom he thought she looked like a pitiful waif from a Charles Dickens novel – her spectacles covered in rain, her piled-up hair hidden under the gaberdine's hood, water dripping down her nose and off her chin while the wind moaned about her. He looked back over his shoulder, at the buildings across the square, and again saw the small hotel that he had noticed when they parked the car there.

'When we've finished with him,' he said, 'we might as well book into the nearest hotel – that one over there.'

'Yes, Jerry,' she replied, wiping rain from her spectacles. 'Now do we ring the bell or not?'

Sighing, feeling an odd reluctance, he rang the doorbell and waited with increasing trepidation for someone to come. The door opened soon enough, letting light beam out into the street, and standing before him was a stoop-shouldered man wearing dishevelled trousers, shirt and braces, his face cadaverous and unshaven, his eyes dark and mistrustful, his teeth, when he opened his mouth to speak, almost rotted away.

'*Ja?*' he asked in an unfriendly manner, his voice a guttural croak. '*Was wunschen Sie?*'

'*Entschuldigen Sie,*' Ingrid replied. '*Sprechen Sie Englisch?*'

'Of course,' the man replied impatiently. 'Who are you? What do you want with me?'

'Are you Klaus Schiller?' Jerry asked, his skin crawling at the sight of the little man, who looked unwashed and, indeed, as degenerate as Helena Barbanell had said he was.

'*Ja*, I am. So who are you?'

'Can we step in out of the rain?'

'No, you can't. Now who *are* you?'

'I'm Jerry Remick, an American writer,' he lied, 'and this is Ingrid Zweig, my research assistant. We're writing a biography on the life of the Comte de Saint-Germain, and were told that you might be able to help us.'

'It's really most urgent,' Ingrid added. 'We're just putting the finishing touches to the book, but our deadline with the English publisher is almost up – which is why we drove all the way here from London.'

'You did that for a few minutes of my time?'

'Yes, Herr Schiller, we did.'

Obviously impressed by this fact, Schiller stared at each of them in turn, then shrugged, stepped aside and waved them inside.

'Okay,' he said. 'Enter.'

Following Ingrid, Jerry brushed past Schiller, heard him close the front door, then was led by him along a short, dark hall filled with bits and pieces of machinery, into a lounge that smelt of decay and had the appearance of a very cluttered junk shop. Antique spears, swords and shields were leaning against every wall, the walls themselves were covered with old paintings and the furniture for the most part was stained and broken. Saucers filled with souring milk for the half dozen cats wandering about were resting on various parts of the floor.

'Here,' Schiller said, indicating the old pine table in the middle of the room. 'Take your raincoats off and sit down while I pour you a glass of schnapps, which should at least warm you up.'

'You speak very good English,' Ingrid said, removing her soaked coat.

'Naturally,' Schiller replied, filling three glasses with schnapps and bringing them to Jerry and Ingrid when they had sat by the table. 'Most Germans do. And I am, of course, an educated man from an illustrious family.'

'A descendant of Prince Charles, the Landgrave of Hesse-Cassel,' Jerry said.

'Quite so,' Schiller replied. 'And I have fallen to this.' He waved one hand disparagingly at the surrounding clutter. 'I sell antiques for a living to abominable tourists. Ach, such is life!'

He drank some schnapps, wiped his unshaven chin with the back of his right hand, then idly stroked the mangy cat that leaped onto the table and started prowling around the very large goldfish bowl in the middle of it. While stroking the cat, he grinned crookedly at Ingrid, looking her up and down in a bold, suggestive manner, which clearly she didn't notice since she was staring in disbelief at the goat that was tethered to the outside handle of the door leading into the back yard.

When Jerry lowered his eyes, feeling slightly embarrassed to find himself recalling Miss Barbanell's description of Schiller as a degenerate and sodomite, he noticed that the design of the fading carpet was that of the occult pentagram.

'You must have heard of me through your researches,' Schiller said in a pompous manner. 'I have heard that I am mentioned in certain books, though I don't read them myself.'

Jerry had already noticed that Schiller's bookshelves contained some of the books he and Ingrid had read in the British Library Reading Room – some of which had, indeed, made fleeting references to Schiller, none of which had been important enough to make them feel him worth following up before Miss Barbanell mentioned him – but he chose to ignore the obvious lie and instead said, lying himself, 'Yes, we came across your name in certain books and were very impressed.'

Smirking, the awful little man continued to stroke the cat, then casually stuck his hand in the goldfish bowl, grabbed one of the goldfish and threw it onto the table in front of the cat. When the cat pounced on the wriggling goldfish, Ingrid averted her sickened gaze.

'So,' Schiller said, watching the cat as it started to eat, 'what do you think I can add to your almost completed book?'

'Can we take it from what we've read that you *do* believe in the existence of the legendary Comte de Saint-Germain?'

Schiller nodded emphatically. 'Yes, young man, I do. He lived in this very town, in my father's former house, and was supposed to have died here and been buried in the graveyard of the Nicolai church. However, it's very unlikely that Saint-Germain was actually buried. More likely he *ascended* from the graveyard, which is why my ancestor, Prince Charles of Hesse-Cassel, was known to have gone there at nights for years after Saint-Germain's disappearance. He went there to consult Saint-Germain when he materialized there, which often he did. When Prince Charles died, his body was buried there – but his spirit joined Saint-Germain.'

'You don't believe that Saint-Germain ever died?'

'As the great Voltaire said: Saint-Germain is a man who never dies. Alas, that is so.'

'Why *alas*?'

Schiller shrugged, then stroked the cat as it gobbled the goldfish. 'Never mind,' he said. 'Let us leave it that Saint-Germain never died – and probably never will.'

He said it flatly, unequivocally, accepting it as a fact, and Jerry found himself thinking of his bizarre experience in the Great Pyramid, of the two men, both wearing snow-white *galabiyehs*, staring at him, surrounded by pulsating light and a magical sky. Those men had emerged from space, from the mysterious world of time, and one of them, the one called Saint-Germain, had somehow spanned the centuries.

It was too much to think about.

'What do you mean,' Ingrid asked, 'when you say he did not die, but *ascended*?'

'Once an ordinary mortal, Saint-Germain emerged from the obscurity of prehistory, probably founded the original, very mysterious Rosicrucian Society, and gradually learned through his alchemy the Hermetic secret whereby he became immortal. Now, as an adept, an immortal, a spirit being, he can take human form at will – and has, in such a form, reappeared on earth throughout the centuries, in many different disguises.'

'And the eighteenth-century Saint-Germain was such a being?'

'Yes. The eighteenth-century Comte de Saint-Germain took physical incarnation as the son of Franz-Leopold, Prince Ragoczy of Transylvania, and Princess Charlotte Amalia of Hesse-Wahnfried, who were married in 1694; was brought up, after his brothers had been taken prisoner by the Austrians and his parents had died, by the executors of his father's will – namely, the Duc de Bourbon, the Duc de Maine and the Comte de Charleroi and Toulouse – and through them was introduced to the courts of Europe as someone of princely blood and almost royal descent.'

'Which is why he never seemed to need any money,' Jerry said.

'Correct,' Schiller replied. 'According to the historical work *Illustri Italiani*, by Caesare Cantu, librarian of the great library in Milan, when this particular emodiment of Saint-Germain came of age, he was educated at the University of Siena, travelled much in Italy and Spain, was greatly protected by the last Grand Duke of Tuscany and eventually inherited his father's considerable legacy. He was certainly no penniless adventurer, as described by certain historians.'

Certain historians, Jerry knew, had a tendency to *change* history, to distort it and create a new truth that more suited their own ends. Thinking about it, he turned cold, knowing that anything was possible, imagining a vast conspiracy, ordained by Saint-Germain, that straddled the whole world and spanned the centuries as if they had never been.

Did such a conspiracy actually exist? And if so, what was its purpose?

He recalled Saint-Germain in the magical light in the Great Pyramid, pointing at him and saying, 'You must know that the first number is "one".' In mathematical terms, it certainly was – but Saint-Germain had meant something other than that . . . The number 'one'. The first number of *what*? The first clue to a vast and incredible conspiracy that had no respect for time nor space, being based on pure magic.

Jerry suddenly felt dizzy with confusion and excitement, and spoke to hear his own voice, to come back to reality . . .

'And when he wanted to disappear, he simply took his spirit form, after arranging for his disciple and partner in alchemical experiments, Prince Charles of Hesse-Cassel, to fake his death and bury *someone* in the graveyard of that church?'

'Quite so. We will never know *who* was buried in that grave in 1784 – but certainly Saint-Germain's name was entered in the church register, and there, as far as history is concerned, the matter must rest.'

Another cat jumped onto the table to try to wrest the remains of the goldfish from its partner, who responded by clawing savagely at the intruder. The cats were hissing, spitting and clawing furiously at one another when Schiller, obviously democratic in certain senses, swept the first cat off the table with a sharp sideways blow, reached into the bowl for another living goldfish, held it up until the second cat had snatched it out of his hands and then watched with interest as it was eaten.

'According to Eliphas Levi, the nineteenth-century occultist,' Ingrid said, repeating what she had read in the British Library and trying to avoid the disgusting sight on the table, 'the Comte de Saint-Germain was born in Lentmeritz in Bohemia, the bastard son of a leading Rosicrucian.'

'A confusion between history and *pre*history,' Schiller responded. 'The details of the eighteenth-century Saint-Germain are as I told you: he was born in the late 1860s in Transylvania and brought up in the court of Vienna. However, Levi's confusion arises because Saint-Germain, in a previous incarnation – either as the son of Christian Rosenkreuz or *as* him – was instrumental in the formation of the original Rosicrucian Society.'

'A society to which you once belonged,' Jerry said.

Schiller spat in disgust into one of his hands, then rubbed both hands together. 'Ach!' he exclaimed contemptuously. 'That bunch! The modern Rosicrucians have their roots in California – and I think that speaks for itself. I joined because I thought they might connect me to my past, but they threw me out because of my loudly proclaimed belief that they had nothing to do with the real Rosicrucians, who emanated in mysterious circumstances here in Germany.'

'Right,' Jerry said. 'I've read up on all that. The first *printed* records we have of the original Order were published, in 1614, in Hesse-Cassel – where Prince Charles, your ancestor and Saint-Germain's disciple, came from. It was that pamphlet, entitled *Fama Fraternitas of the Worthy Order of the Rosy Cross*, that first mentioned Christian Rosenkreuz, saying he'd spent his life wandering the East in search of occult wisdom, found it, and subsequently formed the Brotherhood of the Rosy Cross, now known as the Rosicrucians, and managed to live to be 106.'

'Yes,' Schiller said. 'It is believed that the author of that work, plus two subsequent works on Rosenkreuz and the original Order in general, were written by a minister, Johann Valentin Andraea, in Tübingen, also right here in Germany, where those original Rosicrucians met. Central to the work of Andraea and the Rosicrucian beliefs spread *by* that work were two obsessions: the concept of a Utopia of superior beings – and the nature and uses of alchemy, particularly as a means of transforming men into gods.'

'Could Johann Valentin Andraea have been another incarnation of, or pseudonym for, Saint-Germain?'

'Almost certainly,' Schiller said, smiling smugly at Jerry and stroking the cat as it tore the goldfish to shreds.

'The facts certainly fit,' Ingrid pointed out. 'From 1710 to 1822, Saint-Germain apparently travelled extensively, taking in most of Europe, Africa, India and China. He claimed to have been at the Court of the Shah of Persia from 1732 to 1742, where he reportedly acquired his considerable knowledge of diamonds and other precious stones, as well as learning his most advanced secrets of nature and alchemy. Certainly he was reported as being able to speak Italian, French, Spanish, Portuguese, English, Chinese, Hindu and Persian – a remarkable achievement by any standards. In a letter to the Graf von Lamberg he claimed to have learned his knowledge of melting jewels during his second journey to India in 1755, to where he journeyed with General Clive. He was also reported to be deeply involved in numerous esoteric orders, including the Rosicrucians, Illuminates and Templars.'

'It is my belief,' Schiller said, 'that Saint-Germain, whatever his most distant origins, founded the original Brotherhood of the Rosy Cross, or the Rosicrucians, and that Christian Rosenkreuz and Johann Valentin Andraea were one and the same – in short, Saint-Germain.'

Jerry felt distinctly unreal, as if haunted by ghosts, and found himself staring around the gloomy room, into shadowy corners. He kept expecting to see that strange light, the magical bending of time and space, the materialization of Saint-Germain and his mysterious partner . . . He sensed that they were watching him and Ingrid wherever they went, and would not let them go.

He just didn't know why.

'In the British Museum,' he heard Ingrid say, 'there are pieces of music, dated 1745 and 1760, reportedly composed by, and certainly signed by, Saint-Germain. Do you know of anything else that might more firmly substantiate his existence?'

'Yes,' Schiller said without a pause. 'Although Saint-Germain has been very successful throughout the centuries at destroying, or hiding, most of the evidence for his existence, there *is* a document written by him that still exists and is preserved in the library in Troyes, in France. If you haven't yet read it, you should. It is *most* interesting.'

'Are you willing to tell us what it says?' Jerry asked.

'No. You must view it for yourself. It is well worth the journey.'

Smirking in what seemed, to Jerry, to be an oddly fearful manner, Schiller swiped the second cat off the table and then picked up a third that had been rubbing itself around his ankle. Resting this cat in his lap, he stroked it with one hand, reached into the bowl with the other, pulled out a wriggling goldfish and slowly, sadistically, lowered it over the cat's gaping mouth.

Jerry took a deep breath, feeling nauseous, then lowered his eyes and said, 'What kind of man, or being, is Saint-Germain? Is he good or evil?'

'Is *he* good or evil?' Schiller sneered as the cat snatched the unfortunate goldfish from his grubby fingers. 'Am *I* good or evil? Are *you*? I only know of his existence through my family's written records, as well as those of recorded history, but believe that my personal misfortunes have been caused by my proclaiming that he was actually Christian Rosenkreuz in one of his many former incarnations. It is Saint-Germain's *vengeance*. Of that I am sure. He has placed a curse upon me, ruining me and all I touch, destroying the name of the once illustrious family out of which his own greatest disciple, Prince Charles of Hesse-Cassel, sprung. This is the extent of Saint-Germain's vengeance because I revealed one of the Order's most closely guarded secrets: the true identity of its original founder, the adept known as Saint-Germain.'

'You have no proof of that,' Jerry said.

'I know, young man. *I know!*'

Agitated, Schiller threw the cat to the ground and stood up to go to the back door, where he shuddered and stared down at his tethered goat, his brow furrowed in thought. Jerry caught Ingrid's despairing glance, knew she wanted to escape this dreadful house, but couldn't bring himself to take his leave without asking the disgusting little man some more questions.

'Do you dabble in the occult?' he asked him.

'I *was* a Rosicrucian!' Schiller said, still keeping his back turned to both of them, still studying the tethered goat.

'Rosicrucian occultism is supposedly concerned with the long-term betterment of mankind. Is that what you practise?'

'You think the Rosicrucians are committed to doing good? Perhaps centuries ago. But who knows the purpose or nature of an Order in which the greatest adepts have become immortal and know no limitations? I am frightened of Saint-Germain – as many people are – and have turned from the old ways of the Order to practise their opposite.'

'You mean black magic?'

'Yes.'

'And does the number "one" mean anything to you?'

'No,' Schiller said, and finally turned back to face them, and Jerry saw, in his shadowed eyes, a smouldering malevolence that turned his blood cold. Ingrid gasped, kicked her chair back, stood up and glanced at Jerry, her hand covering her mouth, her eyes too big behind the thick spectacles.

He felt real concern then, and stood up, still facing Schiller, tried to meet that darkly burning malevolence and felt himself shivering.

'You didn't come all this way just because you read about me in a book,' Schiller accused him. 'You must have talked to someone about me. *Who sent you here?*'

The vehemence in his voice startled Jerry, making him step backwards, but he managed to keep his voice calm when he said, 'A woman called Helena Barbanell. She was once a member of the Theosophic Society, but like you was excommunicated when she –'

He stopped talking when Schiller walked slowly towards him, his face contorting with hatred and a great deal of fear.

'*Barbanell?*' he asked hoarsely. 'You talked to Helena Barbanell? *When?*'

'Two days ago. On Friday afternoon.'

Schiller was aghast. 'God,' he said, his voice hysterical, 'don't you know what you've done, you young fools? Whoever killed Helena Barbanell has probably followed you *here!*'

Jerry's thoughts swirled in confusion. '*Killed?*' he said, feeling stupid. 'Helena Barbanell was killed?'

'She was murdered on Friday afternoon,' Schiller hissed. 'The same day you saw her. *Damn you, get out of here!*'

He picked up one of the swords leaning against the nearest wall and swung it wildly over his head. Ingrid shrieked and reached out to pull Jerry away as he

229

ducked and the sword cleaved the air where his head would have been. Schiller kept screaming abuse and swinging wildly with the sword as Jerry pushed Ingrid behind him, then, still facing Schiller and ducking the swinging sword, made his way backwards out of the room and along the dark corridor with the many cats, suddenly galvanized into action, hissing and spitting and biting at his feet in a ravenous, unnatural fury.

He heard Ingrid opening the front door, felt her tugging him out backwards, then he slammed the door closed in Schiller's face as the cold wind beat at him. He found himself staring at Ingrid, at her magnified frightened eyes, then took her hand and hurriedly led her away through the deepening darkness, into the wind and rain.

CHAPTER TWENTY-ONE

Jerry was still badly shaken by his experience with Klaus Schiller when he sat facing Ingrid in the almost empty restaurant of the small hotel opposite Schiller's house, and found himself greatly lacking in an appetite for food, but very keen to drink as much Liebfraumilch as possible. What had started out as an exciting adventure was now turning into a living nightmare, and the knowledge that Helena Barbanell had been murdered shortly after his and Ingrid's departure, combined with Schiller's almost inhuman malevolence and fear, made that nightmare all the more real and his feeling of danger more riveting.

'You always tell me to look after myself,' Ingrid said, 'and now you're not even eating.'

'I'm on a liquid diet,' he retorted.

'That's not at all funny,' Ingrid responded primly. 'You shouldn't drink *at all* on an empty stomach – and it certainly won't calm you down.'

'I don't need calming down.'

'Yes, you do. Your hands are shaking. Every time you fill your glass up, you spill it, so let's not pretend otherwise.'

He wiped the spilt wine off the table with his thin paper napkin.

'Okay,' he said, 'I'm a bit shaken up. Who wouldn't be? I can't get over the fact that that woman was murdered shortly after we left her. I think that's real scary.'

'Yes,' Ingrid replied, 'it's scary. But I don't think

Saint-Germain had anything to do with it. I think my father's men murdered that poor woman. There were two men standing by an Audi car when we left – and they approached Helena Barbanell's building just as we turned the corner. I think they got her to tell them what she told us – and then shut her mouth for good.'

'That sounds logical.'

Ingrid shuddered. 'Oh, yes . . . And now those men know that we were coming here – and they probably *have*, as that revolting Schiller believes, followed us here.'

'Yes, Ingrid. Exactly.'

He picked in a desultory manner at his food, drank some more wine, glanced at Ingrid, yearned deeply to possess her, but knew the time wasn't right. This was no time for love and romance – they were caught in a terrifying web of intrigue, and now it was becoming truly dangerous and increasingly frightening.

'Maybe we should stop this,' he said. 'Get out while we can.'

'It's too late for that now,' Ingrid said. 'My father won't rest until he finds us – and that still leaves our mysterious Saint-Germain. Besides, I won't give in again. I won't surrender my freedom.'

She stared defiantly at him and he felt himself glowing, filled with pride at how far she had come in such a short time. His timid mouse was turning into a formidable lady.

'Let's visit the church before it closes,' he said. 'Let's do that, at least.'

'Yes,' she agreed. 'Let's.'

Feeling fairly drunk, but too shaken to be stupid, Jerry paid the bill and led her out of the dismally empty restaurant into the almost dark, later afternoon *strasse*, with its cold wind and fine rain. While not yet

232

dark, the streetlamps had been turned on, and their light, beaming down on the pavements, had a wan, eerie quality.

Jerry felt disorientated, far removed from his home, disassociated even from the personality he had thought was himself. In this quiet, ancient town, in its rainswept streets, he felt haunted and threatened.

They reached the Nicolai church soon enough and found it still open. The parish priest looked as lonesome as the town, but otherwise was obliging. He showed them the church register, left them with it in the vestibule, departed as Ingrid translated aloud what she could see by torchlight.

Deceased on February 27th, buried on March 2nd, 1784.
The so-called Comte de St Germain and Weldon.
Further information not known.
Privately deposited in this church.

Ingrid kept the torchlight on the register for quite some time while Jerry just stared at the entry in German, feeling that he had stepped back into time and become someone else.

'Well,' Ingrid said, 'there it is. Your authentic church record. And according to the *church*, Saint-Germain was buried in these grounds on the second of March, 1784.'

'Yes, Ingrid, that's right. At least according to the parish priest who wrote this particular entry. But don't forget that Prince Charles *was* the Landgrave of Hesse-Cassel, that he was a man of considerable influence in the community, that he was bound to have given considerable financial aid to the church, and that it would have been easy for him to have either buried someone else here without the parish priest knowing, or even, if the parish priest knew that Saint-Germain had simply fled, bribing him into keeping his mouth shut

233

and writing a false entry about his supposed death. Either way, this particular entry, even if genuine, doesn't necessarily mean what it says. And what we're still left with, according to Helena Barbanell and Schiller, is that the Saint-Germain who supposedly was buried here is in fact still alive and well.'

Ingrid didn't reply, but he knew what she was feeling. Like him, she would be feeling that she was living a dream, slipping into a mysterious zone where time and space had no meaning. Like him, she would be feeling disorientated and increasingly unreal . . .

Behind him, the wind howled, the rain splattered on the ground, and he shivered.

'Come on,' he said, 'let's go.'

They returned the register to the parish priest, thanked him and left, heading back through the narrow rainswept streets, illuminated by lamplight. Then Jerry saw another light, a flickering yellow glow near the square; saw smoke and then heard sirens wailing as they raced towards the fire.

'Oh, no!' he heard Ingrid murmur.

He understood what the phrase signified and, feeling a surge of fear, he tightened his grip on her hand and started running. When they reached the town square, which they did very quickly, a crowd had already gathered to watch the spectacular blaze, and the firemen were fighting a losing battle with the house of Klaus Schiller.

Jerry caught Ingrid's frightened look, then waited impatiently while she spoke in German to the person standing next to her. When she had finished, she stared very intensely at the blazing house, bit her lower lip and then told him, 'It's apparent that Schiller's dead. Before the fire started, he was heard screaming for help – but before anyone managed to get to the house, there was some kind of an explosion, then the whole house went up. Schiller probably died in the explosion; if not, then he's burned to death.'

Jerry just stared at her, not knowing what to say, but sharing the dread he saw reflected in her eyes. She shuddered, shook her head, pressed her forehead to his chest, and he put his arms around her and held her close to him. She was melting in his embrace, letting her body merge into his, but then she stiffened, straightened up, stepped away, and, looking even more fearful, indicated with a nod of her head that he should look behind him.

Looking over his shoulder, at the far side of the street, he saw two men in black gaberdines, standing apart from the otherwise anonymous crowd of on-lookers, their brutal faces illuminated fitfully in the glowing of the flames rising from Klaus Schiller's house.

When they saw him watching them, both men smiled maliciously, then melted back into the darkness of an unlit side street.

Even as he was watching the men disappearing into that side street, he had the distinct feeling that he was himself being observed. Dazed, feeling drugged, he looked beyond Ingrid's head ... and was almost hypnotized by the silvery-grey gaze and diabolically handsome features of the same mysterious man he had seen with Saint-Germain on the deck of the boat cruising along the Nile.

This time, he didn't experience that disturbing, unnatural desire for the strange man gazing so hyp-notically at him, and was, in fact, almost instantly able to jerk himself out of his brief, trance-like stupor and start forward, determined to confront the mesmer-ist. However, before he could reach him, the man smiled in a teasing manner, nodded as if in acknowled-gement, then turned and hurried away, soon losing himself in the crowd of people still watching the blazing fire.

'Christ,' Jerry said. 'They've *both* got people on our tail – Saint-Germain *and* your father. Which one of them had Schiller murdered? That's what I'd like to know.'

'Let's go back to the hotel, Jerry. *Please*. I'm scared. I don't like it here.'

He knew what she meant, actually felt the same way, and so willingly took her by the elbow and led her away from the crowd. Once upstairs in the hotel, they started going to their separate rooms, but then she stopped, stared forlornly at him and said, 'I can't stand the thought of being alone tonight. Can I stay in your room?'

'Sure,' he said. 'Naturally.'

He opened his door and waved her in, closed the door behind her, shivered with cold and rubbed his hands. Ingrid shivered also, then took off her coat, passed it to him and sat on the bed while he hung the coat in his wardrobe.

When he turned back to face her, she was frowning and picking something off the pillow. She held it up in the light, swung it on its short string, and looked closely at it.

It was a tiny, steel swastika.

There was a label tied to the string and Ingrid, holding it close to her spectacles, studied it.

'Compliments, Saint-Germain,' she read aloud, then glanced up with frightened eyes.

Remembering the teasing smile of Saint-Germain's partner, when he had seen him in the square just a few minutes ago, Jerry didn't know whether he should be angry or even more fearful.

'Ring through to reception,' he said, 'and ask them if anyone's been in the room during the past hour or so.'

Ingrid did so, then placed the phone back on the receiver and shook her head from side to side in a negative manner.

'No,' she said. 'The receptionist swears that no one's been in here – no cleaning women, no visitors. She swears that nobody's even been *near* this room since we left it.'

'Did you sense she was lying?'

'No. She sounded sincere. Genuinely puzzled that I should ask. I don't think she was lying.'

'Then how the hell was that swastika left here?'

Ingrid glanced down at the swastika, which she had placed back on the bed. She reached out to pick it up; her hand shook and she withdrew it.

Jerry picked it up instead and studied it closely.

'Well, it's a normal swastika – a good, old-fashioned, Nazi swastika. The question is: what's it meant to tell us? And *I* think it's Saint-Germain's teasing way of confirming that your father's men – not Saint-Germain's – murdered Schiller and set his house on fire. And that in turn confirms that it was also your father's men – not Saint-Germain's – who murdered Helena Barbanell in London.'

'Oh, God,' Ingrid murmured, suddenly looking ill and gazing down at her clasped hands.

'So,' Jerry continued, wanting to sympathize with her but not knowing how, 'we now know we're being watched by two different parties – your father's men and Saint-Germain's lot – and that for some reason Saint-Germain is actually *encouraging* us to continue our search, while protecting us from your father's men.'

'But *why*?'

He shrugged. 'Presumably he has his reasons and we'll discover them in due course. In the meantime, we just have to keep going and try to unravel the mystery as we go.'

Without thinking, he glanced around the room, realized what he was doing, felt foolish and turned back to Ingrid, who, still sitting on the bed with her hands clasped in her lap, looked distinctly uneasy and forlorn.

'And what have we got so far?' he asked. 'We have the extraordinary fact that Saint-Germain is almost certainly still alive; that he seems to have either lived for centuries or been reincarnated many times; that he is considered by many people, such as Helena Barbanell and even Schiller, to be some kind of magical adept, possibly the founder of the original Rosicrucian Society, and maybe even a member of some kind of secret society that had its origins in ancient history and has managed to survive to the present day. What's the purpose of that society? And why's Saint-Germain guiding us to it? At the heart of all this is the number 'one', but we don't yet know how. What we *do* know is that Saint-Germain teased us into investigating him and finding out that he actually still exists. Obviously, he wanted us to know *that* much. Equally obvious is the fact that he wants us to continue tracking down any clue we get. And since Schiller told us to visit the library in Troyes, where the only document known to be written by Saint-Germain still exists – apart, that is, from the music scores in the British Museum Library – then we have to make that our next stop. Are you still game for all of this?'

Ingrid looked up from her clasped hands, her face drawn and pale.

'Yes, Jerry, I am.'

'Are you frightened?'

'Of course.'

'Well, so am I. But fear's a healthy emotion. As long as we feel fear, we'll have our wits about us. Though right now, dear God, I feel tired . . . maybe too tired to sleep.'

'So am I,' Ingrid murmured.

She lay back on the bed, closed her eyes briefly, opened them again, held her arms up and said, 'Come here. Lie down beside me. I want you to hold me – nothing else – I don't want to sleep alone.'

Exhausted, bewildered and more than a little nervous, he was nonetheless touched enough by the sight of her to get a lump in his throat. Taking off his own soaked coat and kicking off his shoes, he lay beside her, drew the cover over them both, took her in his arms, kissed her eyelids and warm lips. She returned his affections, but too quickly closed her eyes, and he held her, stroking her face and hair, until she was sleeping.

He lay beside her a long time, taking warmth and comfort from her, then gently slipped out of bed and went to the window. Down below the crowds had begun to disperse, but the house of Klaus Schiller, which had become his crematorium, was still blazing in the night, sending flames and sparks and billowing smoke into the sky, the sparks cascading brightly around the odd, distant star while the black smoke, dense and a little frightening, obscured the full moon.

The fire blazed a long time.

CHAPTER TWENTY-TWO

Jerry lay on his narrow bed in his shabby room in a small *auberge* in Troyes, still feeling hungover from his drunken evening the night before in Frankfurt-am-Main.

They had arrived half an hour ago in the middle of a heavy rainstorm, and the rain was still beating down outside, falling from thunderous black clouds that only served to make the unattractive town seem even more ominous. Already feeling trapped, depressed and very nervous, Jerry swung his legs off the bed, opened one of the cans of beer he had bought downstairs, then sat back on the bed to have his drink and ponder what had actually happened to him during the past twenty-four hours or so.

After leaving Eckernforde, they had driven all day and spent the night in Frankfurt-am-Main, booking into a small hotel on the left bank of the river and then relaxing in one of the many taverns of the lively Sachsenhausen quarter. They had both felt the need to relax, since their otherwise pleasant journey had been overshadowed by what they had learned from their waitress over breakfast in the hotel in Eckernforde.

According to the wide-eyed, unhealthily excited waitress, the town was rife with rumours that the charred corpse of Klaus Schiller had been found handcuffed to the gas oven of what had once been his house – and that it had been obvious from the remains of the oven that all of the taps had been turned on.

'The bastards probably set a lighted candle near

him,' Jerry said to Ingrid as she drove him away from Eckernforde. 'He was heard screaming for help just before the escaping gas was ignited, but then, when the gas exploded – ffffttt! – that was the end of him. Oh, boy, what a way to go!'

He had regretted his comment when he saw Ingrid shudder, and remembered that the men who had committed the awful deed had almost certainly been in the employ of her father. Instantly ashamed of himself, he patted her knee reassuringly, gave her a smile, then stared straight ahead at the road which, unwinding between the sea and lakes just north of Kiel, had eventually led them to this tavern in Sachsenhausen, in Frankfurt-am-Main.

Relaxing with large beers, beginning to feel like an ordinary tourist, he had gradually started forgetting the fears that had been dogging him and instead found himself falling in and out of romantic reveries about Ingrid, wanting to hold her and be held *by* her; and also thinking, more basely, about the forthcoming night and fantasizing about sharing a bed with her.

When he had glanced sideways at her studious, bespectacled face, slightly hazed in the cigarette smoke that filled the noisy tavern, and thought of making love to her, he flushed as much with guilt as with desire, since he knew that by bringing her with him, he had possibly put her in danger.

'Whenever I start worrying about all this business,' he had told her in the hope of relaxing her, 'I think of quantum mechanics, which now lie at the heart of all modern science. Without quantum mechanics there would be practically no chemistry, science or molecular biology, no knowledge of DNA, no genetic engineering – hardly anything at all. In fact, quantum theory is the greatest single achievement of science, surpassing even the relativity theory . . . and yet, according to quantum mechanics, *nothing is real unless it is observed*. In other words, Ingrid, don't worry too much. Until we actually *observe* Saint-Germain's magic powers, neither he nor they can actually exist.'

'But we *have* observed them, Jerry.'

'No, Ingrid, I don't think we have. I think we've just *dreamed* about them.'

'I haven't observed quantum mechanics,' Ingrid replied, 'so *they* don't exist.'

'What a bright girl you are,' he said.

He had joked with her to hide his own fears, as well as his desire, but his more sensual feelings had nonetheless only been inflamed when, after talking about everything from Saint-Germain to Ingrid's father to antimatter and supergravity, from their respective, *real* childhoods to their magical meeting on the boat in Egypt, he had drunk a couple of whiskys on top of his many beers and quickly became very light-headed.

'This whole business is no more real to me than Schrodinger's Cat,' he said. 'Did you know that a charged pion can transform a neutron into a proton by interacting with a proton that becomes a neutron? Have you worked that out? Good! Now if you want to understand how *unreal* the real world is, you have to accept that your proton, a product of the mathematically sound impossible, can itself explode into a vast network of interacting particles, then vanish back into itself. Having itself appeared out of nothing, the non-existent proton's numerous particles also appear out of nothing, recombine with one another, then disappear before the universe at large even notices that they were present in the first place. Similarly, a photon that doesn't actually exist can create a positron/electron pair that instantly annihilate to produce the photon that created them in the first place, since the photon doesn't know the difference between past and future – something we might also say for Saint-Germain, if what we've so far learned about him is true.'

'Saint-Germain is real, Jerry.'

'Is he, Ingrid? I'm not so sure. We're back to quantum mechanics again. Let's imagine Saint-Germain as an electron, chasing its own tail in a time eddy. What I mean by this – and please stop me if I confuse you – is that according to quantum mechanics, an electron can appear out of nothing, out of nowhere, the non-existent, then travel a short distance, realize its mistake – that it's actually unreal – then turn around and travel back through time to its starting place, thus having never existed in the first place ... and it repeats this again and again, in one sense actually never existing, in another existing eternally in an ever scattering time-event. Does that help explain Saint-Germain?'

'No, Jerry, it doesn't.'

'Then I'm a very poor teacher.'

In his sublime state of drunkenness he had kept talking to her, hardly aware of what he was saying, only recalling later, with no great deal of pride, that at some point in the evening he had simply dropped his hand onto her knee and hoped for the best. She was wearing blue denims, but he had felt her warmth through them, and when she made no move to take his hand away, he just let it rest there, surprised that he could feel so self-conscious about such a small thing.

'It's such a small thing to feel your knee,' he remembered saying in a grand, if slurred manner, 'but it means a lot to me.'

'Oh, good,' she replied.

Becoming more drunk, with exhilaration as well as whisky, he had kept his hand on her knee, even moved it slightly higher, squeezing her there, and was delighted when she simply smiled at him and, instead of removing his hand, once or twice actually patted it affectionately, which he took for encouragement.

'I feel good,' he was certain he had said, 'given what we've been through.'

'Let's hope it lasts, Jerry.'

Unfortunately, it hadn't. His mood of romantic reverie had been brutally disturbed when, over another, doubtless foolhardy, whisky, he suddenly fell back into a sense of unreality by remembering how, when driving earlier that evening through the deepening darkness of the countryside just outside Frankfurt, he had experienced a prickly sensation on the back of his neck, and had the distinct, inexplicable feeling that he and Ingrid were not alone in the car.

Confused, he had glanced back over his shoulder at the road receding behind the car, but saw nothing other than the trees at both sides of the darkening road. Turning back to the front and concentrating on the road ahead, trying to convince himself that he was simply imagining things, he nevertheless was unable to shake off the feeling that he and Ingrid were not alone, that if the unseen presence was not in the car, then it must be outside . . .

In truth, the last hour of that journey into Frankfurt had been hell. As he drove, he kept thinking he could see something out of the corner of his eye, first left, then right . . . could *hear* something . . . or *feel* it . . . just above the car, behind it, sometimes alongside it . . . and for the rest of the journey to the hotel in Sachsenhausen, had found himself glancing frequently out of the car window, scanning the sky, convinced that something unseen, yet something *real*, was somewhere out there in the night, in the sky, quite deliberately following them . . .

Shivering to recall that, he now finished off his beer, washed himself as best he could in the chipped sink in the corner, put on a thick, roll-necked pullover and jacket, then pulled the curtain back and looked down on the dark, rainswept street.

It was very quiet down there, not at all like Sachsenhausen, and he realized that he no longer liked silence . . . nor dark, empty streets.

He checked his watch. They had agreed to take an hour's rest and then meet downstairs in the hotel's small, shabby bar, prior to going together to the library of Troyes before it closed for the evening. Still twenty minutes early, but feeling very unsettled, he decided to go down anyway and have another drink while waiting for her.

Leaving the room, he closed the door firmly behind him, double checked that it was locked, then walked past Ingrid's room, put his ear to the door, heard nothing and walked down the stairs into the lobby where the bar was located. Luckily, the woman behind the bar was bright and cheerful, making him feel instantly better, and he huddled gratefully in a corner with his beer, trying not to think of what had happened the night before, but unable to stop himself . . .

Drunk and light-headed, his conflicting emotions heightened, he had left the tavern with Ingrid and walked with her, not too steadily, back through the gaudy, lively streets of Sachsenhausen to their small hotel, where he had hoped to be suave and casually promiscuous, to seduce her with insolent charm and carry her off to his room, but instead, his thoughts in turmoil, his emotions too chaotic, had simply stopped at her door, in the silence of frustrated longing, to give her a tentative kiss on the lips and whisper good night.

That much, at least, he remembered with certainty.

What he could not know for certain was how he had spent the rest of that evening and early morning . . .

He remembered tossing and turning most of that night in a fever of frustrated desire and vivid imaginings, loathing his own cowardice, cursing Ingrid's painful shyness; wanting to get up and storm into her room, constantly listening for her knock on his room door, for her highly romantic, white-robed, wraith-like entrance . . . But none of those things happened, as he knew they would not, and eventually he had dozed off, falling in and out of sleep, hardly knowing when he was dreaming or simply *imagining* himself with her, hardly knowing the difference between the real and the unreal . . . which was why, when the manifestations came, he thought they might be a nightmare.

He had opened his eyes upon hearing something, or because he had *felt* something; realized it wasn't a sound, but actually some kind of *pressure* – something pressing upon him, invisible, heavy, amorphous, and very unnatural. He had felt crushed, suffocated, touched by an alien heat . . . and then, even as he tried to sit up, and failed, had noticed a faint, pulsating light spreading over the ceiling.

He had managed to turn his head. The light was beaming in through the window. Then at last he heard the sound – or at least somehow *felt* it – a rhythmic bass humming, a pulsating sound that matched the flickering light.

That sound, or that *pressure*, combined with the rhythmic flickering of the pale light, seemed to press him back into the bed and force his gaze to look inward. He saw the tracery of his veins, the cataracts of his stomach, and spiralled down through the whirlpools of his blood to the source of himself.

At first there was darkness, complete, terrifying, then a speck of light appeared, multiplied, became a cascade, and he travelled through somersaulting space until his room reappeared.

Saint-Germain was standing in front of him, by the foot of the bed, his unblinking gaze visible through the light in which they were both held. The other presence was his partner, the diabolically handsome mesmerist, and both men, gazing down through the light, possessed a shimmering beauty.

Saint-Germain had smiled at him. He had tried to speak, but couldn't. He had been numb and struck dumb and paralysed, left with nothing but vision.

The light brightened around the two men, yet didn't hurt his eyes; but he started to suffer in another way – and it filled him with terror.

He felt himself disintegrating, flesh and bone turning to dust. The pressure closed in upon him like an invisible vice, crushing him, breaking him, reducing him to a pulp – and then just as it reached the point where it became unendurable, he found himself jerking upright on the bed, screaming in terror.

He had sat there for a long time, shaking, trying to breathe; had wiped sweat from his brow, licked his parched lips, and gazed around the dark, silent room, at the ceiling, the window.

Everything was normal. He must have been dreaming. He groaned and lay back on the bed and waited for dawn to come, praying that it was a dream, saying aloud, 'It *was* a dream!', but convinced in his heart that it had happened, maybe not for the last time . . .

He didn't want to think about it, but simply couldn't stop himself; though now, in this hotel, in the bright lights of the bar, he had doubts about himself, remembered that he had been drunk, and wondered if he couldn't, after all, interpret what had happened as a terrible dream.

When Ingrid walked into the bar, he felt a lot better. Obviously prepared for the rainstorm outside, she was wearing a plastic mac with a hood, and black leather boots.

Quantum mechanics, he thought. *Because I see her, she is.*

'I might have known you'd beat me down to the bar,' she said. 'Have I time for a drink?'

'No,' he replied, finishing off his own drink and then standing up. 'That library's going to be closing soon, so we better get going.'

Taking her by the elbow, he led her away from the bar, across the hall and out of the building. It was now as dark as night, the wind howled, the rain poured down, but luckily the car was parked right by the door and they were able to get into it without getting completely soaked.

Once strapped in, and before Ingrid, who was driving, could turn on the ignition, he surprised himself by saying, 'Don't start the car yet, Ingrid. I've something to tell you. I want to tell you before we get to the library, but I'm not too sure why.'

Her hand fell away from the ignition key and she turned her head to stare at him.

'Oh?' she said. 'What?'

'Remember I told you about my feeling that we were being followed – or *observed* somehow – as we drove towards Frankfurt yesterday?'

'Of course.'

'Well, I had a bad sleep last night – a *very* bad sleep – and I'm still not sure if something actually happened or if I just dreamed it. You want me to tell you?'

'You think it'll frighten me?'

'It might.'

'Why not try me?'

Taking a deep breath, not too sure that he was doing the right thing, he told her about his dream, or *experience*, of the previous night. When he had finished, she looked surprised rather than frightened, and told him she had had a similar experience.

'A *similar* experience?' he asked, not quite believing it.

'Yes, Jerry. Not the same experience, but similar – at least in the sense that I dreamed about Saint-Germain, and actually felt that I was living the experience with him. Now we better get going.'

She started the car, pulled away from the kerb, and moved off through the heavy storm, along the dark street, keeping her eyes fixed straight ahead, sometimes biting her lower lip.

'Even now I'm not sure if I was sleeping or awake,' she said. 'Though my feeling is that it *was* some kind of real experience – and, just as it was with you, so with me it began with that strange light. In my case, the light materialized out of the wall –'

'Like it did with me in London.'

'Right. Then it expanded and seemed to fill the whole room and, when I tried to sit upright, pressed me back to the bed. Then I saw Saint-Germain – the man we talked to on the Nile – and with him was another man, very handsome, smooth and decadent, whose smile had a strange effect on me, making me dreamy and . . . *wanting* him.'

Her voice sounded hesitant when she said this and he smiled, actually feeling amused.

'He made *me* want him as well, so don't worry about *that*.'

'Anyway,' she continued, 'they both materialized in my room, out of that very odd, bright light, stared at me, both smiling enigmatically, and put me into a kind of waking trance. Then the walls of the room dissolved and were replaced by other walls, other places . . . God, it was shivery!'

'Go on!' he encouraged her.

'First I saw what I somehow knew to be the Anitchkoff Bridge across the River Neva, in old St Petersburg, then a small street named Grafsky, through which horse-drawn carriages clattered; then I found myself wearing eighteenth-century clothing, with a lot of jewels around my neck and arms, sitting in an antique chair, listening attentively to Saint-Germain – also in eighteenth-century clothing and with many jewels on his fingers – as he played a violin that sounded remarkably like a full orchestra.'

'He *did* have that reputation,' Jerry assured her.

'Anyway, when Saint-Germain had finished playing, he turned to another man – one surrounded by beautiful paintings – and showed him a piece of music bound in beautiful red maroquin, which he explained was an air for a harp, composed by himself and to be dedicated to one Countess Ostermann.'

'That makes sense. Saint-Germain *was* in St Petersburg, now Leningrad, in 1762, where he stayed with various high-class folk, including the famous Italian painter, Count Rotare, whose paintings are now in the Peterhof palace. Rotare *did* live in the Grafsky *pereoulok* – which means small street – at that time; Saint-Germain was then well known for his own remarkable artist's talents; and he *did* compose a piece of music in 1760 – the one we found in the British Museum.'

'Very good, Jerry. So –'

'Yes?'

'Saint-Germain then turned to me and smiled, and it all dissolved and became something else . . . It was an eighteenth-century laboratory in a suite of rooms in a great château, and Saint-Germain, surrounded by young men, all wearing similar clothing, was experimenting with what looked like paint. Around the walls of the laboratory were oil paintings of an unnatural vividness

– paintings that seemed to live and breathe, overwhelming the senses.'

'The Renaissance château at Chambord,' he could not resist informing her, 'south-west of Orléans in France. King Louis XV gave Saint-Germain a suite of rooms there in the late 1750s, and the mysterious gentleman turned them into a laboratory for his alchemical experiments, most notably those involving paint and the transformation of diamonds. Other guests at that time included the Princess of Anhalt-Zerbst, mother of Catherine II of Russia; the Marquise d'Urfe; Baron de Gleichen and Madame de Genlis, all of whom mentioned Saint-Germain's experiments in their letters and memoirs.'

'Then that also changed,' Ingrid said, as if she hadn't heard him, 'and became another place, then another; and I saw Saint-Germain – stood beside him, in fact – in another laboratory in Amsterdam, where he turned metal into gold; then, in what was clearly the court of Louis XV, having words with the King; then with Madame de Pompadour and other members of the aristocracy; then playing the violin again, but this time in what I knew was the castle of Raudnitz in Bohemia, in the presence of an old gentleman, obviously Prince Ferdinand von Lobkowitz; then, most unusually, in the dress of an Armenian and wearing a long beard, having lunch with a distinctly flamboyant gentleman in Tournay, in France . . .'

'The flamboyant gentleman was Casanova,' Jerry explained helpfully. 'And the bearded goat *was*, according to Casanova, the legendary Saint-Germain.'

Ingrid nodded then sighed. 'All of these places and people,' she continued, 'materialized and disappeared with a vividness, an almost *palpable* reality, which convinced me that I couldn't be dreaming . . . and then, when I tried to speak, but couldn't do so and grew frightened, Saint-Germain smiled, as if understanding . . . and I found myself back in bed, staring at the opposite wall, watching that brilliant light shrinking back through it, and finally, thank God, disappearing, leaving everything normal.'

She fell silent, kept driving, her brow furrowed in thought, concentrating on the road as they passed industrial buildings, many churches with stained-glass windows and houses that were already lit up to combat the premature darkness brought on by the storm.

'Jesus,' Jerry said, shifting restlessly on his seat, 'this is getting to be a really weird experience. Saint-Germain and his partner seem to be able to materialize at will – anywhere, any time. And *we're* trying to find *him*!'

'You said it yourself, Jerry: he *wants* us to find him. He's leading us to him – or leading us *somewhere*, at least. Only God knows where or why.'

'I'm growing paranoid,' Jerry said. 'I can't help it – I just am. On the one hand, we're being hounded and harried by your father, who initially wanted to get you back – and with his international network of communications would have no trouble in doing so. But he clearly has decided just to have us followed – *only* followed, at least, until it suits him.'

'And right now he's thinking we might lead him to the Tuaoi Stone.'

'Yes, Ingrid. Right on.'

'And on the other hand?'

'On the other hand, my angel, we're being observed and maybe *protected* by another kind of agency altogether – a seemingly supernatural agency that doesn't need modern telecommunications to keep track of our movements. I don't know if that's quite true. I mean, I might be imagining it. But I'm starting to *believe* that it's true, and now I'd just like some proof.'

'Quantum mechanics,' Ingrid said, speaking softly,

to herself. 'Think of Saint-Germain as an electron . . . here, there and everywhere; past, present and future, all at once . . . And now we need proof.'

She slowed down, stopped the car and looked across the dark street.

'There's the library, Jerry.'

The lights of the building were beaming out into the night, illuminating the pavement, slanting lines of silvery rain, and the debris that was being blown along the street by the fierce, howling wind.

'So,' Ingrid said, turning off the ignition, 'are you all set to run?'

'Sure, Ingrid. Let's do that.'

Simultaneously, they climbed out of the car, slammed their respective doors, then ran through the teeming rain and rushing wind into the warmth of the building. Jerry glanced around the lobby, briefly dazzled by its brightness, taking comfort from the surf-like murmur of whispered conversations, then, feeling instantly at home with the rows of books, took hold of Ingrid's hand and led her briskly towards the nearest librarian.

'Okay,' he said. 'Ask her.'

Speaking fluent French, Ingrid soon managed to find the person in charge of the Saint-Germain document. Waiting for the rare text to be brought to them in the reference room, Jerry wiped the rain from Ingrid's face with his handkerchief, kissed his fingers and pressed them to her lips, then held on to her hand. He said nothing to her and she likewise was silent – until the single text was brought in, when she read softly to him.

The text was frequently illegible and often hopelessly obscure, but Jerry's ears pricked up when Ingrid read the following section:

'We moved through space at a speed that can be compared with nothing but itself . . . Within a fraction of a second the plains below us were out of sight, and the

earth had become a faint nebula. I was carried up, and I travelled through the empyrean for an incalculable time at an immeasurable height. Heavenly bodies revolved, and worlds vanished below me . . .'

Jerry felt the hairs stand up on the back of his neck, as if a ghost had sat on his shoulder and thrown its mantle about him. He took a deep breath, trying to choke back his excitement, and looked into Ingrid's studious, bespectacled eyes.

'Jesus,' he whispered. 'He wrote *that* in the eighteenth century?'

'Yes,' Ingrid replied. 'And that's exactly what *I* experienced when that light filled my room. I felt as if I was travelling through space, perhaps through time, before coming back to earth, to another time – and another place.'

'Is that what Saint-Germain is doing?' Jerry said. 'I think it is. It *must* be!'

At that precise moment, as if to confirm what he was saying, there was a faint bass humming sound, a sensation of growing pressure, and the shelves of the reference room shook visibly, as if in an earthquake. The bass humming sound grew louder. All the lights in the room went out. Someone screamed and then the humming sound ceased and the room stopped its shaking.

'Oh, my God!' Ingrid said.

Jerry grabbed her hand, stood up and started running – but the lights were still off, the room was in pitch darkness – and then even as people screamed and bumped into one another, there was a bizarre rushing sound, like air being pumped from a hose, and then another kind of light, very brilliant, striated, poured into the front lobby from outside and temporarily blinded him.

He cursed, held onto Ingrid, started forward again;

but then the light outside vanished, plunging the library back into darkness; the bass humming returned and the shelves started shaking again; then the noise rose on high, cut out abruptly, and the lights on the walls came back on as the shelves stopped their shaking.

Ignoring the sobbing around him, Jerry glanced down at the desk, saw immediately that the Saint-Germain document was missing and looked elsewhere for it.

The document could not be found. The librarian had not grabbed it. The woman stared at Jerry, startled, opened her mouth to say something, but Jerry quickly turned away, grabbed Ingrid and hurried out of the library to see what was outside.

The rain was still pouring down and there was nothing in sight.

'Shit!' he said in frustration. 'We've missed them again! And now the Saint-Germain document is gone, so we better get out of here. Come on, Ingrid! *Let's go!*'

He rushed with her to the car and stood patiently in the rain while she fumbled with her keys, opened her door, slid in, then leaned over to open his door. He got into his seat, saw something outside on the windscreen, thought it was a parking ticket, cursed and reached around to grab it, and was about to throw it away when he saw what it was.

It was a neatly folded note, written on fine, antique paper, now soaked and soggy and just about legible, the writing flamboyant, slightly archaic, and strikingly similar to the writing on the card attached to the tiny swastika they had found in their room in Eckernforde.

Closing the car door, he unfolded the note and read aloud from it:

'*Think only of the individual as being but one of many;*

think of the legend of Faust and know it to be true...'
Signed, *'Saint-Germain'*.

He caught Ingrid's glance, her ever widening gaze, then he stared all around him, saw nothing but rainswept buildings, then looked up at the dark evening sky and saw a pulsating white light.

It was very high up, disc-shaped, dime-sized; but it moved from east to west, stopped briefly in mid-air, then abruptly ascended towards the stars and eventually disappeared.

He studied the sky a long time, seeing nothing but black clouds, then found himself shivering uncontrollably as he reached out to Ingrid.

'That's it,' he said. 'That's my proof. Now let's drive back to England.'

After letting his head rest on her breasts, she drove on to Calais.

CHAPTER TWENTY-THREE

After his unpleasant time in the bleak wastelands of Eastern Europe, Zweig was delighted to be back on his luxury cruiser on the Mediterranean, lying on a sunbed on the upper deck with his fleet spread out around him and Elena supine beside him. She was wearing sunglasses, her long blonde hair was clipped up, her bikini was practically invisible and her belly, unlike his, was as flat and smooth as a skating rink.

He glanced sideways at her, thought of taking her down below, but decided to wait for Hans to bring his report up. The helicopter had landed a couple of minutes ago, and he knew that Hans would be scampering up the ladders this very minute, wiping sweat from his forehead. Zweig liked it that way. Obedience always came through fear. He had learned that in the Fatherland during the war, and had never forgotten it.

Closing his eyes again, he concentrated on the sun, feeling it on his face, on his too-flabby body, and quietly cursed that he had not yet learned the secret of eternal youth. He had tried everything on the market, every capsule, every enema, every kind of injection, but now knew that only Saint-Germain's secrets could return him to good health.

He was in fact beginning to think of the elusive Saint-Germain as a very personal enemy, a formidable foe, a creature of magic, mystery and menace, almost beyond credibility. Yet he believed in the supernatural, in the power of unseen forces, knowing full well that the Third Reich of Hitler, Himmler and Rosenberg had sprung from the sulphurous smoke of a belief in the occult. Yes, he believed it – and belief could conquer all – and he knew that if he wanted it badly enough, he would find Saint-Germain.

And, in so doing, find the Tuaoi Stone and the power it would offer him.

'Herr Zweig?'

Opening his eyes to squint up into the sun, he saw the silhouetted figures of Hans and two much larger men, the latter holding gaberdines over their arms. Seeing them, he sat upright, feeling a twinge of excitement, told the steward to bring him a fruit juice and then removed his sunglasses. The two men with Hans were hired killers, but seemed decidedly nervous.

'Your men do not look too happy,' he said to Hans. 'Can I take it they failed us?'

'Herr Zweig –' one of the men began, but Zweig silenced him by snapping his fingers and saying, 'Shut up and speak only when spoken to. Now, Hans, please elucidate.'

The Filipino brought him his fruit juice and he sipped gratefully at it while listening to the exhausted and sweating Hans give his report, while the two hoods, also sweating, but with nervousness, shuffled their feet.

'As requested,' Hans reported, 'I had Ingrid and the American followed to Eckernforde, in West Germany, where they visited a certain Klaus Schiller. Shortly after they left Schiller's house, my men – these two – also paid him a visit to find out exactly what he had told our young friends.'

'And?'

Hans was just about to respond when Elena yawned loudly, uncoiled like a cat, rolled on to her belly, then arched her glistening spine as she raised herself on to her knees. The two hired hoods, sweating even more profusely, tried to keep their eyes off her.

'God,' she said, yawning, and looking the hoods up and down as if taking their measure, 'this heat puts me to sleep.'

'Then go downstairs and sleep,' Zweig said impatiently. 'I'll join you later.'

'Yeah,' she replied, standing upright and stretching, her breasts bulging out of her skimpy bikini top, her long legs and flat belly gleaming with oil, 'I think I'll do that. I hate business anyway.'

Rolling her hips like a disco dancer, luscious buttocks trembling teasingly, she sauntered across the deck, ducked low, giving a good view of her backside, and disappeared through the hatchway. The large hoods, trying hard not to look, were both visibly moved.

Zweig, taking note of their discomfort, was faintly amused.

'And so,' he said, returning his gaze to Hans, 'these men were extracting information from Schiller. What did he tell them?'

'He told them,' Hans replied, 'that Ingrid and the American had asked a lot of questions about the Comte de Saint-Germain, were particularly interested in his origins, and said that after they had visited Schiller they were going to check the famed Saint-Germain tombstone in the nearby churchyard. Schiller, who is a descendant of Prince Charles, the Landgrave of Hesse-Cassel – the man with whom Saint-Germain was living when his death was reported – told them that Saint-Germain had *not* died at that time; and also that the Saint-Germain of whom we speak is a magical adept, an immortal – a possible protector of the so-called Philosopher's Stone–'

'The Tuaoi Stone, or Lodestone.'

'Correct, and was almost certainly, in a previous guise, one Johann Valentin Andraea, author of the first three books on the original Rosicrucians, more widely known as Christian Rosenkreuz, the original founder of that very mysterious Order.'

'I knew it!' Zweig exclaimed, unable to help himself, suddenly picked up on a wave of excitement that made him feel almost youthful. 'Damnit, I *knew* it! Himmler himself believed that the Tuaoi Stone originated in the Fatherland, and what Schiller said merely confirms it.'

'I'm not sure I –'

Hardly able to contain his excitement, Zweig said, 'Don't you understand? It's widely believed that the Rosicrucians, being a secret brotherhood of alchemists, had discovered the elixir of eternal life – the compound of the Philosopher's Stone, less widely known as the Tuaoi Stone – and now we have confirmation that the Rosicrucians, therefore the Hermetic secret, originated in the original Fatherland – sixteenth-century Germany – just as Himmler had always insisted was the case. The Tuaoi Stone belongs to the Reich! We were *destined* to have it!'

Even more excited, feeling almost orgasmic, he smacked one fist into the palm of his hand, glanced beyond the railing at the fleet of cruisers surrounding him, then took note of the fact that Hans was trying to conceal his scepticism.

Feeling that cold water had been splashed on his face, he studied Hans intently and saw that he was too soft for his own good. Hans was bright and obedient, knew his place, worked very hard, but he clearly lacked certain manly traits and needed toughening up.

'You do not agree, Hans?'

'No – I mean, *yes*!'

'Good, my friend. *Sehr gut!* The Tuaoi Stone belongs to Germany and we are going to find it – and Saint-Germain, who was once Christian Rosenkreuz, will lead us to it eventually.'

'Yes, Herr Zweig. Of course.'

Zweig nodded with satisfaction, then turned to the two hoodlums. 'So,' he said, speaking directly to the biggest one. 'What happened then?'

Confused, the big hoodlum looked at the smaller one, then coughed into his clenched fist.

'*What?*' he asked stupidly.

Zweig sighed with exasperation. 'When this Schiller, this disgusting little sodomite, had finished confession.'

The big man frowned and eventually prepared to speak, but the smaller man prevented him from doing so by stepping forward and offering a cocky grin.

'We handcuffed him to a very hot griddle, then turned the heat up,' he said.

Zweig chuckled at that one. '*Very* good,' he said. 'The old-fashioned methods are the best, so I'm glad you still use them. Excellent . . . Then?'

'Following your instructions,' the smaller hoodlum replied, 'we didn't bother your daughter or the American, but kept watch on the hotel where they were sleeping.'

'They were sleeping together?'

'No, they had separate rooms.'

'That virgin,' Zweig said, feeling nothing but contempt, remembering that his daughter was like her dead mother, a frigid bitch who shortly after their marriage had gone right off sex. That was one of his reasons for killing her – he hadn't been able to take her rejection, particularly when she said he was a pervert who made her feel ill. He knew that wasn't the reason, that the reason was frigidity, and so he had slipped some arsenic into her medicine and got rid of her that way. And Ingrid, his daughter, was every bit as frigid as her mother – and like her, despised him . . . 'And that Yank's just the same,' he added quickly. 'So, please continue.'

Very pleased to continue, the smaller hoodlum

smirked and said, 'They spent a short time watching the house of Klaus Schiller burning down and asking some locals what had happened, then they retired to the hotel across the square for the night – as I say, using separate rooms. Schiller had told us that he'd encouraged them to visit the library at Troyes in France, where apparently they would find confirmation for the existence of the eighteenth-century Saint-Germain – and true enough, they left Eckernforde the next morning and drove down through Kiel and Hamburg, stopped for lunch near Hanover, then drove on to Frankfurt-am-Main, where they spent the night, and . . .'

Here, the small hoodlum stopped smirking and glanced nervously at his bigger partner, as if not entirely sure that he should say more.

'Don't hide anything from me,' Zweig warned him. 'It would not be advisable.'

'Of course not,' the hoodlum said. 'It's just that it's a little . . . Well . . .' He shrugged. '*Unbelievable.*'

'No matter. Continue.'

The small hoodlum sighed. 'We didn't book into the hotel, but instead parked our car just outside it and took turns at keeping an eye on it through the evening and morning. Neither of them emerged from the hotel, but shortly after midnight, when both of us were awake, we saw what we could only describe as a . . .'

'Yes! Yes!'

The small hoodlum shrugged. 'A sort of . . . *flying saucer,*' he said. 'A very large, disc-shaped light that first took shape in the low clouds, then descended vertically – like a helicopter – but with no noise at all, then hovered right over the roof of the hotel and remained there a long time. It glowed and pulsated. It had a dark inner core. It just hovered impossibly in mid-air, making no sound at all.'

'No,' the bigger hoodlum corrected him, looking a

bit embarrassed. 'It *did* make a sound. You could hardly hear it, but there was definitely a sound – a very deep sound – and it actually made our car shake at times.'

'Yes,' the smaller hoodlum said. 'I forgot. That's absolutely correct.'

'And then?' Zweig asked him.

'It remained there for about an hour – scaring both of us shitless – then it rose up as quietly as it had arrived, and disappeared through the clouds.'

'Anything else?'

'No.'

'And the next morning?'

'Your daughter and her boyfriend drove on to Troyes where, in the middle of a heavy rainstorm, we ...' He trailed off nervously, then reluctantly concluded: 'We lost them.'

Zweig felt the rage churn up to blind him, but breathed deeply, controlled himself.

'*You lost them?*' he hissed.

'It wasn't our fault!' the bigger man exclaimed.

'Shut up!' his partner snapped. 'It was the UFO,' he said, looking hopefully at Zweig. 'We couldn't do a thing against that UFO. It came back and harassed us.'

'I am losing my patience,' Zweig said. 'You better make this believable.'

Looking even more uncomfortable, the smaller hoodlum continued: 'They were obviously heading for Troyes and we were following them at a pretty safe distance through a heavy rainstorm when that *thing*, that brightly glowing flying saucer, materialized out of nowhere, tailed us for a short time, then, just on the outskirts of Troyes, almost came down on top of us.'

'Not on *top* of us,' his big partner corrected him. 'I think it was all around us. It looked solid in a way, but it *couldn't* have been solid, 'cause it was suddenly all around us, above us, below us, and we couldn't see a goddamned thing – we were blinded by the light – and the next thing we knew, our car was in a ditch and we were both regaining consciousness, wondering what the hell had happened to us. Right?'

'Right,' the smaller man replied. 'And when we looked through the smashed windshield, at the road we had just been on, we saw what appeared to be the same UFO, that *light*, growing smaller as it shot away through the storm in the direction of Troyes . . .'

'Obviously following my daughter and the American,' Zweig said helpfully.

'Yeah,' the small hoodlum said, sounding relieved. 'We think that's what it did. I mean, we had to leave our car in the ditch and hitch a lift into Troyes – getting there pretty late in the evening – but when we eventually got there, we went straight to the library and we found an awful lot of people gathered together in the street, all gibbering excitedly and gazing at the sky. When we asked what was up, they said a UFO had been seen – and that it had briefly illuminated the whole library before disappearing.'

'And my daughter and the American?'

The smaller hoodlum shrugged for the last time. 'They were gone by the time we got there,' he confessed. 'We hired another car and drove to Calais, but they weren't on the ferry *we* got. Obviously they're both back in London . . . and that's all we know.'

'And that's quite *enough*,' Zweig retorted. 'You both know too much now.'

He enjoyed the startled glances that passed instantly between one hoodlum and the other, was thrilled when they stared directly at him with their eyes filled with fear.

'*What?*' the big one asked.

'Wait a *minute*!' the small one exclaimed, taking a

step back towards the railing, which is just where Zweig wanted him.

'Open the gate, Hans,' he said. 'It's time these hooligans left.'

Hans stood there for a moment, obviously a little shocked, then walked reluctantly to the railing behind the small hood. He opened the gate that normally led to the gangplank, then stepped back and turned around, leaving an empty space high above the trembling blue sea.

Both hoodlums glanced back over their shoulders, then stared wildly around them.

'*Wait* a minute!' the small one pleaded, raising his hands in the air. 'It wasn't *our* fault that we finally lost them. It was that *UFO*, for chrissakes!'

Zweig, having fun, didn't reply, but merely turned to his Filipino steward and said, 'Give me the Luger.'

'I don't think –' Hans began.

'Please don't think,' Zweig interjected. 'These two halfwits failed to do what they were told to – and besides, they now know too much.' He took the Luger from the steward, who had pulled it from his jacket, then aimed it at the smaller of the hoodlums as he backed towards the railing. 'The sea or a bullet in the brain,' he said. 'The choice is all yours.'

'Jesus Christ, this is –'

Zweig raised the pistol and fired, felt the recoil, heard the shot, saw a ribbon of grey and crimson splashing forth as the hoodlum's head jerked back. He disappeared over the side, making no sound of protest, while Zweig calmly aimed at the other, saying, 'Step over there, please.'

The big man waved his hands, but did as he had been told. He stood in front of the space where the gate had been opened, framed by the radiant blue sky and iridescent sea.

'*Please*, Herr Zweig! *Please don't!*'

Zweig raised the Luger, took aim and then paused, taking note of the look of revulsion on Hans's face, his visible trembling. *Oh, yes*, he thought, *he's weak. He is frightened of the real world. He needs a sharp lesson in manly virtues, and now is the time for it* . . . The thought made him smile, wave his left hand, call Hans to him. When Hans reached him, he gave him the Luger and said, 'Either persuade him to jump or help him along.'

'There are *sharks* down there,' Hans said.

'I know. That's the whole idea, Hans.'

Hans was obviously in a state of shock, his eyes widening with disbelief, but Zweig deliberately kept his own stare hard, which soon did the trick. Hans licked the sweat around his lips, controlled himself, turned towards the hoodlum, raised the Luger and took aim.

The hoodlum put his hands up entreatingly.

'*Please*, Hans!' he croaked. 'Don't!'

Zweig watched Hans squeeze the trigger. The firing gun jerked his wrist up. The big man was bowled backwards, his hands flapping at his chest, blood spurting between his fingers as he disappeared over the side and splashed into the sea below.

Hans stood there, shaking visibly, tears springing to his eyes, still holding up the Luger, aiming blindly at the sky, paralysed until Zweig, feeling almost paternal, went up to him, put one arm around his shoulders, gently removed the pistol from his shaking fingers and said, 'Good boy. *Good* boy. You will soon be a man, *ja?*'

Hans didn't reply.

CHAPTER TWENTY-FOUR

'No,' Jerry insisted as Ingrid drove the car at a snail's pace through the peak-hour traffic of Tottenham Court Road, in central London, heading for her hotel in Bloomsbury, 'I absolutely insist. It's now getting too dangerous, so we have to stick together, which means *living* together – either in your place or mine – and I certainly think we'll be more safe in your hotel than all alone in my flat. So, we're going to stay in your hotel, in the same room, and that's all there is to it.'

'My room's too small,' Ingrid replied, feeling cowardly, her cheeks burning, despising herself for her reluctance to accept what she secretly wanted.

'Then we'll simply move into a double room,' Jerry responded. 'It's as easy as that.'

'I'd be too embarrassed to ask,' she said, speaking the truth, though ashamed of its nature.

'Then *I'll* do it, Ingrid. I'll hide you in the lounge where the desk clerk can't see you, and I'll sign the both of us into a far bigger room, maybe even a suite.'

'You don't have to do that.'

His hand dropped on her knee, squeezed it, moved up further and, although it made her feel really good, it also disturbed her. She knew he wasn't like her father – that not everyone was – but she couldn't stop the fear that raced through her when she thought of reality. Sooner or later it would come to that – otherwise it would be unnatural – and although she actually *wanted* it to come to that, she didn't think she could handle it.

'Gee,' he said, 'you have a really nice thigh. It's so *soft*, so . . .'

'Please don't,' she said. 'I can't drive if you do that. Now tell me again.'

'What?'

'I said tell me again. You were explaining what you thought that quote meant, so tell me again.'

'Oh,' he said, sounding disappointed. '*That* . . . Well, yeah, right . . .'

He removed his hand from her thigh, as if hurt by her indifference, so she reached out, took hold of it and planted it back where it had been.

'I like it,' she said. 'I do! *Honestly!* But I have to know certain things.'

He sighed. 'Okay. I'll tell you again. The note said: *Think only of the individual as being but one of many; think of the legend of Faust and know it to be true* . . . Right?'

'Right.'

'Well, I don't think it was a quote, but it *was* some kind of message, and obviously it refers to Faust – not the opera, but the Faust famed in legend and literature as a man who sold his soul to the devil in exchange for knowledge and power.'

'I got that much,' she felt obliged to tell him.

'Okay,' he said. 'Now the fictional and mythical Faust was actually based on a real-life person, one Dr Georg Faust, who was born, if my memory serves me well, in Knittlingen, Germany, around 1480, became famous as a sodomite, magician and mesmerist, and was commonly thought to have concluded a pact with the devil, before dying in Staufin, near Freiburg, in 1540 or early the following year. Assuming, then, that the note was left by our Saint-Germain or one of his minions – and accepting that what we've already learned about him is true – what the note seems to be telling us is that the mysterious Comte de Saint-Germain is, was, amongst other personas, the original, possibly diabolical Faust, who reportedly died 169 years before the death of the eighteenth-century Count Saint-Germain.'

'Of course,' Ingrid said, feeling excited for a moment, swept away by the unravelling mystery. 'The historical Faust died 169 years before the *recorded* death of Saint-Germain. And, if the *recorded* date of Saint-Germain's death in Eckernforde is correct, it makes him 169 years old when he died.'

'Right,' Jerry responded. 'It now seems unlikely that he actually died at that time, but that's the date he *chose* to die, at least as far as the mortal world is concerned. Ergo, Saint-Germain was *supposed* to have died, at the age of 169, exactly 169 years after Faust died.'

'A way of telling us that he and Faust *were* one and the same.'

'*Right!*'

'So he might be telling us that he sold his soul to the devil?'

'Or that he *is* the devil.'

'Or simply antagonistic to us.'

'He hasn't harmed us yet,' Jerry said. 'And he certainly could have. No, what *I* think he's trying to tell us is, simply, that like Faust he's learned the secret of immortality and is, in fact, a man of many lives, possibly spanning the centuries . . .'

Ingrid felt herself unable to look directly at the truth and its awesome, terrifying possibilities. She felt Jerry's hand on her thigh, sliding lightly up and down it, and took a great deal of comfort from it – even though fearing *that* as well.

'So you now believe,' she said, not looking at him but at the traffic, 'that our Saint-Germain *is* a magical being, and possibly immortal.'

'I do,' he responded. 'All the facts point that way.

He's obviously some kind of magical adept – maybe a member of a secret society of such – and the original Rosicrucians, of which Saint-Germain as Christian Rosenkreuz was one, were part of that very ancient band – all alchemists . . . or mystics.'

'God,' she heard herself saying, though she hadn't planned on replying. 'And the Hermetic secret, or Philosopher's Stone, is in fact the Lodestone, or Tuaoi Stone, which was once hidden in the top of the Great Pyramid –'

'And somewhere else before that, ducks.'

He had said it to amuse her, and she couldn't help smiling; but her lingering fear returned soon enough, like a shroud or dark cloud.

'So we're trying to find the Stone,' she said, 'which means finding Saint-Germain . . . And he seems to be encouraging us to do so – though he won't simply approach us . . . It doesn't make sense.'

Jerry sighed again. 'No,' he said, 'it doesn't make much sense . . . But he must have his reasons.'

Thankfully, she was suddenly able to turn off the choked main road and into the relative tranquillity of the Bloomsbury side street that led to the hotel in Tavistock Square, where she parked illegally, since all the meters were taken. They locked the car, removed the cases from the boot and walked into the hotel – but once inside, when they approached the reception desk, Ingrid could not stop her blushing.

The clerk behind the desk looked up with a glacial smile and said, 'Yes?'

'I have a room here,' she began, 'and I . . .'

'Of course. Miss Smith. Room 413.'

'Yes,' she replied, having forgotten that she'd signed in under a pseudonym and relieved to have been reminded of it, 'and I . . '

When the knowing clerk glanced at Jerry with a

sceptically raised right eyebrow, she simply couldn't complete her sentence.

'You would like your room key, Miss Smith?'

'Well, actually . . .'

'I'm *Mister* Smith,' Jerry said to her horror, 'and now that I've arrived, my wife and I would like to move into a bigger room, with two single beds.'

'Two *single* beds, Mr Smith?'

'My wife and I only share a bed when making love, so please make it two single beds.'

The clerk's glacial superiority crumbled into embarrassed confusion. He coughed, cleared his throat and scanned the book on his desk far too intently. Eventually, trying to pull himself together, he turned away, pulled a key off its hook and handed it rather formally to Jerry.

'Room 325, sir. Very nice. With a view of the square.'

'Gee,' Jerry replied, 'that's terrific. Have a good day, pal.'

The hotel had no porter, so Jerry had to carry the suitcases and Ingrid followed him to the lift, feeling as embarrassed as the clerk had looked. When the doors closed behind her and the lift started its ascent, she heaved a sigh.

'What's the matter?' Jerry asked her.

'I don't know how I'm going to walk past the reception as long as that clerk's there.'

'Don't worry, he won't even give you a glance. That English whimp is more embarrassed than you are, so he'll just look right through you.'

'God, Jerry, you're shameless. You really are.'

'I wish I was,' he replied.

Aware that he was gazing steadily at her, she lowered her gaze and studied her own feet until the lift came to a stop again. When the doors opened, she held the button until he had taken the suitcases out, then followed him along the corridor to their new room. He put down the cases, grinned at her, turned the key in the lock, then motioned her inside.'

'I'd carry you across the threshhold,' he said, 'but these suitcases killed me.'

He was trying to amuse her, but she was too tense to smile, and went past him, into the room, feeling very self-conscious. She saw the two single beds, a chest of drawers and wardrobe, and was gazing at the bathroom when she heard the door closing behind her. Jerry brushed by, huffing and puffing melo-dramatically, then placed the suitcases on the slotted racks beside the wardrobe and turned back to face her.

'Well,' he said, grinning broadly but uneasily, 'here we are – man and wife.'

She had never shared a room with anyone before and felt really trapped. Looking at the bathroom, she simply couldn't imagine using it, knowing that Jerry would be sitting in the room, with just that thin wall between them. Then she looked at the two beds. Her mind went blank when she did so. She could hardly focus on Jerry, but she sensed him staring at her, and though wanting to hold him, and be held *by* him, the very thought of doing anything more than that made her shrink back within herself.

With clothes on? *Without clothes* . . . How would she get undressed? Would *he* do it? Or would she have to do it herself, and if so, where and when? *In the bathroom?* . . . Ridiculous – and she would have to emerge . . . Should she be naked, or wearing a night-dress – and whatever, what then?

Oh, God, she thought, *I wish he would* . . . *No!* . . . *Yes, yes, I do love him and want him to* . . .

'Oh, Jerry,' she heard someone say plaintively, like a

lost child – and then, as she realized it was herself, he made a lunge towards her.

She fell back against the wall – or was forced back by his weight – and closed her eyes automatically when he kissed her and groaned at the same time. She felt shocked, excited, helpless, confused, aware of the weight and warmth of him, hearing only his breathless groans. A wave of emotion caught her, picked her up, swept her away; but then it smashed her on the rocks of her own fears and left her breathless and dizzy.

She had a vision of her father, saw his whores, recalled her dreams; felt a hand on her breast – Jerry's hand – and thought of other hands elsewhere . . . No, it wasn't nice. It was base and animalistic. She saw Elena rubbing oil into her father's bulging belly and remembered the many other humiliations going back to her childhood.

God, she wanted him – *Oh, Jerry!* – and her breasts responded to him – but she heard a cry of protest (Was that pitiful sound herself?) and slapped wildly and pushed him away and then turned to the side, her heart pounding, lungs aching.

'No, Jerry! *Please!* I can't help it! I can't! *I just can't!*'

'Oh, Christ!' he groaned softly.

She reached blindly towards him, felt her fingers on his face, touched his lips, the tears on his cheeks, then had to choke back her own tears. None of this was real. It was like a bad dream. She was picked up in a tide of love and grief and swept to the door. She opened it and fled, aware dimly of her actions, heard him calling back, took the stairs, hurried down to the bar. He met her before she got there – he must have taken the lift – and took her by the shoulders and shook her, saying, 'I'm sorry! *I'm sorry!*' Helpless, she burst into tears and let his strong arms embrace her. He hugged her and kissed the top of her head and then wiped her eyes dry. After that, he led her into the bar and sat her down in the corner.

'Here,' he said, putting a glass down on the table. 'I feel as bad as you do. Do you *like* gin and tonic?'

She smiled and calmed down. He reached across the table, held her hand and looked steadily at her.

'I'm no good at this,' he said. 'I don't know how to start. God, I love you and want you, but I'm shy about certain things, and *you're* not exactly the forward type, which doesn't help me a bit. Jesus, I love you. You're the nicest thing on the earth. I want to hold you and kiss you and ... *you* know ... but, Jesus, I'm hopeless. I mean, I know you have your problems. Your father's made you that way. I know and I try to understand, but shit, it's so *heavy*. You know what I mean? I'm probably as scared as you are. I lunged at you because I thought the time was right and I didn't know what to do. We have to share that room, Ingrid. We *have* to share it. So let's try it again.'

'I can't even get undressed there,' she said. 'I'll just feel too self-conscious.'

'Okay,' he said. 'I understand. I mean, I know you're inhibited. So when you want to get undressed, tell me how long it'll take, and I'll go down to the bar and come back up when you're safely in bed.'

'I can't even use the toilet.'

He waved his hands. 'Same thing. Absolutely. When you want to use the bathroom, I'll come down and wait in this bar.'

'All right, then.'

'Good,' he said. 'It's agreed.'

He squeezed her hand and smiled at her, making her feel better, so she finished her gin and tonic, drinking it far too quickly, and walked back to the lift, feeling drunk. Leaning against him in the lift, resting her head against his shoulder, she felt her fear falling away and melting into his warmth. He slid his arm around her, resting one hand on her hip, tugged her to him, squeezed her a little and then stroked her hair. She felt secure and at peace, at last protected by love, and when they left the lift and walked back to the room, she knew their love would survive this.

As soon as they entered the room, they knew someone had been there.

'Shit,' Jerry said.

Spread out on the bed, in the rough shape of a pentagram, were a coiled rope, a lotus flower, and three postcards.

Jerry pressed her against the door. He indicated that she shouldn't move. While she stood there, he checked the bathroom, reappeared, shrugged his shoulders. He rang through to the reception desk, asked if anyone had been in the room; when he shook his head, she knew they had denied it and probably meant it. Then he went to the bed. He picked up the coiled rope. While he did so, she picked up the lotus flower and inhaled its fresh scent.

Jerry studied the postcards. He passed them to her in silence. The first showed the Temple of Diana at Ephesus in Turkey; the second was a reproduction of Sidney Barclay's 1875 wood engraving of the Colossus of Rhodes, once located in the harbour of Rhodes Island in Greece; and the third was a photograph of the ruined statue of Zeus at ancient Olympus, now Olympia, in the Peloponnese.

'Saint-Germain,' Jerry said. 'He's been here. And now the bastard's leading us by the nose. He's telling us where to go.'

Thinking of Saint-Germain and his mysterious partner, one of whom had been in this very room just a few minutes ago, Ingrid slipped back into a fear that quickened her breathing.

'How did he get *in* here?' she asked.

Jerry shook his head in defeat. 'Picked the lock, or . .'

He just stared at her and she remembered that night in Frankfurt, when Saint-Germain and his partner materialized out of a strange light. Then she remembered that same light outside in the library of Troyes, in France, the message found on the windshield of the rented car . . .

'God,' she said, 'I don't like this. I don't like it at all.'

Jerry didn't reply. He simply swung the coiled rope back and forth above the bed, and then, while she sniffed at the lotus flower, stared at her with thoughtful eyes.

'All of these things are connected,' he said abstractedly, looking inward, as if remembering all the books he had read about ancient mythology. 'A coiled rope is the ancient Egyptian symbol for a hundred. A lotus flower represents the ancient Egyptian 1,000.'

'So?' she asked when he stared questioningly at her.

By way of reply, he picked up the three postcards, spread them out in a fan and asked, 'What have these three locations in common?'

Ingrid studied them for a moment, at first feeling baffled, then, with a childish flush of pride, finding the answer.

'They're three of the Seven Wonders of the World.'

'And?'

'They're all located on land masses that are joined by the Aegean Sea.'

'Right,' he said, pleased. 'And the Aegean Sea is the most likely location of the legendary Atlantis.'

'What makes you think he's referring to Atlantis?'

she asked, not too sure what he was driving at. 'He may simply be telling us to visit those three locations – two of which are in Greece, the other in Turkey.'

'He *is* telling us to do that, Ingrid – but he's also telling us to make that journey while keeping ancient Atlantis in mind.'

'I don't see the connection.'

Jerry swung the coiled rope slowly before her face, then placed a finger lightly on the lotus flower.

'The Atlantis myth is derived solely from Plato, who mentions it in two dialogues: the *Timaeus* and *Critias*. According to Plato, the ancient world wasn't devastated once, by one great flood, but many times by different floods – though the greatest was the one that destroyed Atlantis, which, according to Plato, lay beyond the Pillars of Hercules – Gibraltar – and was as large as Libya and Asia put together. However, Plato insists that Atlantis consisted of many islands, rather than being a single continent – most likely the islands of the Aegean Sea.'

Ingrid sat on the first bed, crossed her legs and looked up at him. He again dangled the coiled rope before her face, his eyes bright with excitement.

'Are you with me so far?' he asked.

'Just about,' she replied, smiling at him, 'but don't let that stop you.'

He sighed. 'The most famous attempt to solve the mystery of Atlantis was that of Professor A. G. Galanopoulos. His intriguing theory is that all the figures given in connection with Atlantis are too large, being based on a confusion between the Egyptian one hundred – a coiled rope – and 1,000, whose symbol was the lotus flower. It is believed that Plato, in confusing the numerical symbols of ancient Greece, multiplied the original figures for Atlantis by ten in all cases – in other words, the true size of the original Atlantis became ten times larger in Plato's calculations – which made it impossible to locate it in the Aegean Sea – and he likewise multiplied the date of its destruction by ten, thereby making the date approximately 9,000 years before his own time. However, if all of the figures are based on the coiled rope, rather than the lotus flower – in other words, *divided* by ten – Plato's figures place Atlantis in an acceptable historical context, his description of the Royal City and its plains corresponding exactly to modern Crete, and the date of its destruction, instead of being 9,000 years before Plato's time, becoming approximately 1,500 BC.'

'What does that date have to do with the lost Atlantis?'

'We don't know what existed in that area 9,000 years ago, but we *do* know that Athens existed as a fortified town about 2,000 BC, and that in 1,600 BC there was a high level of civilization in nearby Crete. The sea between Greece and Crete is full of islands which were once part of Greece itself – and the most southerly of these islands is Santorini, which was once circular in shape and five or six miles in diameter. It *is* known that around 1,500 BC there was a tremendous explosion – probably volcanic – that ripped Santorini apart and turned it into little more than the remains of a gigantic crater. *Modern* Santorini consists of three islets, all covered with pumic and volcanic rock. And since the explosion of 1,500 BC was three times as large as the eruption of Krakatoa in 1883, it must have produced a tidal wave of unprecedented size – which would certainly have destroyed any civilization existing in the Aegean Sea area – and would also account for the mysterious destruction of the palaces of Knossos and Phaestus at about that time. So, if we accept that Plato confused the lotus flower and the coiled rope, or mistook one hundred for 1,000, we can take it that

Professor Galanopoulos was correct in assuming that modern Crete is the site of the Royal City of ancient Atlantis, Santorini is the metropolis described by Plato, and the whole empire once extended over the many islands of the Aegean Sea, before being destroyed in 1,500 BC.'

'And that's what Saint-Germain is trying to tell us?'

'Right. He wants us to go to each of these three sites – and he wants us to know that each of them belonged to Atlantis. That's what he wants us to know and do – but don't ask me why.'

Ingrid felt that she was managing to get control of her fear, but her confusion only grew deeper at what she was hearing. Jerry grinned at her, mischievously, reassuringly, and she knew, just by looking into his eyes, just what he was planning.

'We're going to *Greece*?'

'Via Turkey,' he replied. 'We'll arrange it tomorrow.'

He grinned at her again, thus removing her from herself, letting her slip away from the fear and return to her love for him. She forgot about Saint-Germain, about her father and the Tuaoi Stone, and became aware only of Jerry and how close he was. God, she loved him and wanted to be touched by him, but could do nothing about it.

It was fear of a different kind.

She glanced at the two suitcases, looked back up at Jerry, noted his schoolboyish excitement and gave him a smile. She hoped the smile seemed natural, but in truth she still felt nervous, being tired and wanting to go to bed and sleep soundly for once. No matter what he had said, she still didn't know how to start, so she yawned and blinked melodramatically and murmured, 'God, I'm so tired. I really have to lie down.'

'Sure,' he said. 'You want a bath?'

'Yes, I feel rather grubby.'

'Would forty minutes do it?'

'I think so.'

'Then I'll go down to the bar.'

She felt idiotic, but couldn't help herself, so just nodded and murmured embarrassed thanks and watched him walk out. When he had closed the door behind him, she stripped and opened her suitcase, took her dressing gown and toilet bag out of it and went into the bathroom. She thought about him while she had her bath, rubbing her naked skin with the soap, feeling hot and tingly all over, wanting to touch and be touched. She closed her eyes and visualized him, sitting all alone in the bar, imagined what might happen if he walked in and looked at her nakedness. *God, I'm a fool*, she thought. *I might as well be a nun.* Then she pulled the plug out, stood up and wrapped herself in the towel, listening, hoping that the door would open and he would see her this way.

The door didn't open. He was being a gentleman. Disappointed, relieved, yearning and ashamed, she dried herself, put on a short nightie and climbed into the bed. She had already removed her spectacles and she tugged the blankets up to her chin and stared at the ceiling.

Jerry stayed out of the room for an hour, but it seemed like the whole night.

'I stayed away a bit longer,' he said when he returned, 'because I didn't want you to get nervous about running late.'

'I wasn't,' she said, feeling foolish, the blankets up to her chin, her cheeks burning helplessly.

'Can I get ready now?'

'Of course.'

'I'll unpack and take my things into the bathroom. Just pretend I'm not here.'

'Oh, Jerry,' she said.

He grinned and unzipped his suitcase, removed what he required, went into the bathroom, closed the door behind him and then ran the bathtaps. She could hear him singing. He was doing it in the bath. It was a terrible rock 'n' roll song and his voice was quite tuneless. Luckily, he was quick – she heard the water draining out – he gargled and then went quiet and then he emerged again, wearing a lurid Chinese dressing gown that was covered in dragons.

She closed her eyes and pretended to be sleeping as he walked to his bed.

'Good night, Ingrid,' he said.

'Good night, Jerry,' she replied without thinking.

'Ah, ha!' he said. 'Fooled you!'

'Fooled me? *I* wasn't pretending to sleep!'

'Yes, you were.'

'No, I wasn't!'

'Good night, Ingrid.'

'Good night.'

He switched his light off, plunging the room into darkness, and she lay there, keeping her eyes closed. She was tired but couldn't sleep, first thinking of Saint-Germain, of what Jerry had told her, then thinking of Jerry himself, lying there in the other bed. She heard him tossing and turning. That just made her toss and turn. She sighed and yearned for him, was fearful that he might come, listened for him and imagined him coming and then slipped into fantasy. She felt his hands on her naked skin, on her belly and breasts, felt the hard heat of his body against her, almost tasted his lips. He was here and then there – in her bed, then in his own – and she wanted him and feared him and burned with shame and need, and then eventually didn't know if she was dreaming or awake, but opened her eyes, after what seemed like an eternity, to the morning's grey light.

Jerry was still in the other bed, sleeping soundly and snoring. She stared sleepily at him, resenting his contentment, contemplating slipping in beside him and nuzzling against him. She trembled, trying to work up the courage but just couldn't do it.

CHAPTER TWENTY-FIVE

If Jerry had felt a muted confusion when in London, three weeks later, when he was sitting opposite Ingrid at an outside table of a *cafeneion* in the atrociously noisy Constitution Square in Athens, drinking *ouzo* while Ingrid had a *citron pressé*, he felt that he was either losing his mind or living a dream. What he had planned, very carefully, to be work and pleasure combined had become a bizarre, frightening journey into the unknown.

'I still can't believe it,' he said to Ingrid. 'I look back and it's all a dream.'

'It all *happened*,' she replied, reaching out to take hold of his hand, letting him know that he really existed and she still cared for him. 'I was there. We *both* saw it.'

Having another sip of *ouzo*, he wondered just *what* they had seen. He glanced around the noisy square with its hotels, travel agencies, cafés, orange trees and the hellish traffic crawling around the central fountain, and tried to reconstruct in his mind just what he and Ingrid had actually experienced.

Determined to make a holiday out of this second trip financed involuntarily by the revolting Zweig, he had flown with Ingrid to Istanbul, spent a few days there, then hired a car for the drive along the Aegean coast, along the rich, rolling countryside between the higher plateau and the sea, through names that had once lived for him only in mythology – Nicaea and Izmit and Bursa and Troy – and finally through a surprisingly modern Izmir and then on to Ephesus.

Once there, and standing beside Ingrid on the top step of the great horseshoe-shaped odeum and theatre, looking over the solemnly impressive excavated ruins of the temple of Diana, or Artemis, he had realized that apart from the hint that he should come here, Saint-Germain had failed to tell him what to look for. Consequently, for the rest of that afternoon, he and Ingrid had exhaustively explored the widespread ruins of the ancient Ionian Greek city, but failed to come up with anything unusual.

Determined not to give up, and remembering that the previous manifestations had occurred in darkness, he had insisted to Ingrid that they wait in the car until nightfall, when the ruins would be closed to the tourists. Ingrid had agreed, and that evening, when darkness had fallen, they both got out of the car and started walking back towards the ruins.

Everything became confused after that.

Jerry couldn't be sure, but he was convinced that he had fallen into a trance-like condition, that a globe of dazzling, pulsating light had materialized gradually over the ruins of the theatre; that the great columns of the original temple of Artemis, then the great Artemisium itself, had reappeared magically over the illuminated ruins; and that Saint-Germain and his unnamed friend, both wearing Grecian robes decorated with reliefs of animals and bees, both with high-pillared priests' headdresses, had emerged from that shimmering light, from the ghostly pillars of the ancient temple, and smilingly observed him from the lower steps of the theatre while Ingrid, sitting beside him on those same steps, had slumped against him and then fallen asleep. He also had been affected, mesmerized by those two ghosts, and then one of them, Saint-Germain, had approached him and placed a hand on his shoulder.

'You are doing well,' he said. 'Continue to do so. I

have already given you the first number. There are only Seven Wonders in the World. The second number is seven.'

Then Saint-Germain had squeezed his shoulder. That's all he remembered. He had blacked out and awakened in the cold light of dawn, leaning against the still sleeping Ingrid in the vast, circular ruins of the Artemisium, thinking: *Seven.*

Why seven?

When he shook Ingrid awake, she grew frightened, then insisted that they leave as soon as possible, that the ruins were possibly haunted, and that she had imagined, or experienced, exactly the same as he had described. They drove straight back to Istanbul, but even that city now frightened her, so he booked them on the next flight to Rhodes, wondering what he would find there.

The Colossus of Rhodes, a hundred-foot bronze statue of the god Helios, which in ancient times had bestrode the entrance to the harbour of Rhodes, had been destroyed in the earthquake of 277 BC. Where the Colossus had once been, three windmills now stood on the breakwater which terminated at the Agios Nikolaos Lighthouse in the cluttered modern port of Mandraki, with its caiques, yachts and tourists.

Not knowing what to expect, nor where he should go, Jerry had spent that first day touring the capital of the island, walking along the Aegean Sea, by the walls and towers of the old city, past the picturesque old houses of the Street of the Knights, then back in a restless circle to the pseudo-Venetian and Roman buildings of the waterfront where, bearing in mind that the darkness seemed to help, he and Ingrid sat until the early morning.

Bitterly disappointed when nothing out of the ordinary happened, he had returned with Ingrid to their double bedroom in their hotel above the beach.

Ingrid had got over her inhibitions to the degree where she would change in the bathroom while he waited in the bedroom, but they still used separate beds; and very early that morning, when darkness still reigned, Jerry awakened to find the room filled with a light that seemed to emanate from the walls, floor and ceiling, but miraculously didn't even shine out through the window into the darkness. Then, in the brilliant light, which had also wakened Ingrid – who seemed fascinated rather than frightened – Saint-Germain materialized, this time alone and wearing a modern boiler suit, to smile enigmatically at both of them and say:

'You have come a long way. You have more courage than you know. Divide the sum of the first two numbers by two and you will have the third number. Think about it when sleeping.'

And indeed he had slept, going under immediately, adding one to seven and dividing by two and coming up with four in his dreams, which then turned quite erotic. He saw Ingrid naked, swaying slightly, smiling at him, holding up her four fingers and counting them off, one by one. Then she lay down beside him, still naked, still smiling, and he kissed her four times on the belly and heard her soft groanings. The number *four* haunted his dreams, in permutations of lust and loving, and he awakened, still alone in his narrow bed, as dawn lit up the harbour.

They both took the boat to Athens, wondering what was coming next. They were still disbelieving of what had happened, and they thought that a leisurely cruise to Athens would give them time to relax – which in fact it did . . . while it lasted.

Now, sitting in the bedlam of Constitution Square in Athens, breathing the appalling stench of petrol and diesel oil, Jerry looked back on that cruise as something invented – something so beautiful and serene that it had to be fiction. They had cruised through the

Cyclades, around the holy island of Delos, had explored Mykonos, Syross and Paros and many others, and remembered only the beauty of the radiant blue sea, the dazzling white chapels, cubist houses and windmills, all perched on the sun-drenched parched hills beneath the sky's iridescence – and then his shock on reaching Athens, the sudden clamour and chaos, the roaring traffic and the smell of petrol and the sight of an urban sprawl.

He had hired another car, let Ingrid drive him out of all that, south along the toll highway, past more ruins to Corinth, around the Peloponnesian foothills, beneath forests of pine and cypress, high above the Corinthian Gulf, through Patras, with its castle and arcaded street, then sixty-eight kilometres south to Olympia and the ruined temple of Zeus.

This time prepared for anything, they parked the car well away from the ruins of the ancient site and waited until evening was falling and the tourists had left; then they made their way carefully through the olive trees and ageing pines to where the great Doric temple still dominated the sanctuary, though its broken columns lay scattered under the trees. There, beneath the stars, near the pediments of Zeus's temple, he held Ingrid's tender hand and waited, knowing that something would happen.

And this time, for the first time, they saw it properly.

At first it was just a flash, then a brightening star, then it flared out to form an umbrella of light at the far side of the silhouetted peak of Mount Kronion. Jerry blinked, rubbed his eyes, saw stars, looked again, and then saw a glowing disc, a saucer-shaped, pulsating radiance, expanding as it flew down from the mount and over the trees in slow, stately motion. It stopped right above him, high up, like a great moon, an enormous, incorporeal, pulsating light with a dark inner core. He watched it, transfixed, not comprehending what he was seeing, then it grew wider as it dropped down towards him and covered the ancient site.

He started burning and was dazzled, closed his eyes, thought it would scorch him, opened his eyes as the radiant light surrounded him and then covered the ground. Ingrid melted in the haze. He felt her hand, but she wasn't there. His skin had stopped burning, the radiance no longer dazzled him, and just as he realized this, the dark inner core covered him.

There was light in that darkness. It took a human form. Saint-Germain stepped towards him – or, rather, materialized – and he heard that magisterial, icy voice speaking to him again.

'You have the courage and heart of saints. You are both on the right path. Divide the sum of the first three numbers by two and you will have the last number. That is all you will need for now. The rest will come later – when we feel that the time is right. Now relax. We will meet again.'

He relaxed into sleep, feeling Ingrid sleeping beside him, falling down into darkness as the brilliant light ascended and the stars fell about him with the rush of the incoming night. He awoke counting up the first three numbers and dividing by two.

'*Six!*' he heard his own voice exclaiming.

That had happened this morning. Now they were back in Athens. The traffic was causing bedlam as it crawled around the fountain, the stench of petrol and diesel oil filled his nostrils, but he still couldn't quite accept that he was awake and not living a dream.

He was haunted by miracles.

Finishing his *ouzo*, he immediately ordered another, had a sip and tried smiling at Ingrid, hoping to hide his deepening confusion; but when she nervously returned his smile, letting her breath out in a sigh, he slapped the table with the palm of his hand in an affirmative manner.

'Right,' he said. 'So it happened . . . Now let's try to accept that fact.'

'It happened,' she said solemnly. 'We both had the same experience. You thought *I* was sleeping, I thought *you* were sleeping, yet both of us had the same experience. Now let's work out what it means.'

'The numbers,' he replied. 'It's all in the numbers . . . and I *have* worked them out.'

From where he sat, he could see the Acropolis, planted distantly on its high hill, its column scraping the dark clouds drifting lazily over it. That sky only made him nervous, recalling light descending vertically, and he had another sip of his *ouzo* and turned back to Ingrid.

'Saint-Germain gave us the first number,' he said, 'when he materialized in the burial chamber of the Great Pyramid. That number was one. And the other numbers, in the order they were given, were seven, four and six – which makes a magical number.'

'A *magical* number?' she asked him dubiously.

'Yes,' he said. '1746 is a so-called *magical* number. Add up the digits and the sum is eighteen; and eighteen is the sum of three sixes, as in 666 – which is, of course, the number of the beast.'

'I've never heard of it,' Ingrid said.

'It's taken from the Bible. From the book of *Revelation*. I quote: *He that hath understanding, let him count the number of the beast; for it is the number of a man; and his number is six hundred and sixty-six* . . . So, in a roundabout way, that's what we've been given – 666 – the number of the beast – a magical number.'

'But why would he give us that number?' Ingrid asked. 'And why in such a bizarre manner?'

Jerry shrugged. 'I don't know.'

He stared uneasily at her serious, bespectacled eyes and wished he could let down her hair and then stretch out beside her. He wished that a lot, but now, when he did so, he remembered his clumsy lunge at her in the hotel in Bloomsbury and suffered another acute spasm of embarrassment. He believed that Ingrid loved him, could feel it and see it, and that very knowledge made him more frustrated that they still hadn't made love.

More frustrated and more foolish, even ashamed of himself, because it left him exposed to his own lack of sexual sophistication. He wasn't a virgin – no, but now he felt like one, incapable as he was of finding a way to conquer their mutual fear.

Also, growing more desperate to find sexual fulfilment with her, he found himself thinking increasingly of other women, *any* woman, as compensation for the aching need he now lived with. Ironically, then, he realized, it was the very strength of his love for her that was looming as the greatest threat to their relationship.

He no longer trusted himself.

'Well,' she said, obviously not reading his mind, 'what do we do now? Go back to London?'

He shrugged again. 'Yes, I suppose so. There's obviously no reason for staying here. All we can do is go back and hope that something turns up. I don't think we've heard the last of Saint-Germain, so we'll just have to wait for him.'

Yet even as he spoke, he sensed that he was being watched, and looked past Ingrid, over her shoulder, to an outside table at the far end of the café.

Sitting at the table, wearing a perfectly normal off-grey pinstriped suit with white shirt and tie, looking very cool in the sweltering afternoon heat of Athens, his smile seductively dangerous beneath glistening eyes, was Saint-Germain's partner.

'Oh, shit,' Jerry heard himself murmuring automatically. Then, even as he noticed that a perplexed Ingrid was looking back over her shoulder at the man, his attempt at resistance was rendered futile, his will reduced to nothing, and he felt himself melting into the heat of a desire that transcended his normal appetites and made that man's sex irrelevant.

He *wanted* that man, unnaturally, helplessly, and found himself climbing to his feet in order to follow those mesmeric eyes and that slyly seductive smile. He couldn't help himself – and saw Ingrid standing with him – and then followed the man, that beautiful, male creature, away from the café.

'Jerry!' Ingrid exclaimed. 'What –?'

'It's all right, Ingrid. Let's follow him.'

His own voice sounded distorted, reverberating through his head, but he held Ingrid's hand, feeling electric, phosphorescent, ashamed because his only desire was to pursue the man walking ahead, through the noisy, polluted streets.

He wanted that man. He wanted to take him, to be taken *by* him, to lose himself in the intoxicating radiance of the man's inner light. It was love and desire – a primal, pagan, lust – and even as he burned in his own shame, he could not fight the feeling.

He noticed Ingrid glancing at him, perplexed, but could not meet her eyes.

This betrayal was too much.

The man kept walking, casually, gracefully, occasionally looking back over his shoulder and smiling ambiguously. Jerry didn't return that smile, but merely stopped when the man stopped, then started walking again as if tied to his quarry. He was led along Stadiou, through the main shopping centre, then into Omonia Square, where the fountain in the pool dominated the busy intersection above the station, and the touts and peddlers lent to the busy street life a dubious charm.

In a cluttered street just off the square, the stranger, after smiling seductively back over his shoulder, entered what looked like a sleazy *pension*, or brothel.

'Please, Jerry,' Ingrid said, 'don't go in!'

'I have to,' he replied, feeling insane. 'Damnit, Ingrid, *I have to*!'

He had to virtually drag her into the *pension*, but once inside found nothing but an unattended, very grubby reception office at the foot of steep stairs covered in moth-eaten, stained carpet, at the intersection of three corridors, all of which looked equally uninviting, though the fat whores leaning against the walls near certain rooms had a slightly decadent, slovenly allure.

'*Kalimera*,' the nearest one murmured. '*Onomazome Liliane*. You speak English, Mister? I please you. And your friend, she is welcome. *Malista?*'

Jerry didn't respond, but looked at the whore and through her, wondering where the object of his desire had disappeared to.

He hadn't a clue where to go until he heard the stairs creaking . . . on the landing above him.

'No!' Ingrid hissed. 'Don't go up there!'

'*We have to!*' he insisted.

Obsessed with that handsome stranger, seduced by his dangerous smile, he dragged Ingrid up the stairs of the brothel, ignoring her protests. He came to a landing, no carpet, splintered floorboards, a short, bare-walled corridor with three lime-painted doors on either side, only one of them open.

At the open door, Saint-Germain's partner was smiling seductively. He beckoned with one hand, the fingers covered in glittering diamonds, and Jerry, feeling as if he was dreaming, stopped just in front of him, enslaved by the light in those brilliant eyes, unable to help himself.

'It isn't me you want,' the man said, his voice low and extraordinarily melodious, its accent untraceable. 'What you want is inside.'

He nodded, pointed into the room, and Jerry, releasing Ingrid's hand, walked in without thinking.

The door slammed shut behind him.

CHAPTER TWENTY-SIX

It was a small, perfectly square, cell-like room, containing no windows, its only furniture being a bed along the back wall, a hand basin with a surprisingly clean towel beside it, a cracked mirror hanging above it.

Sitting on the bed, her long legs crossed, her voluptuous body covered in a short, see-through black negligé, was a raven-haired, green-eyed woman in her early thirties. When the door slammed shut, she looked up and smiled, then climbed to her feet.

Standing upright, she was utterly breathtaking, all hollows and curves, her pubic hair showing darkly through the negligé, which also flowed sensually over firm breasts and clung to her belly.

Jerry took a deep breath.

'How sweet you are,' the woman said in English, her voice thrillingly sensual. 'I truly never expected this.'

She stepped towards him with a languid rolling of her hips, stopped just in front of him and smiled again, her lips emphasized with moisturizer, her green eyes hypnotizing. He held his breath, drank her in, very aware of her breathing, hearing it as if hearing music, watching her breasts rise and fall. She reached out and placed a hand on his neck, then pulled him to her.

'Feel me,' she said. 'Press against me. Do what you want with me. I am here for your pleasure.'

He knew this was a set-up, but couldn't resist it, his will crumbling in the heat coming from her, his senses slipping away. He thought of Ingrid outside, remembered the man who had led him here, felt a brief spasm of concern for Ingrid's welfare and then heard himself groaning. The whore was rolling herself against him, sliding her belly across his groin, and her large breasts, incredibly soft and warm, were exciting him further.

He pressed his hands to her spine, felt her tongue down his throat, was drawn out of himself by her heat and softness, as she writhed against him and tugged at his clothing. Her fingers found his bare back, slid up and down his spine, and he groaned again and slid his hands up her negligé, slowly drowning in bare skin. He felt her buttocks, pressed her back against the wall, touched her breasts and pubic hair and sweating thighs as she sucked at his lips.

'Yes!' she whispered. 'That's it. Do it! *Yes!*'

She thrust up with her belly, falling back towards the bed. Her hands were clasped around his neck, her lips on his, as her weight pulled him down. He fell on top of her on the bed, sinking into her yielding flesh, excited by breasts and belly and spreading legs, feeling her hands on his back, along his ribcage and hips, even as concern and guilt whipped him at the mere thought of Ingrid.

She was standing just outside, in the company of that mysterious stranger, and this whole thing was some kind of set-up, the motive for which was still hidden. God, he wanted this whore – yes, he did; *God, he did!* – but concern and guilt, based on his love for Ingrid, brought him back to his senses.

He groaned and rolled off the woman and lay flat on his back, lying there for some time, breathing harshly, before sitting up. His loins were still inflamed and he felt dizzy, but he resisted the woman. When her left hand slid invitingly between his thighs, he pushed it away.

'No!' he said. '*Damn you, no!*'

He jumped back to his feet, feeling choked and unreal, and looked down at the woman, She was sitting upright, brushing the hair from her green eyes, smiling at him with what seemed like mockery and admiration combined.

'You don't want me?'

'Just who the hell are you? And why was I brought here?'

'You were brought here to receive satisfaction.'

'I'll have that if you answer me.'

The woman smiled again, this time without mockery, then nodded decisively.

'You resisted me,' she said. 'That's very good. I can be hard to resist. How did you manage it?'

'It was simple. I just thought of someone else. Now who the hell are you? Just a whore? I don't think so. You and him – that bastard outside – you both work for Saint-Germain, don't you?'

'Yes,' she replied. 'We are associated with Saint-Germain . . . and you're trying to find him. Why?'

'He obviously knows that.'

'Ah, yes,' she said, smiling, 'the Tuaoi Stone. You all want the Tuaoi Stone. Why do *you* want it?'

'Because I simply have to know that it exists . . . and because I don't want a man named Wilhelm Zweig to get it. He's after it, and if he gets his hands on it, he'll rule the world with it.'

'You are trying to save the world?' the woman asked, her mocking smile returning. 'Such nobility is truly very rare . . . or is it all for the love of a girl?'

Jerry felt himself burning with resentment *and* embarrassment, then leaned back against the wall, feeling dizzy, mesmerized by the woman's green eyes, sinking into a reverie . . . He saw himself on the Nile cruiser, on the deck, in the moonlight, Saint-Germain waving languidly at the light ascending into the night sky . . . Then Ingrid was there. She was holding his hand and smiling. Her smile vanished when she sat at the table in the boat's bar, beside Jerry, but facing Saint-Germain, who was framed by the window. Jerry saw the dark desert, the riverbank shifting silently, then the scene changed to the gardens of the hotel, with the pyramids and Sphinx in the background. He watched himself bidding Ingrid an anguished farewell, then saw Zweig and Elena chortling with mockery as he boarded the airport bus. When he saw that, his hatred broke his reverie and returned him to the small room, blinking and rubbing at his eyes.

'No,' the woman murmured, 'you are not completely selfless . . . but your heart's in the right place.'

'It doesn't matter what my motives are,' he said firmly to her. 'What matters is that Zweig is after the Tuaoi Stone – and Saint-Germain should know that.'

'Oh, he knows it. Saint-Germain knows *every*thing.'

'Then let him be warned.'

'He doesn't need warning. Wilhelm Zweig will never use the Tuaoi Stone . . . though you possibly might. Saint-Germain can find *you* any time he desires – but until you locate Saint-Germain, you will not see the Tuaoi Stone.'

'He *wants* me to find it?'

'He wants you to *try*. You have been chosen, and so far have been successful, but the test is not over yet.'

'The test?'

'We think you are a good man, a pure man, though you don't know that yet . . . and neither do we. But only the good, the pure at heart, can find the Tuaoi Stone.'

'I don't understand this. Who are you? What are you doing here? And why was I lured here?'

'You were brought here to be seduced. If you had been, you would have failed. Because you didn't fail –

because your love was stronger than lust – I am permitted to tell you what I know – which is not all that much. I know only enough to give you what you need . . . to take you on to the next stage.'

'And what's that?'

'I can't tell. I can only answer.'

'This is crazy. I just don't believe it.'

'But of course you do, Jerry. That's why you're here. It's your belief that has kept you going this far. You have the faith of a saint.'

Suddenly fearful for Ingrid, not trusting this woman's smile, he turned away and tried to jerk the door open, but found it was locked. Even more fearful, he turned back and asked, 'Why am I locked in?'

'The door will open when I've answered your questions. Now what do you wish to know?'

'Is Ingrid still out there?'

'She is perfectly safe. She is destined to make this journey with you, so no harm will come to her.'

The woman's tone managed to soothe him a little, but he still found it difficult to think of what he might ask her.

He leaned against the wall again, taking comfort from the feel of it, but when he closed his eyes, even briefly, he drifted away from himself. The woman's presence permeated him, set fire to his imagination, and he had a vivid recollection of Saint-Germain and his friend wearing Grecian robes and headdresses in the Temple of Artemis; then of that same Saint-Germain in the eighteenth century, his fingers covered in extraordinary diamonds, his powdered hair pinned behind his head.

One vision slid through the other, defeating space and time, and when he came to the Saint-Germain in modern clothing, he opened his eyes again, finally managing to get out the question that brought him back to the present.

'Saint-Germain has given me a magical number – 1746 – the so-called number of the beast. Why has he done this?'

'I cannot answer. I have not been informed.'

'Is it true that the Tuaoi Stone was once the top of the Great Pyramid at Giza?'

'Yes.'

'Why was it removed?'

'You will find out in due course.'

Jerry sighed, feeling that he was being toyed with, wanting to make his escape. 'What is the Tuaoi Stone made from?' he asked.

'What is the difference? Simply think of the Great Pyramid as an instrument of astrology and base all your assumptions on that.'

'The Great Pyramid was a tomb, not an instrument of astrology.'

'It was both – now it is only the latter.'

'It *is*?'

'It was constructed as a vehicle for transcending the material state, for travel in space and through time, into a further dimension. It retains that ability.'

Feeling a shiver go down his spine, recalling not only his own experience in the burial chamber of the Great Pyramid, but also what Saint-Germain had written on the document in the library in Troyes, Jerry found it difficult to think, but managed to speak at last.

'Constructed by the Pharaohs?' he asked.

'The *final* Great Pyramid – the one you know – was constructed by them.'

'You mean there were others?'

'You have to search through prehistory.'

'Beyond our present knowledge of Man?'

'That is so.'

He had a vision, then, of that great civilization which extended across the islands of the Aegean Sea, linking Greece to ancient Babylon and the Pillars of Hercules. He saw a different landmass, gleaming pyramidal cities, a flame that joined the earth to the cosmos, rendering space and time obsolete. The high priests of the civilization, dressed in robes and headdresses, were magical adepts of vast learning and extraordinary powers. Saint-Germain, who also transcended time and space, had been one of those holy men.

Shaken, Jerry stared down at the woman. She was still sitting on the edge of the bed, her white skin showing through the black negligé, her long legs crossed, hands folded in her lap, her smile one of amusement. She had the eyes of a big cat, bright green, and they kept him enslaved.

'Does this relate to Atlantis?' he asked her, trying hard to be logical.

'Yes,' she replied.

'Where and when was Atlantis?'

'You have crossed the length and breadth of Atlantis in your journey to me –'

'The Aegean Sea.'

'– and you also know when it was destroyed – in 1,500 B C.'

'A natural disaster?'

'Yes. A volcanic explosion.'

'And does the Tuaoi Stone – the missing tip of the Great Pyramid – relate to that vanished Atlantis?'

'I know only a little about this. Those who have studied the occult traditions of Atlantis speak of the use which the scientists of the former world made of the tip of the pyramid as a medium for attracting and transmitting solar energy.'

'Which suggests that the Tuaoi Stone was a diamond . . . or some other form of *crystal*.'

'If you think it, it will be.'

'Yet the Great Pyramid is in Egypt – not in the area of the vanished Atlantis.'

'Everything under the sun has its reasons – *and* explanations – but I only know this much. Now you must go.'

'To where?'

'Back to where you have come from.'

'London?'

'Your signposts are the world's Seven Wonders, and there are three more to visit. To learn more you must return to where you have come from – you must visit the Tomb of Mausoleus and brave what you find there. That is all I can tell you.'

'You know nothing else?'

'Nothing else. Now the door is unlocked. Goodbye . . . and good luck.'

The farewell was a command, spoken quietly and firmly, but he found himself unwilling to go, having much more to ask.

He closed his eyes again, concentrating on what to ask, went blank and then saw a great pyramid towering over the much smaller pyramids scattered over a vast plain. The great pyramid was made of stone blocks, but its tip was shining crystal, and the lightning of the elements, phosphorescent and jagged, soared from the tip to the heavens to form, between the stars and the parched plain, a pulsating white haze.

He looked and was dazzled, blinked, then looked again, saw the same great pyramid, but in another time, its crystal tip missing and the sky dark above it, the pyramidal city around it being covered in dust.

The dust presaged the fire and rain of the holocaust that would sweep all before it, leaving nothing but silence.

Jerry opened his eyes again, feeling dizzy and unreal.

He tried to stare the woman down, looking deep into her green eyes, but even as he did so, he started losing his senses, felt desire for her creeping back over him to render him helpless.

He thought of Ingrid outside, of the very strange man with her, and jerked himself out of his sensual reverie to reach for the door handle. The door opened and he stepped into the hall, then looked frantically up and down.

There was no one in sight.

In a panic, he turned back to the room, but before he could speak, the woman waved her right hand in a gesture of reassurance.

'Don't panic. Your friend is downstairs by the desk. No harm can come to her.'

Not reassured, he hurried down the stairs to the entrance – but Ingrid was nowhere to be seen. He rushed into the street, looked up and down it, but saw neither Ingrid nor Saint-Germain's partner. Now truly fearful, cursing under his breath, he hurried back into the brothel, up the stairs and rushed into the one room with its door open.

The strange woman had vanished.

Almost sobbing at his own stupidity, he rushed back and forth, from one room to another, from one floor to another, finding nothing but fat whores and their sad, bedraggled clients, none of whom knew anything about a European girl or the well-dressed man with her, none of whom even recalled seeing them. Choked up, in a fever of despair, he rushed past the empty reception office and out into the street, where he continued his panic-stricken, fruitless search, finding neither the seductive stranger nor his beloved Ingrid.

They had vanished completely.

CHAPTER TWENTY-SEVEN

Ingrid couldn't help herself. In despair over Jerry's behaviour, shocked at how he had left her, horrified by her own behaviour after returning to the hotel, she hurried out of her room, walked down to the lobby, entered the shop and started pacing around, possessed of the urge to steal.

She knew she shouldn't do it, but couldn't help herself. The miseries of her past, mostly caused by her father, were as nothing compared to the pain she had felt when Jerry walked into that room in the brothel and, worse, started groaning passionately with that whore soon after the door closed. Standing just outside the door, hearing the groanings from within, and held in the mesmeric gaze of the man who had led them there, she could not doubt for a second what was happening and had burst into tears.

Her heart had been broken at that instant and would never recover.

She glanced around the shop, wondering what she could steal, horrified that she should be doing this again, but unable to stop herself. She was suffering the anguish of grief and had to somehow release it.

Blushing, shaking, aware of her racing heart, she waited until the Greek salesgirl wasn't looking, then slipped a silk scarf off its hanger and sneaked it into her pocket. She held her breath when she did it, closed her eyes and waited, at once hoping to be caught and dreading it, feeling excitement and shame.

When she heard no sound, no cry of protest, she opened her eyes again.

Jerry was watching her.

Shocked, she just stood there, burning up, shaking terribly, then watched as he hurried through the shop towards her, his lips pursed in a grim line. When he reached her, he leaned very close to her and spat his words out.

'Put it back!' he snapped.

'No!'

'*Put it back!*'

'No, I won't!'

'Damn you, Ingrid, do as I say or *I'll* call the sales-girl!'

'All right, call her, then!'

He grabbed hold of her right wrist, jerked her hand from her pocket, then took hold of the scarf, pulled it out and hung it back on its hook.

'Come with me!' he hissed. '*Now!*'

Still holding her by the wrist, he dragged her out of the shop and turned to face her in the hotel's busy lobby, again leaning very close to her and glaring furiously at her.

'Just what the *hell* do you think you're doing?' he demanded.

'Nothing! It's none of your business!'

'None of my *business*? I catch you stealing like you used to do before and it's none of my business? What the hell does *that* mean?'

She tried to jerk her wrist away, but he refused to let her go. 'It means whatever you want it to mean. Now let me go, Jerry.' She tried to break free again, but he still refused to let go, so instead, unable to look him in the eyes, she burst into tears.

He immediately pulled her into his embrace and

303

stroked the back of her head. 'Hey, hey,' he said. 'What's up? What started all this?'

'You know, Jerry! *You know!*'

She pulled away from him, but he didn't let her go too far, still holding onto her right hand and letting her step back only as far as his arm would stretch.

'If you mean –'

'Yes, I do! How could you? Oh, God! Just leaving me with that man in that brothel while you . . .' She couldn't say any more. She couldn't bear to *think* about it. Just remembering the sound of his groaning was enough to . . . 'I've never been so ashamed in my life. How could you? *How could you?*'

This time she managed to wrench her wrist free and instantly hurried off across the lobby, wondering where the bar was. He caught up with her quickly, grabbed her shoulders, turned her around to face him once more, looking more hurt than angry.

'Hey, hold on,' he said, 'I just refused a very nice piece of ass for your sake.'

'Oh, charming! What language!'

'I did! Swear to God!'

He let her go in order to cross his heart, so she started walking away again, wiping the tears from her eyes and feeling increasingly foolish.

'Come back, Ingrid!'

'No! I can't stand you! You're just lying to me. I heard your awful groaning from that room. I even heard the bed creaking. Oh, God, how disgusting!'

'Well, I don't get too much from *you*, sweetheart – so, you know, what the hell?'

She burst into tears again, saw the bar, hurried into it, took a seat in a dimly lit far corner and pulled out her handkerchief. His last remark had hurt her more deeply than she could bear, and was compounded by the guilt it resurrected by reminding her that she and Jerry had *still* not consummated their love.

It was a sorry state of affairs, perhaps even unnatural, and his remark, while wounding her to the quick, also filled her with shame. She was depriving him, as well as herself, and she couldn't forget that fact.

Sniffing back her tears, she glanced across the bar and saw Jerry standing in the doorway, staring angrily at her. She wanted him to leave, was frightened that he might do so; was shocked by what she had heard in that brothel, but more shocked by herself – not only because she had attempted to steal again, but because of what she knew had led up to it.

She dabbed at her eyes with the already soggy handkerchief, then saw Jerry's anger changing to despair as he walked over to her, stopping right in front of the table and looking down at her.

'I'm sorry,' he said. 'I shouldn't have said that. You just made me angry, so I hit back, but what I said wasn't true. I swear to you, Ingrid, I did nothing. Now are you willing to listen?'

She sniffed, glanced around her and saw a few people watching her over their drinks.

'All right,' she said wearily.

Jerry sighed with relief. 'Good,' he said. 'Now let me get you a drink and explain the whole thing. What will it be?'

'A brandy.'

'It's too early for that.'

'Damn you, get me a brandy!'

'Okay, Ingrid! Okay!'

He retreated to the bar, where she saw him having words with the barman, obviously trying to master the language and using his hands a lot. She tried to calm her emotions. She felt foolish and ashamed, frightened of what she had attempted, and then the love that she felt for Jerry welled up and threatened to drown her. When he came back towards her, holding a glass in each hand, she thought of what had happened in her hotel room and felt even more ashamed.

He placed a double brandy in her hand, then sat down with his beer, raising his glass in a mock toast.

'Cheers,' he said.

She sniffed again, then had a sip of the brandy and felt it rush to her head. Jerry leaned across the table towards her and took hold of her free hand, squeezing it tenderly.

'I swear to you,' he said, 'I did nothing with that woman. I followed that bastard because I didn't have a choice – because he sort of *mesmerized* me – and when I walked into that room, I swear to God, that woman did the same – she almost hypnotized me – and I *wanted* to make love to her – yes, I did – but then the thought of you stopped me. I wasn't myself. I swear to you, I wasn't! She tried to seduce me, and she almost succeeded, but the thought of *you* jerked me back to my senses. I was stopped by my love for you.'

'That's true?'

'Yes, it's true.'

She felt like crying again, though this time with joy; but instead she had another sip of brandy and squeezed his hand in return.

'You were an awfully long time in that room,' she said. 'What kept you in there?'

'It was a test,' he responded. 'This whole trip has been a test. I'm still not sure why, but Saint-Germain actually *wants* us to find the Tuaoi Stone – though apparently we have to earn it first. Don't ask me to explain that. I'm just as confused as you are. But if I'd let that woman seduce me, we wouldn't have got any further – Saint-Germain would have deemed me a failure and left us without a clue. He's not leading us on a wild-goose chase – there's a purpose to this madness – and the only way to find out what it is, is to keep playing the game.'

'You mean that woman told you something else?'

'Yes,' Jerry replied, looking more excited. 'The Tuaoi Stone *is* the missing tip of the Great Pyramid, it's probably made of some kind of crystal, and the original Great Pyramid was at least an instrument of astrology – though of a very particular kind. Remember that remarkable statement made by the eighteenth-century Saint-Germain in that document in the library of Troyes? I quote from memory: *We moved through space at a speed that can be compared with nothing but itself . . . Within a fraction of a second the plains below us were out of sight, and the earth had become a faint nebula. I was carried up, and I travelled through the empyrean for an incalculable time at an immeasurable height. Heavenly bodies revolved, and worlds vanished below me . . .* He wrote *that* in the eighteenth century? It sounds just like space travel!'

'So?'

'Well, that woman in the brothel – who later vanished – told me that the Great Pyramid in its intact state – in other words, with the magical crystal, or Tuaoi Stone, as its apex – was a vehicle, quote, for *transcending the material state, for travel in space and through time, into a further dimension* . . . And if what we've both witnessed is anything to go by, Saint-Germain is able to do just that – him *and* his partner.'

Recalling Saint-Germain's mysterious partner, Ingrid shivered helplessly and lowered her gaze to the table, too frightened to look up. She was frightened by the whole affair – by Saint-Germain and his partner, by her father and his henchmen, by where this bizarre search might be leading them and what it could mean – but most of all, she was frightened of what it might be doing to her, particularly in view of what she had just tried in that shop a few minutes ago.

She had thought that meeting Jerry had changed her forever, that she would never steal again, nor try to set fire to anything; but now she wasn't so sure.

'I don't want to go on,' she said.

'We've got to,' Jerry replied fervently. 'We can't leave it now. *We've got to get to the end of it!*'

'I don't want to. I'm frightened.'

'We've got to go back to Turkey,' he said, as if not really hearing her. 'To the ruins of the Mausoleum, the tomb of Mausolus, in modern Bodrum. It's another of the Seven Wonders of the World and it's next on our list.'

'I'm frightened, Jerry. *I'm frightened!*'

She had to look up at him, to show him her terror, then moved her gaze to focus on the man, that diabolically handsome, mesmeric creature who, looking perfectly normal in a light-grey suit, white shirt and tie, had walked into the bar a few seconds ago and taken a seat near the door.

Jerry caught her glance, looked over his shoulder, studied the man a moment, then turned back to face her, his brow furrowed in sudden confusion.

'Come to think if it,' he said, 'what *did* happen when I entered that woman's room? What happened while you were waiting outside? Where did you and he *go?*'

She blushed furiously and finished off the brandy, letting it go to her head. She believed what Jerry had told her about him and that woman . . . she believed – because it had happened to her and she would never forget it.

'I couldn't bear it,' she said. 'I could hear you groaning with that woman. I heard you both falling onto the bed, and then I walked out. I was crying. I remember that. I thought you were making love to that woman. I rushed down the stairs, but he followed me and took hold of my arm. When he did that, I calmed down a lot . . . I mean, I calmed down immediately.'

She caught Jerry's gaze, tried to hold it but didn't succeed and lowered her eyes again.

'He waved down a taxi and brought us back here,' she said. 'He told me not to worry, that you'd be perfectly safe, and that everything in life had its purpose, including what you were doing.' She didn't know how to go on. She felt a deep shame and bewilderment that made her heart race. Then she coughed and continued, 'He kept talking to me quietly, hypnotically, telling me not to worry, that everything was preordained, and then, when we got here, he personally asked for the room key and led me up to our room and let us both in.'

'And you didn't *resist*?'

'No, I didn't resist.'

Jerry released her hand and started pulling his own hand away, but she reached forward, very quickly, instinctively, and took hold of his fingers. Gently, insistently, in a trance, she pulled his hand back towards her.

'You said it yourself, Jerry – that man almost hypnotized you. Then the woman in that brothel did the same – and almost seduced you. Well, that happened to me. Christian Grabbe almost seduced me. Yes, he called himself Christian Grabbe, complimented me, hypnotized me, and was stretched out beside me on the bed before I knew what was happening.

'God, yes, I wanted him – so badly I was hurting – I wanted him to take me, to devour me, obliterate me – but all the time I knew that it was wrong, that it wasn't quite natural.

'Still, I was overwhelmed – I thought I was losing

my mind — but then I thought of you, thought *desperately* about you, and when I did, I was able to roll away from him and get back my senses. When I did that, when I rolled away and told him to leave, he just smiled — not in malice, but in simple amusement, then told me I was surprising, quite exceptional, and then walked from the room, promising that he would see me again in the very near future . . . and now he's sitting right there, smiling at both of us.'

Glancing up, she saw Jerry staring back over his shoulder, then he turned and looked directly at her, his gaze clouded with anger. She didn't know if it was directed at her or not, but felt compelled to explain herself.

'I was hypnotized, Jerry. Just as you were hypnotized. But when I fixed my thoughts on you — as you fixed your thoughts on me — I was able to break out of that trance — exactly as you did. Nothing happened between me and Christian Grabbe. It *almost* did — but that's all . . .'

He stared very steadily at her, his eyes bright with rage, but then, when he gently squeezed her hand, she knew who he was angry with. He dropped her hand, then stood up and turned around, clearly about to go across the room and confront Christian Grabbe.

However, Christian Grabbe stood up also, smiled mockingly and nodded, then walked casually out of the bar. Jerry followed him, looked out, shook his head in exasperation, then came back and stood directly in front of her.

'He's gone already,' he said. 'But you and I are still here. So . . . let's head back to Turkey.'

'I'm frightened,' she said again, meaning it, feeling it.

'So am I,' Jerry said.

CHAPTER TWENTY-EIGHT

'I own the whole island,' Zweig said, waving his right hand languidly, as if it were nothing. 'I bought it from a movie star whose career was virtually over and who built laboratories here to *help* the natives. However, once he had his *Geld*, I kicked him off the island and started showing his noble natives what *I* wanted them for.'

He could tell that Kuragin was impressed as, wearing white shorts and shirt with sandals on his feet, he walked along the beach beside Zweig, exploring the island after a very heavy lunch.

The island, in French Polynesia, had 750 acres of lush vegetation, with half a dozen small atolls surrounding it and a reef outside, beyond which his fleet of heavily armed yachts was anchored. The idiot film star, bored out of his mind with wealth and wanting to set the world to rights, had bought the whole island, moved onto it with his family, and built the laboratories in order to help the natives survive the onslaught of civilization by trying to make use of solar energy, develop native-grown products into food, protect the giant crabs and turtles from extinction, and even transform plankton into food. Zweig, highly disgusted by such a waste of the lush island, had emptied the laboratories and turned them into military barracks; razed a great many trees to the ground to turn the land into firing-ranges; placed barbed-wire and sand-bag fortifications along the once immaculate, virgin beaches; and drained and then filled in a lovely natural lagoon in order to build himself a small airstrip and landing-pad for his aircraft and helicopters.

'As you can see,' he said, 'I have put the island to good use. And the natives, formerly living an idle life, have *also* been put to good use. I work them very hard and, of course, they come in handy when it comes to the training of my men. Here my men learn armed combat, physical torture and psychological interrogation techniques – and the natives are used as fodder in this, when not actually working. Very good, *ja?*'

'Most impressive,' Kuragin said, the compliment dropping from his fat lips with obvious reluctance.

Zweig sighed, trying to contain his frustration, furious that he had been reduced to allowing sub-human Soviets on his island. He really wanted to use Kuragin as a guinea pig in a torture session; he wanted to see him writhing under the electric prod, not looking so smug.

'Anyway,' Kuragin said, glancing at the band of men who, all wearing old Brown Shirt uniforms, were on a fully equipped forced march around the island's perimeter, with the sea spraying languidly over them where it broke on the rocks, 'my time is strictly limited –'

'You enjoyed the long lunch, yes?'

'– and I think,' Kuragin continued, ignoring the jibe, 'it's time to get down to business.'

'*Every* time is time for business,' Zweig insisted. 'As you know, I believe this.'

'Quite,' Kuragin said, not smiling as Zweig led him away from the beach and up over a fairly steep slope of white sand and palm trees. He was pleased to note that Kuragin was already starting to sweat a bit, and he wanted to get him away from the cooling breeze in order that he might sweat some more.

'So, *what* business?' he asked the Soviet. 'Everything

seems to be going well. I have kept my promise to route more of my products in your direction, and I trust that your request for the supply of high-tech devices – normally forbidden to you under the Concom convention – has been going through smoothly. Afghanistan, was it? I believe so. You are doing good work there.'

'I can do without compliments,' Kuragin said. 'Let us stick to the issues.'

Instantly enraged, Zweig had to control himself, and he did so by picking up some stones and hurling them, one by one as he walked, at the birds chattering overhead.

'Of course,' he said, with the uncomfortable feeling that he was on his hands and knees before the Russian, 'I understand.'

'The Kremlin is not pleased,' Kuragin continued as they crossed the brow of the low hill and he dabbed at his sweaty face with a handkerchief. 'As our part of the agreement, we have distributed considerable monies to your numerous bank accounts in various tax havens. We have also, as you requested, distributed to your numerous administration centres and private homes a great many of the works of art which we found in various locations in Nazi Germany. In return for this, you were to do two things for us – first, increase dramatically the flow of embargoed technology to us; and, second, get us the legendary Tuaoi Stone. The former promise you have kept; the second you have still failed to deliver.'

At the bottom of the slope they came to a sandy clearing in which, beneath a green umbrella of large palm leaves, some of Zweig's stormtroopers were practising hand-to-hand combat under the supervision of a well-muscled mercenary. All the young men looked beautiful, stripped to the waist and sweating, and

Zweig, taking note of their radiant fitness, yearned for what he had lost.

'Impressive?'

'Yes,' Kuragin replied.

'They are devoted to me,' Zweig said. 'Completely . . . And would be killed if they weren't.'

'That's the best kind of devotion,' Kuragin said. 'Now what about the Tuaoi Stone?'

Annoyed that he hadn't managed to change the subject, Zweig led the flush-faced Russian away from his young gods of war and along a winding path through coco-palms.

'I am on the trail of it,' he said, 'but you will have to be patient.'

'The Kremlin has never been long on patience – and it is now running out. We wish to know what is happening regarding this. We need more specifics.'

'*Specifics*, Kuragin?'

'Don't play with me, Zweig. You said you had a lead, but refused to state what it was. Since you have still not delivered – and have refused to discuss the matter – we wish to know exactly what you are doing and what progress is being made. After all, this could all be a hoax – and the Tuaoi Stone may not exist.'

'I wouldn't lie to you, Kuragin.'

'You would if you could.'

Zweig sighed. 'All right,' he said, 'I will tell you. I didn't tell you before because my own daughter is involved; but clearly I have no choice any longer. The Tuaoi Stone exists, my friend.'

They emerged from the trees into another sunlit clearing where a thatched hut, raised high on stilts, was spread out before them. At either side of the steps leading up to the entrance were two guards in tropical battle dress. Both of whom, seeing Zweig, snapped smartly to attention, bringing their Swiss 5.56 mm assault rifles to their shoulders and saluting, before returning to their at-the-ready positions.

A scream of agony emanated from the hut, then tapered off to a sobbing whimper, interrupted by a harshly barked command, and another short scream.

'My school for torture,' Zweig explained. 'We use the natives, of course. This is not only useful to my men, but keeps the natives in check. Thus the school serves a double purpose and is most economical.'

'I don't like to hear screaming,' Kuragin said. 'Can we go somewhere else?'

'Of course,' Zweig said. 'This way.'

He started forward past the hut, but then, when the roar of guns split the silence ahead, he remembered that the firing range was there and so instead took the path heading west. While they were walking through the shade, under drooping papaya trees, he reluctantly told Kuragin about Ingrid and the American, then about his own magical encounters with the mysterious Saint-Germain. Kuragin looked increasingly incredulous and finally stopped walking.

'This is true?'

'*Very* true. My men have been following my daughter and the American, and wherever those two go, they are also followed by Saint-Germain or *his* men . . . And when Saint-Germain appears strange things happen . . . *miraculous* things – beyond our logic and science. Saint-Germain has the magical powers of one who has found the Philosopher's Stone.'

'And he knows your daughter and the American are pursuing him?'

'Yes.'

'Then why doesn't he use his miraculous powers to prevent them from doing so?'

'The only explanation is that he *wants* them to find him eventually.'

'Why?'

'Perhaps because they've been chosen.'

'To join him as adepts?'

'Yes. It is possible.'

Kuragin started walking again, forcing Zweig to rush to catch up, his smile hiding resentment. There was the sound of gunshots from the firing range, but this time more distant.

'And what have your daughter and the American found out about the Tuaoi Stone so far?'

'I don't know,' Zweig said. 'My men haven't approached them yet. We keep hoping they will lead us to Saint-Germain, but that hasn't quite happened yet.'

'*Quite?*'

Zweig shrugged. 'I have already described some of the events my men witnessed when Saint-Germain materialized to my daughter and the American – miraculous events. However, at no stage could they get to Saint-Germain before he vanished again – and, indeed, it is doubtful if they could do anything if they had managed to do so.'

'Then what is the point of this pursuit?'

'Because I am convinced that sooner or later Saint-Germain will lead my daughter and the American to his lair – to where the Tuaoi Stone is hidden. And then, and only then, can we act – not necessarily by confronting Saint-Germain, but by stealing the Tuaoi Stone when his back is turned and then, hopefully, using its power to defeat him.'

They emerged from the trees into the expansive open space that had once been a lovely lagoon and now was a tarmaced airstrip, crossing the breadth of the island, and with quonset huts and hangars along one side of it. Zweig's half-dozen light and transport airplanes and four helicopters were lined up along the strip, with the Hawker Siddeley HS 125 passenger plane just roaring into life, preparing to take Kuragin to Honolulu, on the first leg of his lengthy journey back to Eastern Europe.

Kuragin stopped walking, studied the airplane, then his own feet, furrowed his brow as if struggling to think, then raised his eyes again.

'It is clear from what you tell me,' he said, 'that this Saint-Germain knows that your men are *also* following your daughter and her American boyfriend.'

'Yes,' Zweig admitted, 'that is so.'

'Good,' Kuragin said. 'Let us speed things up a little. You are to inform your men to stop simply *following* your daughter and the American, and instead to try to capture them. Should they succeed, they are to interrogate both of them to the limit – I repeat: to the limit – to ascertain just how *much* they have discovered about the Tuaoi Stone or Saint-Germain. When they have done that, they are to terminate both the captives.'

'*Terminate* them?'

'Naturally. Why not?'

'I should remind you,' Zweig said, 'that one of the subjects to be terminated is my own daughter.'

Kuragin laughed at that. 'How sentimental you are,' he said. 'However, my personal KGB file on you indicates with no uncertainty that filicide would not be alien to you. It also indicates that you have never treated your daughter with the greatest concern. So let's not play games, Zweig.'

Refusing to acknowledge this below-the-belt jibe, Zweig merely forced a smile, nodded and then said, 'Let's assume I were to do as you ask – what point would it serve? If we terminate Ingrid and her American, we might lose Saint-Germain.'

Kuragin thought about that, his bullish brow furrowed again, then turned away rudely and started walking towards the roaring aeroplane.

'A good point,' he acknowledged with ill-concealed

bad grace, 'so let us proceed in a different manner. Should you be able to capture your daughter and the American –'

'We will.'

'You will, as formerly suggested, interrogate them both to the limit, to ascertain exactly what they know. You will then pass your daughter on to me personally, tell the American that he is to continue his search for the Tuaoi Stone alone, and inform him that if he refuses to do so, I will personally execute the woman he appears to love so much. In this way, we will find out exactly what is going on, and also have more control over the situation – rather than risk losing both of them, as we do at the moment.'

They had reached the steps leading up into the aircraft and Kuragin, turning around to face Zweig, had to shout in his face.

'So! Is it agreed?'

Zweig had no choice – and he knew it – since if he failed to agree, the Soviets would spill the beans about his assets and then leave him to the mercy of the financial and legal eagles of the European and American governments. No, he had to do as he was told . . . at least for the time being.

'Yes,' he said, forcing a smile. 'Of course. It's agreed.'

The Russian smiled smugly back and reached out his hand; Zweig shook it, wanting to crush every bone in it, then watched the fat bastard mount the steps and go into the airplane. He waved once and disappeared, and then Zweig walked away, heading towards the quonset hut at the edge of the airstrip. When he reached it he went inside, took a seat in the small lounge, snapped his fingers at the Polynesian steward and demanded some champagne.

The steward jumped to attention, brought the champagne very quickly, and Zweig sat there by the window, watching the airplane take off, wished he had planted a bomb in it and then drank his champagne.

When the plane had disappeared, taking Kuragin to Honolulu, Zweig stood up and walked out of the hut and went back to his main house, where Elena, stretched out on a hammock on the porch, fanning herself and drinking a cocktail, was moaning to the sweating, nervous Hans about the terrible heat.

'Stop your whining,' he said angrily to Elena. 'And you, Hans, come inside.'

As Elena slid her sunglasses down her nose and looked at him with an unusual hint of anger, he led Hans into the cool interior of his palm-thatch house, conveyed Kuragin's demands to him, and finished by telling him that this time the men must not fail.

'If they do,' he said, 'they might as well kill themselves, because I'll just hunt them down. And then, when I have disposed of their sorry lives, I will personally take over this whole affair and ensure that it's handled right. Is that understood?'

'Yes, Herr Zweig, it is.'

He stared at Hans for some time, wondering what the young man was thinking, and then, remembering what he had made him do not so long ago, had to suppress a shudder, shocked that the ravages of old age could make him so desperate.

Yet Hans's face was unreadable, making Zweig uneasy, and he decided to show the young man that what had occurred between them was not a sign that Hans could take liberties.

'Good,' he said curtly. 'So get to it immediately. And when you leave, tell that whore to come inside and attend to my needs.'

When Hans nodded and left, Zweig took off his clothes, stretched out on the bed, spreadeagled himself, and waited for Elena to walk in. When she did so, sweating nicely, her body lush in the thin bikini, he told her to go to the wardrobe and put on some proper clothes.

Elena did as she was told, but with a kind of dumb insolence. She withdrew his favourite clothes, stripped in front of him and put them on, then pulled out some leather thongs and a short-handled whip. Then, wearing the jackboots, S S jacket and black stockings, she crossed the room and started tying him to the bed while he licked his parched lips.

'It's terrible to grow old,' he murmured. 'Hurt me gently, Elena.'

'You can depend on it,' she replied, spitting her gum out into the palm of her right hand, then pressing it down on his forehead. 'It's all in a day's work.'

Zweig closed his tired eyes.

CHAPTER TWENTY-NINE

Driving the sixty miles back from al-Hillah to Baghdad, along dusty flatlands parallel to the Euphrates river, Jerry felt like a very different person to what he had been. He was haunted by miracles, by the deep well of the unknown, and he couldn't shake off the startling images of what he and Ingrid had been through since leaving Athens three weeks ago.

That three weeks seemed like three years – or like a timeless, bewitching dream – and he knew Ingrid felt the same way. He wasn't sure just how, but he knew it to be true – he and Ingrid had changed, were no longer quite human, had been touched with the reality of magic and now believed all was possible.

They could never go back to being what they had been, because of what they had witnessed.

Even now he could see in the back of his mind the unveiling of miracles . . . In Bodrum, in Turkey, above the ruins of ancient Halicarnassus, they had seen the great Mausoleum materializing out of the night, its thirty-six columns supporting a twenty-four-step pyramid, which itself was surmounted by a four-horse marble chariot, the whole towering edifice with its numerous statues of kings and queens shimmering in the pulsating light cast down from the night sky.

And that light, beaming down, flattened out as it descended, soon covered the mighty tomb, obliterated it and shrank back into a dark core in a shell of luminous energy, out of which, with the ambiguous smile of a Sphinx, stepped a different Saint-Germain.

Different, but only slightly, dressed in Anatolian robes, his face more lined than it had been before, more Asian in features. He had emerged from that haze, walking lightly, as if on air, and had passed through the barriers of time and space a very real, if crumbling, piece of parchment on which, drawn in what appeared to be a fading paint, was an illustration of the Ishtar Gate of ancient Babylon.

Having done that, he returned to the light, which then flared up and disappeared, leaving everything normal once more.

Jerry remembered it vividly. He didn't remember it – he still lived it; as he still lived what had happened in Babylon.

He and Ingrid had returned to London, overwhelmed by their experiences, had holed up in another hotel while applying for visas to Baghdad, had managed to get them after much reluctance by the Iraqi embassy, and had then ventured forth again, to visit ancient Babylon in al-Hillah, sixty miles south of Baghdad . . . this time to an adventure which even for them had no parallel.

Jerry tried not to think of that adventure as he drove back to Baghdad . . . it was too much to contemplate.

Instead, he glanced sideways at Ingrid, who was obviously exhausted, and asked, 'Are you sleeping?'

'Yes,' she said. 'Please don't waken me.'

'Ah,' he said. 'Right!'

'I want to sleep, but I'm frightened of dreaming, which makes sleep impossible.'

'I know what you mean,' he said.

And indeed he did, since sleep eluded him also, the very closing of his eyes being an invitation to recollections almost beyond the comprehensible.

They had arrived in Baghdad yesterday and drove straight to al-Hillah, a modern town built from the bricks taken over the centuries from the ruins of Nebuchadrezzar's Babylon. Driving up to the replica of the Ishtar gate at the entrance to the site, with its baked clay bas-reliefs of sacred animals, arched door and twin towers, he had experienced a sense of eerie desolation and the hauntings of silence. They had arrived in the afternoon. Because of the war there were no tourists, and so they spent a leisurely few hours exploring the extensive ancient ruins by the Euphrates River – including the remains of Nebuchadrezzar's palace where Alexander the Great died; the Emakh temple; the banquet hall where Belshazzar saw the handwriting on the wall; the site of the Tower of Babel; and finally, the foundations of the Hanging Gardens – deemed in Hellenistic times one of the Seven Wonders of the World – where they decided to wait for the sunset and their next magical experience.

When the sun set they *had* that experience, and would never forget it.

'Are you sure we're on the right track?' he asked Ingrid, feeling anxious.

'Yes,' she replied patiently or, perhaps, wearily, looking down at the map of Baghdad spread out on her knees. 'It's a street in a bazaar near the Mosque of Kadhimain, a few miles north of the city, on the west bank of the Tigris. Don't worry, we'll find it.'

'I just wonder if that blind seer exists.'

'He'll exist,' Ingrid said. 'Saint-Germain wouldn't tell us to go there if he didn't exist. He just doesn't work that way.'

When she said that, he realized just how completely he had come to accept the fact of Saint-Germain's magical existence – which may, as he also realized, have been Saint-Germain's purpose in exposing him and Ingrid so gradually to his incredible world.

What should have been impossible to comprehend,

323

let alone accept as fact, now seemed like the only reality in what had once been, at least to him, a material world. Now, he was adjusting to it – or at least accepting that other world – and he sensed that part of the purpose of this great search was to aid that adjustment.

They eventually arrived at the Mosque of Kadhimain, a few miles north of Baghdad, and parked the car near the bazaar marked so clearly on Ingrid's map.

As they walked through the labyrinthine lanes and alleys, past stalls and shops filled with copper and silver and cloth, brushing shoulders with Arabs, Afghans, Armenians, Kurds, Lurs and Sabaeans, hearing the sharp chatter of Arabic in Kurdish, Turkish and Syriac dialects, he realized how he, who had never left America before, had also begun to accept as perfectly normal the diverse strangeness of foreign peoples.

In fact, as he searched with Ingrid for the shop drawn on the map given to him in a miraculous manner, the very strangeness of the environment, instead of overwhelming him, made him think back on all the places he had seen since beginning this journey: Athens, Olympia, Crete, the Cyclades; then Izmir in Turkey, now here in Baghdad, the foremost city of ancient Mesopotamia, in an Islamic country at war. These places, and his experiences with Saint-Germain, had changed him completely, perhaps irrevocably.

'Here it is, I think,' Ingrid said.

They were at a shop selling copper pots and pans, at the very far end of the bazaar, where the narrow lane broadened into waste ground, over which much rubbish was strewn. In the distance, beyond the rooftops of the bazaar, they could see the golden domes and minarets of the magnificent Mosque of Kadhimain, over which a few grey clouds were drifting; but here there was an air of desolation and poverty.

An old turbaned woman was sitting on a wooden chair in the entrance to the shop, wiping sweat from her face with the hem of a faded blouse and watching the bright-eyed Arab boy who was rearranging the pots in the open window. Ingrid spoke to the old woman in faltering Arabic, and the boy, hearing her speak, looked up and offered a radiant smile.

'English?'

'Sort of,' Ingrid replied.

'I speak English,' the boy said.

'We've come to see the blind man,' Ingrid said. 'Hasan al-Takriti.'

'You wish to buy something?'

'No. We wish to speak to him.'

'Okay. Follow me.'

They were led into the cluttered front part of the shop, then through the small, equally untidy room behind it, and finally into a spartan bedroom, lit only by the striations of sunlight beaming in through one open window.

The room was dusty and smelt of human decay.

Propped up on a small, rickety cot was a very old man with a white beard and unshorn hair, a head seemingly far too big for his shrivelled body, and enormous, glassily brilliant blind eyes.

He had no arms or legs.

Jerry twitched with shock, but managed to control it; and felt, rather than heard, Ingrid sucking in her breath beside him. Also taking a deep breath, he focused his gaze on the lips of the old man, avoiding as much as possible the limbless torso below those glassy, sightless eyes in that unnaturally large head.

The man moved his head slightly, left to right, up and down, as if trying to observe the room through his ears. The boy spoke to him in Arabic, then, smiling encouragingly at Jerry and Ingrid, took a chair by the bed. The old man moved his head in their direction, his sightless eyes turning towards them while his lips, shaking slightly beneath his moustache, finally spoke in a whisper.

'Hadim says you are English.'

'I'm actually American,' Jerry replied. 'My name's Jerry Remick. And this is Ingrid Zweig. German by birth, but educated in England and Europe.'

'You wish to see me?'

'We were *sent* to see you.'

'Ah,' the old man said. 'I understand. You have visited Babylon.'

'You were expecting us?'

'Yes. I have been aware of your approach since yesterday. I was told you would come here.'

'Told by whom?'

'The only one I can see. The one who often comes to me.'

'Saint-Germain?'

'He has many names. And has lived many times.'

The old man's head looked almost as big as his limbless torso, and again Jerry felt a shiver go through him at what he was seeing: a blind accident of fate, life's hidden nightmare, the unthinkable moulded in flesh and blood by some demon creator.

As if sensing what he was thinking, the old man smiled at him.

'Were you prepared for me?' he asked.

'No,' Jerry replied.

'I was born like this, my son, so know of no other way. The pain was greater for my mother than for I, the nightmare more lasting. We are all born in innocence. Nothing can change that fact. In my innocence I accepted my condition as being the normal; I only knew that I *was*. And why should I know otherwise? I was fed, clothed and bathed. I grew into manhood like a baby, taking what I was given, protected by blindness. I have never seen a human being. I cannot touch with my fingers. I can only *imagine* what humans look like – though you are forced to see me. Only later, in adolescence, was I told what I was, and suffered great horror and revulsion for a long time thereafter.'

Although he was sweating, Jerry went cold all over, imagining what that creature on the bed had endured when his innocence was replaced with the knowledge of what he actually was to those who could see. He would have screamed in terrible silence, falling backwards through his terror, then turned over with the lurching of his heart to see the face of insanity. Somewhere, down there, in the dark hole of his Self, imprisoned in a mind supported by a limbless torso, he would have quivered like a fly in a spider's web, viewing God as a nightmare . . .

Yet he had somehow survived it.

'I retreated into myself,' he explained, 'into the hidden depths at my centre, and found that my spirit was more abiding than the shell of my body. I took faith from that, ignoring the flesh, exploring the spirit, and found sanity in this dialogue with myself, the acceptance of *being*. I found that the world of mind, which is the spirit, had no limitations – that I could travel back and forth at will, through time and space, gaining sight by so doing. The material world, which before had been but darkness, took shape inside me, and I no longer needed eyes to see, nor limbs to feel with. I recreated the material world within myself and took my place in it.'

Jerry looked at Ingrid, aware of what she must be feeling, observed the tight line of her lips, the teeth biting her lower lip. His heart went out to her, but the voice of the limbless blind man, a deathly whisper, drew his reluctant gaze back to the bed, to the nightmare ensconced there.

'Thus, I found serenity, the absolute of existence. A nightmare to others, I transcended my physical prison and located the beauty of the Self that few mortals see. Sightless, without limbs, I saw and touched the All, and because I was in that state of grace, he recognized me and came to me.'

'Saint-Germain?'

'To me, he is nameless. He simply appears in the radiance of his light – as he also appeared to you. I saw him approach you in ancient Babylon, where he passed on my name. He passed my name and address through space and time and brought you to this room. He has his reasons. I know them not.'

Listening, Jerry was transported back to the ruins of ancient Babylon, to when he and Ingrid had waited in the full moon for something to happen – and in that instance they not only observed it, but were actually sucked into it . . .

The light had materialized through the low clouds, first a pinprick, then a large, silvery plate, then that familiar globe of magical light with a dark inner core. It grew bigger as it descended, finally hovered above the ruins, spreading out until it covered the ancient stones and made them seem to dissolve.

Saint-Germain did not emerge immediately. Instead the dissolving ruins started changing. They changed shape, becoming what they had been, and then Babylon reappeared, the largest city in the world, spreading out magnificently on both banks of the Euphrates river, the older city on the east bank, the rebuilt city on the west, the great walls forming a triangle placed flat on the earth, with the Palace of Nebuchadrezzar II enclosed in its apex, north of the Greek Theatre and Main Citadel.

Jerry first saw it from a distance, his gaze drawn to the blue-glaze temple surmounting the 300-foot high Tower of Babel, then taking in the other four temples in the eastern half of the city, then dissolving *into* the city with Ingrid beside him. And then, by some miracle, he found himself in what he knew to be the suburb of Esagila, where the quays were packed with trading vessels, warehouses and hundreds of workers, most of whom were swarming in and out of the warehouses, and up and down the many gangplanks, carrying copper goods and leather, baskets bulging with dates, sacks of wheat and barley and trays stacked with goat's cheese.

It was a scene of extraordinary industry, exotic, cacophonous.

Jerry stood there on a quay, wearing common robes like Ingrid, feeling unreal as they waited for Saint-Germain to appear on the deck of the sailing ship which, looming over them and creaking against the river, its decks also swarming with labourers and seamen, was obviously being prepared for another journey across the high seas.

Then Saint-Germain appeared, a Chaldean regent, dressed in finery, and came down the gangplank with armed men in front and rear, their swords glittering in the brilliant light of noon, their leather straps and sandals covered in dust and gleaming with sweat.

Jerry felt that he was dreaming, yet was vividly aware, and witnessed himself taking the parchment that Saint-Germain handed to him. Saint-Germain smiled at him. Brilliant sunlight flashed around him. He dissolved into that light, as did the ship eventually; then the light became blinding, filling his eyes with stars, and he glanced sideways and saw Ingrid melting into that silvery haze. He called out to her, felt her hand, grasping her fingers desperately, then slipped into the arms of Morpheus and dreamed the dream he was dreaming.

When he awakened, he found himself beside the sleeping Ingrid, both of them in the ruins of the Hanging Garden in the grey light of dawn.

In his hand was a ragged, fading parchment on which was drawn a map of the bazaar near the Mosque of Kadhimain in modern Baghdad, with a spindly arrow pointing to a particular spot in the maze of alleys, and a message, written in that now very familiar, slightly archaic hand, saying: '*Visit the blind seer in the shadow of the Temple — for only the blind can truly see . . .*' It was signed: *Saint-Germain*.

Now, staring at the blind seer, who was also without limbs, Jerry shuddered to think of how he had been brought here, still unable to credit it. He placed his hand on Ingrid's shoulder, squeezed it encouragingly, then returned his attention to the old man, who, as if sensing that he had done so, tilted his head again.

'So,' he said, 'you were sent here to learn something. What is it you wish to know?'

'I have been led to believe that Saint-Germain might be thousands of years old. I want to know if that's true or not.'

'You had your proof this morning, my son, at the ruins of Babylon. What more do you need?'

'How did I receive this message to visit you?'

'You *know* how you received it, young man — through time and space, from Saint-Germain.'

'Was I really in ancient Babylon?'

'If you perceived it, you lived it.'

'I could not receive a parchment from my thoughts.'

'What parchment? Where is it?'

Jerry looked at Ingrid who had been holding the ancient map, but she was staring down, amazed, at her hand, which clearly was empty.

'Where –?'

'I don't know,' Ingrid said, anticipating his question. 'I was holding it a couple of minutes ago. I swear, *I was holding it!*'

They both glanced down at the boy, but he was still in the chair, his feet hooked under its supports, his chin in his hands; then they glanced around the spartan, gloomy room, but the floor was completely bare. When Ingrid shrugged, looking very bewildered, Jerry turned back to the old man.

'We've lost it,' he said.

'You might never have had it,' the old man replied. 'On the other hand, perhaps you did – either way, you came here.'

'Where did Saint-Germain come from?' Jerry asked him.

'From prehistory – from beyond human knowledge – from the world that was then.'

'Atlantis?'

'Some would call it that. Others say it was Eden.'

'It is said that Atlantis was in the Aegean sea, and that it was destroyed in 1,500 BC when Santorini exploded. Was Saint-Germain alive at that time?'

'Naturally.'

'So that's where he came from?'

'No. It was simply one of his resting places. Saint-Germain has been to many places, and that was but one of them.'

'But all my indications are that he originated in Atlantis.'

'There is no single Atlantis. All the legends of lost civilizations such as Lemuria, Mu and Atlantis itself are based on the numerous lost civilizations throughout the history that preceded our own.'

'Modern historians would argue that point,' Ingrid said, 'claiming that there *were* no civilizations before our own.'

'They are wrong. The earliest of those civilizations existed millennia ago when the landmasses of Africa and India were joined. That was the first great maritime civilization, which eventually, through migration by land and sea over the centuries, found its way to another landmass in the Atlantic ocean, where a new civilization was formed from the influx of the old – and was, accordingly, called Atlantis.'

'Do you know anything about it?' Jerry asked.

'Not much. Only that it was highly developed and possessed a sacred stone called the Tuaoi Stone, or terrible crystal; but it suffered three periods of great destruction by natural causes, mainly volcanic. However, before the final destruction of that mighty civilization, the high priests removed the sacred stone from its location at the peak of their greatest temple of learning – which was in fact a pyramid, as were most of the Atlantian buildings – and took it with them when they fled by boat across the North Atlantic Ocean to the Mediterranean, past the so-called Pillars of Hercules, to the Aegean Sea between Crete and Santorini – to form another civilization, the one commonly mistaken for the original Atlantis.'

'And Saint-Germain was one of the high priests?'

'At that time, yes. Saint-Germain is a magical adept from that original Utopia – the one that existed about 200,000 years ago in the single landmass of Africa and India. He was one of those who migrated from that mighty civilization to form a new civilization, Atlantis, in the Atlantic Ocean. Between the three great catastrophes which destroyed that civilization – over a period of approximately 5,000 years, ending about 10,000 BC – Saint-Germain became a magical adept, discovered the Philosopher's Stone – the compound of the Tuaoi Stone – and through it learned the secrets of immortality, disappearing from and reappearing on earth when necessity called.'

'So he must have been one of the highest of high priests,' Jerry said.

'Yes. It was he who forecast the final destruction of that Atlantis, and thus fled with the sacred Tuaoi Stone and his higher adepts – just before their civilization had disappeared under the waves of the Azores and Sargasso Sea – to the welcoming islands of the Aegean Sea, and there formed the foundations for another civilization. Over the next centuries, that great and powerful civilization conquered North Africa, including Egypt; and in the latter, about 4,000 BC, more pyramids were built and the Tuaoi Stone, or terrible crystal, was placed at the peak of the mightiest of those constructions – the Great Pyramid of Cheops at Giza.'

'Which was built about 2,500 BC,' Ingrid said.

'In 2170 BC, to be precise,' the blind seer corrected her. 'The higher adepts of the Aegean Atlantis travelled by sea to Egypt because they wished to build their great instruments of astronomy and alchemy – the pyramids – at the exact centre of the world's land mass, which at that time was at Giza, in Egypt. In 2170 BC, when the Great Pyramid was built, its summit pointed to the sun at noon – and at midnight of the autumnal equinox, it pointed to Alcyone in the constellation Pleiades, the centre of the then known universe. The number of days in the solar year is set in the measurement of the Great Pyramid's base perimeter, a hundred pyramid inches being given to each day. The pyramid inch, 1.001 of the modern inch, is exactly one five hundred millionth of the polar axis of the earth.'

'I don't wish to be rude,' Ingrid said gently, 'but how do you know all that? You are limbless and blind and have spent your life in that bed, so how could you –?'

'I have been taught all these things by Saint-Germain, who also told me that in the pyramid's inner chambers students of the mystery religions – astrology, alchemy, and other esoteric traditions – were initiated, including Plato and Pythagoras. Yes, the Great Pyramid was first an observatory, then a temple of occult learning, and only in its final stages a burial chamber – though even this was merely an acknowledged ritual, since no actual persons were buried there, but only the symbols of life.'

'So the Tuaoi Stone was placed at the top of the Great Pyramid about 270 years before the Atlantis in the Aegean Sea was destroyed, about 1,500 BC, in the tidal waves caused by the explosion of Santorini. Presumably it was later removed from the tip of the Great Pyramid by the magical adepts who were then looking after it – but why? And where did they take it?'

'It was removed because a corrupt civilization was encroaching upon Egypt and the magical adepts fled from that encroachment. Where they went eventually, I cannot say – since the whereabouts of the Tuaoi Stone is only revealed to those who are chosen in their own lifetime to become an adept. I have not been so chosen, but am hopeful that that day will be soon. That is all I can tell you.'

'Does the society of magical adepts still exist?'

'Yes, my son. Naturally. After all, *Saint-Germain* exists – and he is the highest of the high – though where they are, I do not know.'

'Are any of the adepts,' Ingrid asked, 'apart from Saint-Germain, human beings with whom we could identify?'

'Yes,' the old man said. 'I have already mentioned two of them – Plato and Pythagoras – and the others I know only as names that have sprung from Saint-Germain's lips over the years: Nebuchadrezzar, Jesus, Buddha, Mohammed, the wizard Merlin, Roger Bacon, Christian Rosenkreuz, Georg Faust, Paracelsus, Christopher Marlowe, Lord Lytton ... the list goes on, my son. It is a thread running back to the darkness of prehistory, winding around the present and then on to an as yet unknown future. They exist. They are here and now.'

'Did you say *Georg Faust*?' Jerry asked him.

'I believe so,' the old man replied. 'That name rings in my head with all the others.'

'Is there anything else you can tell me?' Jerry asked, feeling removed from himself. 'Anything at all?'

'No,' the old man said. 'You were sent here to learn all I know – and that *is* all I know.'

Jerry took a deep breath, glanced at Ingrid, and saw that she was looking slightly dazed, her gaze lost in the infinite mysteries of history and the problematical future. He thought of Saint-Germain as a Chaldean regent in ancient Babylon, wearing Anatolian robes in another time and place, sitting urbanely in a neat suit in the boat on the River Nile, of his impossible presence here, there and everywhere, in the past and the present. He was one or many men, possessed extraordinary powers, and was part of some secret society that had emerged from the distant past, survived throughout the ages, and now had tentacles reaching out across the globe for some obscure purpose. Yes, it was a conspiracy, a vast, complex plot, and he and Ingrid were being sucked into it and might never escape.

Shaken by these thoughts, he reached out to Ingrid and took hold of her shoulder, feeling her reality, the warmth and softness of skin and blood. Then he stepped towards the old man, wanting to touch him as well, to place his fingers on that large brow, above the bllnd eyes, and let that creature without arms and legs at least *feel* his gratitude.

He was just about to do so – had actually reached the old man – when the woman outside screamed, copper pots fell to the floor, and two Caucasians, both wearing light grey suits, burst into the room, slapping Ingrid aside, pushing Jerry against the wall – one of them staring stupified at the *thing* on the bed, the other pressing his pistol against Jerry's forehead and spitting into his face.

'Make one move and you're dead,' he said.

CHAPTER THIRTY

Ingrid pressed herself against the wall and tried to avoid the murderous gaze of the hoodlum in front of her, which only caused her to look across the small room to where Jerry was likewise pressed against a wall, but with the barrel of the other hoodlum's pistol tapping his forehead.

That sight only made her heart race all the more, so she glanced obliquely at the blind man on the bed, saw his head tilting as he concentrated on what was happening; beside him the boy slid off his chair and stood upright, his lovely brown eyes flicking from one hoodlum to the other in disbelief and excitement.

Then the hoodlum in front of her slapped her face again, took hold of her chin, shook her head viciously and snarled, 'Keep your goddamned eyes to the front; otherwise I'll get nervous.' He pulled something from his pocket and a glittering blade snapped open before her eyes. '*Verstehen Sie mich?*'

'Yes,' she replied, ashamed to be shaking. 'I understand.'

'Good,' he sneered. '*Very* good!'

He waved the blade threateningly in front of her eyes, then turned his gaze towards the door of the room as, accompanied by the clatter of more falling copper pots, the old woman who had been sitting out front was thrown roughly into the room, followed by a third hoodlum, this one wearing an immaculate tropical suit and matching shoes, his lavender shirt open at the collar, his black hair thick with grease. He stared calmly around the small room while the other woman whimpered, then fixed his gaze on the limbless blind man on the bed and said, 'Christ, what's *that*?'

'He's blind,' Ingrid said.

'He's more than *blind*!' the man said. 'So,' he continued, looking directly at her, 'you're Zweig's runaway daughter.' When she didn't reply, he turned his calm gaze on Jerry. 'And you're the American he wants. Well, nice to know you kid.'

Looking at the man from under the barrel of the pistol leaning lightly against his forehead, Jerry likewise didn't respond.

'You're being very wise,' the man said. 'Silence is golden. But it won't be so golden if you try to avoid answering my questions.'

'Go to hell,' Jerry said.

'You're not as smart as I thought,' the man said. 'I'm real disappointed.'

He glanced down at the old Arab woman, who was whimpering on hands and knees, at the bug-eyed boy, then looked intently at the blind, limbless man, the *thing*, on the bed. Seeing him fully, he shook his head from side to side, as if in weary perplexity.

'Can he at least *hear*?' he asked the boy.

'Yes,' the boy said.

The smooth hoodlum looked at Jerry, grinned crookedly and said, 'And you were sent to see *this* old fucker? What the hell could *he* know?'

'Nothing,' Jerry said.

'You lying shit,' the hoodlum replied. 'If you came here to see him, he must know *something* – though God knows what it is.' He grinned laconically again, almost amiably. 'Never mind,' he added. 'We'll find out soon enough. Hey you! You on your hands and knees. Stop all that snivelling!'

The old woman stared up at him, her eyes wide and

frightened, then crawled away and huddled up in a corner while the old man's head moved.

'Who are you?' the old man asked, his voice firm. 'What do you want here?'

'Shut your mouth,' the smooth hoodlum said. 'You'll have plenty of time to talk. Only then, when you do, you'll be *answering* questions, not asking them, buddy.'

'I don't like your tone of voice,' the old man said. 'I refuse to talk to you.'

The smooth hoodlum stared at him, then walked up to the bed. He gave the old man's face a short, sharp slap, then stepped away again.

'Be careful, my friend,' he said. 'Don't get on my nerves. You could soon find yourself without a tongue, without ears or nose, let alone arms and legs – so try not to annoy me.'

'Who are you?' Jerry asked. 'Do you work for that bastard, Zweig?'

'He wouldn't like to hear you calling him names. Believe me, Remick, he wouldn't.' The man turned to Ingrid, looking her up and down as if examining merchandise, then settling his gaze on her face. 'I'm Louis Palladinos from New York. I freelance. These two goons belong to your old man, who wants you back home real quick.'

'And what about him?' Ingrid asked, indicating Jerry.

'Your dad has a use for him.'

She closed her eyes for a moment, thought of her father, felt a wave of revulsion wash through her and opened her eyes again. She caught Jerry staring at her, saw a flickering smile, then returned her attention to Palladinos.

'How did you find us?' she asked him.

'*Find* you? We never lost you in the first place. You know your old man, lady. He's got eyes and ears everywhere. This is the age of telecommunications and secret agents, and I'm just another one of the many who work for your Dad.'

Ingrid felt like a fly caught in a spider's web. She could actually visualize that great web, a network of electric cables and satellite links and fax machines, of anonymous spies in airports and hotels and parked vans – and there, in the middle of it, biding his time, watching distantly, was the spider that would eventually destroy them – namely, her father.

She looked at Jerry, felt a rush of love for him, then reluctantly returned her gaze to Palladinos, whose crooked grin was malicious.

'What I want to know,' he said, 'is exactly what you've found out about the so-called Tuaoi Stone and that guy who knows all about it, the Count of Saint-Germain. Now do *you* want to tell me?'

'No,' Ingrid said, surprised at her sudden lack of fear and urge to defy him.

'Are you sure?'

'Go to hell.'

Palladinos sighed. 'I like a woman of spirit. I've surely got to admire that.' He then turned slightly, pushed the barrel of the other hoodlum's pistol aside, and stared intently at Jerry.

'You're sweating,' he said.

'It's hot in here.'

'I'm cool as a cucumber,' Palladinos said, 'but you're sweating a lot.' His grin broadened as his gaze flickered towards Ingrid, before returning to Jerry.

'Okay,' he said, 'are *you* going to tell me what Zweig wants to know?'

'No,' Jerry said.

'I think you might.'

'I won't.'

Palladinos nodded, as if understanding, then snapped

his fingers at the hoodlum in front of Ingrid and said, 'Get her prepared.'

The hoodlum grabbed her by the collar of her blouse, tightened it into a noose, then used it to jerk her upwards, until her toes were barely resting on the ground. He placed the blade of his knife under her nose and stared coldly at her.

'We've been following you for so long,' Palladinos said, 'and now you won't even talk to us. My feelings are hurt.' He turned back to Jerry and said, 'She won't look so good when her nose is gone, so why not save her embarrassment?'

Ingrid tried to call out to him, but the collar of her blouse, being like a noose, was choking her.

'No!' she croaked. 'Don't tell him a thing. Don't give my father that pleasure!'

Jerry, though unable to move his head because of the pistol, at least managed to turn his eyes towards Palladinos.

'That's Zweig's *daughter*,' he said. 'I don't think that even a bastard like Zweig would let you cut up his daughter.'

Palladinos just chuckled mockingly. 'Oh, really?' he said. 'I think he'd let me do *more* than that. A man who poisons his wife wouldn't hesitate to kill his kid as well. And it was this bitch' – here he nodded to Ingrid – 'whose mother he poisoned . . . so this bitch can be cut up.'

Hearing those words, Ingrid felt a dreadful pain, something geysering up from her centre and exploding right through her.

'No!' she muttered. 'No . . . you couldn't know . . . I don't believe . . .'

'I couldn't know, lady? Who the hell are you trying to kid? I work for a lot of people and each one of them has some dirt on all the others. I did some work for the

KGB before I worked for your father. I was *following* your father for the KGB and they gave me his file. Not all of it, of course, but enough to describe him . . . and one of the items enclosed was about the death of your mother. Your old man poisoned your mother, kid, and the KGB know it.'

Ingrid felt sick, filled with pain and disbelief, almost dizzy with shock at receiving confirmation of something that she had tried to deny for years. She had learned through relatives long ago of the mysterious death of her grandmother in a car accident that rumour said had been arranged by Zweig; of the equally mysterious death of her mother's parents when they opposed Zweig's plans to marry her; and, most horribly, of the widely held belief that Zweig had been instrumental in murdering his last wife, Ingrid's mother – officially reported as suicide – by feeding her cyanide . . . but Palladinos's words resounded in her head with a shocking finality.

It was true, then, and could no longer be doubted, that her father had throughout his lifetime murdered anyone who stood in his way, even including her mother.

Yes . . . he had murdered her mother. Now she had to accept that fact.

The tears sprang to her eyes before she could control them, blurred her vision when she tried to stare at Jerry and take comfort from him. She saw his flushed cheeks and raging eyes, then was drawn back to Palladinos's icy grin and the murderous leer of the larger hoodlum holding her by the throat, with his knife at her nostrils.

'First I'll smash your specs into your eyes,' he said, 'then I'll chop off your nose. That's some lover you've got.'

'What are these barbarians doing in here?' the blind man said. 'Remove this filth from my home.'

Startled, Palladinos glanced down at the *thing* on the bed. 'Jesus,' he said. 'We got a bean-bag with a talking head on top – and it's trying to *threaten* us. Franz,' he added, looking at the hoodlum guarding Jerry, 'when we've finished with the Yank, we'll start on that freak. He should sing like a bird. And now to Miss Zweig . . .'

He was just turning to give his instructions to the goon holding Ingrid when the Arab boy by the chair, incensed by the threat to the blind old man, dived at the goon threatening Jerry and sank his teeth in his leg. The man bawled and kicked the boy aside, spinning away from Jerry, while the man holding Ingrid let her go to glance over his shoulder. The old woman screamed, the boy rolled across the floor, and Jerry grabbed a copper pot that was resting on a table and brought it down heavily on the bawling hood's head. The hood dropped his pistol, staggering sideways as he did so, and as the second hood raised his pistol to take aim at Jerry, Ingrid stamped brutally on his toes and started *him* bawling.

Jerry picked up the pistol, and started fumbling inexpertly with it while Palladinos, seeing the weapon in his hand, fled from the room. The pistol went off by accident, sending a bullet into the ceiling, and as plaster rained down upon them the other two hoodlums also fled.

Jerry rushed out of the room in pursuit and Ingrid rushed out after him, frightened at what he was doing and calling him back. She caught up with him outside, by the door of the shop, just as he took aim with the pistol and fired at the three men as they tried to make their escape in a Jeep.

Ingrid winced when the pistol fired, the noise whipping through her, then she saw one of the men jerking violently, grabbing at his shoulder, losing his balance and falling out of the Jeep. He fell sideways

343

into the road, sending up a cloud of dust, then rolled over and yelped loudly with pain.

Jerry looked down disbelievingly at the pistol in his hand, blew the smoke away from its barrel, then hurried along the road to where the hoodlum was trying to sit upright, holding one hand over the bleeding hole in his right shoulder. With a brutality that Ingrid had never seen in him before, Jerry grabbed the man by the collar of his jacket and, ignoring his yelps of pain, dragged him roughly along the street and back into the shop.

'Oh, Christ!' the man yelped. 'It hurts! *Don't hurt me no more!*'

'Shut up!' Jerry said, then turned back to Ingrid and added: 'Stay outside, Ingrid. I don't want you to see what I'm doing, so don't come back in until I tell you.'

'Oh, God, Jerry,' she said, 'what on earth are you going to do to him? Don't –'

'There are things I've got to know,' he replied grimly. 'And there comes a time when civilized rules don't apply any longer. Stay outside and try not to listen.'

'Oh, Jerry –'

'*No*, Ingrid!'

He pushed her away from the doorway, then disappeared into the shop. She could hear the wounded man groaning. Jerry told him to shut up. There was silence, then the clattering of copper pots falling over, then the man cried out, 'No! Oh, God no! Not that! Please don't do that!'

She couldn't stand to listen and walked further along the street, stopping in front of a shop selling lace and leather goods. She heard a cry of protest, shuddered and covered her ears with her hands and licked her dry lips.

Jerry was obviously torturing the man. She couldn't accept that he was capable of it. As she tried to imagine what he might be doing, then remembered her father, she began to think that Jerry wasn't much different, that inflicting pain thrilled him.

She uncovered her ears. 'No, please!' the man screamed. *'Don't!'* Horrified, she pressed her hands over her ears again, then closed her eyes.

She thought of her mother lying ill in bed, of Zweig murdering her and making it seem like suicide – she thought of that and *still* couldn't condone Jerry's torture of her father's hired hoodlum. She remembered her father's cruelty, the many times he had humiliated her – and even that didn't reconcile her to what Jerry was doing.

What Jerry was doing was wrong, and that's all there was to it.

Determined not to let him sink to the same depths as her father, she removed her hands from her ears and hurried back to the shop. However, just before she reached it, the wounded man was thrown out of the doorway into the street, where he fell on his hands and knees, looked despairingly at her then stood up, still holding onto his bloody shoulder, and suddenly raced away from her.

Jerry followed him out and watched him rush off, then he took hold of Ingrid's elbow and led her away, heading back along the narrow, crowded lane, between shops and stalls piled high with goods and attended by voluble Arab traders.

She tried to break free of his grip, to stop walking, but he just dragged her on.

'I've already said goodbye on your behalf,' he said. 'There's no need to go back there.'

'I don't want to go back. I just want to –'

'Be quiet,' he interjected rudely. 'Just keep walking.

We have to go back to the car and then drive to our hotel. We have lots to talk about.'

'Yes,' she said. '*Lots!*'

She wanted to talk about how he had changed – about how he had tortured that wounded man, about how corruption bred corruption, about how he would not be able to live with himself after what he had done – but he didn't give her the chance, kept shutting her up when she tried to speak, and only let her get her words out when they were back in their hotel in central Baghdad, in their room overlooking Al-Tahreer Square, with the traffic creating a constant bedlam below them, the air hot and stifling.

'How *could* you –?' she managed to get out, before he cut her short again as he ripped off his shirt, threw it angrily on the floor and, standing bare-chested before her, said: 'I got that bastard to talk. He sang like a bird. He told me that your father's made some kind of pact with the Soviets, that they've finally insisted he find out just what we've learned about Saint-Germain. You were going to be taken hostage and, unless I played ball and continued the search for Saint-Germain and the Tuaoi Stone, you were going to be terminated. Now do you understand my main point, Ingrid? Your father, the uncivilized bastard, would even have *you* killed!'

'*Uncivilized!* And do you think you're any better? What did you *do* to that poor man? Pull out his finger-nails?'

'Poor man?' Jerry looked astounded. '*What* poor man? That *poor man* was going to deliver you to some Soviet who would kill you if I failed to find the Tuaoi Stone – and you're worried about *him*!'

'You tortured him! That makes you no better than he is! God, you're despicable!'

'*Tortured* him?' Jerry said. Then slowly a mischievous grin broke on his face. 'Oh, yeah,' he continued, 'I

346

tortured him all right. I submitted him to the worst torture of all. I told him that if he didn't tell me what he knew, I'd pass on his whereabouts to Zweig – along with the news that he had failed to capture us. You heard how he responded.'

She felt confused at first, then she realized what he meant, and the irony made the laughter bubble up and pour out of her, setting her free. Still laughing, she fell backwards onto the bed, her feet resting on the floor, and stared up at him, wanting to feel him, to touch and be touched by him.

When she understood that and couldn't deny it, she suddenly stopped laughing.

'Kiss me,' she said.

She was shocked by her own words – or by what they had implied – yet as he stood over her, looking down at her, she knew that she wanted him to fall upon her and crush her out of existence. He didn't quite do that, but he did at least lean over her, supporting himself on his hands, his legs pressed against her knees, his face just above her face, then smiled like someone being given a gift and lowered himself gently onto her.

Lying upon her, he kissed her.

That kiss made her die, resurrecting her as someone else. She opened her eyes and saw his smile, his loving gaze, his bare chest, and knew she was about to escape at last from her father's bleak influence.

'Touch me,' she said. 'Do what you want. I want to *know* what you want. I want to *be* what you want. Touch me now. Touch me everywhere!'

He kissed her again, sliding his tongue between her lips. He kissed her a lot on the lips and then moved elsewhere. She felt his lips on her throat, on her shoulders; and she drowned in what he was doing, lost herself and was reborn. When he unbuttoned her

347

blouse and slipped it off her shoulders, she was warmed by an ethereal heat, radiated an inner light.

She *wanted* to be reborn, to become someone else (a woman), and she moved herself in towards his hands and the length of his body. She felt his fingers all over, on her shoulders, breasts and hips, then they tugged her denims down her legs as she kicked her shoes off. She heard the shoes fall to the floor, first the left one, then the right; and the air, which had been warm, seemed much cooler when it covered her bare legs.

'God, I want you,' he said.

His words came to her like magic, igniting her desire, blowing away former inhibitions as she gave herself to him. She arched her spine, became a bridge, thrusting up to feel his hands, subsided beneath the pressure of his fingers when they pressed on her stomach. Her heart started to race. She had great difficulty in breathing. She thought briefly of the fear that her father had instilled in her, then felt herself smiling, her defiance like a soft flame, and let the fingers sliding along her body defeat that fear forever.

'God, I love you!'

'And I love *you*, Ingrid!'

'Come inside me,' she said to him.

She hardly recognized her own voice (it was too husky and sensual), but she knew that the fire spreading through her came from her own flesh. She was aware of his fingers (where they touched her, she glowed) and felt the whole length of him against her, felt herself melting into him. She wanted him – yes, and wanted to *be* him – and when he gently rolled upon her, when he moved between her legs, when he entered her and seemed, at that instant, to *become* her, she lost awareness of everything but sensation, *pure* sensation, and heard nothing but the languorous groaning that emerged from her lips.

'Yes!' that husky, sensual, stranger's voice said somewhere above her. 'Oh, Jerry! *Oh, yes!*'

Then all thought slid away from her.

CHAPTER THIRTY-ONE

For the next seven days, the time of creation, Jerry lost and found himself in Ingrid's body, thus recreating himself.

With her spectacles removed and her long hair loose at last, with her slim but curvaceous body divested finally of its protective clothing, Ingrid was no longer a demure, childlike woman, but a voluptuous, wanton creature of the night, her lips swollen from kissing him.

Her naked body was a revelation, an alien, wondrous object, an exquisitely smooth terrain that rose and fell and kept yielding surprises. He was dazzled by its revealed shape, its sensual hollows and curves, its ability to repose itself endlessly and keep him entranced. He loved the long length of her legs, their curves accentuated by arched feet; was thrilled by the sight of her brown nipples on her creamy-white breasts.

'God, I love your breasts,' he told her. 'I could play with them all night. I love squeezing and licking and stroking them or just simply holding them. And I love the way they feel against my face when I'm having a rest.'

'Don't have a rest,' she responded. 'It's too early to rest.'

The mind was *not* all. He was learning that at last. What counted was his newly discovered feelings and his body's release. He felt incandescent, in a constant state of excitation, and he wanted the glory of his love to lift him out of his mortal shell.

Her body was joined to his, and moved with his to

love's rhythms, and he found himself losing himself inside her, body and soul. He went winging into the ether, somewhere outside time and space, and caught a glimpse of his transcendental other half, with its heady potential. He was temporarily inviolate, beyond fear or self-doubt, and felt that he was gliding through a cosmos created by love.

The foreplay and the fulfilment soon became one and the same, a seamless merging of tactile sensation with great emotional release. He often felt himself melting, dissolving into her pores; becoming *her* other half, her alter ego or *doppelgänger*, even as he was conquered. What he gave, he received – he only won what he surrendered – and her body and spirit became extensions of his newly found Self.

'God,' he said at one stage, 'I can't believe this is you. I can't even believe it's *me*. I always thought we were both so inhibited. How did *this* start?'

'It just did,' she replied. 'It was bound to happen sooner or later, and finally it did. I think those men had something to do with it. At least *my father* certainly had. I finally accepted what he had done to my mother, and in doing that lost my fear of him. That excited me, Jerry. I was free as a bird. When I knew that, I also wanted you and couldn't wait any longer. So, here we are.'

'I'm delighted,' he said. 'I'm gonna stay here forever. You feel as soft as a bed of feathers beneath me, but you're warmer and smoother.'

'I'm glowing. I'm burning. I feel like an electric light-bulb. I never imagined a man's body could do that to me. Only you. Oh, you *sweet* man!'

She bit his ear, stroked his flanks, curled one leg languidly over him, licked his lips with the stem of her tongue and then kissed him passionately.

'Yes!' she whispered. '*Again!*'

After that, they would make love, have a bath, eat and drink; return to bed and make love again, letting daytime turn into night and back into day. They got their food from room-service, usually consumed it half-heartedly, and invariably returned to their passionate lovemaking, with the blinds always drawn and the room in half darkness, the traffic roaring and honking in the square outside the hotel as their bodies inter-twined athletically, their sweat soaking the tangled sheets.

He worshipped her naked body, was obsessed with its shape and touch, lost and found himself upon it, below it, inside it – and also in her voice, her sighs, her moist, hazel eyes.

Indeed, her eyes were a revelation – without the spectacles they were lovely – and he studied their misty depths, their beguiling warmth and lurking wickedness, and adored them even more when they were framed by the long hair that had, at last, been set free to enrapture him further.

Her long hair was erotic to him, soft as silk, fine as gossamer, and he often wiped his face with it, simply wanting to feel it.

'Your hair's fantastic,' he said. 'I never knew it was so beautiful. Don't ever pin it up again, Ingrid. Let it hang loose and glorious.'

'Oh, no!' she protested. 'Not in public!'

'Why not?'

'Men might think I was trying to attract them, and I couldn't stand that.'

So they made love again, with more confidence, even expertly, learning from one another, taking and giving what was needed, and sobbing and groaning their way into a trance of delight. Jerry felt that he was hypnotized, enslaved by his own raptures, but his journey into sensuality, while electrifying and uplifting,

352

gradually made him think of other travels and their accompanying mysteries.

He saw the stars of boundless space, disc-shaped lights in the ether, himself gliding over the green breast of Earth to snow-covered mountain peaks. And there, in the mountains, in a cavern hacked from the rocks, he saw Saint-Germain and his mysterious partner, both wearing dark robes . . .

He returned when Ingrid cried out, winging back through time and space, and found himself sheltering in her arms with his heart racing madly. He was here – and also there. He was with Ingrid – and then with them. He recovered, as she did, by eating and drinking lightly, then lay back beside her on the bed, distractedly stroking her.

'Sooner or later . . .' he began.

'Yes, Jerry, I know.'

'Sooner or later we'll have to leave this room and go back to the search.'

She sighed. 'I suppose so.'

'No *supposing* about it. This isn't the *only* hotel room in the world – and we'll soon have to move on.'

'Where to this time?'

'I'm not sure,' he said. 'Let's discuss what we've got so far and work out what it means.'

This time she sighed forlornly. 'I suppose we better discuss what that blind man told you,' she said, wrapped up in his arms and not sounding very interested at all as she breathed into his ear.

'Yes,' he replied, as his breath started quickening. 'I suppose we should.'

'You think all that stuff he told you about earlier civilizations was true?'

'Well,' he said, again possessed of the urge to talk, sorting the facts out in his mind and wanting to check them, 'he said that that civilization existed about

200,000 years ago, when Africa and India were joined by a landmass – and it *is* now known that 180,000 years ago the land masses of Africa and India were adjacent, which is why there are startling resemblances between fossils found in both countries, and one of the reasons why nineteenth century scientists thought that the adjacent land masses of that time had formed a single great continent, which they called *Lemuria*, after the lemur, a mammal still found in both countries.'

Ingrid took a deep breath, let it out again, then took his limp penis into her hand to tenderly stroke it. 'Well, *that* certainly sounds interesting,' she said, sounding very distracted.

'Well,' he replied, looking down in wonder as his limp penis twitched a little in her delicate hand and then started hardening, 'I've just remembered something that has certain startling parallels to what that blind seer told us – and *he* certainly wouldn't have known about this.'

'Oh,' Ingrid crooned. 'Really?'

'Yes,' Jerry said, becoming excited for two reasons. 'According to Edgar Cayce, the great American clairvoyant, Atlantis was a vast island in the Atlantic Ocean, bigger than Europe, extending from the Sargasso Sea to the Azores and suffering three periods of destruction, from 15,600 BC to 10,000 BC, the first two splitting a single island into three smaller islands, the third destroying everything.'

'Well, *that* certainly matches what the old man was saying,' Ingrid murmured huskily, bending over to breathe warmly upon him and greatly distract him.

'Right,' he managed to say. 'And *also* according to Cayce, that Atlantean civilization was highly developed and possessed some *crystal stone* for trapping and utilizing the rays of the sun. He further claimed that the Atlanteans date back as far as 200,000 years – which could certainly place them in the joined continent of Africa and India 180,000 years ago – and that they were very headstrong, had great powers of extrasensory perception and telepathy, and also had electricity and invented the airplane.'

'Not an *airplane*, dear – it's an *aeroplane*,' she corrected him; then, obviously agitated, murmured, 'God, I feel like a whore . . . and I don't give a damn.'

She proved it by leaning over him, breathing upon him, kissing him, and then he lay back, closed his eyes and surrendered to what she was doing.

'So you think that Cayce's *crystal stone* was actually the Philosopher's Stone that we're all trying to find?' she asked him, running her tongue lightly down his chest and onto his belly.

'Well, as I've just remembered – dammit, why didn't I remember before? – it was Cayce who actually visualized that early Atlantean civilization and did claim that the source of their magical energy was a, quote, *terrible crystal* or *Tuaoi stone*, unquote, and also said that it was eventually so misused by that increasingly aggressive civilization that it brought about their final destruction in 10,000 BC.'

'Your belly button's so sweet,' Ingrid murmured. 'I could lick it all day.'

'What's *really* interesting,' he managed to continue, even though finding it difficult to breathe properly, 'is that Cayce also prophesied that the Atlantis which disappeared under the waters of the Azores and the Sargasso Sea would rise again in 1968 or 1969 . . .'

'Fascinating,' Ingrid murmured.

'. . . and in 1968, long after Cayce's death, airline pilots photographed what appeared to be underwater buildings in that very area – off the coast of Bimini, to be exact – and undersea explorations since then, in that same area, have uncovered on the ocean floor what appear to be the remains of ancient roads, walls, pyramids and even circles – reminiscent of the circular walls of Plato's Atlantis.'

'Mmmmm,' Ingrid murmured, sitting up a little and looking disconsolate.

'So, it's possible that a civilization *could* have existed 200,000 years ago in the African-Indian continent, migrated to what was then the landmass between the Azores and the Sargasso Sea, and been destroyed in approximately 10,000 BC – as the old man believed.'

'And what about Plato's Atlantis, which was destroyed about 1,500 BC?' Ingrid asked, rolling onto her back and pulling him gently upon her.

'Well,' he responded, breathing deeply and finding it difficult to concentrate, 'Plato may have been right about that *particular* Atlantis. The existence of a few famous ancient maps – all since proven to be authentic – has offered substantial proof that there was a worldwide maritime civilization thousands of years before the Egyptians or Babylonians – and that being so, if, as the old man claimed, the highest of the high priests of the Atlantic civilization *did* flee before its destruction in 10,000 BC, they would have had no great difficulty in sailing from the Azores or the Sargasso Sea to the islands of the Aegean.'

'I like lying beneath you,' Ingrid said. 'I like being your bed.'

'And according to Plato,' he continued, trying to ignore her, 'who claimed that the story of the lost continent of Atlantis was originally told to Solon by *Egyptian* priests, the civilization of the Atlantis located beyond the Pillars of Hercules – in other words, in the Aegean Sea – built their major city in concentric rings around a temple of the sea-god Poseidon, shaped like Santorini, in fact, and they accomplished great feats of engineering and architecture, then conquered North Africa, including . . . *Egypt*.'

'Which would explain why,' Ingrid added in an urgent manner, 'if a select few of that Aegean Atlantis *had* removed the Tuaoi Stone from its leading temple and fled with it *some* time after 10,000 BC, when they first arrived in the Aegean, they *could* have taken the Tuaoi Stone to Egypt and there built another great temple of learning and astrology – the Great Pyramid, built in 2170 BC – and placed the Tuaoi Stone safely on its peak before the destruction, in 1,500 BC, of the civilization of the Aegean, from which they had also fled.'

'Right,' Jerry said. 'And they've since taken the Tuaoi Stone somewhere else . . . somewhere *we're* trying to find.'

Ingrid sighed, as if losing something precious, then gazed forlornly at the ceiling and said, 'I wish we could stay here forever and forget that whole business.'

Yet they knew it was impossible, wishful thinking, an unreal fantasy, and as the fifth and six days passed, and as the need for sleep returned to normal, they talked more and more about Saint-Germain and their search for the Tuaoi Stone. It seemed they were addicted to it, or at least trapped by past experiences, now more desperately needing to know what it all added up to. And so no matter their personal feelings, no matter how deeply they now loved one another, no matter how much they wanted to touch and be touched, they knew by the morning of the seventh day that they were ready to leave.

How surprising, then (though utterly predictable with hindsight), that early that morning, when breakfast was left outside their door by room service, Jerry found on the tray, when he set it down on Ingrid's lap, an envelope containing air tickets for flights from Baghdad

357

to London and from there to Tel Aviv, a postcard of the Temple of Solomon in Jerusalem, and a calling card on which was scribbled, in that increasingly familiar, elegantly flamboyant writing: *Compliments, St Germain*.

'Please note,' Jerry said. '*Saint*-Germain.'

Thus reminded that both of them were on a quest more important than their own immediate happiness, that they were still being watched, that the joy they had found together could not prevent what was to come, the naked, dishevelled and very voluptuous Ingrid pinned up her long hair, put on her clothes and spectacles, lowered her head demurely, and let Jerry lead her away from the rumpled bed, out of that sweltering room, back into the material world and its numerous mysteries.

They caught a cab to the airport.

CHAPTER THIRTY-TWO

As he walked out of Baghdad airport with Hans and Elena, Zweig had only one thought in his mind: to have a talk with the three hoodlums who had, according to his Arab spies, let Ingrid and the American escape once more from their clutches.

'And you still have those three imbeciles under lock and key?' he asked his Baghdad contact, as he impatiently waved Elena and Hans into the back of the limo.

'Yes, sir,' the Arab replied. 'We have them in a farmer's house just outside al-Hillah, where in fact they were hiding. Naturally, when they asked for a doctor for the wounded man, the farmer knew that something was wrong and informed the police at al-Hillah. One of the policemen got in touch with me, and that's how I found them.'

'You did well.'

'Thank you, sir.'

Zweig climbed into the back of the limo and seated himself beside Elena, thus putting her in the middle, between him and Hans, the former chewing gum and fanning herself with a lace handkerchief, the latter simply gazing out of the window, as if lost in thought.

'I don't know why *I* had to come,' Elena whined. 'You *know* I can't stand this heat and dust.'

'Please be quiet,' he said, again noting her growing insolence. 'The heat and dust are unavoidable – and certainly bearable.'

'So why couldn't I stay on the boat? Or at least on the island?'

'Don't you *want* to see Baghdad?'

'It's just another noisy city.'

'What would I do without you at nights?'

'Find a whore,' the whore replied in a knowing manner. 'I'm sure the hotel would provide one.'

He held his anger in check and settled into his seat as the Arab climbed into the front and told the driver to start. As the car sped away from the airport, heading for al-Hillah, Zweig puzzled over the whereabouts of Ingrid and Remick, and started feeling distinctly nervous at the thought of the possible repercussions should they fail to be found. Kuragin, for a start, would not take kindly to their loss; and would, indeed, withdraw Soviet assistance and leave him defenceless.

He would be ruined overnight.

Yet what could he do? He couldn't work out what was happening. If Saint-Germain actually existed (and his own bizarre experiences indicated that he did), and if, as it seemed, he was the keeper of the Tuaoi Stone, then why had he protected Ingrid and the American over the past few months?

It didn't make sense.

Gazing out of the window of the speeding car, observing the dreary flatlands and the grey Euphrates river, which appealed to him not at all, he thought with growing rage and humiliation of what Ingrid had done to him.

The ungrateful whore. A frigid bitch like her mother. He had raised her in luxury, educated her at the best schools, sent her to the finest sanatoriums for her problems – and she had repaid him by stealing his money and running away with her Yank.

You could never trust women. He had always understood that. Although needing them, he had never really liked them, had always sensed their dislike of him; and had realized at an early age that they basically hated sex and only tolerated it in order to get their own way – just like Elena.

It was always the women. Deep down, he knew that. He'd had trouble with women all his life, particularly with the older ones, the mothers, who obviously could sense more than their daughters. No mother had ever liked him. That's why he had killed a few. He had certainly arranged the deaths of his first wife *and* her parents (that bitch mother, who had despised him) and, later, did the same for Ingrid's grandparents, before killing her mother. He had done it for money, to obtain their inheritances, but had doubtless also done it as an act of revenge against women. Every woman he had known had turned against him, forcing him to destroy them.

And now Ingrid. God, yes! Just like all the others. Frightened of him, even more frightened of sex, and possessed of a whore's urge to steal from shops, not to mention from him.

She hated him. He knew that. She had always done so. Like her mother, she had feared *and* envied his masculine strength, then blamed him for her lack of self-esteem and growing neuroses. He should have killed her, just as he had killed her mother, to put himself out of misery.

Certainly, when he finally caught up with her, that's what he would do.

Her *and* the American.

'Hey, Hans!' Elena said. 'Close that window. The wind's blowing my hair about.'

'Yes, Elena, of course.'

Hans did as he was bid, rolling the window up very quickly; and taking note of the fear that was always in his eyes, Zweig remembered that day in Eforie Nord, in the thermal treatment centre, when he had made Hans go down on his knees to offer obedience. He hadn't meant to go that far, still wondered why he had done it, and could only conclude, glumly – indeed, with increasing dread – that it had been caused by his age, by his loss of potency in *normal* sex, and by his subsequent need to make up for that loss, no matter the methods. Thus, Hans on his knees, Elena in Nazi uniforms, his own nostalgic memories of his Hitler Wolfcub comrades, his increasingly romanticized thoughts of the glorious Third Reich.

He wanted his past back.

Shuddering, he turned away, looked straight ahead instead, stared at the empty road cutting through the arid flatlands and remembered, again, that Hans could use their moment of intimacy against him, if only with idle talk.

One should never be intimate with one's minions. It only leads to rebellion. And Elena, just to take one example, was already showing signs of that.

Yes, his enemies were everywhere . . .

Such gloomy thoughts, which had increased in recent weeks, continued to torment him until, an hour later, the limo pulled up outside a crumbling, mud and stone farmhouse, near the Euphrates river. There were a few goats wandering loose, some chickens, a couple of cows; the air smelt of wild flowers and manure, was stirred by a faint breeze. Two armed Iraqi policemen were guarding the front door of the farmhouse, and a third one, a sergeant, as fat and slovenly as the other two, emerged as Zweig climbed out of the limo, relieved to be doing so.

'I'm not getting out,' Elena said. 'I'm not getting goat shit on my new shoes, so I'll just wait in here, thanks.'

'Of course,' Zweig said. 'Naturally.'

Taken aback once more by the extent of her insolence, he turned away from her, held his rage in check, then with Hans and the Arab driver, approached the police sergeant and his armed minions.

As soon as the driver had introduced him to the police sergeant, he asked if his three men were still alive and well in the farmhouse.

'Yes,' the potbellied, pleasant Iraqi sergeant replied. 'We had to discipline them once or twice, but they're still alive.'

Zweig had to smile at that. 'And my daughter and her American boyfriend? Any news about them?'

'Yes, Herr Zweig. One of our men has just called us from Baghdad airport, telling us that your daughter and the American took a flight to London shortly after you landed. We have also learned from hacking into all the airline computer systems that they have been booked onto flights from London to Tel Aviv exactly one week from now.'

Zweig couldn't believe his ears. It was too painful to be true. He had missed them by a matter of minutes and now they were gone.

'Tel Aviv?'

'Yes, sir.'

Zweig suddenly felt bewildered, hot and bothered, even nauseous, but kept a firm grip on himself and displayed no emotion.

'Very good, Sergeant. You've done an excellent job. Now please bring those three men out here. I *want* them out here.'

'Of course, Herr Zweig.'

'I suggest that you then leave with your men and let *me* handle the prisoners. Believe me, I will deal with them.'

The Iraqi sergeant picked his nose and flicked something off his finger, then frowned to display his disapproval. 'I'm afraid I cannot permit –'

'Yes, yes,' Zweig interjected, waving his hand

impatiently. 'Hans here will pay you for your troubles before you depart. Now take the money and go, please.'

Hans stepped forward, took the police sergeant aside, slipped an envelope into his hand and whispered into his ear. Looking a lot happier, the sergeant slapped his fat belly, spat on the ground, and waved at his two uniformed guards; then all three of them, after climbing into their battered Jeep, waved goodbye and were driven away, disappearing in clouds of dust.

When the police had gone, Zweig nodded at his Arab informer who pulled a pistol from his jacket pocket, cocked it and walked into the house. He could be heard barking commands, then, a few seconds later, the three hoodlums emerged, obviously having been kicked out by the Arab holding the pistol. Two of them looked up pleadingly at Zweig through blackened eyes, while the other, badly bruised, and also with blood caked around the bullet hole in his shoulder, groaned weakly and fell into the dirt.

'Pick that miserable wretch off the ground,' Zweig said, 'and support him between you.'

The two men did as they were told, jerking the wounded man up onto his knees and, as he groaned louder, supported him by putting their arms around him. He hung limply between them, blubbering pathetically, his head bowed; and Zweig, studying the other two, was pleased to note that Louis Palladinos – who had once been hired by Colonel Andropov Kuragin to keep his eye on Zweig – had lost his aplomb and, with his face badly bruised by the police, was a sorry reflection of the man he had formerly been.

'Tell that bastard to hold his head up,' Zweig ordered.

'He can't,' Palladinos replied. 'He's been losing blood for days and is nearly unconscious.'

'Nearly unconscious, is he?' Zweig said. 'Well, we'll soon fix that.'

Leaning forward, he grabbed hold of the wounded man's bloody shoulder, squeezed it tightly and bit into the area around the wound. The man screamed in anguish, quivered like a puppet on a string and jerked his head up, opening glazed, tearful eyes.

Zweig smiled at him and stepped back.

'So,' he said. 'Now that you are all awake and attentive, let us commence . . .' He stared at each man in turn. 'You have failed. All *three* of you have failed and I want to know why. I send you out with the simple task of locating two people, we have helpful operatives in every major city, we have telephones and bugging devices and numerous informants – and still you have managed to lose your quarry. You were supposed to be in charge, Palladinos, so maybe *you* should explain.'

'Yes, Mr Zweig, of course. Whatever you say. Naturally.' Palladinos wiped sweat from his battered face and licked his parched lips. 'It wasn't our fault,' he said. 'We were taken by surprise. We followed your daughter and the American into the shop of a blind old man, in the bazaar near the Mosque of Kadhimain, north of Baghdad, and found them discussing Count Saint-Germain and the Tuaoi Stone. We were going to beat the truth out of them when a large group of men burst into the shop and started beating *us* up.'

'Oh, really?'

'Yeah,' Palladinos replied, obviously lying through his teeth. 'As I said, it was a fairly large group – probably Saint-Germain's men – and they attacked us and then chased us from the shop. We managed to get into the Jeep, but then, when we were driving away, one of them shot at us, badly wounding poor Kramer, as you can see.'

Poor Kramer, still holding his bloody shoulder, nodded his battered head.

'And then?' Zweig asked.

'Well, Mr Zweig, the rest you know. Determined to look after Kramer – refusing to leave him alone while he was wounded – we stayed with him in this house and sent for a doctor – but instead of going for a doctor, the farmer sent for those cops, who informed you of our whereabouts before we could do so ourselves, which is what we intended.'

'I see,' Zweig said. 'So you *were* going to get in touch with me, just as soon as Kramer had received medical attention?'

'Exactly, Mr Zweig,' Palladinos said, smiling with relief. 'The minute Kramer was fit enough to be moved, we were going to get a plane directly to you, and then tell you precisely what had happened.'

'An honourable thing to do,' Zweig said. 'Almost *noble*, in fact.' He turned to glance across the broad, muddy expanse of the famed Euphrates river, remembered that he was standing in the cradle of civilization, received no ecstatic feeling from that particular knowledge, so said, 'Wasn't that noble of them, Hans? Don't you agree?'

'Yes, sir,' Hans said, nervous as always. 'Very noble, indeed.'

Zweig nodded judiciously, took a deep breath, then turned to Palladinos, slapped his face and hissed, 'You lying bastard! No group of men attacked you! My Arab friends went to the blind man's house and were told the true story! There *was* no band of men! You let my daughter, the American and the Arab boy put you to flight – and were in fact shot at by the *American* as you made your escape!'

'No, Mr Zweig! Please let me –'

Zweig slapped his face again. 'Shut your lying

mouth. You were put to flight by a bunch of amateurs! And only went back to the bazaar– when my daughter and the Yank had gone – because you didn't want anyone to find *this* wounded idiot. Then, when you collected him, you drove out of al-Hillah and hid in this farmhouse, hoping to escape from my wrath by going into Baghdad, you inept, treacherous bastard!'

'No, I –'

'Shoot this pig! *Shoot him now*!'

'No! No! Please don't – *no*!'

Palladinos was still bawling his protest when Zweig cut him short by slapping him sideways into the dirt and the Arab, moving very quickly, stepped forward, leaned over him, placed the barrel of the pistol against his head and pressed the trigger. The pistol jerked in the Arab's hand, blood and brain matter splashed him, then Palladinos twitched once and was still.

As the wounded man rolled his eyes and his friend burst into tears, the Arab grabbed the lifeless Palladinos by the collar of his jacket and dragged him like a sack of maize across the dusty earth. He kicked the body to make it roll down the incline into the river, then returned to aim his pistol at the other two hoodlums while Zweig, feeling slightly out of control, glared fiercely at them.

When the wounded man stared up at him with glazed eyes, he gave him a soothing smile.

'Come, my friend,' he said. 'Like myself, you are a German. Please tell me what happened after the other two fled, leaving you all alone.'

The wounded man bit his lower lip, shuddered with pain and said, 'It was terrible, Herr Zweig. Really terrible. That American, he was a demon. He dragged me back into the shop, submitted me to torture, and interrogated me as to why we were pursuing him. I told him nothing, Herr Zweig.'

'Nothing?'

'I swear it!'

Zweig leaned forward and grabbed hold of the man's wounded shoulder again. The man screamed and jerked violently, but Zweig slapped his face, bawled at him to be silent, then, while he shuddered and whimpered, stepped back and studied him.

'Now what did you *really* tell him?' he asked.

At great length, and with much sobbing and whimpering, the man managed to confess that he had told Remick all he knew – which wasn't all that much, being essentially the simple fact that Zweig had originally been letting Ingrid and Jerry run free in the hopes that they would lead him to Saint-Germain, but that the Soviets had then insisted that he capture Ingrid and force the American to continue the search for the Tuaoi stone.

'And that's *all* I told them, Herr Zweig. That's all I *know*!'

Feeling outraged but not wishing to show it, Zweig placed a hand gently on the man's good shoulder, shook him affectionately, then told him to stand up beside his companion. When he had climbed to his feet and stood trembling before him, he gave both men a smile, nodded and said, 'You are men. *German* men. And should be treated as such. You should be accorded the respect and dignity reserved for all soldiers.' Then, turning rather sadly to Hans, he said, 'Execute them.'

Without a word, the increasingly pale-faced Hans nodded at the Arab with the pistol. Also without a word, and ignoring the sudden outbreak of entreaties from the two doomed men, the Arab raised his pistol and shot each of them in the head, then dragged their bodies, one by one, to the river and kicked them down into the muddy water.

Zweig walked back to the limo without a word and climbed in beside Elena.

'Are we going back now?' Elena asked, looking terribly bored.

'Yes,' Zweig replied. 'And then we're flying under false passports to Jerusalem, via London, for a little vacation.'

'Jesus, why *there*? That place is knee-deep in yids.'

'That much I know.'

He sighed in despair, wiped the sweat from his face, and looked out of the window as Hans climbed in the other side, the Arab got in beside the driver, and the limo moved away from the old farmhouse, churning up clouds of dust and sand as it headed back to Baghdad.

As they travelled across the flatlands, past goats and Arab farmers, moving parallel to the broad, muddy swathe of the Euphrates river, which had continued to flow while mighty civilizations rose and fell, Zweig contemplated time, wondered what it really was, tried to separate the past from the present, but gave up in defeat. The glorious days of his youth were as real to him as the present, the great dramas of the Third Reich and its aftermath as vivid as yesterday. Yet through Saint-Germain he had found himself soaring through time and space to view first the stars of the cosmos, then snow-capped mountains.

It was too much to comprehend.

He remembered his experience in the park in Bucharest, could not forget the bizarre events experienced by his men, and now knew that in his pursuit of Saint-Germain, he had found the ultimate enemy.

Victory over the ultimate enemy was the greatest victory of all, and the Tuaoi Stone would be but the icing on that particular cake. Yet there was more to it than that – he needed the Tuaoi Stone for himself – to own it was to possess the whole world, and even, if what he had heard was true, to find immortality.

He desperately wanted that. He was growing terrified of old age. His erections were less frequent, usually hardly worth mentioning, and his other ailments were multiplying every day, no matter what he did to keep them at bay. Yes, he was growing old, going to seed, *decaying*, and he dreaded that more than anything else on earth, could not abide the thought of mortality, to be one of the common herd.

Hitler could have been a god, inviolable, immortal, but instead had been betrayed by his flesh and the facts of mortality. But he, Zweig, could do what Hitler had only imagined: conquer not only the earth, but also the mysteries of time and space, and through them, the secret of life, and . . . *immortality*.

God, he hungered for that.

Yet he was being thwarted. His own daughter was betraying him. That bitch and her surprisingly bright American were making a fool of him. They were doing it with Saint-Germain's help. That much was obvious. And now Saint-Germain's bizarre scenario was propelling him, with his daughter and her American, towards the ultimate test.

'Jerusalem!' He sighed. 'My hell on earth! Why is God punishing me?'

God did not answer.

CHAPTER THIRTY-THREE

As he watched them walk barefoot into the cool interior of the Mosque of Omar, or the Dome of the Rock, in the Noble Enclosure in the Old City of Jerusalem, Ibrahim Dayieh thought the young lady and her American boyfriend seemed just like any other tourists.

Wondering if they knew they had been chosen, or if they were being tested in ignorance, he followed them as they made their way around the magnificent temple, under the brilliantly coloured tiles and Koranic inscriptions of the great dome, past marble panels in muted pastel shades and across floors decked with oriental carpets, to the railing around the mosque's focal point – the Rock. There, surrounded by other whispering tourists and Islamic worshippers, they gazed at the rock from which Mohammed – blessed be His name – was said to have ascended to heaven and which even now contained the unmistakable imprint of a human foot.

The young lady and her American boyfriend stared at it, as if in a trance.

Watching the couple, Ibrahim stroked his grey beard and started feeling as old as he was, which was close to seventy. As he padded barefoot alongside the wall of the Mosque, in order to get a better look at the couple whom he had been told, by Saint-Germain, would enter the mosque at exactly this time, he realized that he was suddenly feeling old for the first time because of his understanding that his time had come. His new sense of *age*, then, was not at all unpleasant; but was in fact slowly filling him up with the peace of contentment.

He was proud that he had been chosen and would now soon be called; would soon become one of that secret, illustrious line that included Mohammad, Moses, Abraham, Jesus, Buddha, Rama Krishna, Nebuchadrezzar and many other of the world's most noble men, from both East and West. Yes, the present guardian of the sacred stone, the emissary, St Germain, had come to him years ago, in the midst of his meditation, to begin that other, more relevant education and show him the way. He had been chosen as an adept, as one of the immortals, and soon would be relieved of his mortal shell and find the bliss of transcendence. His sudden ageing, then, was not a sign to be feared, but a cause for rejoicing.

Stopping parallel to where the group of tourists were gathered in front of the sacred Rock, he stared surreptitiously at the girl and her American boyfriend.

He had always found Western women to be thin, pale and insipid in character, but this one seemed even less impressive than most. She was much too thin, had small breasts, was stoop-shouldered; her hair was piled untidily on her head and she wore a pair of unattractive spectacles.

In truth, he couldn't imagine what the young American saw in her; nor could he imagine her *nor* that young American, in his scruffy jacket and blue denims, even being *considered* by the Master. However, St Germain had told him to contact them and that's what he was doing.

Standing beneath the superb stained glass windows and black and gold mosaics, the couple had turned their attention towards the small tabernacle as the far end of the Rock, which contained a few hairs of the Prophet. Ibrahim stared at them, willing them to sense his presence, and eventually the American turned his head and looked directly at him.

Ibrahim smiled at him, then turned away and walked towards the exit.

As he walked on bare feet across the oriental carpets, past jostling Christians and Moslems kneeling in prayer, he knew that the girl and her American would be close behind him. Smiling, he thought of how St Germain had appeared to him that morning – as if in a dream, but in his essence, very real – to tell him that the time for his transcendence had come, that he would leave the earth this day, but that before this great event came to pass he had one last earthly duty.

There was an American and young lady who had been chosen and were being tested; they had reached the Seventh Station – this great Mosque and Temple of Solomon – and had been told that they would be recognized and contacted by someone – and that someone was he.

He would tell them what they needed to know . . . and then death would release him.

Stepping from the cool shade of the interior of the Mosque to the blazing light and heat outside, he slipped his feet into his sandals and turned back towards the entrance. The girl and her American appeared soon enough, blinking against the brilliant light, then, as they put on their shoes, they both stared very intently at him. After glancing at one another in a questioning manner, they walked forward and stopped directly in front of him.

'You're the one we're supposed to meet,' the American said. 'Aren't you?'

'Yes,' Ibrahim replied, knowing without doubt who they were and so speaking with confidence.

'I saw you looking at us.'

'Of course.'

'How did you know us?' the girl asked him.

'I was shown your likeness by our Master, St Germain, when he asked me to speak with you.'

'I'm Jerry Remick,' the American said, 'and this is Ingrid –'

'Your names are not important,' Ibrahim said. 'Come. Walk beside me.'

He led them away from the octagonal Mosque with its gold and polychrome tilework, across the flat stones of Solomon's Platform, the El-Haram-es-Sharif, towards the sealed Golden Gate in the wall of the Old City, not unaware of the great history around him, of the ghosts of the centuries rising up from the hot, sun-scorched stones.

'It is believed that right here,' he said, pointing at the ground, 'is where Abraham prepared to sacrifice his son, Isaac. The Prophet Mohammed, as you doubtless know, was said to have ascended from the rock enshrined in the Mosque. Here Solomon reigned, the Romans had their temple to Jupiter, Herod built his fortress, Pontius Pilate condemned Christ to death, and the Crusaders tried to convert us with violence. This place is a fitting end to your journey; now your journey begins.'

'That's a contradiction in terms,' the American said.

'No, my son, it is not. All endings are the beginning of something else. Thus the circle is given shape.'

As the sealed Golden Gate loomed over them, he turned north towards the Antonia Tower, where Pontius Pilate had condemned that other adept, Jesus Christ, to death. The tower cast its great shadow on the flat stones, obscuring the tourists.

'So,' Ibrahim said, 'what do you wish to know?'

'Every time Count Saint-Germain sends us to see someone,' the American said, 'they ask us what *we* want to know – but we don't know what to ask.'

'He is not Count Saint-Germain,' Ibrahim felt obliged to correct the American. 'He is a saint – *Saint* Germain – and if, as you say, you do not know what to ask, you have come a remarkably long way on no information.'

'Okay,' the American said, grinning with considerable charm. 'Is it true that this meeting with you marks *some* kind of end to our journey?'

'That is correct. You have managed to make your way to the seventh of the Seven Stations; after this, you will commence *another* journey, east or west, one the right way.'

'And one the wrong way?'

'Correct.'

The American glanced at the girl beside him, and she smiled in return. In that smile, which illuminated her drabness in a magical manner, Ibrahim saw the light of her love and blossoming sensual self.

Clearly there was more to this couple than met the eye ... a mutual affection and trust, a spiritual innocence. Perhaps that's why ...

'What are the Seven Stations?' the girl asked. 'Are they the Seven Wonders of the World?'

'That is a self-evident fact,' Ibrahim answered, warmed by her gentle smile. He sensed a certain mischief in her, which suggested that she might have more spirit than he had given her credit for.

'What *isn't* self-evident,' the American said, 'is why we were sent there.'

'And *here*,' the girl added.

'You were sent to be tested,' Ibrahim said. 'I do not know how or why. I only know that if St Germain arranged it, it is not without purpose. Obviously, since you have managed to come this far, you have been satisfactory.'

'Satisfactory for *what*?'

'That is not for me to say. Only St Germain can know that. I only know that you were sent to the Seven Stations as to the seven rungs of a ladder; if you fail to climb beyond a certain rung, you can only descend again.'

'So, what were we tested for?'

'For belief and self-belief, faith and courage, for the will to continue. It is important that your motives be as pure as the love you have for each other.'

The young lady blushed at that, lowered her eyes, squeezed the hand of the man. Both of them, Ibrahim observed, not without a certain amusement, looked much younger at that moment than they were.

'Our motives for *what*?' the American asked, almost aggressively.

'Your motives for wishing to find the Tuaoi Stone – since the Tuaoi Stone can only be shared by those with pure minds.'

They took the steps down from Solomon's Platform and started along the crowded path that led alongside the northern wall of the Old City to the nearest exit, which was via the Lion's Gate. They were hemmed in by Moslem traders and Christian tourists, but seemed very alone.

'We passed all those tests?'

'So far, young lady.'

'He tested our love and commitment?'

'And the depth of your purity.'

'Excuse *me*,' the American said sardonically, 'but I just don't *get* this. I mean, *I'm* not particularly pure, I believe in little, and my love ... Well,' he added tentatively, glancing sideways at the young lady and blushing as she had previously done. 'I mean, that's *natural*, isn't it?'

'Love is generally a form of self-deception,' Ibrahim said, 'that cannot last for too long. You are pure at heart – both of you – more than you know . . . and such love is quite rare.'

'And belief?'

'You do not know you believe, but it is part of your nature. You have faith in the ultimate goodness of Man – and that, my friends, is the only true belief at the heart of existence.'

They went through the Lion's Gate, thus leaving the Old City, walking out between two stone walls lined with gypsy beggars, mostly children, and Arabs selling their wares to noisy tourists. Across the Jericho Road was the Valley of Kidron, and beyond that, and the Moslem graveyard in it, they could see the church of Gethsemane on the lower slopes of the Mount of Olives, with the golden spires of the Russian Orthodox church gleaming through light-green olive trees.

'Assuming what you say is true,' the American said, 'that we were in fact tested and have so far passed every test – why were we tested in those particular places? Why not where we were?'

'Those places where you were tested were themselves part of the test. It is the knowledge of the significance of those places that will make you begin again.'

'The end of this journey and the beginning of another?'

'Quite so.'

'Then what is the significance of those places?'

'I cannot tell you what you have already learned.'

'We haven't learned it.'

'You have.'

'Oh?' the American said, raising a questioning eyebrow.

'Yes,' Ibrahim explained. 'You have simply not accepted it. You have discussed it together, but so far not managed to recognize it. You have talked together about it, without actually knowing you were doing so.'

'If we know it, you can tell it.'

'That is so.'

'Then tell it. Please *tell* it.'

The American was looking exasperated, making Ibrahim smile. 'I can only tell it when you ask the relevant question – and that question you know.'

The American stopped walking, stared at him with increasing exasperation, then raised his hands and shrugged his shoulders in despair. Ibrahim started walking again, but then the girl darted in front of him, making him stop.

'Why are those particular places – the Seven Wonders of the World – representative of your so-called Seven Stations?'

Ibrahim nodded at her. 'Yes,' he said, 'that's the question.'

'And the answer?'

As the American looked in a surprised manner at the girl he clearly loved, Ibrahim took hold of the girl's elbow, gently tugged her in beside him, then continued walking along the Jericho Road, with the American falling in at his other side.

'Did you ever learn about magic squares when studying mathematics?' Ibrahim asked the American who, in a rather naive way, seemed very bright.

'Sure,' the American replied. 'I used to have great fun with them – and often, when still in high school, tried inventing my own.'

'I don't know what they are,' the young lady said, obviously put out by her own ignorance.

'Magic squares,' the American explained to her, 'are blocks of numbers that produce the same sum whether added in horizontal rows, columns or diagonals. In other words, let's say you had a block of numbers in columns of three – three up, three down, three across, giving a total of nine numbers in a square. If it's a so-called *magic* square, then you should be able to add up any three lines across, any three lines down, or any three lines diagonally, and you'd always get the same number as your sum total. They're mathematical freaks that are mostly found in puzzle books or used as the basic structure for crossword puzzles.'

'Correct,' Ibrahim said. 'However, they were rightly regarded by the mathematicians of antiquity as numerical illustrations of cosmic laws; they believed, again rightly, that the numbers of magic squares were cosmological keys to the mysteries of the universe – and so seven of those squares became traditionally attached, each to a particular planet in our cosmos.'

'I remember that,' the American said, hardly able to hide his growing excitement. 'The smallest of the seven is the Square of Saturn, which has nine numbers, totalling forty-five, but arranged so that no matter how any individual block of three numbers is read – diagonally, horizontally or as columns – the sum is always fifteen.'

'You have a good memory,' Ibrahim told him as they left the Jericho Road and walked south, with the wall of the Old City on their right, the Valley of Kidron and the Silwan village falling away to their left. 'And what you both have sensed, but not yet recognized, is that the places you have visited – the Seven Wonders of the Ancient World – form an astrological system, with each of the sites representing a centre of cosmological influence, as revealed by their relevant magic squares. The original buildings, as they stood, were actually instruments for the control of a particular aspect of cosmic energy, and their construction was based firmly on the dimensions suggested by the numerical pattern of their individual magic squares . . . Now think of the beginning as an ending – of the first as the last – and relate this to the places you have visited.'

379

'The first place we visited was the Great Pyramid at Giza,' the American said, looking directly at Ibrahim, his eyes growing brighter with revelation while the girl frowned beside him. 'And that's where we received the first digit of the magical number 1746.'

'Exactly,' Ibrahim replied. 'And since the beginning is the ending, let us see what your travels have revealed.'

'Yes, let's,' the American said.

'The Temple of Diana, or Artemis, at Ephesus, represents the Square of the Moon,' Ibrahim informed him. 'The Colossus at Rhodes represents the Square of the Sun. The Temple of Jupiter, or Zeus, at Olympus, represents the Square of Jupiter. The Tomb of Mausoleus, in Turkey, represents the Square of Venus. The Towers and Hanging Gardens of ancient Babylon represent the Square of Mars. The Temple of Solomon, right here in Jerusalem, represents the Square of Saturn. And finally, taking the beginning as the end, the pyramids of ancient Egypt, themselves represented by the Great Pyramid of Cheops in Giza, represent the Square of ... *Mercury*.'

He laid particular emphasis on the last word – and was pleased when the young American said without a pause: 'The Moon, the Sun, Jupiter, Venus, Mars, Saturn and ... *Mercury*. So all of those ancient monuments, as well as representing astrological systems and being used for astronomy, were also instruments of ... *alchemy*?'

'Do not doubt your own wisdom.'

Smiling, Ibrahim led them through the Dung Gate, past Arab traders, armed Israeli soldiers and the mandatory hordes of Christian tourists, then led them in a circular direction back around the Western Wall – better known as the Wailing Wall – and into the narrow streets threading through the Jewish quarter, towards the Street of the Chain.

The American had seemed deep in thought, and now he stopped walking.

'Okay,' he said. 'So the secret of the riddle is in *alchemy*. Now what –?'

Ibrahim waved his right hand, cutting the American off in mid-sentence. 'I can tell you no more than that,' he said. 'It is all I know.'

'It's all that you *know*?' The American looked sceptical.

'Yes,' Ibrahim insisted, starting to walk again. 'I was told to discuss no more than that – and I *know* no more than that. For the rest, you must wait.'

'Wait *where*?' the girl asked in a practical manner.

They had just crossed the El-Wad Road, which was narrow, stepped and busy, and Ibrahim stopped where it intersected the Via Dolorosa and stared steadily at them. Yes, he felt old now, and this couple seemed very young; he tried remember what that was like, but it was too long ago.

'Where are you staying?' he asked them.

'In the American Colony Hotel on Nablus Road,' the American replied.

'Then remain there,' Ibrahim told him. 'Why move when you have nowhere to go? Let events take their course.'

'And how long might that be?' the girl asked.

'As long as it takes.'

The young lady blinked behind her spectacles, wrinkled her nose and glanced at her boyfriend. The American shrugged as if defeated, then tried one last time.

'And the Tuaoi Stone?' he asked. 'How does that relate to –?'

'No,' Ibrahim said quickly, cutting him short again.

'I have told you all you will learn this day. *Sabah el kheir* – goodbye. And good luck, my young friends.'

He walked away hurriedly, leaving them standing on the narrow road to Calvary, and turned down a side street that led him back to his modest house in the Moslem Quarter, just behind the Lion's Gate. Entering the house, which was made of brick and mud, spartan and painted white, he thought of his wife, who had died many years ago, and of his children, both boys, who had died in the war against the Jews. He felt no rancour, understanding Man's foolishness, and only wondered how his own end would come and what transcendence would be like.

Casting off his robes, he knelt cross-legged on the stone-flagged floor, bowed his head and closed his eyes, thought of the American and his girlfriend, wondered why they had been chosen, then began the meditation that normally sent him winging across space and time, beyond the material world, to frozen lakes and snow-covered mountain peaks and, finally, to that great monastery hacked out of the rocks, where St Germain, surrounded by other Masters, protected the sacred stone – the Tuaoi Stone that the American had asked about and must find for himself.

He was just about to fall into the depths of his meditation when the unlocked front door of his house was opened.

Looking up, Ibrahim saw a large man walking in, stooping over to do so, and being followed by two other men as he entered the room.

At that moment Ibrahim stopped wondering how and when he was going to die.

'*Scheisse!*' the big man exclaimed. 'What a hovel! God, how I hate Arabs!'

Straightening up again, and flanked by the other men, all three of them wearing jackets and trousers and open-necked shirts, he stopped directly in front of Ibrahim, towering over him like a monolith, and gazing down at him with the coldest eyes that Ibrahim had ever seen.

'Stand up, you old goat,' he said. 'I have some questions to ask you.'

'I cannot answer any more questions,' Ibrahim replied. 'Now do what you will with me.'

The large man turned purple, reached down very quickly, grabbed Ibrahim by the beard and tugged him brutally onto his feet. Then, while Ibrahim tried to blink the tears from his eyes, he saw that evil face up close, smelt his bad breath, heard his venomous voice.

'My name's Zweig,' the large man whispered. '*Wilhelm* Zweig. You hear me? And you've just been talking to my daughter and her filthy American. Now what did you tell them?'

'These are my last moments,' Ibrahim said, 'and I will spend them in silence. Now do what you will with me.'

What they did to him was beyond his belief, a catalogue of torture and humiliation that went on for ever. He took it all in silence – they has stuffed a cloth into his mouth – and as his agony mounted, as the pain became unendurable, he first found himself wondering how St Germain could let this happen, then found himself accepting it as his penance for the rewards yet to come.

He then flew out of his pain, hovered beyond it, above it, and looked down from the peaceful shore where he was dying to see himself on the stone floor. There was blood all over his body. His bones were broken, his flesh was torn. He was spitting a bloody cloth from swollen lips as their knives probed his open wounds.

He observed himself being tortured, slipping in and

out of consciousness, then saw them give up in disgust, or perhaps just exhaustion. The large man shouted at him, kicked him, spat upon him, then dragged his bloody body across the floor and rolled him against the wall.

'I am leaving my calling card,' he said. 'You might remember me by this.'

Returning from his peaceful shore, dropping back down through his pain, Ibrahim opened his swollen eyes when he heard a ticking clock, focused painfully and saw a hand turning on the yellow clock of a time-bomb.

'You see this, you old goat?' he heard that venomous voice whispering. 'It's set for one minute and it'll blow you and this house sky high, then your friends will blame the yids for what's happened and all hell will break loose. Are you sure you have no final words for me? If you have, I might stop it.'

Ibrahim tried to smile, but his lips cracked and bled again, so he smiled in his mind because he knew that the German was lying. It didn't matter what he said – that bomb would go off anyway – and he knew, as that single hand turned in the clockface, that the ticking was counting off the seconds at the end of his life.

'No?' the voice asked again. 'You still have nothing to say? Then goodbye, you old goat!'

He heard them leaving his home. He tried to move, but was too weak. He lay there for an eternity, trying to think of his past life, instead thinking of the young lady and the American and St Germain, and then glowing with a radiant, inner peace as he drifted out of himself. The ticking faded away. The yellow bomb faded from sight. He had counted off the seconds in his head and he knew that his time had come.

Then his whole world exploded.

CHAPTER THIRTY-FOUR

Ingrid and Jerry left the Old City by the Damascus Gate, crossed the busy Sultan Suleiman Road, then walked up the Nablus Road towards their hotel. The sun was still blazing down with unrelenting fierceness, and Ingrid felt herself longing for the rain that would make Jerusalem green.

Hardly believing she was here, she glanced back over her shoulder, saw the domes and minarets within the walls of the Old City, gleaming pink and golden in the light beating down from an azure sky. She looked ahead again, squeezed Jerry's hand, smiled at him, sticking close to him as they made their way along the pavement, which was crowded with Arabs and Jews and young Christians with rucksacks. She felt slightly unreal, as if removed from herself, and squeezed Jerry's hand a second time, wanting to feel skin and bone.

He had been looking straight ahead, his brow furrowed in thought, but now he turned his head and grinned at her.

'Sorry,' he said. 'I was distracted. It's all too much for this puny brain.'

'Yes,' she replied. 'The plot thickens with every encounter. And I sometimes feel that the more we know, the less we know – that we're just running in circles.'

'I don't think so, Ingrid. I'm sure we're not wasting our time. And as for circles, remember what that old Arab said: *All endings are the beginning of something else; thus the circle is given shape.*'

'So we're about to begin another adventure.'

'Yes, Ingrid, that's it.' He tugged her towards him and kissed her on the forehead. 'Let's go for a drink,' he said.

'No,' she replied, surprised by her own shamelessness. 'Let's go back to our hotel and make love. I want to forget all this.'

'You know something?' he replied. 'I can't get over the difference between the private and public Ingrid – between the Ingrid who strips naked and lets down her hair and this prim and proper creature walking beside me. Straighten your shoulders, Ingrid! Let your hair down! Let the world see the real you.'

'No, thanks,' she said, helplessly blushing. 'I'm *afraid* of the real me.'

'Not any more, surely.' He sounded terribly English. 'Surely not after what we've done together. I mean, didn't that change you?'

'When we're together it's different. I mean, it's different when we're in private. But outside, in the real world, I can't forget my father. His influence can't be shaken off that easily; unfortunately, I'm still his child.'

'But you still want to return to the hotel and make love?'

'Yes, Jerry – in private. And don't look so smug.'

He grinned and nodded, as if saying he understood, then glanced across at the bus station, which as usual was thronged with passengers of every conceivable nationality, then started walking more urgently, his brow furrowed in thought again.

'*Alchemy*,' he said eventually, as if savouring the word. 'How about that? The Great Pyramid, and all those other sites, had *alchemical* purposes.'

She didn't want to talk about it, but obviously couldn't avoid it, so moved closer against him as they walked, and asked, 'So what does it mean? I thought alchemy was a process for turning metal into gold – and certainly that's what Saint-Germain did.'

'The original Count Saint-Germain and the probable keeper of the Tuaoi Stone, namely *Saint* Germain, now being one and the same person,' he reminded her.

'Yes, Jerry, I *know* that.'

'Anyway,' he continued, 'contrary to the widely held belief that alchemy is *only* a chemical process, it is also, as Helena Barbanell told us, considered to be a *mystical* process, a symbol of a spiritual transformation in Man. Jung, for instance, believed that the alchemical texts were concerned with psychic transformations and symbols rather than chemistry; and Gurdjieff also took this attitude, believing the human body to be the vessel for alchemical change, in the sense that it transmutes lower energies into the greater powers that we already possess but lack the will to call forth.'

'*Mercury!*' Ingrid said, unable to resist beating him to it. 'The old Arab said that the Great Pyramid of Cheops represents the Square of *Mercury* – and mercury is one of the two basic elements of alchemical transmutation: male and female, sol and luna, sulphur and . . . *mercury*.'

'Right!' Jerry exclaimed.

'Those elements have to be mixed with some kind of secret fire and heated in a sealed vessel, which marries the elements, which then purify and blacken, this process being known as the nigredo. Then, with further heating, the so-called *soul* of the nigredo is driven out of the black mess and turns white to become the albedo. After lots more processes, the substance turns green – the Green Lion – and finally red . . . the Philosophers' Stone.'

'Right,' Jerry said again, actually hugging her with excitement as they passed the site of the Garden Tomb. 'That's the process for *chemical* alchemy. However, for

Jung and many others those processes were purely symbolic. For instance, the heat that produces the nigredo is a dark night of the soul which ends with the first stage of self-transformation; the other chemical processes are actually further stages in that largely *spiritual* transformation; and the last stage – the Philosophers' Stone – is actually a symbol of the final, complete transformation of mortal man into a new kind of being – a higher, purely spiritual being.'

'Like that legless, armless, blind old man in al-Hillah might have been on the way to becoming.'

'Right.'

'And possibly a being like St Germain.'

'Yes,' he said. 'Maybe.'

As he practically dragged her up the steps and into the American Colony Hotel, which had once been a pasha's palace and still retained that atmosphere, his excitement fused with hers and was being transmuted, she realized with a hot flush, into *sexual* excitement. Shocked by this knowledge, then amused and thrilled instead, she let him take her across the lobby to the reception desk, where he collected their room key.

'*That's* why,' he continued, 'the famed nineteenth-century alchemist, Mary Anne Atwood, described alchemy as a *philosophical* system which – and I quote – "by fermenting the human spirit, purifies and finally dissolves it". In fact, Synesius, the last author in the famous Venus-Paris alchemical manuscripts, had already defined alchemy as a, quote, "mental operation, independent of the science of matter", and –'

'And the so-called *magical* number of 1746,' she couldn't help pointing out, 'being a numerical disguise for the number 666 – the so-called number of the beast – was itself the most renowned of alchemical incantations.'

'Yes,' he replied, briefly annoyed that she had got

there first. 'So the magical number of 1746 – or, more precisely, 666 – is obviously related to the *alchemical* properties of the Great Pyramid ... and so to the missing tip of that same pyramid.'

Opening the door, he stepped aside and pushed her into the huge room with its beamed ceiling and oriental traceries, then closed the door firmly behind him and turned the key in the lock. Breathing deeply, leaning back against the door, he shook his head, and smiled at her.

'So that's it,' he said. 'That's the message we've been given. The Tuaoi Stone is *undoubtedly* the missing tip of the Great Pyramid; it is also a Philosophers' Stone that can cause spiritual transformation, and possibly *chemical* transformation as well; it is, further, the so-called *Lodestone* or *terrible crystal* of a very ancient race; and its present guardian, Count Saint-Germain, now St Germain, an original member of that ancient and *magical* civilization, is now one of the leading adepts of the remaining descendants of that civilization – a civilization that had discovered the Lodestone, chemically *and* symbolically, and had used it to transform the highest of its high priests, or adepts, into creatures who could transcend the material state. And some of those creatures, such as our elusive St Germain, still exist to protect the Philosophers' Stone which, in its physical form, is the Tuaoi Stone, or terrible crystal, and in its symbolic form is the Secret Knowledge.'

'So where *are* they?' Ingrid asked, feeling frustrated.

'Ah, yes, *there's* the rub!'

He rolled his eyes, grinned, walked up to her and placed his hands on her shoulders.

'*Where* are they, indeed?'

She looked up at him, amused, but also feeling very sensual, then stood on tiptoe, closed her eyes and waited for him to kiss her. Instead, the room shook slightly, making her open her eyes again, and even as she saw Jerry glancing at the window, she heard a distant explosion, obviously emanating from the direction of the Old City.

Without a word, Jerry rushed across the room to the window and looked out. He was still there when she reached him, wriggling in beside him, and saw a cloud of smoke billowing up in the east, obviously from a part of the Moslem Quarter, close to the Lion's Gate.

'Shit,' Jerry said, 'that must've been a bomb. Nothing else would make *that* noise.'

'It might have been a gas explosion.'

'It was a bomb, Ingrid. *Definitely*.'

Even as she felt a trickle of fear course through her, the wailing of sirens split the air as military vehicles and ambulances raced towards the scene of the explosion. She kept staring at that smoke, watched it billowing up from the rooftops, drifting south on the wind and turning the blue sky black above the magnificent golden dome of the great Mosque in which they had met the old Arab. Then she remembered Germany, the man who died in the gas explosion, and the trickle of fear within her became a torrent when her thoughts circled back like the smoke and made her dwell once more on the old Arab they had left a short while ago.

Unable to stand the noise of the wailing sirens, she stepped away from the window, straightening up as Jerry turned to face her.

'It's my father's men,' she said.

'What?' he replied, confused.

'Remember that German, Klaus Schiller, whom we interviewed in Eckernforde?'

'Yeah, of course.'

'He was burned to death in his own home after being handcuffed to a gas oven. And remember the woman who sent us to see him? Miss Barbanell, in London?

She also was murdered in her own home after talking to us.'

'I don't think –'

'I do. That old Arab we just talked to probably lived in the Moslem Quarter – and was certainly heading in that direction after parting from us. That explosion is too much of a coincidence, Jerry. I think that old man's been killed . . . killed by my father's men.'

Jerry gave a low whistle. 'Oh, boy,' he said. 'You mean, you think they're right here in Jerusalem?'

'Yes.'

'That's too close.'

She had wanted to let her hair down and take off her clothes, to make passionate love to him and lose herself in him, but now she was only conscious of the fear that was pummelling at her. It was not fear for herself – she knew her father wouldn't harm her – but for Jerry, who would, if he was caught, be forced to pay some terrible price for having stolen her away – which is obviously how her father would view her flight from him. So, her heart raced, being pumped by her fear, and she glanced automatically at the room door, as if someone might be there.

'We've got to get out of here,' she said.

'Correct,' he replied. 'We've got to get across the Old City and find out if you're right. We've got to find out if that old Arab was killed – and if so, who did it.'

'It was my father's men, Jerry.'

'Probably. Yeah. But we might as well find out for sure, before running away.'

'I *want* to run away.'

'We can't, Ingrid. *We can't!* We have to wait for a message from St Germain. We can't let it end here.'

'Damnit, Jerry, you might be killed!'

'Come on, Ingrid, let's go.'

He unlocked the door and ushered her out of the

room, then hurriedly led her along the corridor. Even as they bounded down the stairs and into the lobby, they could hear other sirens, alarms, going off all over the city. Jerry threw his room key onto the reception desk, took Ingrid's hand and was just about to rush her towards the exit when the desk clerk grabbed him by the wrist, holding him back and then shrugging apologetically.

'I'm sorry, sir,' he said. 'I didn't mean to be rude, but we've just received a call from the security services, telling us to recommend to all our residents that they remain indoors until the All Clear sounds.'

'The *All Clear*?' Jerry said disbelievingly.

The desk clerk shrugged again. 'There's been an explosion in the Moslem Quarter of the Old City,' he said. 'Apparently an old Arab, one of the Moslem Quarters' most respected religious leaders, has been killed in that explosion, and the Moslems naturally think it was an assassination carried out by the Jews. Already there are riots all over the Old City, and it's expected that the violence will soon spread out into East Jerusalem. The Army's being brought in to protect the city, but they haven't arrived yet.'

Ingrid had time to catch Jerry's knowing stare, then she was being dragged across the lobby, past other excited residents, and out through the doors, onto the front steps. Just as the sunlight dazzled her vision, she heard a siren very close, rubbed her eyes, blinked, then saw a Jeep containing six armed soldiers rushing right past her. It growled away along the road, leaving a sudden, startling silence ... then she heard rifles firing, a machine gun roaring in the distance, obviously within the walls of the Old City where a battle was raging.

'We can't get in there,' she said. 'The troops won't let us go in. And since we already know that the old man was the victim, we also know the assassins. Not Jews . . . my father's men.'

The machine gun roared again. The rifles answered immediately. Jerry jerked his head around, looking towards the Old City, and she followed his gaze and saw more smoke and heard louder explosions.

'Hand grenades,' Jerry said. 'That'll be the Arabs. Jesus . . . your father.' He shook his head in disbelief, then squeezed her hand. 'Okay,' he said. 'Now we know his men are here. So let's get the hell out of this hotel and go somewhere else. We've got to stay here until St Germain contacts us – and we've got to hide out.'

'Then St Germain may not be able to find us.'

'St Germain has *always* been able to find us and he'll find us again. Now let's pack and get out.'

Collecting their key again, they hurried back to the room, locked the door and went across to the window to look out once more. The rifles continued firing, the machine guns roared, the grenades exploded; and now some troops were jumping out of a truck below to guard the hotel doors.

'They must think the Arabs will soon be attacking *us*,' Jerry said.

'They might not let us out.'

Ingrid looked out over the rooftops of East Jerusalem, at the domes and minarets of the Old City and the black smoke trailing over them, listened to the gunfire and exploding hand grenades and distant shouting, and thought with rage of what her father had begun for his own selfish purposes. The rage burned up and consumed her, releasing her from her fear, and then bubbling up out of it came amusement at the thought of her victory.

She had been what her father wanted – a frightened child, a crushed woman; forced by his base sensuality into being ashamed of her own desires, her shame then making her hide her own charms – with stooped shoulders, in the clothes of an old lady, behind very thick spectacles.

What would he think if he knew her now? If he knew of her love for Jerry? What would he do if he saw her wearing tight clothes, her long hair tumbling free?

He would turn purple with rage.

Feeling as though she had been transformed by the very alchemical process that Jerry had discussed, she turned away from the window, drawing Jerry's gaze towards her, then faced him when she stood before the bed, the back of her legs pressed against it. Jerry stared at her, sensing something, not quite sure what it was, and when she saw his confusion, his sweet and tender concern, she smiled at him and then removed her glasses and threw them onto the nearest chair.

'I don't *really* need glasses,' she said. 'I can see *you* without them. I only wore them because I was frightened of people and the glasses made me feel hidden. I won't wear them any more.'

'No,' Jerry growled, 'don't.'

Surprised and thrilled by his husky tone, even more thrilled when he stepped towards her, she stopped him with a raised hand, listened to what was happening, heard the roaring machine guns, the rifles, the explosions, then removed the clips from her piled-up hair, very slowly, one by one, and then, as Jerry was taking a deep breath, let her long hair come tumbling down.

'In future, I'll *always* have it like this,' she murmured throatily. 'I *do* hope you like it.'

'Oh, Ingrid . . . Oh, baby!'

Once more he started towards her – but again her raised hand stopped him; then she let that hand fall upon her bosom and started unbuttoning her blouse.

She did it slowly, with amusement, teasing him, wanting to please him, and when she heard the audible quickening of his breath, she felt like a queen.

She let the blouse hang loose, took a deep breath, started slipping it off her.

'Jesus, Ingrid. Oh, Christ!'

His words came at her as a groaning, a helpless sign of surrender, then she felt herself falling upon the bed with his body on top of her. He was kissing her, stroking her, stripping the clothes from her, and she raised and lowered herself to help him as his fingers tugged at her.

She felt deliciously wanton, shameless, almost mischievous in fact, but then started losing herself in his heat and hard muscle. He divided her, entered, radiating heat through her, and she melted from her insides to her skin and then flowed all around him.

She became *him* at that moment. She was him and he was her. They joined together, congealed, burned as a single flame, and she came to life as him, who was her, and through that found herself.

So she made love like a whore, voluptuous and proud, while outside machine guns roared, rifles fired, grenades exploded, and the world seemed to come to an end and be renewed on the instant.

Putting an end to her old self, accepting the new, she felt him come inside her, let her spasms match his, gasped, got her breath back, then chuckled and kissed his damp forehead.

'Terrific!' she whispered.

CHAPTER THIRTY-FIVE

Jerry was feeling really proud of himself when the noise of machine guns, rifles and exploding hand grenades reminded him that a minor war had started in Jerusalem and was, by the sound of it, rapidly spreading out beyond the Old City and approaching the hotel. Sitting up on the bed, he was about to go to the window when an odd sound near the door of the room made him look the other way.

An envelope was being slipped under the door.

Glancing down at Ingrid, he saw her tangled hair, sleepy eyes and swollen lips; then he got out of bed, hurriedly put on his underpants and picked up the envelope. He opened the door and looked along the hallway, but there was no one in sight. Sighing, yet feeling slightly amused by St Germain's bizarre games, he closed the door and walked back to the bed, tearing the envelope open as he did so.

Ingrid, stark naked, sat shamelessly upright and stared at him as he pulled out the contents of the envelope and carefully studied them.

'Well?' she asked him.

He shook his head and grinned at her. 'Two air tickets to Calcutta,' he said, holding the tickets up in front of him and waving them in a teasing manner, 'along with false passports and air and train tickets to take us on to Darjeeling, which is at the base of the Himalayan Mountains, in India. You better put on your walking shoes.'

'And when do we leave?'

'Right now. The first leg of the journey starts this evening, but I assume that this is St Germain's method of also getting us away from your father's men – so let's leave the hotel right now and go to the airport, before they actually find out where we are.'

'Do you think they'll let us out of the hotel?' she asked him, indicating the window, through which could be heard the increasingly loud sound of conflict.

'It was only *recommended* that we remain in the hotel,' he told her. 'And if we're heading for the airport, rather than into the city, I don't think they'll bother us. So let's shower and get dressed.'

They shared the shower, soaping one another down, became aroused and rushed back to the bed and made love again. After that, they wisely took turns with the shower, then dressed, packed their suitcases and left the room without bothering to call a porter.

Downstairs in the lobby, an armed Israeli soldier was standing guard inside the main doors and, when Jerry checked, he saw two others guarding each side of the door outside. He asked the soldier if it was okay to go to the airport, was told that it was, then returned to the desk, paid his bill and ordered a cab.

'Let's wait outside,' he said to Ingrid. 'Let's see what's happening.'

Carrying the suitcases, he led Ingrid outside where, while they waited for the cab, they listened to the sounds of battle from inside the Old City and saw black smoke billowing up into the bright, afternoon sky.

'A regular little riot,' he said to Ingrid. 'Nice to live where the action is.'

'I don't think that's at all funny, Jerry.'

'So sorry,' he said.

He was stirred to note that even when trying to be severe in that very English manner, she was – particularly minus specs and with her long hair falling over her shoulders – a pleasantly attractive young woman, not to say sexy. Suddenly brimming over in a flood of emotion, he put his arm around her, pulling her to him and kissed her pale cheek. She made a soft purring sound, like a cat when its throat is stroked, and was just about to turn in against him when the taxi arrived.

The sounds of battle had moved out of the Old City and were slowly progressing up the Nablus Road when the cab driver suddenly stood on his brakes and started honking his horn.

Releasing his grip on Ingrid, Jerry glanced around him, noted that a large group of Israeli soldiers were stepping *backwards* along the Nablus Road as if retreating from a mob, so picked up the suitcases and hurried with Ingrid down the steps to the honking cab.

He hadn't actually put a foot on the pavement when he heard the other noise – a noise louder than the sounds of battle – then felt a sudden, sharp wind. Almost swept sideways, he was jerked back by Ingrid, then looked up as the roaring became deafening and the wind whipped more furiously. He was dazzled by the sunlight, briefly blinded by dust, rubbed his eyes and shook his head and looked again and saw, descending quickly and noisily, a helicopter with no markings on its bodywork.

'Shit!' he said. 'What –?'

Deafened by the roaring, beaten back by the swirling air, he dropped the suitcases and heard another noise – a loud screeching of tyres. He heard Ingrid shouting – first his name, then a warning – and lowered his gaze to the road as a canvas-topped truck screeched to a halt just beyond the parked cab, disgorging a lot of heavily armed soldiers, all of them wearing old SS uniforms and looking terribly young.

'Christ!' he exclaimed. 'It must be your father's men!'

He instinctively grabbed Ingrid, pulling her against him, as the cab driver jumped out of his car and fled, the Israeli soldiers by the entrance started shouting, and the adolescent soldiers in front of him spread out and lowered their weapons, preparing to fire.

The helicopter dropped lower, a machine gun roared, then all the soldiers began firing their weapons.

'Get down, Ingrid! *Get down!*'

He pulled her closer, heard her gasp as if amplified, then dragged her down onto the steps, writhing backwards, and tugged her against the nearest wall. The noise was catastrophic. He glanced back up the steps as plaster exploded around the door and one of the Israeli soldiers, after jerking like an epileptic, collapsed and bounced, lifeless, down the steps.

'Oh, God!' Ingrid cried. '*No!*'

She turned her head away from the dead man, from that rattling, bouncing corpse, and hid her face in Jerry's chest as he looked back up the steps and saw the other Israeli soldier dropping low and bawling, then quivering to the bucking of his sub-machine gun, which was aimed at the road. More plaster and brick exploded around him, dust spiralled up from the steps, and Jerry looked to the front and saw the horde of SS youngsters swarming across the road towards the hotel, firing their weapons, screaming like lunatics, pirouetting and dropping dead.

'*Don't move, Ingrid!*'

She had started scrabbling across the steps, but he grabbed her and pulled her back, looking up as the helicopter dropped dangerously low, its rotors whipping the air into a tornado, its roar almost deafening.

'Oh, God, *it's my father!*'

Even as Ingrid's breathless, heartbreaking wail stabbed him to the core, he recognized, through the swirling dust, in his panic and confusion, the broad-shouldered Wilhelm Zweig, who was leaning out of the shuddering helicopter and bawling instructions to his troops through an amplified megaphone.

'*Don't harm the American and the woman! Bring them both in alive!*'

Deafened and dazed, Jerry felt a bubble of insane laughter expanding inside him. This whole affair was a bad dream, too ridiculous to be true – and yet another soldier screamed and quivered epileptically as the wall behind him was perforated with bullet holes and spat clouds of dust.

'It's my father! *Oh, God!*'

Hearing that singular lament of grief from the woman he loved, Jerry suddenly vaulted out of himself and became someone else.

He saw the dead Israeli, the hand grenades and bayonet that had rattled down the steps scattered around his tattered, bloody body like obscene decorations.

He glanced up at the helicopter, saw Zweig hanging out, saw the megaphone, the rotor blades above, then pushed Ingrid away.

He hardly knew what he was doing. He was a dreamer in his own dream. Ingrid cried out as he hurled himself forward. The dead man was very dead. He knew that when he touched him. He reached down, inexperienced, risking all, and picked up a hand grenade.

'Oh, shit!' he said. 'Jesus!'

He had only seen it in movies, so that didn't help too much, but he lay on his belly, seeing bullet holes and blood, then rolled onto his back and pulled the pin out. He saw the adolescents charging, firing their weapons from the hip; then he threw the hand grenade, saw Ingrid crawling towards him, grabbed her, pulled her to him, rolled upon her and prayed that the throw was right.

'Get them!' Zweig bawled through his megaphone. *'Bring that pair in alive!'*

The hand grenade exploded with a godalmighty roar – something tearing at the air, ripping through all Jerry's senses – and he saw a pall of smoke in which Zweig's stormtroopers were staggering and screaming. They broke, then, and ran as more trucks materialized out of nowhere and disgorged other soldiers – Israelis, tough and trained, firing methodically and precisely, cutting down those in flight like so many ninepins.

Those not dying were screaming, scrambling back into the truck, were pursued by the Israelis as the vehicle growled into life and lurched forward through a fusillade of gunfire and more scattered explosions.

Jerry looked up, saw the helicopter ascending, watched it shrinking above him, ennobled by sunlight, then looked back at the road and saw Wilhelm Zweig's truck bouncing and swaying through a hail of gunfire and cascading dust. It soon screeched around a corner with the Israelis in hot pursuit – and then Jerry felt a movement and realized that he was still lying on Ingrid who, as the sound of battle receded, gave a smile like the dawning sun.

'Oh, my hero!' she crooned.

Zweig couldn't believe it. As his helicopter soared above the rooftops of East Jerusalem he looked down and saw his troops in his rented truck fleeing from the scene of the debacle. Zweig couldn't believe their incompetence, their woeful lack of courage, and as the sirens continued wailing and more Israeli troop carriers closed in on the hotel, thus blocking off all chance of escape for his men, he let out a bellow of rage, hammered his fist into his palm, but had to keep looking down, transfixed by defeat.

It was more than he could bear. Ingrid's boyfriend,

the American, had managed to put Zweig's troops to flight by simply giving them a taste of their own medicine with a neatly flipped hand grenade.

All that training! That iron discipline and order! All destroyed by an . . . *amateur*!

'You scum!' Zweig shouted down at the earth, waving his clenched fist at the truck that was skidding to a halt inside a circle of Israeli troop carriers, under dense, streaming dust. 'May you all rot in hell!'

Finally, just before the helicopter soared too high for him to see properly, he managed to make out his daughter and the American embracing on the steps of the hotel, while a horde of Israeli soldiers – despised Jews swarming like ants on an ant hill – appeared from all directions to fill the streets around the hotel and capture the last of his men.

Zweig let out a cry of rage and vowed to himself that he wouldn't rest until he had Ingrid, the American *and* St Germain in his clutches.

'Now get me out of this Jewish cesspit!' he hissed at the pilot. 'I can't stand the stench of it!'

Too frightened to speak, the pilot nodded and obeyed; then the helicopter shuddered and climbed rapidly towards the sun, carrying Wilhelm Zweig, shocked and outraged, away from his personal hell on earth.

PART THREE

THE
SECRET KNOWLEDGE

CHAPTER THIRTY-SIX

St Germain had thoughtfully arranged for Jerry and Ingrid to have a few days' rest in Calcutta before going on to Darjeeling; and Jerry insisted that they recover from jet lag by making love until midnight local time, after which, as he helpfully pointed out, they could sleep arm in arm like babies and awaken feeling refreshed and normal. This they did, since Ingrid now loved lovemaking, and indeed awakened refreshed and more prepared to face the strangeness of India.

'Calcutta's the largest of all Indian cities,' Jerry explained as they got their breath back in bed, 'and is, in fact, the second biggest in the British Commonwealth, outranked only by London. It spreads over 270 square miles, has a population of approximately ten million, and is filled with industrial plants and textile mills, in which jute is processed.'

'That's fascinating, Jerry.'

'You think so?'

'Absolutely.'

'I like learning these odd little facts. It makes me feel at home.'

Aware that they hadn't seen the last of Ingrid's father, but convinced that he would not be able to trace them for some time, they delighted in their luxurious accommodation (which had been paid for in advance by 'a European gentleman who did not wish to be named') in the Oberoi Grand Hotel in Jawahharlal Nehru Road, overlooking the sweeping lawns of the Maidan, and during the next couple of days used it as a base for their exploration of the vast, noisily overwhelming city.

Glowing beautifully after that first evening of passionate lovemaking, Ingrid more than once tried to persuade Jerry to take her to the Ashutosh and Indian Museums, the Marble Palace or the various temples and mosques of the sprawling city; but he had no intention of wasting his time on seeing the things he could see in books and instead insisted upon seeing the *real* India which was, according to him and clearly to Ingrid's horror, to be found in the Howrah Station, where hundreds of passengers hung out of the carriage windows like bunches of dark grapes, whole families camped out on the platforms for days until they could depart, and peddlers of rice and sweetmeats, water vendors, tea-serving waiters, newsboys and rampaging, shrieking children added their relentless noise to the cacophony of the hundreds of loudly chattering Bengalis and Hindus, the bawling of porters, and the whistling and clanging of the oil-covered, red-rusted locomotives, which, in clouds of smoke and fountains of steam, were disturbingly ghostlike.

'The *real* India,' Jerry said. 'Not your usual tourist rubbish. These are the sights, sounds and smells that you'll never forget.'

'It's awful,' Ingrid replied. 'I can't stand it. Let's get out of here.'

'You're joking,' he said to her. 'You can't mean that. Let's do some exploring.'

Making it clear that she was repelled by the swarm of humanity that virtually lived in or passed through the smoky, chaotic station, Ingrid persisted in trying to guide Jerry towards some culture; but considering himself already well educated, his brain already crammed with facts, he instead returned time and again to the overwhelming hustle and bustle of the station – and when in need of a change only took her out of it to join the throng of penniless peasants and holy men in dhotis and saris, who poured by bus, car, truck, bicycle, ox-cart, rickshaw and foot across the immense, cantilevered Howrah Bridge, its web of girders casting shadows on the muddy, slow-flowing Hooghly river, the shores of which were crammed with barbers and masseurs who plied their trade by the water's edge while the sacred cows roamed amongst them, untouchable, safe.

The shores of the Hooghly frightened Ingrid even more than the station, particularly during the evenings when the atmosphere changed dramatically, becoming unfriendly, dark-shadowed and threatening – and she certainly smiled a lot more readily when, after two exhausting days in the swarming city, they left, took the forty-five minute flight to Bagdogra, and boarded the famous 'toy' train at New Jalpaiguri, for the seven-hour journey to Darjeeling.

'I feel like a kid again,' Jerry said. 'It's like being in Disneyland.'

'It's lovely,' she replied. 'I'm enchanted. Now *this* is the India *I* love. I can't wait to get started.'

The 'toy' train consisted of three coaches and a baby locomotive that huffed and puffed its way laboriously along a two-foot gauge track, first winding through the solid walls of vegetation in the jungle just outside Bagdogra, then beginning the exceptionally steep, twelve-miles-per-hour climb uphill, until the palm trees and dense forest had been replaced by a lush green landscape of terraced tea plantations, which rose, one on top of the other, to a crystal clear sky.

While Ingrid observed the scenery with eyes bright-ened by delight, Jerry, who preferred the squalors of urban life to landscapes, found himself wondering just what would be in store for them once they arrived at Darjeeling. They were heading for the Himalayas, and he wondered why that was so; wondered if those legendary peaks hid St Germain's secret.

'And why not?' he asked her. 'To the Tibetans, the Himalayan peaks are the sacred ground for an awful lot of gods and demons, and are credited with *supernatural* powers of defence. In fact, so sacred was Kanchenjunga considered to be, the British expedition of 1955 turned back five feet from the summit in order not to offend their Sherpas. The area hasn't been explored much at all, and to hide in it wouldn't be too difficult.'

He caught his first glance of Kanchenjunga from the small village of Kurseong, where the train's track seemed to run through Main Street and the shops were so close that the passengers could haggle with the vendors without leaving their seats.

While Ingrid purchased a silk scarf from one of the shopkeepers who was only an arm's length away, Jerry contented himself with studying the snow-capped peaks of Kanchenjunga.

The names of the mountains reflected a mystical tradition, with the highest of them all, Everest, being the Mother of the Earth, Annapurna translating as Giver of Life, and the mountain richest in mythology – the one he was looking at, Kanchenjunga – being the Five Treasures of the Eternal Snows, since the Tibetans believed that the god of wealth lived there, storing in its five peaks the five treasures: gold, silver, copper, corn and sacred books ... perhaps, in fact, the Secret Knowledge – the Philosophers' Stone.

'I wonder where we'll end up,' he said to Ingrid.

'I don't care,' she replied. 'Right now, I'm just enjoying the trip. I think I'm in heaven.'

'You *look* like you're in heaven. You're all suntanned and glowing.'

'I don't want to remember the past or even think

about the future. I just want to soak in the landscape and live for the moment.'

'Good thinking, Ingrid.'

Leaving Kurseong, the 'toy' train continued its journey up through gloriously varied, exotic scenery, moving so slowly that every car on the adjoining road passed it easily and children were forever jumping on the running boards of the coaches to talk, make faces or beg for money.

Ingrid seemed ecstatic, more so as the train climbed higher, but Jerry felt confused. On the one hand enthralled by the beauty of what he was seeing, he was, on the other, becoming increasingly disorientated, overwhelmed and crushed by the distant, snow-capped mountains, obsessed with the thought that they might not be distant for too long, might in fact be his final destination, the place from which he would not return.

That thought was unavoidable, unshakable, terrifying, and as the small train climbed higher yet and the air became more rarified, he felt himself becoming light-headed and more divorced from himself, as if he was indeed being prepared for some dramatic, irrevocable change.

For that very reason he smiled and joked a lot with Ingrid, but with each passing hour, with each subtle change of scenery, he felt himself slipping into another, more alien skin, burning with a disturbing mixture of excitement and fear.

'It's really weird,' he said, 'but I'm still convinced we're being watched, that somehow or other St Germain has his eye on us.'

'I feel the same,' Ingrid replied. 'I keep thinking I'm being stared at. The most innocent glance makes me nervous, I'm growing so paranoid.'

'Yeah,' Jerry said. 'Right.'

Eventually, after nearly seven hours, the journey

ended at the world's highest railway station, Ghoom, at 8,000 feet, which was 1,000 feet above Darjeeling itself.

Exhilarated and fearful, mentally alert and physically exhausted, he and Ingrid explored the brightly painted, red and blue Tibetan Buddhist monastery of Ghoom – where the monks were of the yellow sect and worshipped a large image of the Coming Buddha – then took a rickshaw down to the Oberoi Mount Everest hotel on Ghandi Road, with its glorious views of Kanchenjunga.

St Germain was being kind to them, since they soon discovered that they were able to view the mystical mountains even as they lay naked together on the bed and made love, which they did often throughout that first afternoon, evening and morning.

The next day, satiated for a while, they checked if there were any messages for them – fully expecting to find one from St Germain – and, being told that there were none, and that their suite had been booked for a 'maximum of one week' which had been paid for in advance by 'a well-dressed European gentleman', Jerry realized that there was little they could do except wait for events to take their course and meanwhile enjoy the town.

'Let's go out and explore,' he said to Ingrid. 'We might as well be tourists for the time being. Have we any cash left?'

'Enough to last for a couple of weeks if we're economical.'

'Aren't we always, my pet?'

He couldn't help but feel delight at the thought of having spent most of the money Ingrid had pilfered from her old man. Any thought of Zweig was inevitably tinged with dread, but the fear *could* be defeated, at least temporarily, by imagining the fat pig flushed with rage. He must have been flushed a lot like that since Ingrid fled from the hotel in Cairo, and Jerry savoured his little bubble of joy at the thought of him suffering so.

Yet the fear always returned. It was something he hid from Ingrid. He joked to hide his concern over where they were headed and, perhaps more relevant, his fear that the actions of her father must be secretly tormenting her.

Her escape from Zweig's clutches had changed her profoundly, given her self-esteem and strength, but Jerry knew that she still felt dread and shame in the knowledge of what her father was – a murderer, a monster, possibly a psychopath – and he sensed that that knowledge was something she had not learned to live with. She couldn't accept that it was true, didn't want to believe it, and would not be a completely whole person while Zweig's shadow hung over her.

A confrontation with Zweig would come sooner or later; and Jerry, while occasionally frightened for himself when thinking about that, was even more concerned for Ingrid and what it might do to her . . .

As if contaminated with Ingrid's fear, reminded of how far from home he was, and suddenly realizing he didn't even know that he would ever return, he left their room in the hotel to let Ingrid wash and dress, padded furtively down the stairs, picked up the telephone, dialled his mother in New York, and after considerable difficulty, actually managed to get her.

'Hi, Mom, it's me.'

'Jerry? Where *are* you? Why haven't you come home yet? I'm in the middle of a game of bridge, and the girls keep asking embarrassing questions about you. I mean, why aren't you *home*, dear?'

'I'm in India, Mom.'

'I *beg* your pardon?'

'In India. I can't explain everything just now, but I'm calling from India.'

'You're still . . . *sight-seeing*, Jerry?'

'Yes, Mom, you might say that. I mean, I'm travelling around here on my own, living cheaply and enjoying it, so I'm not too sure when I'll be coming home.'

'You're living . . . *cheaply*?'

'Yes, Mom, real cheap. I have a rucksack and I hitchhike everywhere and I'm having a great time.'

Even as he said that, he had the distinct feeling that he was being watched. He looked over his shoulder at the busy hotel lounge, thought he saw eyes staring at him, blinked, then saw nothing, scanned the people in the lounge to no effect and then felt pretty foolish. He was brought back to reality by the sound of his mother's voice.

'It sounds absolutely dreadful. That country is filthy, Jerry. I just hope you're taking malaria tablets and avoiding all food and drink.'

'I just called to say I love you.'

'Well, that's very sweet, dear. But I suspect that there's more to it than that. . . . Is some *woman* involved?'

'Of course not, Mom.'

'Not that awful German's daughter!'

'I promise you, Mom, I'm just travelling around. There's no woman involved.'

'So when are you coming home?'

'What's that, Mom? I can't hear you.'

'I said, when are you planning to return? I mean, it's *weeks* since I've seen you.'

'I just rang to say don't worry. I mean, I'm having a great time, Mom. I just rang to say I love you, that I'll try to keep in touch. I'm probably going hiking in the mountains and won't be near a phone for a while.'

She sighed melodramatically. 'If you say so, dear.'

He used the uncomfortable pause that followed to

scan the busy lobby again. He noticed a man turning away from him, almost *too* quickly, and watched him move off through the other people and turn up the stairs. *Had* that man been watching him? Was he only imagining it? He sucked his breath in and let it out while his heart settled down again.

'I'm all right, Mom, I promise,' he said without feeling too confident. 'You don't have to worry.'

'I *do* hope you're not involved with some woman.'

'Cross my heart, hope to die.'

He heard her sigh again. 'Well, all right. Enjoy yourself. Just remember to avoid food and drink and not to talk to strangers.'

'I'll remember, Mom. Honest. I've had a good time so far. And don't worry if you don't hear for some time – I'll write sooner or later. Okay?'

'Well . . .' Her hesitation was profound. 'If you insist. . . . I suppose.'

'Goodbye, Mom.'

'Goodbye, dear.'

He hung up, feeling guilty, wiping sweat from his brow, wondering when he actually *would* return home – if, indeed, he would ever do so. Stepping out of the phone booth, he glanced around the lobby, trying to catch someone staring at him, but the people, mostly middle-aged men and women, seemed routinely pre-occupied.

Feeling foolish in his nervousness, he returned to the room, found Ingrid washed and dressed, felt like stripping the clothes off her, but instead growled, 'Let's go.'

'Of course, darling,' she murmured in an in-describably sensual, seductive manner. 'Whatever you say, dear.'

Darjeeling, if thoroughly enchanting, was a place to be

climbed. Built on the side of a steep hill, overlooked by the distant splendour of the peaks of the Kanchenjunga mountain range, it sat on a series of natural landings linked by steep flights of steps and narrow, almost vertical lanes. The top level of the village was the main tourist area, with the larger hotels, cafés, shops and attractive villas lined along the busy Mall, or Main Street; the middle level more authentically Indian, with smaller hotels, more shops and restaurants; and the lower level the most colourful of all, being filled with Darjeeling's working population of Nepalese, Tibetans, Bhutias and Lepchas, most in colourful tribal costumes, forming an exotic, noisy throng in the bazaars and market places.

Determined to keep active while he waited to be contacted, and not wishing to give either himself or Ingrid time to dwell uncomfortably on Zweig or the magical unknown into which St Germain was drawing them, he dutifully led Ingrid around the town and surrounding area, but always circled back automatically, as if in a trance, to the ravishing, three-tiered town, drawn by its natural beauty, exotic colour and vibrancy – but even more than that, by the thought that he and Ingrid would soon be facing St Germain.

That expectation was exciting, but also increased his fear, and as he tried to pass the time, seeing the sights, playing the tourist, he was increasingly frustrated by his impotence at this stage, by his knowledge that he was now at the mercy of St Germain's whims. His paranoia was increasing, perhaps even infecting Ingrid: he was haunted by shadows, by the sounds of stealthy movement, imagining eyes upon him, agents always on his tail – and was frightened that those in pursuit would not necessarily be St Germain's allies.

No, Zweig would not give up. He would be following them as well. And if he and Ingrid, at least so far, were being *guided* by St Germain, they would not be handled with such care if caught by Zweig's men.

Jerry felt trapped, caught between opposing forces, and trying to keep himself busy, yet also looking for signs, he continued to explore the teeming town.

'They might *come* to us,' he said. 'But they might expect us to *find* them. Without guidelines, there's nothing we can do except keep our eyes open.'

'The more I do that,' Ingrid replied, 'the more I imagine things. Even my own shadow scares me.'

'Maybe that's part of the test as well. We'll just have to brave it. Let's check out a few cafés.'

If the lower part of the town was rendered exotic by its throng of brightly costumed Indians, it was also noteworthy for its collection of Western hitchhikers, adventurers and shady characters who drifted restlessly from one meeting place to another, trading anecdotes and information, buying and selling drugs, and generally giving Jerry a different sense of danger and intrigue.

'These guys are brigands,' he told Ingrid. 'They're all here for adventure. They're the last of the existentialists, living just for the moment, into drugs and sex and quick thrills, contemptuous of capitalism, of *materialism*, and into spiritual things.'

'They're mostly just bums,' Ingrid responded. 'And they all need a bath.'

'But they know what goes on here,' he said, 'and they might tell us something.'

Using this as his excuse, he dragged the reluctant Ingrid down the steep steps and narrow lanes of the town to its colourful lower level. Once there, he led her from one noisy café to another, smiling brightly enough to encourage any passing stray, whom he would then engage in lengthy, sometimes drunken or drugged conversations about quantum mechanics, the theory of relativity, life after death, the mind-expanding potential of hallucinogenic drugs, and the lore and lure of the magical mountains that loomed over the town.

He was careful not to mention the real reason for his and Ingrid's presence in Darjeeling, and when asked lied blandly that they were here simply as tourists. But during those conversations, with the air smelling of curry, beer, cigarette smoke and marijuana, and filled with the cacophony of tinnily amplified Western music, he learned from more than one long-haired, bearded youth that it *was* generally believed that the sacred mountains of the Himalayas, particularly Kanchenjunga, were rumoured to harbour a secret colony, or colonies, of ancient mystics.

'Yeah, man, this place is *weird*,' he was told. 'Strange things happen in the mountains. There's hidden valleys up there, fabulous riches, strange forces, a lot of things that can't be explained and make the Sherpas real nervous.'

'Right,' Jerry said to his stoned friend. 'I've heard a few stories.'

'Fucking A,' his friend replied, drinking beer, smoking a joint. 'But it's best not to look too carefully, man, 'cause that can bring bad luck. I mean, people disappear. They don't ever find the bodies. The Sherpas say they got too close to forbidden places and were stolen away. There are *weird* people up there. No one knows who they are. Some say they're Tibetan monks, but others say they don't even come from Earth, that they're not of this time.'

'Wow,' Jerry said. 'Far out!'

'You ever see the lights, man? Lots of *strange* lights up there. People climbing up there have been *attacked* by those lights and driven all the way back down the slopes. There are places you just can't go. You even get the lights right here – flying down from Kanchenjunga.

They're really *weird* lights – disc-shaped, like god-damned UFOs – and they're often seen flying down from the mountains and hovering over Darjeeling. Sometimes they land. You can see them glowing beyond the lowlands. Then they ascend again, very quickly, no noise, and wink out in the higher slopes of Kanchenjunga, just like lightbulbs. *UFOs*, man! Really *weird* . . .'

That news changed Jerry's attitude, encouraged him out of the cafés, seduced him into studying the mountains and exploring, particularly in the darkness, the hills around that jewel of a town at the base of the mountains.

He always took Ingrid with him, frightened of being parted from her, and he loved her more than ever in those dark, scented hills, her eyes reflecting the moon, her long hair blowing freely in the breeze and touched by the starlight.

The stars were in her eyes and hair, seemed to make her white skin gleam. He realized how much she had changed, how much of a woman she was now, and wondered how much of the change, that magical metamorphosis, had been caused by the extraordinary experiences that St Germain had put them through these past few weeks.

So he walked her over the hills, in love with her, fearful for her, but after a few days, seeing nothing but moon and stars, took her back down to Darjeeling, to a smoky, noisy café and, holding her hand, gazing deep into her eyes, reminded her that this was, in all likelihood, their last evening in town.

'It's got to be tonight,' he told her, shouting against the noises of the café, scanning the other tables for a familiar face amongst the mostly young men and women who were drinking beer and coffee and smoking pot in a blue haze. 'Our room was booked until tomorrow. That means that whatever's going to happen is going to happen tonight.'

'Did you *see* it?' their bearded friend said, suddenly leaning over their table, breathing the smell of beer into their faces while he puffed on a joint, his eyes large and brilliant. 'It was a UFO. Jesus Christ! Or at least some kind of strange light. It came down from Kanchenjunga, hovered over Main Street, then shot off and stopped above Observatory Hill and seemed to settle down on it. A couple of guys zapped up there. They took a Jeep and went like bats out of hell. As they were driving there, half of Darjeeling was watching that goddamned light. It illuminated the Mahakala Temple, pulsating rapidly, then dimming; then it flared up and rose to the sky again and shot back towards the mountains. Then the guys in the Jeep returned. They all looked a bit shaken. They said they got there too late – that the light had gone when they arrived – but that the ground around the Mahakala Cave – the Bhutian shrine devoted to Siva – was charred black and warm to the touch, as if lightly scorched. Those guys went off to get drunk in another bar, but they were clearly scared shitless.'

'When did all this happen?' Jerry asked.

'About half an hour ago,' was the reply. 'Jesus, man, what a sighting!'

'That's it!' Jerry heard himself exclaim automatically, as if the voice belonged to someone else. 'Come on, Ingrid, let's go!'

Taking her by the hand, he dragged her out of her chair, then out of the noisy bar, and kept tugging at her as they made their way hurriedly up the steep steps and almost vertical lanes, through the various levels of the crowded and exotic hillside town until, out of breath and excited, they reached the hotel.

They saw him immediately.

It was not St Germain but his equally strange partner. He was standing in the lobby, very close to the entrance, wearing a light tropical suit with white shirt and old school tie, his hands clasped together in front of him, his wintry-grey, almost silvery eyes staring steadily, hypnotically at them, a slight smile on his lips.

'Hello,' he said, his voice deep, melodious and exquisitely caressing. 'I often use the name Christian Grabbe, but you may call me. . . .'

Here he paused to lower his head in a slight, theatrical bow, his smile one of dry amusement and mockery . . . and diabolically charming.

'You may call me . . . *Mephisto*.'

CHAPTER THIRTY-SEVEN

As he stared at Christian Grabbe, or Mephisto, perhaps even Mephistopheles, Jerry felt himself surrendering to those silvery-grey, mesmeric eyes, to that quietly seductive smile, and realized that once more he *wanted* the man with an insatiable, unnatural, shaming lust.

He had come such a long way for this – and now hardly knew how to react, let alone what to ask. The man staring so hypnotically at him, as if sensing his dilemma, smiled smoothly and stroked his ink-black hair, his amusement plain on his diabolically handsome face.

'Why are you blushing?' he asked, his voice mellifluous. 'Does my name mean that much to you?'

Jerry didn't reply. He felt confused and embarrassed. He had never had a homosexual thought in his life, and yet he felt a very powerful need for the man smiling at him – as indeed he had had each time he had seen him before.

'It's all right,' Mephisto said softly. 'There's nothing to be ashamed of. *Everyone* feels that way about me – it's part of my curse.'

'Your . . . *curse?*'

'Try looking at Ingrid,' the man replied, ignoring the question. '*She* wants me as well. If you love her, your jealousy will protect you from what you are feeling. You can *talk* to me, then.'

The mockery was quiet and unmalicious, almost weary, perhaps *self* mocking. Jerry glanced at Ingrid and noted her blushing cheeks and glistening gaze.

Yes, she wanted Mephisto – her slim body was straining towards him – and Jerry filled up with a fierce, blinding rage that transcended his own lust. His desire for Mephisto fell away – as Mephisto had said it would – and he was able to view the man's extraordinary charm with surprising detachment.

'*Mephisto?*' he asked. 'Why *Mephisto*? Obviously that can't be your real name – so just who the hell *are* you?'

Mephisto smiled. 'So many questions,' he crooned. 'Which one should I answer first?'

'Why Mephisto?' Jerry repeated. 'Any relationship, by any chance, to Mephistopheles? Are you an old friend of Doctor Faust?'

'Doctor *Faust*? *What* Doctor Faust?'

'It's generally thought that the name Mephistopheles was invented by Georg Faust, the sixteenth-century magician and charlatan, famed in legend and literature as the man who sold his soul to the devil in exchange for knowledge and power.'

'Really? I was conceived by a magician and charlatan? How terribly undignified!'

'I didn't say you were *conceived* by him. I just think you might have adopted the name, that's all.'

'And why would I do that, young sir?' Mephisto asked, his smiling lips moist and sensual.

'Why? I'd love to know. Christopher Marlowe described his fictitious Mephistopheles as a fallen angel, torn between satanic pride and dark despair. Goethe, on the other hand, saw *his* Mephistopheles as cynically witty and cold-hearted. Which one are you?'

Mephisto shrugged, clearly amused and pained at once. 'What does it matter? Your Faust was not well known in life, but only in death, his posthumous fame due to the anonymous author of a collection of tales about the ancient magi: wise men skilled in the occult sciences –'

'Tales retold in the Middle Ages,' Jerry interjected, 'about other famed wizards, such as Merlin, Albert Magnus and Roger Bacon.'

'Quite so. And Mephistopheles was created in those magic manuals of Faust, and as such is a creature of fiction. Why, then, should I be him?'

'Maybe Mephistopheles *wasn't* a creature of fiction. Maybe, like a lot of fiction, he was more real than reality.'

'I'm glad I seem *real* to you,' Mephisto said. 'That *will* be helpful.'

'I want to know why you call yourself Mephisto in the twentieth century.'

Mephisto shrugged again. 'My name is Mephisto,' he said. 'That's all I know. It is the name I was given.'

'By whom?' Ingrid asked, and blushed more brightly when Mephisto stared directly at her.

'St Germain,' he said. '*Naturally.*'

Jerry felt oddly chilled, suddenly filled with trepidation, caught in what seemed increasingly to be some kind of waking dream. Glancing distractedly around the hotel's modern lobby, he noted, with a shock, that most of the women present were staring either blatantly or surreptitiously at the man calling himself Mephisto, some of them visibly flushed, others obviously embarrassed or confused by their own helpless behaviour. Disturbed, he returned his gaze to Mephisto, wondering who, or what, he was truly facing.

'And who's St Germain?' he asked. 'Did *he* sell his soul to the devil in exchange for knowledge and power?'

Mephisto stopped smiling. 'I wouldn't know,' he said quietly.

'Or wouldn't say?' Jerry ventured.

'You are impertinent.'

'I just want to *know*.'

'We don't always get what we want. Shall we talk sitting down?'

Without waiting for a reply, he turned slightly sideways, indicating with a nod of his head that they should all take a seat around a small table. Seated, he clasped his hands under his chin and stared at them with his silvery-grey eyes.

'So,' he said, 'you have actually come this far. You must be very keen to meet St Germain . . . or to get your hands on the Tuaoi Stone.'

'We don't want the Tuaoi Stone,' Jerry responded. 'And we *never* actually wanted it. At first we simply wanted to warn its keeper that Ingrid's father was after it –'

'Which we knew.'

'We soon found *that* out. And then, once we'd started our search, and you'd placed various clues in front of us, we just had to see it through to the end.'

'*What* end?' Mephisto asked, his fine eyebrows raised in amusement. 'What do you hope to find?'

Jerry looked at Ingrid, and was shocked to note that she was still gazing at Mephisto, her cheeks flushed, eyes glowing with adoration, her lips slightly parted. Very aware of Mephisto's magnetism, knowing it to be at once unnatural and irresistible, he still couldn't help feeling betrayed by her shameless behaviour.

He looked back at Mephisto.

'I don't know,' he said. 'I can't work it out. I only know you could have stopped us at any point in the journey – your powers are such that you could have done that – but instead, you protected us and led us here. That man in Israel said we were being tested. Tested for *what*?'

'That is not for me to say,' Mephisto replied. 'You will have to ask St Germain.'

'I will – *when* I see him. So when will that be?'

'To see St Germain, you must go to him – and that journey, in its simplicity and hardship, is the final, most dangerous test.'

'I thought our journey had ended here.'

'The journey has ended for *Ingrid*,' Mephisto said, smiling at her. 'But for you the real journey has just begun.'

'The *real* journey?'

'Your final test. The one you must make alone.'

'I won't go anywhere without Ingrid,' Jerry responded automatically.

Mephisto smiled in weary cynicism. 'Oh, yes, you will.'

Ingrid looked confused, first glancing at Jerry, then blushing with what seemed like guilt.

'I'm going wherever Jerry goes,' she whispered. 'I wouldn't leave him at this point.'

Mephisto spread his hands in the air. 'Well, we will see.'

The way he said it chilled Jerry to the bone, forcing him to remember all that he and Ingrid had experienced so far, and convincing him that in getting involved with Mephisto and St Germain, he was getting in over his depth and could easily drown.

These were not normal people – they were possibly inhuman – and as he gazed at Mephisto, wondering who or *what* he was, he pondered the fine line between good and evil. Mephisto, through St Germain, had protected him and Ingrid from Zweig – but why should they bother doing that when even Zweig was no threat to them?

They were testing him – they had let him know that much – but he didn't know why . . . and what he didn't know frightened him.

'Anyway,' he said, 'where *would* I find the elusive St Germain, assuming I *did* make the journey?'

Mephisto pointed in the general direction of the windows at the far side of the lobby. 'Up there,' he said.

'Kanchenjunga?'

'Correct.'

Jerry thought of the far-off, snow-capped mountain peaks of the shroud of clouds which hung over them, obscuring the summit. Even experienced climbers had been lost in trying to climb those slopes, so he couldn't imagine himself, city born and bred, getting anywhere near them. The very idea that he might was ridiculous – but he let that fact pass.

'St Germain's up there?'

'Yes,' Mephisto replied. 'I myself came down from there a short while ago – but *you* can't go up that way.'

'That light – the thing everyone thinks was a UFO. You came down in that?'

'Not *in* it, but *of* it – part of it . . . but I can't quite explain that.'

'You mean it's not a flying saucer?'

'People have been seeing such things for years and calling them flying saucers. If a flying saucer is what you see, then that's what it is.'

'Except that it isn't.'

'No, I'm afraid not. At least not in the accepted sense. It's a means of transportation, certainly, but it's not actually *physical*.'

'Are *you* physical?'

'Yes. Right now I am. At least physical in the sense that you know it – a very deceptive sense.'

'I'm confused.'

'You will learn more if you go up the mountain – if your courage sustains you.'

Jerry glanced at Ingrid, saw her flushed cheeks and radiant eyes, hated her with all the venom of true love and then looked around him. The women at the other tables, most bored with their husbands, were still staring helplessly at Mephisto, as if at a movie star. Jerry wanted to scream.

'What I've learned about you so far,' he managed to say in a civil manner. 'Is that all true?'

'Substantially, yes.'

'What do you mean, *substantially*?'

'You have yet to learn the truth, the whole truth, and nothing *but* the truth.'

'Which I can only learn by talking to St Germain.'

'Correction: which you can only learn by going up the mountain.'

'I won't do that. That's the one thing I won't do. I *can't* do that, and you know it, so why ask me to try?'

'You'd be surprised what you can do if you have to – and in this case, you have to.'

Jerry felt foolish, as if acting in a pantomime. He wanted to shake the truth out of Mephisto, but knew that he wouldn't.

'So you and St Germain are hiding out in the mountains. What *else* is up there?'

'Just ourselves and those like us. Those chosen to be the keepers of the Secret Knowledge, without which the Tuaoi Stone is useless.'

'So why do I have to climb a mountain I'm obviously not equipped to climb? Why can't I just hire a helicopter and get up there the easy way?'

'You can't do that, my clever young friend,' Mephisto answered calmly, 'because a helicopter won't help you find what you are looking for. No, the only way to St Germain is up the ancient Sherpas' path – to the monasteries that have been there for years. Once there, in the monasteries, assuming you ever get there, you will learn what you need to know in order to take you higher. We are very well hidden up there – and that route is the final test.'

'I've come as far as I'm going to go,' Jerry said. 'Your secrets aren't worth that much. I won't expose Ingrid to the risk, so I'm going no further.'

'Whether or not you succeed remains in doubt – but you will certainly try it.'

'What makes you so sure?'

'Because *we* have ordained it.'

He raised his right eyebrow, smiled with cynical charm, then turned and offered a different kind of smile to Ingrid. She stared back at him as if hypnotized.

He reached out and placed his hand on her knee, as if already possessing her.

'Are you all right, my dear?' he asked, his voice once more mellifluous and seductive. 'You look rather . . . *warm.*'

'I'm all right,' Ingrid whispered.

'You have been very courageous to come all this way. It would not be right to make you climb the mountain, so perhaps you should stay here.'

'With *you*?' Jerry asked.

Mephisto didn't bother to turn his head when he gave his reply.

'Perhaps I'll stay here. Perhaps not. Who knows what the night will bring?'

'I'm not going up that mountain,' Jerry said. 'The game stops right here.'

'Really? You think so? You really believe so? The game, once started, can only stop when it's finished – and it doesn't finish until you climb that mountain – which you will do, believe me.'

'Take your hand off my girl's knee.'

'Of course. I'm *so* sorry.'

Winking at Ingrid, Mephisto removed his hand and turned back to Jerry, his gaze steady and challenging.

'I've booked into the hotel for the night,' he

informed them both, but then, to Ingrid, added, 'Room fifty-eight, *should* you need me.'

'She won't,' Jerry said, growing angry at how Ingrid was reacting to Mephisto, even though he knew she couldn't help herself. He was jealous – that's all there was to it – and it made him feel awful.

Clearly aware that he was no longer wanted, Mephisto stood up, took note of the many women who were staring intently at him, then gazed down again.

'We will meet again soon,' he said smoothly, 'but not here – up there.' He pointed in the direction of the distant mountains. 'For there, indeed, is where you will go, one way or the other. Now good night, my young friends.'

He bowed slightly at both of them, then turned away and walked out of the lobby, looking very distinguished. When he had gone, Jerry turned back to Ingrid who, still flushed, obviously nervous, tried to avoid his gaze.

'Well?' Jerry said, feeling hurt and choked up.

'Well what?'

'You obviously found our friend Mephisto fairly attractive – or is that putting it mildly?'

'Please, Jerry, stop this.'

'I can't stop it. I *saw* it.'

'I couldn't help it. You *know* I couldn't help it! He even affected *you* that way! He can do it to *anyone*!'

Jerry felt outraged, humiliated that she had noticed. 'At least I managed to control myself. I didn't make it that obvious.'

'He released you,' she replied, her cheeks now flushed with anger. 'He can turn his magnetism on and off, and he just let you go. He was playing with you, Jerry – you were sport – and then he simply released you.'

'Christ!' he responded automatically, ashamed of what he was saying. 'I'm going to bed!'

Without giving her a chance to reply, he hurried across the lobby, collected his room key, then walked just as urgently towards the lift. He thought he heard her calling him back, but couldn't be too sure; however, he soon sensed her coming up behind him, so walked even faster.

When he entered the lift, she got in beside him, staring at him with moist eyes.

They didn't speak as the lift ascended. It only went up two floors. As they walked out, Jerry thought about Mephisto, another three floors above them. A bolt of fear lanced through his rage, deflating him instantly, making him wonder, as he hurried along the corridor, just what he was dealing with. Still, his childish anger won, defeating the fear for the moment, and after opening the room door and following the chastened Ingrid inside, he slammed the door loudly behind him and made her twitch visibly.

God, he thought, when she turned around to face him, *the bitch really is beautiful*.

And was ashamed to think that, at least the 'bitch' part, and walked past her, further into the room, to hide his suddenly burning cheeks.

'To hell with it,' he said. 'I'm fed up with all of it. I'm sorry, Ingrid. I'm sorry. It's not you; it's this whole thing. What the hell's going on? Who *is* that bastard, Mephisto? What's his real relationship to St Germain? And why do we *still* have this goddamned mystery, this cat-and-mouse game? I'm just tired. I can't take any more of it. I want to sleep and forget it.'

Filling up with remorse, he turned around to kiss her cheek. She kissed him back, then pressed herself to him, hugging him with a fearful desperation that gave him a shock. And then remembering how Mephisto had stared at her, his fear returned worse than ever.

'Be very careful,' he told her. 'You have to try to

resist that man. I think he's going to try to separate us, though I'm not too sure why. So be careful when we meet him again. Think of him as a mesmerist, a hypnotist, and try to fight his demands on you.'

'I will, Jerry. I promise,' she said. 'Now let's *both* go to bed.'

Struck by the change in her, remembering what they had been through together, he reached out in a flood of emotion and passionately kissed her. The very feel of her inflamed him, but also filled him with more emotion; and relieved to be forgiven, brimming over with love and longing, he took off his clothes, watched her doing the same, sucked his breath in at the sight of her pale, curvaceous beauty, and lay beside her on the soft, yielding bed like a man resurrected.

He soon lost himself in her, finding protection from his fear, stroked her, fondled her, became a child again, then fell into the last peaceful sleep he would have for a long time.

The sound of the door clicking shut made him open his eyes again, and he grabbed automatically at the bed-sheets but found no one there. Glancing across the moonlit room, he saw the closed door, and knew without having to look elsewhere that Ingrid was gone.

'Oh, no!' he groaned.

Ripping the sheets off him, he slid out of the bed, dressed himself and rushed from the room, then took the lift to the lobby. It was just after midnight, the lobby was deserted, and he was aware, as he hurried through the silence, of his heart racing dramatically.

'The lady sharing Room Twenty-four,' he said to the desk clerk, who looked up in surprise. 'Did you see her just leaving here?'

He hadn't thought to check Mephisto's room. He knew it wasn't necessary. He knew, as his heart sank and pain swept through him, that Mephisto wouldn't be there.

And Ingrid had gone with him.

'Yes, sir,' the desk clerk said, confirming what he had been thinking. 'She just left with the man from Room Fifty-eight. It was a couple of minutes ago. The man, Mr Grabbe, said you might be making enquiries. He told me to tell you that they've gone to Observatory Hill – though why they should go *there* at this hour rather baffles me, sir.'

'And he told you to *tell* me they were going there?'

'Yes, sir,' the Bhutian clerk said. 'I was told to inform you.'

'*Shit!*' Jerry exclaimed without thinking, then raced from the hotel.

It wasn't worth taking a taxi, so he started to run, first through the cluttered streets, then up the steep steps, eventually into the silence and darkness above the tumbling town. There was a great moon above him, a mottled cheese, appetizing, and around it the stars streamed like sparklers on a Halloween night. He ran, his heart pounding, intoxicated by fear, and looked up to see the slopes of Kanchenjunga, its snow-capped peaks glittering. Moonlight and stars and snow merging into midnight – he saw all of it out of the corners of his eyes as he raced through his own steaming breath in a state of blind anguish.

He can't have her, he thought.

He thought, also, as he ran, of what they had been through together – their shared terror in the burial chamber in the Great Pyramid of Giza; their mutual excitement and love in the British Museum Library; their fear and exaltation during their magical experiences in Greece, Turkey, Germany and Israel – and knew, as it all flooded over him, that he would never forget it. What they had shared was part of him, *was* him, as he was Ingrid; and he ran faster, aware that he was being robbed, knowing how much he wanted her.

The town was now far behind him, leaving moonlight and silence, and when he looked at Observatory Hill, he was chilled to the bone.

There, on the dark breast of Observatory Hill, the Mahakala Temple, sacred to Hindus and Buddhists, was starkly silhouetted, not by the moon and stars, but within a great fan of pulsating, striated white light.

'Oh, God!' he gasped, hearing his own voice as a faraway echo, indistinct and unreal. 'Oh, Jesus! Oh, no!'

He ran more urgently up the hill, the sweat dripping from his forehead and into his eyes, blurring his vision as he tried to see what was happening beneath the pagodas. Then a sob burst from him – unexpected and loud – when the fan of light shrank rapidly and became a glowing orb, which abruptly shot off towards the mountains at remarkable speed.

He stopped running then.

It was hopeless and he knew it. That was Ingrid up there. She and Mephisto were racing away from him in that quickly receding light. The light soon reached Kanchenjunga, stopped abruptly, moved sideways, then glided down, as if into a ravine, and suddenly winked out, leaving nothing behind but what had been . . . the white slopes and dark clouds in a star-bright sky rippling with moonlight.

He couldn't stop his tears. They rolled relentlessly down his cheeks. He wiped them off with his fingers, but kept sobbing as he did so; then continued wearily up the slope, feeling helpless and broken.

He walked uphill realizing what Mephisto had tried

to tell him, finally knowing exactly why he would climb that mountain as Mephisto had said he would.

He would climb it for Ingrid, to get her back and prove his love ... and when finally he stood on Observatory Hill, in the shadow of the Mahakala Temple, with the lights of Darjeeling burning romantically beneath him while the moon and stars cast their splendour into his weeping eyes, he choked back his pain but still wept like a child, then raised his right fist to the mountain and defiantly shook it.

'Okay,' he said. '*Yes!*'

He had made his commitment.

CHAPTER THIRTY-EIGHT

'So remember, Hans,' Zweig said, stepping naked out of the shower on the sun-deck, glancing down at Elena where she lay in a bikini on one of the two sunbeds, then taking the towel extended by the Filipino steward, 'when Kuragin arrives, say nothing about our affairs. He's obviously going to demand that we hand back what they've given us, but I've spread it too far and wide for that – and besides, it *belongs* to me. So don't mention anything about our finances; let the fat pig stew in it.' Drying himself with the thick white towel, he looked up at the sky and saw the helicopter in the distance, glinting in sunlight. 'Here he comes,' he said to Hans, 'so bear in mind what I've told you.'

Hans didn't reply and Zweig didn't expect him to. If anything, his young assistant had become quieter than ever since that incident in the Eforie Nord thermal treatment centre by the Black Sea, and Zweig, who had himself been disturbed by the incident – which had been so out of character and, like his temper fits, sometimes filled him with the fear that he was going mad – tried to hide his concern by convincing himself that it gave him yet another hold over his former accountant.

'So,' he said as he dressed, '*has* the money given to us by the Soviets been completely disposed of?'

'Yes, Herr Zweig,' Hans said. 'The money has been placed in bank accounts in Switzerland, Gibraltar, Monaco and the Channel Islands; while many of the paintings and antiques have found their way into

Christie's and Sotheby's in London and New York. Those that remain will be disposed of through the Biennale Internationale at the Grand Palais in Paris this year; and others will eventually turn up in the more reputable galleries of Florence, Milan and, again, London and New York. I can assure you, Herr Zweig, that the distribution has been extremely wide ranging – and most of it will be difficult, probably impossible, to trace.'

'Very good,' Zweig said.

'You could have shoved some of it *my* way,' Elena said. '*I'd* look after it for you!'

'You wouldn't know the difference between one painting and another,' Zweig said. 'And you can't even count. But thanks for the thought.'

He was in fact growing more impatient with the whore's stupidity, and in keeping with his increasingly explosive mood, often wanted to beat her. She had often whipped him in order to give him pleasure, but now he found himself wanting to whip her because she got on his nerves. She was a sexy bitch, yes, but his sexual desires were waning; and without lust to bind them together, he found her impossible.

'You don't have to be sarcastic,' she said as the helicopter, rapidly approaching the boat, started whipping the wind up. 'I mean, I'm just bored, that's all. It's all right for you, playing tin soldiers on your island and boats, but *I* need to get back to a *normal* life, preferably on dry land. I'm fed up lying here, drinking and reading novels, when I could be out *living*. I've had more than enough of it.'

'The only dry land you're likely to set foot on is the floor of a brothel in Recife – and if you don't shut up, that's where you'll *end* up. Now is that understood?'

Elena, instead of replying, slid her sunglasses down

her nose, stared defiantly at him, then slid the glasses back into position and eased her legs off the sunbed. She then stood up and walked away from him, brushing past the steward and disappearing through the hatchway into the lounge to go below decks.

He couldn't help sighing, feeling weary and confused, not too sure of just why he had antagonized her so, but aware that he had been doing it often recently. His physical health was still degenerating, his many capsules and suppositories were showing side effects, and he knew that his terrible tempers, which now came more frequently, were being caused by his general deterioration.

Perhaps he *was* going mad. It was certainly very possible. And when he thought of that likelihood, of his imminent loss of control, he was filled with an overwhelming terror and heightened lust for the Tuaoi Stone.

He completed dressing, putting on long trousers and a short-sleeved shirt, then squinted into the beating wind as the helicopter, roaring loudly, settled onto the swaying helipad on the deck just below him.

Kuragin climbed out of the helicopter and was escorted across the deck and in through the hatchway that led to the upper decks. The Russian arrived eventually, breathing heavily, his right hand outstretched.

'Ah, Kuragin!' Zweig said, smiling falsely at the unsmiling Russian and shaking his hand. 'How nice to see you again. Did you have a good flight?'

'One flight is like another to me. So, how are you, Zweig?'

'In excellent condition as always. Would you care for some schnapps?'

'No, thanks. I never drink before lunch.'

'Some tea, perhaps?'

'You sound like an English gentleman in his garden. Can we get down to business?'

Zweig gripped the railing beside him and squeezed it, as if trying to crush it. The violence shot down his arm, made his fingers contract, then dissipated itself in the railing, after which he relaxed a bit.

'Of course,' he said. 'Naturally. I notice that the helicopter is still running. You intend leaving quickly?'

'Yes,' Kuragin said. 'I'm annoyed that I had to come here in the first place. It's a long trip to make – and one that should *not* have been necessary.'

'Would you care for a seat?'

'I'm happy standing, thanks.'

Zweig sighed again, studied the azure sky, trying to look unconcerned.

'So why *was* it necessary?' he asked.

'We have been sending you telexes and communiqués demanding progress reports on your search for the so-called Tuaoi Stone, or Lodestone, and to date have received no response. We do not find this pleasing.'

'I am doing my best,' Zweig said, 'but things don't happen overnight.'

'*Overnight* has nothing to do with it – it has now been quite a few weeks since you promised either a quick delivery of the stone or definite proof that it does *not* exist. This infraction would be bad enough on its own, but that all our attempts to communicate with you have been blatantly ignored has only incensed the comrades even more.'

'I confess,' Zweig said, defeated, 'that I didn't reply for the simple reason that I had nothing to communicate. I have found out who owns the Tuaoi Stone, but I don't know *where* he is – and unfortunately I lost track of my daughter and her boyfriend in Jerusalem, where I tried to abduct them. I haven't seen or heard of them since, but will find them eventually.'

'Ah, yes, *Jerusalem*,' Kuragin said acidly. 'We know all about *that* particular farce.'

Humiliated by Kuragin's mockery, as well as by the memory of the incident itself, Zweig burned up with a terrible, smothered fury ... smothered at least in the sense that he *had* to smother it when he turned back to the Russian.

'We all make mistakes,' he said lamely. 'We *learn* by our mistakes. And I can assure you, they will not escape again.'

'*If* you ever find them,' Kuragin sneered. 'There was no record of them having left Israel that day – we checked – which means that they travelled under false passports. But where did they *go*?'

'We'll pick up their trail eventually,' Zweig said, taking a deep breath, controlling himself, and hoping to bluff his way, since in truth he didn't know where to start.

'So how do you intend finding them?' Kuragin asked.

'We are running a computer check on the passenger lists of every plane that left Israel within a week of the incident. Aware that they probably used pseudonyms, we are checking the destinations of every couple their age who travelled together. Should that fail to produce results, we will then check each individual passenger in that same age group. Sooner or later, we'll find out where they went.'

Kuragin was clearly not impressed. 'But that could take weeks,' he sneered, 'by which time they could have left and moved on again.'

'We have to take that chance,' Zweig replied, feeling foolish and increasingly humiliated.

Kuragin banged his fist on the railing. 'This is hopeless,' he said. 'Your daughter and the American could be anywhere in the world – they could even be still in Israel. It's hopeless. Just hopeless . . .' He trailed off in disgust, scratched his blue-veined nose, glanced thoughtfully around him at the encircling fleet of other boats, then turned back to offer his most frosty stare. 'But you do *know* who has the Tuaoi Stone?'

'Yes,' Zweig replied, relieved to at last be offering *something*.

'So the stone actually exists?'

'Yes. Definitely. And my daughter and the American are going to meet its keeper soon.'

'So, who *is* he?'

Reluctantly, but realizing that he had little choice if he hoped to appease the clever Russian, Zweig told him what he knew about Saint-Germain, including his extraordinary history and the magical powers he possessed. Yet even as he spoke, he knew he was losing Kuragin, could see it in his face, his rising incredulity, and so finished his tale, not with relief, but with deepening gloom.

The silence, after he had finished speaking, lasted a long time. Kuragin simply stared at him then shook his head wearily.

'And you say this man has lived at least since the eighteenth century and can move back and forth in time and space?'

'Yes,' Zweig said firmly.

'Do you *really* expect me to take this nonsense back to the Kremlin?' Kuragin asked, sounding strangled.

Suddenly inarticulate, Zweig shrugged and raised his hands. 'Well –'

'I won't do it, Zweig. I'd find myself in Siberia. We think the Tuaoi Stone may exist, though we don't know what it is – its legendary powers could be material or simply symbolic; it may be some kind of extraordinary jewel or just worthless stone – but until we *know* for certain what it is, we have to keep up the search for it ... But Saint-Germain! You really expect me to *believe* in him? That he's hundreds, perhaps thousands of years old and can defy space and time? Are you going mad? Are you losing your mind completely? Whether you expect me to believe that, or whether *you* believe it, is surely a sign that you're demented. What *is* going on here?'

Startled to hear Kuragin suggest the very thing he secretly dreaded – that he might be losing his mind – Zweig felt his heart suddenly racing to make his cheeks burn.

'He exists, I tell you,' he insisted, almost stuttering. 'I personally have been exposed to his magical powers, and I know that –'

'Enough, Zweig! *Enough!*'

Shocked by Kuragin's vehemence, Zweig glanced left and right, noted that Hans and the nearby stewards were staring studiously at the deck, and felt smouldering fury at the knowledge that he was being humiliated by this Soviet pig. Trembling, clenching his fists, taking a deep breath, he fought to control himself while Kuragin, his peasant's face outraged, stepped close to him and stared directly at him.

'And now I will tell *you* what's going to happen,' Kuragin said loudly, deliberately, so that Hans and the stewards could hear. 'Your time has run out, Zweig – or *almost* run out. You have exactly one week in which to either produce the Tuaoi Stone or offer the final proof that it doesn't exist. Should you fail to do so, we will be demanding back everything we've given you; and will also put pressure on the West to classify this fleet of yours unlawful, remove the boats from your ownership, and sequester all you own until such times as your finances have been investigated. Since the West is already finding you a considerable embarrassment to them, I do not think they can ignore such pressure from us.'

He nodded, letting what he had said sink in. 'Do you understand, Zweig? All of this –' and here he indicated Zweig's whole fleet with a circular wave of his hand – 'will disappear. And you will fade away with it . . . and eventually be nothing.'

'I don't –'

'Shut up, Zweig. Keep your mouth shut. Don't speak until I walk off this deck. Now *I* call the shots.'

Zweig exploded. He just couldn't help himself. The rage boiled up like a furnace, burned through his arms and hands, made him leap forward and grab the Russian by the throat. He started strangling Kuragin, banging his head against the bulwark, bawling, 'Who the hell do you think you're talking to? I'll *kill* you, you *schweine*!' Then Hans was shouting at him, tugging at him, pulling him off, and he had to remove one hand from Kuragin in order to slap Hans away. He heard the loud smack, felt the stinging, saw Hans reeling, then Kuragin clenched his other fist and swung a punch at him. He thought his head had split open, saw stars, then felt his knees buckling under him.

'*Please*, Herr Zweig,' he heard Hans whisper in a frightened manner, helping him to his feet, 'you mustn't do anything foolish or –'

Zweig slapped him again, saw him falling to the side, then clambered to his feet, swayed dizzily, feeling sick, as Kuragin backed towards the nearest door, whispering, 'You're crazy! Now *that* much is obvious! You're mad, Zweig – and you'll pay for this!'

'Come here, you Russian peasant! *Come here!* Let me –'

He launched himself at that hated figure, but lost his balance and fell, felt pain and rolled onto his back and opened his eyes again. The sky was spinning above him, a white and blue whirlpool, and he found himself shaking all over, felt nauseous and weak. *Heart attack?* he wondered fearfully. *High blood pressure? What . . .?* He almost sobbed, feeling frustrated and fearful, then saw Hans looking down at him.

'Are you all right, Herr Zweig? What happened? Here, let me help you up.'

'*Get that bastard, Kuragin!*'

'It's too late. He's gone.'

Even as Hans spoke, Zweig heard the helicopter's soft throbbing turn into a roar and knew that it was about to take off again. Humiliated and shocked, but taking strength from his rage, he lay there a few more seconds, until the sky had stopped spinning, then pushed himself up with Hans's help and climbed to his feet.

He heard the helicopter, was battered by its slipstream, then was forced to watch it ascending and start to fly westward.

His self-pity turned into rage, and that in turn gave him back his strength.

Watching Kuragin being borne away, he remembered World War II, his exciting days as a Hitler Wolfcub, then the abrupt descent into nightmare when the Russians entered Berlin. He had just turned eighteen, was a golden-haired, handsome boy, and when he was wounded near the Tiergarten and trying to hide in a bombed-out cellar, a group of drunken Russian soldiers had found him and had some sport with him. They had squeezed and prodded his wound, poured salt onto his opened flesh, kicked him, cut him further with bayonets and then finally raped him.

The last had been the worst, a nightmarish degradation, and when they had had their way with him, one after the other, they had left him for dead in the ruins and gone off for more prey. Naturally he hadn't died.

He had been kept alive by hatred. First hatred of the Soviets, then of all humanity – and it had helped him to cast off the last of his decent feelings and seek only self-satisfaction, no matter who paid for it.

Now, as he watched the helicopter taking Kuragin away, that same hatred returned on a wave of memory and gave him his strength back.

'Damn you, *no*!' he exploded and jumped to his feet, shook his fist at the helicopter, then ran to the telephone in the bulwark, picked it up and screamed into it, 'Get that helicopter! Shoot it out of the sky! You hear me? This is Zweig talking. *Shoot that helicopter out of the sky!* Destroy it! *Destroy it!*'

'No!' Hans exclaimed fearfully into his right ear. 'If we do that, the Russians will –'

'Be quiet, Hans! *Shut up!*'

He slammed the telephone down, grabbed Hans by his collar, shook him violently, bounced him off the wall and then cast him aside. Hans fell to the deck and rolled onto his back as the missile launcher, making a humming sound, emerged from its opening steel covering like a giant silver bullet.

Zweig stared at the sky and saw the helicopter reflecting the sunlight as it headed towards Ascension Island. He shook his fist at it, screamed more abuse, then heard the SAM missile leaving its launcher, saw its smoke trail shooting up like a ball of thread and forming a great loop. Then the helicopter exploded and became a smoke-ringed ball of fire that caused debris to fly out in all directions and fall into the sea.

The ball of fire disappeared, the smoke drifted off . . . and soon there was nothing.

'Oh, God,' Hans groaned. 'We're finished.'

The sound of that voice – and the unpleasant truth it had uttered – enraged Zweig even more. He hurried across the deck, to where Hans was sitting upright, grabbed him and hauled him to his feet and started slapping his face. He kept slapping and screaming, losing himself in the process, hovering somewhere above and looking down at himself beating Hans. It was like playing with a rag doll, something light and loose, and he slapped it, threw it against the bulwark, watched it fall and then kicked it.

'We're *finished*?' he bawled at the bloody thing at his feet. 'You think the Soviets are going to avenge that bastard's death by destroying my empire? Well, they won't! I won't let them! Those Russian pigs will get nothing. I now know enough about the Tuaoi Stone to know I don't need them. *I'll* find the Tuaoi Stone! And I'll do it myself this time. I'll find Ingrid and the American *and* Saint-Germain, and when I've done that I'll put an end to them and take control of the Tuaoi Stone. You think I'm *finished*, you defeatist bastard? Well, I'm not, I'm just *starting*! Now get back on your feet!'

Hans did as he was told, rising painfully, his face bloody, his eyes blazing with uncommon fury out of badly bruised flesh.

Zweig noticed, but didn't care, thinking only of the Tuaoi Stone, and turned away to take hold of the railing and look up at the sky. Strands of smoke were still drifting. Below the smoke, the sea was littered. He studied that wreckage, felt a deep satisfaction, then looked at his fleet of boats, the very heart of his worldwide empire, and accepted that what he had done had put him beyond the pale.

Now he had no choice. He had nothing more to lose. He would go in pursuit of them himself, no matter the risk.

He would find the Tuaoi Stone.

CHAPTER THIRTY-NINE

Even here, on the lower slopes of Kanchenjunga, Jerry already felt very different from what he had been just five days ago. While his two Sherpas stopped to let their mules rest, he looked back at the winding River Tista, low-lying tropical jungle and higher forested hills of Sikkim, through which they had travelled to get to here. He could scarcely believe that beyond was the town of Gangtok, surrounded by rice and maize fields, where he had picked up the Sherpa guides, and further on, south-west of that, Darjeeling, where he had lost his beloved Ingrid and which now seemed five years, not five days away.

Choking up just thinking about that, he turned back to the Sherpas and looked beyond, to where the forested hills gave way to the almost barren slopes of the mountains with their snow-capped, cloud-shrouded peaks. They looked dauntingly high and decidedly frightening; and he shivered, hardly believing that he was heading there, feeling slightly possessed.

One of the Sherpas nodded at him and they moved forward again, heading up, so the guides had informed him in broken English, to a Sherpa hill station located high in the Tibetan Plateau but well below the mountain's glacial peaks. He had told them that he wanted to go higher than that, but they had vehemently refused, saying that the mountains were 'possessed' and forbidden to normal men. He therefore didn't know what he would do when he reached the hill station, only knew that he had to get as far as he could and then hope for the best.

Walking behind the Sherpas and the heavily laden mules, feeling the deepening cold starting to bite at his nose and ears, yet still sweating from exertion in his fur-lined leather overcoat and hide boots, he was relieved that they were nearing the hill station on the plateau, since already they had been climbing the lower slopes for two days and he felt badly bruised and exhausted, not capable of going too much further without a good rest.

When he glanced around him at the increasingly desolate scenery, the rolling hills with sparse scrub, the green slopes receding below him, the sky above grey and malignant, his sense of divorce from the self only became more acute.

Indeed, when he thought back on how he had come here – a taxi from Darjeeling to Gangtok; a restless night in the Tashi Delek hotel, then a hired Land Rover the next day to take him through the richly forested Tista valley, to the Sherpas' base camp at the foot of the Tibetan Plateau; then being fitted with clothing, the Sherpas laughing at his inexperience; then two days and three nights on the lower slopes of the mountain, leaving the greenery behind and moving up into the barren, brown hills, not believing where he was when he lay at night beneath the stars, seeing the sky as through an inverted telescope, far away, shrinking rapidly – when he thought back on all that, it seemed like a dream, no more substantial than the wind that crossed his path and passed on invisibly.

Sweating even as he shivered, he saw, across the slopes, some *kyangs*, wild asses, with their noses nuzzling the earth. They looked sleek and well fed, as all the animals on the plateau did, and he wondered abstractedly what they could find to eat in this arid wilderness. Raising his eyes, he looked at the towering slopes, first ochre, then glistening white, the melting snow forming a web of streams which, when seen in a certain way, in a certain light, turned into a great, glittering necklace suspended in space.

He rubbed his eyes, licked his chapped lips, imagined his teeth were aching, realized that he had started imagining a *lot* since beginning this journey. He hadn't been sleeping well because he had felt he was being watched; he even felt that in the cold light of day when the tiredness took hold of him.

He had cursed himself for his lack of exercise, for not looking after his body, and accepted that some of his worst imaginings were the price to be paid for that. He had ached and breathed harshly most of the way up these hills, and knew, with a helpless, throttled dread, that he hadn't even begun yet; that the real climb was past the hill station, where the browns and greys turned to a glistening white that sometimes soared almost vertically.

When he thought of going beyond the hill station, he felt dread and disbelief.

Closing his eyes, he tried to imagine New York, his mother's plush apartment, his own untidy, beloved room, yet couldn't really see it, but only a blur of vague detail, as if viewing it through a smeared lens. It was too far away, too much a part of what he *had* been, and he knew, as he heard his own heartbeat, that he was now someone else.

Now he was part of Ingrid, as she was part of him; and both of them were part of St Germain and the network of riddles and clues that he had spread far and wide, from the Great Pyramid of Giza, the terrestrial centre of the earth, to Jerusalem, the centre of the spiritual world – and finally to here, where the mountains, with their peaks in the clouds, held the answers to all of it.

When he thought of Ingrid, and of what they were involved in, he was shaken with a terrible anguish and disturbing confusion, since he also thought of Mephisto, alias Christian Grabbe. He had hoped she could resist him, that his love would give her strength, but she had gone with Mephisto, resplendent as a star, to disappear into the mountains' most secret place.

The question was: why? Had she been hypnotized or wide awake? Had she just wanted him with an over-whelming desire or had he abducted her? God, he hated Mephisto then – loathed his Machiavellian charms – and thought of Ingrid with a mixture of rage and heart-numbing grief.

He opened his eyes again, saw the backs of the Sherpas, looked beyond them and saw the track levelling out onto a broad plateau sheltered by soaring hills. In that sheltered space there were half a dozen shacks, made of brick and earth, with roofs of cor-rugated iron, smoke trailing out of their chimneys and streaming off in the wind. It was obviously the hill station. Donkeys were tethered to posts outside the huts, and Sherpas and mountaineers were wandering about in the clearing.

The Sherpas tethered their mules to a wooden post outside a hut which the other men, mostly mountain-eers, were entering and leaving with great regularity. Since it was clearly a bar or café, Jerry wanted to go inside, but the English-speaking Sherpa pulled him back and shook his head in denial.

'You won't go further up the mountain,' Jerry said, 'but those mountaineers will.'

The Sherpa shook his head again in a negative gesture. 'No,' he said. 'No good for you.' He then pointed to indicate the mountain peaks in the west.

'There,' he said, 'the mountaineers climb there. But you –' and here he jabbed his finger at the peaks to the east. 'You must go there, where those men do not go. You must go where no-one has explored – and *they* cannot take you. Come! You come now.'

Before he could refuse, the Sherpa grabbed him by the elbow and guided him across the clearing, through the black shadows cast by the soaring hills, to the door of a dilapidated wooden hut whose chimney was smoking.

'In here is the old wise one,' the Sherpa said. 'He who goes where we cannot go. He once belonged to a monastery, but came down from it years ago. He lives alone and meditates, and knows the secret places in the mountains where we Sherpas will not go. Maybe he take you to the first monastery, maybe not. If he do, he will not take you higher, since he frightened as well. It is the land of the dead up there. Now you go. Go inside.'

Without knocking, the Sherpa opened the door of the hut and pushed Jerry inside, letting the door close behind him, swinging shut from its own weight. The inside of the hut was gloomy, being illuminated fitfully by two spluttering oil lamps, and the air was further darkened by the smoke billowing out of an open fire.

Jerry coughed into his fist, rubbed the tears from his eyes, smelt urine and then squinted through the smoke at the old man who was squatting on the earthen floor, near the flickering flames. He was very old indeed, his face like a wrinkled walnut, and he was wearing a dark-red, Nepalese robe, belted at the waist, over thick black woollen trousers which were tucked into leather boots.

He was rocking back and forth, chanting softly to himself, but eventually, when Jerry coughed again, he stopped and looked up, staring very steadily at him with rheumy eyes, but not saying anything.

'You speak English?' Jerry asked him.

'I do,' was the reply. 'And you have come here to find the first monastery and search for those who hide higher.'

Startled, Jerry took a deep breath, then let it out in a long sigh.

'You *knew* I was coming here?'

'Of course,' the old man said. 'I am always informed. They speak to me across the great divide when I travel down through myself.'

'You mean when you meditate?'

'Yes.'

'They communicate by *thought*?'

'That is so. I am informed when someone is coming and needs showing the way.'

'The way to the monastery?'

'The way to the *first* one, yes. The one *you* want is higher.'

'How do you know which one I want?'

'You are one of the pure at heart. You have come to search for truth. To find that truth is arduous, requiring strength and courage; if you succeed you will find what it is you most want; if you fail, you will return back down the mountain and know nothing but misery.'

'And you'll take me up there?'

'I will only guide you close to the first monastery; after that I will leave you. I am not allowed inside the monastery, since I am not pure at heart.'

'The monastery is a halfway house?'

'More than that: a house of learning. But from there you must climb even higher, into the zone of the dead.'

Jerry saw his own shadow elongated and stretched up the wooden wall, a giant figure, trembling to the rhythm of the flickering flames. That shadow was himself, just as he was *not* himself, and as he gazed down at the old man, who was ghostlike in the smoke, he felt removed even further from reality, as if no more than a player in a bizarre, wide-awake dream.

'Is that where I'm supposed to go?' he asked. 'To the zone of the dead?'

'What will be, will be. You will try to get there. Whether or not you succeed is something I cannot say.'

'Is St Germain up there?'

'I know no names, just that they *are*. I only hear them, though sometimes in meditation I see them as well. They are of every nationality, every creed, but they all sound the same.'

'English?'

'It is not a spoken language. It is sound in the head.'

Gazing down at the old man, who seemed too frail to climb anywhere, he thought of the visions he had had of St Germain, of the reality of his presence, his voice, when he stepped out of the shimmering light. He had clearly heard the voice of an apparition, just as he had with Mephisto. Was this madness or truth?

'So to get to that hidden place, to the zone of the dead, I have to first pass through the monastery?'

'Yes, that is so.'

'Then someone from the monastery will take me higher?'

'No. You must ascend yourself – it is part of the test.'

He thought of Kanchenjunga, of those towering, snow-capped peaks, was crushed even visualizing them, felt a thin blade of terror.

'I can't get up there myself. I know nothing about the mountains. I'm not equipped and don't have the experience. What they ask is impossible.'

'Nothing is impossible where the heart decrees otherwise. If you want it enough, you will do it. Failure is a sign of bad faith and contains its own punishment.'

He wondered what could be more punishing than having to climb that mountain, then realized that he didn't want to know, that some futures were best ignored.

'You say you're informed when someone is coming. Does that mean I'm not the first?'

'Of course you are not the first,' the old man replied, almost contemptuously. 'They have come here, one by one, over the centuries. More will come with your passing.'

'Are you always the one who receives them?'

'No. I am of the Earth. I live the life of a normal mortal. But my father and his fathers before him were here to receive.'

'When do we leave for the monastery?'

'When I climb to my feet.'

'I'm tired – and I need to eat and drink.'

'No. You just *think* you do.' As if to prove his point, the old man, who had seemed so frail and weak, jumped to his feet with surprising agility. 'Hunger and thirst are much exaggerated,' he said. 'And weariness is only a state of mind which can be easily denied. This you will soon learn or not – and if not, you will come back down. My name is Yaksa.'

'Hi,' Jerry said automatically, then, feeling foolish, added, 'Jerry. My name is Jerry.' He didn't put out his hand, but simply smiled at Yaksa, to which the old man responded with an almost imperceptible nod, before brushing past him and opening the door of the hut.

'We're going *right now*?' Jerry asked him.

'Why wait?' Yaksa responded.

Apart from hunger, thirst and increasing exhaustion, physical and mental, Jerry knew, the minute he stepped out the door, why he had wanted to wait.

It was late in the afternoon and already growing dark, and when he looked beyond the huts, at the soaring peaks, he saw the great shadows creeping down as the sun quickly sank. Now the mountains looked more ominous, mysterious, certainly dangerous, and as he followed the old man across the clearing, his heart sank like the sun.

'We won't be able to see,' he said with shame. 'It's too dark to go up there.'

'I can see in the dark,' Yaksa replied, 'and you will learn to do so. The object is not to perceive, but to lean on your faith. Do not trust your eyes, trust your senses, and thus choose the right path.'

'If there are paths why do others not go up there?'

'Because they depend on their eyes – and the eyes reveal nothing. The paths are like our souls – divided into good and evil – and you must make your choice, left or right, by what your senses reveal. In this way your faith will be known. Now be quiet. We must concentrate.'

Jerry shut his mouth, feeling as if he had been slighted, kept his eyes fixed on the back of the old man as they walked away from the camp. The flat road climbed soon enough, curving up between the hills, and gradually the hills closed in upon them and formed two towering walls. The walls shadowed the path, the shadows darkened, turned black, then a ribbon of stars materialized above, given shape by the jagged cliffs.

The moon moved along that ribbon, disappeared, reappeared, seemed to pace them, remaining directly above them like a malevolent eye. Jerry lowered his gaze, feeling spied upon, naked, saw white stones that looked like polished glass spinning over his boots. His own breathing seemed very loud, an oddly amplified discordance, and he imagined that he could hear his heart beating, then tried to forget it.

The old man was still there, just ahead of him, moving quickly, surprisingly agile for someone his age, and with the eyes of a cat. He stopped where the track forked. Jerry took the right turning. He didn't know why, indeed hardly thought about it, and was surprised to find the old man by his side, his smile revealed by the moonlight.

'Very good,' he said. 'Faith.'

Time seemed to stop. Space closed in upon him. The track became narrow, very steep, full of turns, and the wall at his right gradually shrank and disappeared, until there was nothing but dark space and an umbrella of stars. The track was curving around a cliff face. He was certain of that. He had a moment of vertigo, of flesh-burning dread, stopped to press himself into the cliff at his left, then saw the old man's smile. That calmed him instantly, making him feel ashamed, and he grinned back and stepped in front of the old man and started up hill again, aware of the growing cold, the snow-capped peaks moving towards him, convinced that he was divorced from time and space, at the top of the world.

'Are you tired?' the old man asked from behind him, no trace of breathlessness in his voice.

'Yes,' he replied, gasping. 'I'm damned near exhausted.'

'Let yourself dissolve into the night. Become *part* of the mountain. In that way, you will conquer it. What is willed, will be done.'

He did as he was told, tried to will the exhaustion away, felt foolish, then almost tripped and fell into that vast, inky-black void. Terrified, he jerked awake, all his senses resurrected, felt the pores of his skin opening to drink in the icy air.

He dissolved into the air, let its coldness percolate him, and felt the track melting beneath his feet as if no longer solid. It was still there all right, illuminated by the moonlight, disappearing between another narrow canyon that offered protection on both sides. He moved into the canyon, saw the band of stars narrowing, came to a fork and took the left path, knowing instinctively that this was the way.

He didn't have to think about it. He had dissolved into the mountain. He glanced up at the snow-capped peaks, gleaming distantly, hardly real, and was drawn to the starlit darkness around them, to that infinite grandeur.

She was somewhere up there. The girl he loved. His Ingrid. Her image shone like a light in his mind and guided his footsteps. He wondered what had become of her, prayed to God that she was safe, sensed she would be, that her presence up there was the carrot being dangled before him. He smiled, gaining strength, losing himself in the process, saw the ribbon of stars growing wider above the cliff tops, the peaks snow-capped looming ever larger as he made his way uphill.

The track forked again. He turned left without thinking. He felt light-headed, confident, released from his aching body; but then the climb became more arduous, the track rising almost vertically, and the exhaustion, which he had thought had left for good, returned worse than ever.

He fell to his hands and knees, heard the old man's chuckle behind him, felt rage and clawed his way up the steep incline and then felt the snow. He stopped and saw the snow beneath him; then saw it above him, a luxurious carpet covering everything, white and glittering in the darkness, deceptively beautiful.

'Shit!' he murmured to himself, giving voice to his frustration, then glanced back over his shoulder, saw the old man's smile, stoked up his defiance and crawled forward into the biting cold. He had not gone very far, though it seemed to be so, when large snowflakes started falling about him, lying upon him and soaking him.

The misery began then, eating into his body and spirit, making time slow down to a standstill, each metre a mile. Sometimes he managed to walk, stooped over against the wind, but often had to fall back on his hands and knees, when the track became too steep. It rose and fell frequently, curved around sharp-edged rocks, became lost under thickening snow as more snow fell about him. He felt battered and bruised, his strength draining away from him, sobbed when his numbed fingers started stinging and his lips cracked and bled. He looked up, squinting, saw snow falling from the moon, the stars all around it dripping snow, the peaks hiding beneath it.

He tripped then and fell, lay face down, weeping softly, determined not to move another muscle, content to die there. Then something dropped on his right shoulder, took hold and shook it; he turned his head and saw Yaksa's gnarled hand, his walnut brown face.

'You have done well,' he said. 'Very well. Come. Follow me now.'

With surprising strength, the old man pulled him to his feet, wiped the snow from his face, smiled, then nodded and proceeded to lead him up the steep path. Jerry fell in behind him, automatically, in a trance of gratitude, lumbering uphill through the cutting wind and swirling snow until the track started levelling out. He glanced back, saw the snow-covered rocks, and below them a vertiginous darkness towards which he was drawn.

At that moment he was convinced that the earth was not down there, but only boundless space; that somehow they had left the real world behind and were moving into another world. Looking up, he saw the moon, a great eye staring at him, but the stars, which were weeping snowflakes, were not the stars that he knew. He was disorientated, felt as if he was looking *down*, actually did so and thought he saw the sky he knew, but as if it was reflected in water, its moon and stars clearly visible. Then he felt a stab of fear and turned away and hurried after the old man.

Now everything was mountainous, but white in the moonlight, the crags and outcroppings like gargoyles, the stars, which were not the stars he knew, forming a glittering, fairy-tale tapestry around the peaks towering over him. He felt light-headed and lost, torn from his anchorage, cast adrift; and as the biting wind grew stronger, as the falling snow thickened, his stinging flesh lost all sensation and his reasoning slipped away.

He saw Yaksa in front of him – or thought he did; he wasn't sure – and then the snow swirled about him, filling his mouth, blinding him, and he rubbed his eyes and looked uphill again and saw nothing but more snow.

Yaksa had vanished, leaving him all alone, and he cried out in panic, calling the old man's name, heard that name borne back on the wind and felt it slapping his face. He recoiled from that blow – since in fact it was his terror – then hurled himself forward in desperation, praying for comfort. No comfort was to be found – the old man had disappeared – and all he found was the snow-covered track winding into the darkness. He followed it, fell upon it, crawled uphill, his lungs on fire, seeing nothing but the soaring mountain peaks, the stars streaming around them, the snow pouring out of the large moon that glared down malignantly.

The wind howled, the snow fell. His body was numb, his mind screaming. He crawled uphill, sobbing, wanting to give in, unable to, impelled forward by the brightening image of Ingrid that floated in front of him.

It was his rage that kept him going. He was refusing to let them have her. He imagined her, saw her, felt her, was rescued by her, then he fell forward in exhaustion, rolling over downhill, gathering snow as he went.

He waited for that final drop, his endless descent down the mountainside, the death that would be his when he plummeted to earth – and so closed his eyes, expecting it, whispering, 'Ingrid, my love –' and then ploughed through soft snow, stopped moving, choked and coughed, spat snow from his mouth, rubbed his eyes and looked up in wonder.

He had rolled down an incline, causing a cloud of powdered snow, and as that white veil floated around him, obscuring his vision briefly before settling down, he saw in the white-flecked moonlight an edifice of stone and mortar, its chortens like strange pyramids – a Tibetan temple, a monastery – materializing out of the moonlit darkness as the snow ceased to fall.

He lay there, beneath the moon and stars, above the blackened, lost earth, listening to his own heartbeat.

There was that . . . and the silence.

CHAPTER FORTY

He climbed painfully to his feet and noted that he was on a flat plateau above a precipice beyond which he could see nothing but darkness below a sky filled with glutinous stars. The biting wind had died away and now the silence was complete, emphasizing his feeling of frightening isolation, his conviction that he had somehow left the real world and was living a dream.

Then he looked at the monastery stretched out below a towering cliff face. It was built of stone and *chan* – Tibetan moulded clay cement – and was composed of a series of block-shaped, flat-roofed buildings surmounted by elaborate pagodas and dominated by the great buoy-shaped chorten – a dome-like stone structure symbolizing the one Buddha – which, though also covered in crisp white snow, was undeniably exotic and formed the gateway into the monastery courtyard.

The monastery looked unreal in the moonlight, a mirage wrapped in snow.

Feeling unreal himself, and certainly bruised and exhausted, he tramped the short distance to the high gate chorten, walked through it, crossed the courtyard in which some shaggy, horned yaks were tethered, then stopped in front of the door directly facing the gate. There was a bellcord hanging down beside the door, and he tugged it and waited.

He stood there a long time, shivering with cold, feeling drained, but nobody came to the door, so then, on an impulse, he simply pushed it . . . and it swung open, creaking, letting striations of pale, flickering light beam out into the night.

He stepped inside, closed the wooden door behind him, and then looked around him.

He was standing in an immense, austere assembly hall, the floor and walls of which were plain stone and mortar and partially covered by two carpet-sized wall-hangings made from brown yak wool and decorated with a series of white swastikas whose right-angled flanges, he realized instantly, were going anti-clockwise instead of the other way, indicating that they were in this case Hindu swastikas, not related to their unpleasant Western counterparts. Lined along each wall, from one end to the other, like soldiers keeping vigil, were tall, ornately carved stands upon which burned many tall, fat candles of every colour, giving off a smell like incense. At the very far end of the hall, close by another large door that obviously led into the inner sanctums of the monastery, were rows of long brown tables, all neatly laid out with plates and earthenware jugs, as if ready to seat a few hundred monks, though there was no-one in sight.

Realizing that this was so, and thinking it odd, he stepped further into the hall, heard his own footsteps reverberating, and looked up at the balcony that ran around the great rectangular hall, high up, below the ceiling in which a skylight of ornate tinted glass was an eye-catching focal point. Behind the dark polished wooden railing of the balcony were a series of chapel-cells, obviously used by the unseen monks, their small bay windows crisscrossed with wooden laths arranged in intricate patterns.

He called up to those small rooms, hoping that *someone* was there, but the only reply was the ghostly echo of his own voice, resounding eerily under the roof before fading away.

Feeling very strange indeed, he continued along the great hall, his boots scraping on the flagged stone, until he had reached the rows of long tables. Stopping, he examined the nearest table and noticed that the plates and utensils were perfectly clean, but covered with a fine film of dust, as if they had not been used in a long time. He called out again, his voice echoing 'Hello! Hello!'; then walked through the door beyond the last of the tables into a deeper gloom.

He was in another rectangular hall, though this one was much smaller. The walls were covered in more hangings decorated with the Hindu swastika and more tall, fat candles were lined along each wall, though no balcony or chapel-cells could be seen above, but only a flat, unadorned roof which, in this case, had no skylight. However, at the far end of the hall, in the wall directly facing him, was an open door surrounded by latticed windows, and from inside the room came what sounded like a monk chanting prayers.

Feeling a rising trepidation, not sure what to expect, he walked along the hall, stopped by the open door, and looked into a smoky, candlelit gloom to see a bald-headed monk, wearing a faded crimson wraparound coat, a *chuba*, and with a ceremonial silk scarf, a *kata*, hanging down to his waist. He was sitting cross-legged on the floor, his back turned to a Buddhist shrine, and chanting prayers as he rocked back and forth.

He stopped chanting the instant he became aware of Jerry's presence, straightened up and raised his face as if looking at him, but in fact tilting his head a little to the side, as if locating his whereabouts by listening – since, like the old seer in al-Hillah, this lama was blind.

At first Jerry was too shocked to say anything. The fact that the lama was blind was shock enough; even more shocking was the fact that he was so thin as to be almost translucent, his veins frighteningly visible through skin that was stretched on his bones like plain tissue paper. This man was rag and bone, an apparition at death's door; he had faded away to nothing and seemed to float just above the floor – though this was an illusion.

'You are the Westerner,' he said, his voice no more than a whisper. 'You came – as expected.'

'As expected?'

'I was informed from above.'

'St Germain?'

'I do not know his name. He is my *tulpa* – my guide to the other world – and he said you would come here.'

'How did you know it was me?'

'You are standing right there in front of me – so why should I *not* know?'

'Aren't you blind?'

'I can see you with my third eye – my mind. I am only blind because I have meditated here for years and no longer need normal sight. Here,' he added, pushing an earthenware bowl towards Jerry's feet. 'Be seated and eat. The food and drink were prepared for you when your arrival at the outer door was witnessed.'

'Witnessed by *who*?' Jerry asked as he sat cross-legged on the carpeted floor, pulled the bowl closer to him and saw that it was filled with rice and *dahl* – lentils boiled in a little curry. It smelt delicious and almost made him reel, and he tackled it greedily.

'Some of the other monks,' the lama said simply, as if that fact were self evident.

'And where *are* the other monks?' Jerry asked, as he tucked into his food.

'The other monks, who are few, are not allowed to look upon you; they must not be touched by anything foreign, nor even be led to think about such things. I am the Head Lama, their spiritual teacher, which gives me that right. I am beyond such temptations.'

While Jerry scooped up the rice and lentils with his fingers and awkwardly pushed it into his mouth, the blind lama picked up a long-necked pitcher and poured its contents into two earthenware cups, one of which he handed to Jerry, the other being raised before his own lips. The liquid in the cup was bubbling slightly, smelt a bit like cider, and when Jerry had sampled it, following the lama's example, it tasted absolutely delicious and went straight to his head.

'I no longer eat,' the lama said, 'but am still allowed drink. Alcohol in moderation can truly warm the hearts of men, and this is *chang*, brewed from barley, yeast and water, which will help to sustain you. You will speak to me and then you must leave immediately, which is why you must eat and drink.'

A second sip of the *chang* made Jerry feel even better, almost rejuvenated in fact, and he scooped up some more rice and lentils and ate while they talked, feeling the return of his strength and optimism, a pleasantly drunken intoxication, an increasing lightness of spirit.

'Have you ever been higher than this monastery?' he asked the old lama.

'No. I came up to this monastery as a child, and have not left it since. No monk in this monastery has climbed the mountain, since the gods reside there.'

'You're a Buddhist,' Jerry said, between mouthfuls of rice and *dahl*, 'and I don't understand how that relates to those who seem to guide you from above. Are they Buddhists, too?'

'Buddhism is not a religion in the Western sense of that word; it does not speak of God or the soul as you conceive them, but is a doctrine that can encompass many faiths – and it is based on the belief that life is an illusion of the senses, an imperfect state, and that only Nirvana, the absolute truth, is real. Those above, with whom I communicate through my third eye, have achieved the state of Nirvana; they are not Buddhists, but have transcended the material state and can roam freely at will.'

'In an out-of-the-body state?'

'That is so. And it is what I am suffering for. I have lost my sight because I no longer need it, I have not eaten for years in order to free myself from the flesh, and soon I hope to transcend my body and rise to Nirvana.'

Studying the lama's almost incorporeal body, Jerry was reminded about Mary Anne Atwood's description of alchemy being a *philosophical* system which 'by fermenting the human spirit, purifies and finally dissolves it'. The body of the old lama did indeed seem to be dissolving as if, over the years, he was evolving through meditation and lack of movement into a form of pure mind . . . like St Germain.

'What kind of Buddhism do you practise in this monastery?'

'It no longer matters,' the old lama replied, sipping some more of his *chang*, his large eyes staring sightlessly. 'We live by the rule of numbers —'

'Alchemical numbers?'

'Yes — and our meditation, which is based on the contemplation of such numbers, will lead us to that ultimate transformation, from flesh into spirit. We originated, I believe, from the Amda Tibetan Buddhists, reportedly once the rulers of the world, a nation of kings.'

Having finished his food, Jerry wiped his hands on his jacket; he felt drunk and increasingly excited by what he was hearing.

'Do you believe that?' he asked.

'Yes,' the lama replied. 'The world of Man is older than those in the West believe, and it originated here,

200,000 years ago, when this land mass was joined with another, now known as Africa. That great race spread out from here as far as the islands of the Atlantic Ocean where it formed another great nation which, though ruled by magic and faith, was eventually destroyed. Those above are the descendants of the survivors of that mighty destruction. They returned here, to their origins, many years ago, and are protecting the Knowledge.'

'The Secret Knowledge?'

'Yes.'

What the lama was saying supported what Jerry had already learned.

'Have you ever heard of Atlantis?' he asked.

The old man actually smiled. 'Many tales are told about it,' he said, 'most of them untrue. There is no single Atlantis. Many civilizations were lost throughout history – but they all began here.'

'And was that civilization a magical one?'

'What might be magical to you may be normal to others.'

'You can see through your third eye,' Jerry said. 'Did the high priests of that former civilization do similar things?'

'They believed in the contemplation of numbers and derived their power from them; they had a sacred stone that was constructed to the dimensions of such numbers, and that stone, both symbolically and materially, was the source of their ability to read minds, dematerialize themselves and others, leave the body behind them and transcend space and time. In that sense they were a magical race, but to them it was normal.'

'Was that stone called the Tuaoi Stone?'

'Yes, that was its name.'

'Do you know if that great civilization ever settled in Egypt?'

'So it is written. The Tuaoi Stone was pyramidal, its dimensions magical. The pyramid, though without those original dimensions, thus became a common structure throughout that great civilization. Even here, in India and Tibet, our chortens are shaped like elongated pyramids. In this manner, then, there were once pyramids on the islands of the Atlantic Ocean and the Mediterranean Sea; and according to what is written the Tuaoi Stone once surmounted a great pyramid in Egypt, at the world's very centre. Now it is back where it belongs – up there, where no mortal goes with the hope of returning.'

He nodded, indicating the ceiling, meaning the mountain peaks outside.

'So the adepts, the high priests of that civilization, returned to their home high in the mountain, where they protect the Tuaoi Stone and its Secret Knowledge?'

'Yes, that is so.'

'And those adepts can transcend the material state?'

'Naturally.'

'Do you know the number 666?'

'Yes. It is the magical number upon which the dimensions of the Tuaoi Stone have been based.'

'It is also known as the number of the beast.'

'It is only called that in your Bible. It is not so called by others.'

'In our Bible that number refers to a beast coming up out of the earth and another beast coming out of the sea. What beasts would they be?'

'I have not read your Bible, but discussed this with others. The beast coming up out of the earth is clearly a volcanic eruption or earthquake. The beast coming out of the sea would be the great tidal wave caused by such an earthquake. The previous civilizations of man – those of prehistory – were all destroyed by volcanic

466

eruptions, earthquakes and the great tidal waves caused by them. So the number refers to the destruction of those civilizations. But please note that your Bible, in *Revelations*, states that the number of the beast is also the number of *the man* – in other words, again, the civilizations of man that were destroyed before our history was written. Thus do magical numbers tell their tales to those who can read them.'

'And what of those, like me, who can't do so?'

'You are venturing up there to learn.'

'Do you think I can make it up there?'

'If it was willed, it will be.'

The rice and *dahl* had replenished Jerry, and the *chang* had given him back strength and courage and the nerve to continue. What he had suspected had been confirmed: that the man calling himself St Germain was a magical adept, an immortal, and now, with other adepts, protected the Tuaoi Stone where he and others resided higher up the mountain.

Yet what did they want with him? And what indeed was their general purpose?

He sighed, seeing these as final questions, then climbed to his feet.

'I take it that I can't even sleep here?'

'No, you cannot. Once you have asked all you can, you must be cast out again. Have you anything more to ask?'

'No.'

'Then goodbye.'

'Where did you learn English?'

'From my *tulpa*.'

'Do you have any final words for me?'

'Go in good faith.'

Jerry nodded and turned away, walked along the spartan hall, glanced back once at the old man, then went out through the door. Passing the empty tables in the main assembly hall, he again saw the dust on the plates and knew that no one ate here. These monks had gone beyond that. They were weaning themselves off food. They lived on liquids and hid in their chapel-cells, ignoring the outer world. His footsteps echoed around that great hall, desecrating its silence, then he stepped into the world they were ignoring and was slapped by the freezing cold.

He was shocked into alertness, forced to remember what he had just left, and tugged up the fur collar of his jacket and started walking immediately, cutting around the walls of the monastery courtyard and then up the steeply winding track.

The monastery fell away to his left, was replaced by a soaring cliff face, and to his right was what appeared to be a steep drop into a dizzying, snow-flecked darkness. The snow was thick on the track, but being blown by a rising wind and, knowing that it was going to get worse, he started losing his drunken glow. His face began to sting, his eyes wept, his lips were cracking, and he saw the snow-capped peaks as jagged edges cutting into the brilliant stars.

Exhaustion came soon enough, followed by aches and pains, then the stinging of his skin turned to a numbness that made him feel paralysed. He started gasping for breath, sometimes slid and fell down, once nearly rolled over the edge and flipped away in sheer terror. He stood up and stumbled on, aware of that dizzying drop to his right, and was relieved when the track cut into the mountain, under snow-laden outcroppings.

Not far on it branched again, and he turned left without doubt, imagining that it would at least lead him deeper into the mountain, away from its unprotected outer face. He looked up and saw the peaks, gleaming whitely, eerily beautiful and seeming to tilt towards him, as if about to fall on him. He thought of Ingrid up there – somewhere up there: his beloved – and that thought kept him going for a while, until things started changing.

The mountains were all around him, soaring above, falling below, the white slopes plunging into pools of darkness which he did not dare look at. Instead, he stared up at the stars, tried to place them, couldn't do so; watched the moon in its translucent flight through an alien sky. That moon was too big to be true, too wafer-thin to be real, and when he glanced down he saw it reflected in the featureless inky depths, perhaps in a lake.

He shivered and looked ahead, disorientated, losing his senses, and thought he saw other lights, not the stars, winking on and off fitfully.

Lights? *What* lights? He rubbed his eyes and looked again. He saw the lights all around him, above him, in the distance, but thought that they might be the moonlight reflecting off ice.

The cold wind swept the snow across the steep, narrow track. He leaned into it, so far he was almost bent double, feeling the pain of frostbite on his face and hands, his eyes weeping helplessly. Now his misery was total, his will going with his strength, and he thought of what this place was called – the zone of the dead – then dwelt on mortals transcending the physical state and knew the mountains were haunted.

The wind howled like a living creature. The snow swirled and attacked him. His footsteps made the sound of small animals scurrying. He sobbed aloud with terror, bit his lower lip, felt ashamed, surrendered to the terror again and tried desperately to conquer it. Then he remembered the old guide, Yaksa, and what he had told him: that he should let himself dissolve into the night and become *part* of the mountain. He tried to do that, giving himself to the wind and snow; but this time it was too much, his misery was too great, and he fell to his hands and knees and started crawling up the slope like a mule – undignified, shameless.

'Dissolve!' he sobbed. *'Damn you!'*

How long had he been going? An hour or all night? He looked in vain for a sign of the dawn, but saw only the moon and stars. Those and the lights – *Yes, damn it, they were lights!* – and he stopped, breathing deeply on hands and knees, trying to focus his eyes. They were not reflected lights, but individual living things, and they were bobbing up and down, occasionally moving left and right, and seemed to be closing in upon him as if to surround him.

He couldn't believe his own senses, so sobbed and started crawling again, moving up an almost vertical slope while the snow slid around him. The lights were closing in on him, growing larger, ever brighter, and soon they had formed a large, pulsating orb that was gliding towards him. Then his terror fused with his misery, ordaining his collapse, and he fell face down into the snow, taking deep, anguished breaths.

He let himself dissolve, becoming part of the mountain, and rolled over with his body wrapped in snow to gaze up at the stars.

The stars had disappeared. He was blinded briefly by brilliant light. The light turned into an immense, pulsating disc that grew wider and brighter. He felt its ethereal heat. The snow was melting off him. He squinted into the light as it fell about him and quietly ingested him.

He was filled with a wondrous awe. Though dazzled, he could still see. What he saw, as he grew warm and started dissolving, was a shadow-filled bright haze. The shadows seemed to be watching him. They were *there*, but out of reach. He reached out to where he thought they were, but couldn't quite touch them.

At that moment, he lost his senses. He was completely disorientated. He didn't know left from right, the vertical from the horizontal, and felt that he was floating in space and somehow leaving his body.

He knew, then, that it was true – that he was actually dissolving – and remembered in a sudden rush of infantile terror, as the brilliant light winked out and he was plunged into blackness, that given the relationship between light and the human eye, an invisible man would have to be blind.

In his blindness, in that terrible womb, his terror rendered him senseless.

CHAPTER FORTY-ONE

As he drove the hired car from Darjeeling to Gangtok, Hans kept thinking of what he had done. Elena was sitting beside him, wearing a sky-blue jacket with figure-hugging jeans and sweater, and each time she touched her knee against his, his heart lurched with fear as well as lust.

He was concerned that Zweig, sitting in the back, might eventually notice.

Hans had always known he would live to regret his surrender to the drunken Elena that time; and indeed, since then, she had importuned him repeatedly, and he (though terrified that Zweig would find out) had not been able to resist her practised whore's charms. He thought about her night and day, was hardly able to keep his hands off her, but with his lust went his dread of discovery – a dread based on his knowledge of what Zweig would do to him if he found out.

To make matters worse, Elena knew this and played on it, exacting a perversely heightened pleasure from touching and stroking him behind Zweig's back, though very much in his presence. More dangerously, she had also started *openly* displaying her contempt for Zweig – and he had started to notice it.

'Zweig can't get it up any more,' she had confided to Hans more than once, usually when they were together in bed, both naked and sweating after sex, 'and he's growing more stingy. I want to get away from the bastard, and I know you do, too.'

While that was true enough, Hans was frightened

that she could see it – since if she had seen it, Zweig might also have seen it and would not let it pass.

Indeed, ever since that dreadful day in Romania when, after being seduced by Elena, he had been sexually humiliated by Zweig, he had sensed that Zweig was watching him more closely and turning much colder. Hans was growing more frightened of Zweig – even more so than he had been – and was not being helped by the fact that he and Elena were now secret lovers and she was being increasingly obvious about this when in Zweig's presence.

Sooner or later she would let it slip out – and then he, Hans, would be a doomed man, with no hope of reprieve.

So, as he drove and felt Elena's knee touching his, he twitched and glanced fearfully in the rear-view mirror, expecting to see Zweig's cold eyes growing wide with rage. Luckily, Zweig continued to stare out the window, at the Indian coolies in the lush fields bathed in morning's pearly light, obviously immersed in his unhappy thoughts about what he had done.

Apart from his fears over Elena's loose tongue, Hans wanted to get away because he sensed that Zweig was losing control. What had happened between them in the Eforie Nord thermal treatment centre had been the first indication that Zweig was not his normal self; and many incidents since then, mostly outbursts of mindless rage, had convinced him that his boss was going insane.

Any doubts he had had about this issue had been put to rest when Zweig murdered Andropov Kuragin, thus guaranteeing the deadly enmity of the Soviets and the loss of his only remaining ally.

Zweig certainly knew this, would have faced it when his rage subsided; and it was doubtless why he had, since leaving the South Atlantic to come here, alternated between periods of moody silence and inexplicable, frightening rages.

'He's going crazy,' Elena had said more than once. 'We should get out while we can, Hans.'

There could be no arguing with that, but it didn't soothe his fears.

Remarkably, no more than an hour after having received a telex from Zweig's office in Calcutta, informing him that Ingrid and the American had taken a train to Darjeeling, Hans had been surprised to find in his mail a note giving him the same information. The note had been signed 'St Germain' in an elegant, rather archaic hand, and Zweig, when he read it, had growled, 'I think the letter's genuine. He *wants* a confrontation with me. Now why would that be?' And two days later, when Hans had arranged everything, they had flown out from Paris.

The journey here had been awful. Zweig had picked fights with people at every stop along the route – at the airports, in the hotels, with taxi drivers – and Hans had heard him, through the wall dividing their rooms, screaming abuse at Elena. For this reason alone, he was pleased to be out in the open again, away from the claustrophobic confines of the hotel with Zweig throwing tantrums, and instead driving through the increasingly tropical greenery of Sikkim towards the vast, snow-capped mountains.

They had been met at the station in Darjeeling by another of Zweig's informants, a local government official, who told them that Ingrid and Jerry had been staying in the Oberoi Mount Everest hotel, that their room had been bugged, and that by this means it had been ascertained that they had an encounter in the hotel lobby with someone calling himself Mephisto, after which Ingrid had sneaked out of her room, not to return, and the American, leaving the same room to pursue her, had returned all alone.

Also, according to the findings of a perfectly routine check with all of the government official's rail, air and car hire contacts in Darjeeling, the American had hired a taxi the following morning to take him to a car hire company that was located on the approach road to Gangtok, from where, according to the English owner of the company, he had intended taking a hired Land Rover through the Sikkim valley, prior to attempting to persuade some Sherpas into taking him up the mountains.

What the bent government official had *not* been able to ascertain, and what still puzzled Hans and Zweig, was the whereabouts of Ingrid, since the American had made all his arrangements alone and had certainly gone to Gangtok on his own. They had therefore assumed that the American's insane hope of scaling the mountain, at which he was singularly inexperienced, was an indication that Ingrid, somehow or other, had ended up there – no doubt in relation to Saint-Germain.

'We must be close,' Zweig said from the back seat. 'Where *is* the damned place?'

'The town's just a couple of miles from here,' Hans replied, 'so the car hire firm should be fairly close.'

The road here was winding through upland forests and meadows, with spruce, pine, oak and magnolia trees rising out of a bright profusion of yellow, pink and crimson rhododendrons and broad swathes of blue irises, with the peaks of the Kanchenjunga mountain range scraping a cloudy, grey-blue sky.

Hans shivered when he saw the mountains, feeling as if they were calling to him, and was relieved when they approached the outskirts of the small town of Gangtok and he saw a wooden building by the side of the road, surrounded by trucks, vans, cars, and a single, very battered helicopter.

'Here it is,' he said and pulled into the side, directly in front of the building, which looked like a small wood-plank house with a raised verandah at the front.

Turning off the ignition, he jumped out of the car and hurried to open the rear door and let Zweig out. Zweig did not seem too happy as he studied the helicopter, seemed less happy when Elena got out the other side, languidly stretched herself, spat her chewing gum at the ground and said, 'Shit, what a dump!'

'Stop talking like a tramp,' Zweig said curtly.

'I should've stayed back in Darjeeling,' Elena replied defiantly, then, very foolishly, smiled at Hans. 'I mean, what am *I* doing here?'

'You're here because I can't trust you in that hotel. Now shut your mouth and don't bother me. Let's go inside.'

Shocked that Elena could be so stupid as to smile at *him* while defying Zweig, Hans was glad to walk up the steps, onto the verandah of the small roadside house. Glancing sideways at Zweig, he saw that his fleshy face was grim, his eyes smouldering beneath the wrinkled brow and balding forehead. Zweig looked like a monster, not quite human, certainly dangerous, and Hans felt his stomach heaving nervously as he knocked on the door.

'Come in!' a cheerful English voice cried out immediately. 'We're always open for business!'

What they entered was a very untidy office, with a couple of cluttered desks, a few typewriters and telephones. The walls were covered in maps, charts, timetables and pin-up calendars from various tyre manufacturers; and a lot of agricultural and mechanical tools were scattered about the place. A long counter divided the office from the reception area, and behind it stood a small, plump, ruddy-cheeked Englishman, whose eyes, bright blue and crinkled with lines of humour, matched his naturally cheerful grin.

'The first customers I've had today,' he said. 'How do you do?'

'We're fine,' Hans said. 'Are you David Stewart?'

'I certainly hope so. I'm the only English resident in the area, but I sometimes forget that fact.'

'My name is Hans Mayer. I and my friends are travelling about the area and would like –'

'You are German? Yes?'

'Yes,' Hans agreed, 'we are.'

'Damned good soldiers, I have to admit. Let bygones be bygones.'

'Yes,' Hans said. 'Of course. What we want is –'

'I have Land Rovers and trucks and vans and ordinary cars. I have the only helicopter in the area – so just say the word.'

'That is *most* kind,' Hans said, feeling flustered by what was clearly a touch of English eccentricity. 'What we want is –'

'I would suggest, if you intend travelling further, that you take a Land Rover. Of course, if you'd like to *fly* over the mountains, I could be your pilot.'

'We were thinking of –'

'Ah, yes, a flight *along* the mountains. The lady *would* find that heavenly. And I don't doubt that –'

'We're looking for someone,' Zweig interjected rudely, stepping up to the counter, spreading his large hands upon it and staring down without warmth at the small Englishman. 'An American named Remick. We were told he wanted to hire a Land Rover and would have to get it from you. Has the bastard been here?'

The cheerful expression left the Englishman's face and he looked up at Zweig with detestation.

'I *beg* your pardon?' he said.

477

'You heard me,' Zweig whispered. 'An American bastard. His name's Jerry Remick.'

'This is not the police department,' the Englishman replied. 'I am here to hire out cars or give helicopter trips. I'm not here to listen to such language or disclose the names of my clients.'

'Actually,' Hans began, hoping to smooth troubled waters, 'we just wanted –' But he trailed off in despair when Zweig went to the end of the counter, walked into the office area, grabbed the small Englishman by the collar of his jacket and raised him bodily off the ground. The Englishman hung there, eyes bulging, cheeks bright red, kicking his feet helplessly in the air while the huge Zweig glared at him.

'I detest English fairies,' Zweig said. 'Now has he been here or not?'

The Englishman was choking on the tightened collar of his jacket, opening and closing his mouth like a fish out of water. Zweig shook him like a rag doll, making his flushed cheeks pale, then hurled him bodily at the nearest wall.

He picked up an axe, glared at the Englishman, then started swinging the axe with a frightening efficiency, bringing it down on the typewriters, the telephone lines, the desks, then smashing all the chairs to smithereens before attacking the walls. He went at them with cold fury, muttering under his breath, hacking great lumps out of the planks, smashing lamps and pipes, ripping electric cables out of the plaster – taking the whole office to pieces while its owner, crouching back against a wall, looked up in horror and dread, his eyes like two polished spoons.

Eventually Zweig finished, let the axe fall to his side, took a deep breath, then swung the axe back over his head and brought it down on the Englishman.

The Englishman screamed and rolled away just in

478

time, the axe burying itself low down in the wall where his head would have been. Then Zweig reached down, grabbed him and jerked him up to his feet again.

'The *Schwein*'s name was Remick,' he said. 'Now did he come here or not?'

The Englishman simply nodded his head.

Zweig opened his large hands and dropped the Englishman to the floor, where he flopped forward, gasping for breath, then rolled onto his back.

'Yes,' he gasped, 'he was here. He took a Land Rover. He wanted to drive through the Sikkim valley to the base of the mountains. From there he was planning to hire some Sherpas to take him up to the peaks. I thought he was mad and told him so, but he insisted on going. He kept mumbling something about some girl. I didn't catch what it was.'

'What *part* of the mountains?' Zweig asked.

'I don't know.'

'You're sure?'

'*I don't know!*'

The Englishman propped himself against the wall, his legs outstretched before him.

'Is that helicopter outside ready to go?'

'Yes, I can take you –'

'I can fly it myself. *Danke sehr* for your helpful information. Hans, kill this English *Schwein*.'

Hans felt a deep surge of horror and disbelief as Zweig turned away and walked back through the opening in the counter. He opened his mouth to speak, was lost for words, saw Zweig's steely eyes fixed upon him and turned away to face Elena who, for the first time since he had known her, also seemed shocked.

'Jesus Christ, Zweig,' she said, 'you can't really mean –'

'Shut up. This is none of your business. Hans, do as you're told.'

'Herr Zweig, I really don't see any reason for –'

'Goddamnit, Zweig,' Elena interjected, 'don't be such an ass. You're acting like someone going crazy. Show some sense, for Chrissakes!'

Zweig snapped his fingers at Hans.

'A weapon! *Give me the pistol, Hans!*'

Hans did as he was told, removing the pistol from the holster under his jacket. As he handed it to Zweig, he could hardly think straight, was only aware of a growing horror and bewilderment, not sure what new diabolical ploy his master was cooking up.

He soon found out. Zweig held the pistol in front of his face, studied it thoughtfully, then turned around and held it out to Elena, who stepped back, shaking her head in protest.

'No!' she spat. '*No!*'

'You whore!' Zweig growled. 'Telling *me* what to do. You're getting too smart for your own good; it's time you learned to take orders.'

'I won't do it! *I won't!*'

Though ashamed of himself, Hans was too terrified to move, and didn't do so even as Zweig reached out for the protesting Elena, grabbed her by the throat and waved the pistol threateningly in her face.

'Take this pistol and kill that English *Schwein*. It's him or you, you whore. Now take the pistol and kill him!'

Choking, Elena took the pistol out of Zweig's hand, glancing despairingly at Hans, looking more human than she had ever been, then walked, breathing too harshly, through the gap in the counter.

Hans stared pleadingly at Zweig, met that coldly ferocious gaze, turned away to see a shaking Elena slowly raising the pistol. She was no longer a whore, but a woman stripped naked, trembling with terror and revulsion, trying to choke back her shame. At that moment he loved her, understanding what she was feeling, and realized that she and he were bound together in the same stinking trap.

He had to get them both out.

The Englishman whimpered 'No!' and Elena started to cry, the hand holding the pistol shaking visibly as she tried to take aim. '*Please*, miss!' the man pleaded, his voice hoarse and shaking – but Elena's hand jerked, the report ricocheted around the room, the man's heels kicked the floor and he quivered once or twice as Elena stepped back and covered her mouth with one hand, her streaming eyes turning towards Zweig to display her revulsion.

'Oh, you *bastard*!' she sobbed.

Without a word, Zweig stepped around the counter, walked up to her and slapped her face. It was a sharp, brutal blow, making her head jerk to the side, and she dropped the smoking pistol to the floor.

'You're mine,' Zweig said. 'You do as I say. Now let's get out of here.'

He practically dragged her from the office, pushed her through the front door, then indicated with a nod over his shoulder that Hans should follow them out.

Hans rushed into the office area, picked up the pistol, put on the safety catch, then slipped the weapon back into his holster. He looked down at the dead man, saw pieces of brain and blood, an anguished contortion of outflung limbs, and almost heaved up. However, he managed to control himself, looking away and breathing deeply, then hurried out of that place of death and back into the fresh air.

Zweig was standing by the helicopter, holding on to the sobbing Elena, both of them framed by the snow-capped mountains and a cloudily pock-marked sky. Zweig was gripping her very tightly, his large hand crushing her shoulder, as she shook like a leaf in a storm, suddenly frail, almost childlike.

The sight of her tears shocked Hans, but also filled him with fear. He and Elena were in the hands of a madman. Zweig had given up everything, was losing his mind, collapsing, and the dream of attaining the Tuaoi Stone was all he had left.

That stone may not exist – and if it did, so what? Zweig was in no condition to deal with it or anything else. No, he was going mad, inviting destruction with every step, and sooner or later that need to destroy would be turned on Hans, also.

'No,' he muttered. 'It's too much.'

He had been a prisoner too long and now he wanted his freedom, the touch of human warmth, Elena's flesh, that ecstatic renewal. He wanted her and a future – a bright place, without fear – and as he walked towards her and Zweig, putting a smile on his face, he realized that at last he was willing to risk all for that.

'I'll fly it,' Zweig said, then stepped aside, his eyes watchful, to ensure that Hans and Elena climbed up before him. He followed them in, huffing and puffing very badly, sat in the pilot's seat and switched on the ignition, then expertly took them up above the clouds to the vast, sweeping sky – a clean place, well lit, an empty space where birds could spread their wings and had nothing to fear.

CHAPTER FORTY-TWO

Something changed the silent darkness. A hint of light, distant sound. A faint murmuring, like water on sand, reflecting moonlight and stars. No, something else ... not reflected sky, just lights: streaks of light that undulated through the darkness and hinted of substance. No splashing water either: encircling voices, closing in. A heartbeat that resounded like a gong and filled up what he was.

I am, he thought as sensation returned to him. *Jerry ... I am Jerry.* His pulsing blood warmed his skin. *Where am I? What's happening?* He remembered going blind. A spasm of terror whipped him, then receded when the streaks of light widened.

The resounding heartbeat was his own, but it faded away as sound returned: the shuffling of feet, murmuring voices, the words now more distinct ... 'He's coming around ... doing fine ...'

The streaks of light had joined together to become a general brightness; it spread through the darkness, letting him know that he had sight, and he finally opened his eyes, looked up from where he was lying, and saw two faces looking down, both distinctly familiar.

One was diabolically handsome, the other silvery-haired and distinguished, and they smiled and then moved away, leaving his view unobstructed. He felt his body, pinched himself, realized that he was whole, then looked up at a very strange, high ceiling, wondering what he was seeing.

'You're all right,' a familiar voice said smoothly. 'You can sit up now, Jerry.'

He realized that he was lying on some kind of hard bed, and turned his head towards the sound of the voice. St Germain and Mephisto were standing a few yards away, side by side, both wearing Tibetan robes, or *chubas*, in a great hall remarkably similar to the monastery he had left the night before – smooth walls of stone and *chan*, a spartan stone-flagged floor, Tibetan carpets and odd bits of Indian furniture placed here and there.

There were, however, a couple of differences . . . and coming awake, surprisingly free of fear, he took a deep breath, sat upright, and gazed more carefully around him.

The smooth stone and *chan* walls did not rise to an ordinary ceiling, but appeared to have been cut into solid, irregular rock, which he assumed could only be the interior of the mountain. More bizarre was what appeared to be an immense, steel plated dome that formed the high roof of the great chamber, rather like the inside of an observatory.

In the exact centre of the floor of the great hall, directly below the high dome, was a five foot tall, rectangular, solid stone pedestal, on top of which rested, inside a protective transparent case, a light-reflecting, crystal pyramid, about five inches high.

It was obviously the Tuaoi Stone.

Without thinking, he swung his legs off the bed of stone – a solid block, as he noticed – and walked the few yards to the middle of the great hall, stopping in front of the pedestal supporting the legendary sacred stone.

He reached out to touch the glass case, stopped, stared at the two men; when they simply smiled and nodded, he touched the glass to confirm that that's *all* it was.

Yes, it was glass – or certainly something very similar – and he looked through it at the miniature crystal pyramid, which, in reflecting the light, was unusually dazzling.

He stared at that small pyramid for a very long time, then eventually raised his gaze from the tip of the pyramid to the steel-plated dome high above him.

The tip of the pyramid was aimed directly at the centre of the dome.

'Can I touch it?' he asked, still looking at the pyramid.

'No,' St Germain said.

The sound of that distinct voice, which he had first heard on the Nile, jerked him gently back to reality and made him study the two men. Since he had recently seen Mephisto there was no great surprise in store, though once more he was aware of a certain jaded weariness behind his diabolical attractiveness and uncannily erotic, slightly mocking smile. However, since that first encounter during the Nile cruise, he had only seen St Germain in dreams or hallucinations, as a mirage or shimmering ghost, mostly slightly erased and distorted in the pulsating white haze; but now he could see him clearly and was singularly impressed, forcibly struck by his distinguished features, his grey eyes and silvery hair, his air of quiet authority, perhaps arrogance, his indivisible sense of self.

'What happened to me?' Jerry asked. 'I thought I was going blind.'

'You were temporarily dematerialized,' St Germain replied, 'and teleported up to here inside that plasmoid mass. You are now back to normal.'

'I thought it was a UFO.'

'That's what most people think when they see them.

What they're seeing in fact is a pocket of the infinite, a movable point where the world we know doesn't exist, and material objects or persons, as if caught in a black hole, can circumvent space and time to reappear elsewhere.'

'I'm supposed to believe that?'

'Why not? You're very keen on mathematics. You have a particular interest in quantum mechanics and at least *understand* their implications. Think of the electron that can appear out of nothing, out of nowhere – the non-existent – then travel a distance which is both finite and infinite, realize its mistake – that it is actually unreal – then turn around and travel back through time to its starting place, thus having never existed in the first place.'

'Right,' Jerry said. 'And it repeats that again and again, in one sense never actually existing, in another existing eternally in an ever-scattering time event.'

'Correct, Jerry. If you see me, I am. If you do not, *I* am not. The secret of immortality is to be found in quantum mechanics: with the Secret Knowledge, with power, we can transcend time and space, materializing and disappearing at will, existing even in death.'

'And that's how you and Mephisto get around?'

'Yes.'

'Like the lamas?'

'Yes, like the lamas . . . but much more advanced. The lamas can only project *themselves* out of their bodies; we can do the same to others, whether they want it or not. Rather like creating a *tulpa* – a willed materialization of another person.'

'Then Ingrid's up here? She's safe?'

'Of course,' St Germain said.

He nodded at Mephisto who turned and walked away without a word, leaving the great hall by a doorless exit in one side. Then, while St Germain stared steadily at him, smiling slightly, Jerry was able to see something that he had not noticed previously: that this man, for all his outward appearance of youthfulness, was much older, a *lot* older, than he appeared to be. It was as if a youthful patina had been placed over the mouldering tissue of the centuries, a second skin on the verge of shedding, to reveal . . . who knew what?

'What is this place?' he asked.

'A sort of monastery,' St Germain replied. 'We can only leave our material bodies temporarily, and here, when in the material state, we meditate and ponder the Secret Knowledge which, in its learning, sets us free from mortality's strictures.'

'Has this place been hollowed out of the mountain?'

'Yes. Many centuries ago. It was created by normal, mortal men, before they transcended. From outside it cannot be seen unless that is our wish. Nor would you have found it had you wandered these mountains for days. No one has *ever* found this place – unless *we* wished them to.'

Jerry was willing to believe that, remembering his tortuous journey, his increasing conviction that the mountain was playing tricks on him and confusing his senses. He wondered if that path really existed, or if they had placed it there for him, but instead of asking was moved by another, more personal concern.

'Has Mephisto gone for Ingrid?'

'Yes. He's bringing her to you. We brought her here to make you come after her – and you did, as we thought you would. Without the strength of that love you would not have got as far as even the first monastery. You are one of the pure at heart.'

'I seriously doubt that.'

'The pure at heart are possessed of the kind of

humility that even they may not recognize. We are rarely, if ever, what we think we are – and you are more than you know.'

Gazing around the great hall, which had precious little furnishing and made voices reverberate, Jerry felt very removed from what he had been, different, much older and wiser, as if changed overnight. He felt no fear at being here, but only a burning curiosity, a rising excitement that filled his head with light and heightened perception.

There was so much he wanted to ask, but he didn't know where to begin, and was still gazing around him, in a trance of expectation, when the sound of footsteps approaching outside the hall made him look at the doorway to his left.

Ingrid entered with Mephisto, the latter holding her elbow, and she smiled with surprising naturalness and joy, putting her hands out even as she hurried to him, to embrace and kiss him. He felt her softness and warmth, her femininity, and took it into himself, almost weeping at the emotion she gave him. When she stepped away, flicking hair from her eyes, her smile shone like the sun.

'They told me you'd come after me,' she said. 'And I knew you would, too.'

'You're okay?' he asked.

'Yes, I'm fine. A little bit dazed, but looked after. I can't believe this is happening.'

He shared her feelings, but realized with a touch of amusement that it was something they had both expressed often during their journey to this place.

I can't believe this is happening.

No, he couldn't believe it, yet still felt no fear, was moved only by a mounting impatience to find out what the end was.

Mephisto, who had been staring steadily at him,

offered a slight, mocking smile, making him blush with anger and embarrassment, speaking hurriedly to hide it.

'Why did you lure me up here?' he asked St Germain. 'And why, if you're protecting the Tuaoi Stone, did you actually help us to find it?'

'You are here,' St Germain replied gravely, 'to meet your manifest destiny.'

Startled, slightly shocked, and embarrassed in an odd, almost childish way, he stared at Ingrid, received a smile of encouragement, glanced at the thinly smiling Mephisto, then turned back to St Germain.

'You now know the secret of civilization,' St Germain said. 'That civilization began here, when what is now Africa and India were one land mass, and that original civilization eventually became even more advanced in its intellectual and scientific achievements than the most advanced societies of the present day. It was a civilization based on kabbalistic geometry, or numerology; and having discovered that everything in existence is bound together in a great design, and that the design is numerical, the philosopher-leaders of that society soon uncovered many of the great mysteries of the universe and created a civilization in which mental telepathy, extrasensory perception, precognition, the pineal eye, levitation and other so-called paranormal powers were commonplace – at least amongst the philosopher-leaders, or high priests.'

He sighed and glanced around him, as if seeing faraway places, then stared at the Tuaoi Stone.

'Knowing that every number has certain given properties – male and female, active and passive, positive and negative – the leaders of that civilization based all of their creations on the dictates of given numbers, with the names of things or persons encoding their essential characteristics in the numerical values of the letters used. In other words, each letter in the alphabet had a corresponding number, and all words in the spoken language were created from the numbers containing their characteristics. In time the language of words became the predominant language, and the *original* language – the language of numbers – became the secret, magical language of only the most powerful, magical adepts at the head of that great civilization.'

St Germain walked up to the glass case containing the Tuaoi Stone, placed his hand upon it, above the pyramid, and lovingly left it there.

'In the secret language of numbers, the perfect number is six, with all other numbers grouped around it; and the most perfect shape, according to the numerical law, is the shape of the pyramid. Thus, the dominant architectural shape of that great civilization became the pyramid which, in its numerous variations – such as the Tibetan chorten or the oriental pagoda – spread across the world in the wake of the migrations of the people of that civilization about 200,000 years ago, in a time when there were no written records and all was held in the mind.'

'And were you,' Jerry asked, 'in one of your previous incarnations, a high priest, or magical adept, of that civilization?'

'Yes,' St Germain said, not looking at him, but simply staring down at the crystal pyramid in its glass case, and continuing to speak as if addressing it. 'The language of numbers is based on the first eight digits, one to eight, the most important of which is six, with the most magical of all combinations being the so-called number of the beast, 666, which has often been disguised as the sum of its three digits, eighteen, or 1746, the digits of which, when added together, also make eighteen. The Tuaoi Stone is therefore a perfect pyramid whose dimensions are based on that magical number – and thus embody in alchemical terms what the number represents: the fusion of Earth and sky, male and female, sulphur and mercury – the very secret of life. Thus the Tuaoi Stone, when placed on the Great Pyramid, created a fusion between Earth and the cosmos, between the terrestrial and the celestial, creating a bridge across time and space, rendering human mortality obsolete. Through the Tuaoi Stone, immortality and limitless power could be gained – and for that very reason only the high priests of that great civilization – the absolutely pure at heart – were taught the secret language of numbers, became magical adepts, and explored the mysteries of the universe in increasing secrecy, becoming the keepers of the sacred stone throughout the centuries.'

'So the Tuaoi Stone is actually the Philosophers' Stone?'

'Yes, my young friend, it is.'

Glancing at Mephisto, whose eyes glittered mesmerically, Jerry recalled the bizarre journey that he and Ingrid had made to get here, the many clues and leads they had been given – all based on numbers. That whole journey had been a mathematical riddle and they had asked him to solve it. They had helped him the only way they could: with the language of numbers.

'And that civilization later spread out,' he said, remembering all he had learned, 'to the Atlantic Ocean, then the Mediterranean Sea, and finally to Egypt?'

'Yes. And of course, in the inept language of words, became known as Atlantis. Over the centuries of prehistory, while that great race was still progressing, it eventually found its way by boat to the Atlantic Ocean, built other great pyramids and founded another civilization there, on the various islands between the Azores and the Sargasso Sea, and suffered three periods of destruction by fire and rain – in other words, by volcanic eruption, earthquakes and subsequent floods.

However, after the first two catastrophes, and knowing that another was imminent, the high priests, including myself, removed the sacred stone from atop its great pyramid and travelled by boat across the Atlantic to the Mediterranean, finally settling on the various islands of the Aegean Sea, between Crete and Santorini. Not long after, about 10,000 BC, the civilization we had left in the North Atlantic was destroyed in the third of its periods of destruction and buried beneath the sea. Some of its remains are still there to this day, beneath the waters off Bimini.'

When St Germain said that, Jerry remembered the photographs he had seen at various times of the circular walls and pyramidal structures recently discovered at Bimini, off the coast of Florida. He also remembered the visions he had had of great pyramidal cities, with pyramids of all shapes and sizes stretching away to the horizon, of the same constructions being covered in tidal waves and the dust of the centuries. He had seen magnificent civilizations flourish and die in his most vivid imaginings – and now knew that what he had imagined were visions of a former actuality, given to him by St Germain.

He lowered his head and rubbed his eyes, trying to take all this in, then looked up again at St Germain, trying to see the bones of his skull beneath his distinguished, oddly youthful features.

Perhaps he saw weariness.

'The magical powers of numbers,' St Germain continued, 'incorporated in the magical crystal, or Tuaoi Stone, brought great prosperity and joy to the peoples of that growing civilization in the Aegean Sea, but this in turn led to great arrogance and base ambition. While the high priests protecting the Tuaoi Stone became more withdrawn and secretive, the less religiously inclined embarked on campaigns of conquest and soon conquered North Africa, including Egypt. By that time, the high priests, who by now were gifted with mental telepathy and precognition, had prophesied that the island of Santorini would erupt and subsequently destroy that civilization in the Aegean Sea – which many people now call Atlantis. They therefore removed the Tuaoi Stone from its pyramid on an island in that area and placed it on the deliberately truncated peak of the immense pyramid which they had built at Giza, in Egypt, in approximately 2,170 BC. Since that pyramid was to be their great temple of learning and, being located at what was then the exact centre of the terrestrial Earth, was an instrument of fusion between the Earth and the cosmos, it eventually became known as the Great Pyramid.'

Jerry glanced at Mephisto and saw him smiling at Ingrid. She blushed, as helpless as a child, but didn't lower her gaze. He felt nervous just seeing that.

'In about 1,500 BC,' St Germain went on, 'Santorini, as had been prophesied, erupted and destroyed that so-called Atlantis in the Aegean Sea; and the high priests of the new civilization in Egypt guarded even more zealously the Secret Knowledge found through the Tuaoi Stone, educated many new adepts – including, of course, Plato, Pythagoras and Jesus Christ – in the inner sanctums of the pyramid; and used the Tuaoi Stone – whose magical numbers represented the sum of the two basic elements of alchemical transformation, namely sulphur and mercury – as an instrument of such transformation to a higher, purely spiritual plane. Then, when they had succeeded – and had, in so doing, created a small, select group of magically gifted adepts – they removed the Tuaoi Stone from the top of the Great Pyramid, left the now useless pyramid to the encroaches of modern times, and returned with the Tuaoi Stone to the Himalayas, their natural home. I am one of that original group, a magical adept – and you, too, have been chosen.'

Feeling a wave of disbelief washing over him at the sound of those last words, Jerry shook his head, tried to grin it off, and decided not to pursue that point too quickly. Instead, having glanced once more at Mephisto and Ingrid, and been rendered more nervous by Ingrid's helpless response to the former's charms, he choked back his resentment and said to St Germain: 'The adepts actually found the secret of immortality?'

'In time, yes.'

'And you and Mephisto are both immortals?'

'Yes, that is so. We exist inside a physical form, but can transform it at will, can leave it and move back and forth through space and time. We are here – and there, also.'

'And the legendary Comte de Saint-Germain was actually you?'

'Yes, that was me in one of my many manifestations. I was compelled to intervene in the affairs of men and was thus very noticeable. My true history, however, was deliberately rendered obscure and contradictory to confuse those who would try to identify me as who and *what* I truly am. But I was, and am, he: the Comte de Saint-Germain – in truth, St Germain of this secret Order devoted to the Tuaoi Stone.'

'And what's the purpose of the society?'

'Individually, to pursue the Secret Knowledge, which is finite and infinite, and learn the secret of existence, which is finally unknowable; to find through the Secret Knowledge, the Unknowable, the inner peace of Nirvana, the one true reality. Collectively, in mutually finding Nirvana, creating a new Kingdom on Earth, a magical civilization, in which terms like "life" and "death" will become interchangeable, physical journeys through space rendered unnecessary, contact with those in far-flung galaxies perfectly commonplace, and knowledge of the nature of life and time made freely available.'

'That's a purely spiritual quest.'

'Yes, it is.'

'Then why do you sometimes intervene in the affairs of men?'

'We only do so when the secrecy of our Order is threatened – or when the affairs of mortal men are a threat to their future salvation. Plato and Merlin, for instance, in their different ways kept alive in the minds of men the legend of our magical civilization whilst ensuring that our society remained secret. It was the function of Pythagoras to instil in Man the knowledge that reality, at its deepest level, is mathematical in nature and that philosophy can be used for spiritual purification. Jesus Christ, another adept, returned to Earth in human form in order to help Man rise from his barbarism and create a culture based on love instead of primitive fears. You already know about my own many interventions, as the Comte de Saint-Germain, in the troubled politics of the eighteenth century. You may also be aware of the rumour that Hitler had a secret, so-called magical adviser who persuaded him, by referring to his stars, *not* to encircle the besieged British army on Dunkirk beach. That decision cost Hitler the war – and *I* was the widely reported secret adviser who deliberately led him into making that decision – which for him was disastrous, but which saved the free world from subjugation.'

'And what about Ingrid's father?'

'We protected you from Zweig because your purpose had not been fulfilled and he was threatening that. And, in protecting you, we foiled his dream of capturing the Tuaoi Stone and using it for his own evil purposes.'

The thoughtful St Germain was being very persuasive, but Jerry felt that something wasn't quite right, that certain fabrications, or perhaps omissions, were gilding the truth. He had doubts about what he was hearing, didn't quite know why, so decided, instead of giving voice to them, to let St Germain say what he wished.

'And me,' he said. '*I'm* one of the pure at heart? I find *that* hard to believe!'

'Yes, you are one of the pure at heart. You may not recognize that yourself, but your actions have proved it. Your journey to here has been an elaborate one, dangerous and frightening, and throughout it you have acted with courage and the goodness of faith. You are one of the pure at heart. It embarrasses you, but it is so. You have a fine mind, but lack material ambitions. Your pursuit of knowledge is not tainted by base motives, and your journey here, designed to test your courage, also tested your goodness. Although intelligent, you have managed to remain a child – and that innocence blesses you.'

'There must be many like me.'

'Many are chosen, few pass. You were chosen when I met you on that boat on the Nile and recognized your potential as one of us. Everything that has occurred since then has been designed to either bring you here successfully or let you fall by the wayside at the first sign of failure. I knew you were one of the pure at heart, though obviously not knowing it, and your innocence, combined with your intelligence, clearly confirmed this. Likewise, your interest in esoteric matters, both scientific *and* spiritual, was another factor in your favour; and your specific interest and faith in the magical properties of the Great Pyramid of Giza was yet another confirmation of my belief that you were destined to join us.'

'And Ingrid?'

'Ingrid, also, is pure at heart, your mirror-image and helpmate, and her involvement since your meeting on that boat was also encouraged by me. Zweig was after the Tuaoi Stone and therefore had to be stopped; but I also wanted him to be your adversary in the final, most crucial test – in the conflict between good and evil of which you are part.'

'Then it hasn't yet ended?'

'No. The final test has yet to be, but it *is* close at hand, and I am confident that all is as it should be, that you *will* remain here as one of the pure at heart, only leaving to help inaugurate the new Kingdom on Earth.'

Aware that he was caught up in something of startling import, Jerry couldn't help but feel a slight amusement at his own continuing, very human concerns. He felt this when he found himself looking again at Mephisto and Ingrid, fearful of a liaison between them – but when he smiled at her, she returned his smile warmly and, feeling an awful lot better, he turned back to St Germain.

'So,' he said, 'I've been chosen. I'm to become an adept and help create a new Kingdom on Earth. When will that be?'

'Since the Secret Knowledge has been hidden from the mass of normal men by the use of kabbalistic geometry,' St Germain replied, 'the heart of which is the number 666, the new Kingdom on Earth will be inaugurated when 666 mortal men have been rendered immortal by their experiences in this magical monastery. So far, 665 men have done so – and you are the last.'

'And that's why I'm here.'

'Yes, Jerry. Precisely.'

Jerry glanced at Ingrid and was struck by her calmness, the lack of fear or confusion in her eyes, the steady warmth of her gaze. His heart went out to her, like a bird, on wings of love, and then he studied

Mephisto, saw that sly, mocking smile, and wondered what truly lay behind it, if the joke was on him.

'I find most of this unbelievable,' he said. 'I'm only human, after all, and don't believe in immortality. Nor do I believe in the powers you've ascribed to the Tuaoi Stone. It's just a tiny pyramid – a symbol – and its power lies right there.'

'No,' St Germain replied. 'You're wrong. The stone is as I have described it. It can cause physical *and* spiritual transformations, some of which you've actually witnessed during your journey to this place. The Tuaoi Stone can fuse the Earth to the cosmos, it can obliterate time and space.'

'I'm sorry, but I still don't believe you. I'm just a mere mortal.'

St Germain sighed, looked at Mephisto, then returned his attention to Jerry. 'Intervention in the affairs of men is sometimes necessary,' he said, 'and now is just such an instance. We have protected you both from Zweig because he threatened you *and* us; now, before we take you any further, we must pit your goodness against his evil and observe the results. This is your final test, which will strengthen or destroy you; and if, as we hope, it ends with your victory, it will rid you of the last of your doubts and help you accept us.'

'Where and when will this final test take place?'

'Here and now,' St Germain replied calmly. 'Zweig, who mistakenly thinks he has pursued us, has actually been *guided* to this place and is arriving right now. Be prepared to defend yourself.'

Jerry heard the short gasp of shock that burst from Ingrid's lips at the mention of her father's imminent arrival, and he saw her turning white and placing her hands over her lips.

Almost hating St Germain for what he was doing, he was about to say something when he heard a bass humming sound coming from above, and when he looked up, saw the great dome slowly opening, its metal plates parting like the petals of a flower, showing triangular patches of sky, the morning light, drifting clouds; then more sky, more light, as the panels drew further apart, eventually disappearing completely above the rocks, until only an immense, jagged hole remained up there, exposing the white-cloud sky, its centre directly above the glass case protecting the Tuaoi Stone.

Jerry looked up at the morning light and drifting white clouds, entranced by the real world, feeling that the sky was spinning magically and drawing him up to it.

CHAPTER FORTY-THREE

Looking down on the gleaming snow-white valleys and peaks of Kanchenjunga, from the pilot's seat of the roaring, shuddering helicopter, Zweig felt that the mountains were drawing him towards them, luring him down. He had to look away frequently, feeling dizzy and disoriented, but then he was just reminded of Hans and Elena, both of whom were sitting slightly behind him, both obviously chastened. That gave him some pleasure – the knowledge that he still had power – and feeling more lively, not as old as he had been, he took the helicopter higher, watched the slopes slipping below him, and searched every gorge and ravine for a sign of a hideaway.

'*Scheisse!*' he snapped. 'Nothing but rock and snow! They could be anywhere! *Anywhere!*'

'We won't find them,' Hans said behind him. 'They'll be very well hidden. If no one has found them before, even by accident, then we're unlikely to do so.'

Zweig was shocked by what he was hearing. Hans actually sounded rebellious. He sensed a rising antagonism in his young assistant, and thought he understood why.

'Shut your mouth, Hans,' he told him. 'You're missing the point. The point is that we thought we were *pursuing* Saint-Germain, when in fact he's practically *invited* us here. He must *want* us to find him.'

'Why?' Hans replied, sounding agitated. 'That's what *I* want to know.'

'It's a trap,' Elena joined in. 'There can't be any

other reason. We should fly the hell out of here before we get into trouble.'

If no longer impressed with Hans, he was even less so with Elena, and felt like throwing her out of the helicopter, lock, stock and barrel. He loathed her stupidity, her crass behaviour and crude tongue, but mostly he loathed her voluptuous, whorish beauty, which had gradually become a slap in the face to his waning potency. She reminded him of his age, the rapid decaying of his mind and body, and for that reason, as well as a few others, he now wanted rid of her.

'I didn't ask for your opinion, Elena, so please don't say any more. Your voice grates on my eardrums.'

She didn't respond and he didn't expect her to; she had been growing more impertinent lately, but he had managed to crush the bitch – making her murder that squawking English fairy had certainly done the trick. She had been frightened and horrified, shocked out of her wits; and just as with Hans, when he had been forced to shoot the hoodlum, so, too, the very fact that she had squeezed the trigger would render her helpless. She would not forget it easily, would dwell on possible repercussions, and would subsequently now treat him with the respect he deserved.

Satisfied, he stared at the mountain peaks all around him, brown rock in pure snow, the snow melting and forming a necklace of streams that ran hither and thither, glittering brightly in the late morning sunlight, before disappearing into great pools of shadow – deep ravines, winding gorges. It was empty down there, fiercely beautiful and vast, and he felt that he was flying over an alien landscape, perhaps a different planet.

These days everything seemed unreal and he didn't like that; it was caused by his age and failing health, by the crushing knowledge of his mortality, but also by the pursuit of his daughter, her American boyfriend and St Germain. They were all somewhere down there, perhaps waiting for him; and as he glided between the white-capped peaks, through pools of shadow and streams of light, he burned with a murderous hatred that threatened his reasoning.

He was frightened, yes, of things he couldn't see or grasp, felt haunted by the magical unknown, represented by Saint-Germain. He was frightened, but also angry, wanting revenge, then immortality; wanting to see his daughter, that bitch who had betrayed him, suffer as her mother had done when he fed her the poison. And with that, he wanted the Tuaoi Stone, the Secret Knowledge, immortality, the conquest of all his buried nightmares, the key to the world.

'*Scheisse!*' he muttered again. 'Where *are* the bastards? Why don't they show themselves?'

He decided to go higher, towards the most majestic peaks, also known as the Petals of the Golden Lotus created by Vishnu – the first step in the creation of the universe. Somewhere up there, he remembered, Siva was supposed to sit in a state of eternal meditation, generating the spiritual force that sustains the cosmos. That force existed, he now realized, not in Siva, but in the Tuaoi Stone, and was the only thing that could possibly stand between him and oblivion.

Looking down, he pondered that fact and what it meant to him: he had thrown everything away in a fit of mindless rage, in what might have been an attack of madness, and now he had nothing left to live for, except what was down there.

'We're too high,' Hans admonished him. 'The winds are treacherous up here. This machine isn't made for such an altitude or these weather conditions. Please, Herr Zweig, take us lower.'

Again reminded that Hans, though still frightened, was gradually growing more defiant, Zweig took the helicopter higher and soared over more peaks. He looked carefully at them, every shadow, each gorge, saw nothing but an awesome desolation, a vast and immaculate white carpet covering nothing but rock.

His anger grew immediately, when he thought of what they had done – that wimp, Hans, and that painted tart, Elena . . . sometime . . . somewhere.

Yes, it was obvious; such things couldn't be hidden: the wimp and the whore had fornicated and wanted to do so again.

His heart raced when he thought about it; his cheeks burned and he trembled. He took the helicopter higher, flew across the loftiest peaks, looked down at the glittering snow and irregular pools of shadow, a vast, surrealistic, ominous jigsaw of brown and white, and contemplated hurling them both to their deaths, one after the other.

'We're too high!' Hans said through gritted teeth, breathing into his neck. 'Damnit, Zweig, *we're too high*!'

He couldn't help himself. It was just too much to bear. His heart raced and he felt his cheeks burning as the blind rage coursed through him. The impertinent young pup! Him and that whore, Elena. He took the helicopter higher, ascending far too rapidly, and gleaned comfort from Elena's gasp of fear as they bucked through the wind.

'Christ!' Hans exclaimed.

'Shut up!'

'We're going to crash!' Elena shouted. 'Christ, Zweig, you stupid bastard, take her down! She won't *go* any higher!'

'Whore!' he bawled, unable to contain himself. '*Shut your mouth, you fat whore!*' Forgetting the controls, he twisted around in his seat, feeling as if he was in a furnace with everything burning – his body, his mind – and screamed at her, 'Get out, you bitch! *Out!* Get out or I'll kill you!'

'Out? What the –?'

'You mean, *jump*?' Hans enquired.

'That's right! What do *you* think? I want the worthless bitch to jump out. You hear, Elena? *Get out!*'

She was shocked out of her wits, and just stared at him, speechless, then turned pleadingly to Hans, reaching out for his hand.

That was too much for Zweig (he saw himself from a distance now) and he twisted further out of his seat to slap at her face. He missed, fell forward, hanging from his safety belt, as the helicopter tilted to the side and was pummelled by wind.

He heard Hans shouting something, his voice filled with fear, then Elena letting out a piercing scream that almost ruptured his eardrums. He yelled something at her, tried to punch her in the face, saw her big eyes disappearing, the top of her head, then a swathe of glistening white snow and outcroppings of rock.

Hans tried to get at the controls, but he swiped him away, took a deep breath and managed to check himself. The helicopter levelled out, stopped shaking, quietened down, then flew rapidly between sheer walls of snow and frozen rock, its shadow leaping up and down on the land below like a bird seeking food.

'Jesus,' Elena whispered. 'Did you see that? He nearly killed us all, Hans!'

He was just about to twist around and lunge at her again when Hans shouted, 'Look!'

'What?'

'Oh, my god . . .'

Hans' voice trailed off in a stutter of disbelief, and Zweig glanced out to where two soaring snow-capped peaks fell down to a shadow-filled gorge with level ground at its base. It was like a small valley, almost hidden from the sky, and the cliffs that soared up on either side darkly shadowed the plateau.

'*Wunderbar!*' Zweig exclaimed without thinking. 'That *has* to be them!'

He had seen what at first he had thought was a small hole in the snow; but now, as the helicopter flew towards the gorge, he saw that the hole was growing bigger – as if hot water had been poured onto the frozen snow, melting it – and that the irregular edges around the rim of the hole were glinting like metal.

In fact, even as he accepted that he was looking at glinting metal, the separate pieces took shape as immense triangular plates which, like the petals of a flower, moved away from one another, opening up to the sky, to reveal an artificially illuminated space just below – a space enlarging as the helicopter approached it across a glittering white plateau.

Aware that only the most highly developed technology could have constructed such a thing, let alone transported the material to the peaks of the highest mountains in the world, Zweig knew it could only have been the keepers of the Tuaoi Stone – which meant that Saint-Germain was down there.

Filling up with a dangerous mixture of excitement and dread, sensing that he had come to the beginning of the end, he throttled down and let the helicopter hover grumbling above that great hole.

The steel plates had opened completely, folding back over the rocks, enabling him to look down into some kind of large chamber. He thought he saw movement down there, but couldn't be sure – white snow glittered around the rim, merging into a hazy greyness, and below it, defying sense and credibility, was an artificially illuminated cavern containing, he now saw, several human-shaped shadows.

Perhaps four human beings.

'We'll have to go down there,' he said. 'I'm going to land in that place.'

'It's a trap,' Elena said. 'If we fly through that hole, those steel plates are going to close over the helicopter and trap us down there. We'll all be prisoners, Zweig.'

'I don't care. I've got to see the Tuaoi Stone. Nothing else matters now.'

'Not to you, maybe,' she replied like a petulant child. 'But it matters to *us*. *We* don't want to go down there. We don't have a clue what's waiting for us, so let's turn back while we can.'

'No,' he replied, too excited to think straight. 'I've got to see the Tuaoi Stone. *I'll get it somehow!*'

It was madness and he sensed it, but he couldn't turn back. As the helicopter descended, as the great hole widened below him, he knew for certain that he had been led here, that they *wanted* him here, and that until he understood the reason why, he wouldn't be able to rest.

'Yes!' he whispered as the helicopter was buffeted by the wind that howled demonically across that man-made hole. 'Let it end here!'

Then he felt the barrel of a pistol tapping the back of his head.

'No,' Hans said. 'We're not going down there. If you want to go, *you* go.'

Zweig couldn't believe it. He looked over his shoulder, but couldn't see Hans — only Elena's eyes, moving frantically to and fro, and beyond her, outside the roaring, shuddering helicopter, a swathe of steel plating in gleaming snow.

'Take that pistol away from my head. I'm going in there *right now*.'

There was a click as the safety catch on the pistol

was released, then he felt the barrel tapping his head again.

'Elena and I are getting out of here,' Hans said, his voice surprisingly calm. 'You're going down there alone. Elena, take hold of that joystick and try holding the helicopter steady. Zweig, get out of that seat and go to the door.'

Shocked almost speechless, unable to believe that he had miscalculated so badly and that his mistreatment of Hans, instead of paralysing him with fear, had made the dog turn on its master, Zweig wanted to scream with rage, knew that would be foolish, so simply clenched his fists by his sides and took a deep breath.

'You're crazy, Hans,' he said, letting his breath out again. 'Elena can't fly this machine. We'll just crash if she tries.'

'*I* can fly it,' Hans said, waving the pistol. 'Now get out of that chair.'

Scrambling awkwardly around the chair beside him, Elena took hold of the joystick just as he let it go. He studied her briefly, saw her fear give way to triumph, and accepted that she had also turned against him in favour of Hans. He felt shocked and humiliated, ashamed of his own bad judgement, and realized that the abuse he had heaped upon them was now coming back at him.

Well, so be it. He would take his strength from that. He had always despised them both, as he did most human beings, and now he would let his contempt be the base of his strength. He had been suffering from old age, from the fear of his mortality, but his rage would be enough to sustain him through what was to come.

'Of course,' he said to Hans. 'As you wish. Anything to oblige.' And with a contemptuous chuckle, slid out of the chair and went willingly to the open door where

Hans, no longer timid, indeed looking quite aggressive, was aiming the pistol at him, his hand surprisingly steady. 'You want me to jump out?' Zweig sneered.

'Why not?' Hans replied. 'You were going to make Elena jump out. But no, you don't have to jump; you can use the rope ladder. Let it down, Zweig. *Then* get out.'

'And what do you think you can do without *me*?' Zweig asked. 'You and this bitch, here?'

'You thought you owned me, didn't you? And that's why you trusted me. You thought I was too frightened to disobey you or use my initiative. Well, I didn't disobey you, but I *did* use my initiative – by transferring a lot of your assets into my *own* Swiss bank account. I think I've earned it, Herr Zweig.'

'Yes, perhaps you have.'

'I'm going to be rich, Zweig. Elena and I will have it made. We'll live in luxury for the rest of our lives – and at *your* expense. Now winch the ladder down, you fat pig, and let us get out of here.'

'If I ever –'

'You won't, Zweig. You won't ever see us again. I doubt that you'll even get back down the mountain. Now do as you're told.'

Feeling disconnected from what he was hearing, oddly lacking in anger, wanting only to get down there and face Saint-Germain, Zweig studied Hans a second, saw new strength in that handsome blandness, and finally felt a sneaking admiration for him.

'Yes,' he said. 'You *are* a smart boy. I knew that when I hired you as an accountant. And was, as usual, absolutely correct in my judgement – which is what makes me a leader of men. *Sehr gut*, Hans, you have proved my point.'

Satisfied that he had subtly put Hans back in his proper place, he threw the end of the rope ladder out through the door, then began winching it down as the helicopter, roaring and shuddering, swayed dangerously from side to side.

'I can't control this thing!' Elena cried out despairingly. 'I don't know what to do!'

Hans slithered backwards towards her, keeping his pistol aimed at Zweig, took hold of the joystick with his free hand and gave Elena the pistol.

'Keep him covered until he's out on the ladder,' he said. 'If he tries anything, shoot him.'

'My pleasure,' Elena said.

Zweig winched the rope ladder down to its full extent, saw it flapping out wildly in the wind created by the rotor blades, which were also sweeping the snow in dense clouds across the hole below, further obscuring his view of what, or who, might be down there. When he had finished, he locked the wheel and turned back to Elena, who was smiling with what seemed like real pleasure, perhaps because of the pistol.

'Have a good journey,' she said. 'It's been a real pleasure knowing you.'

'*Auf Wiedersehen*,' he replied, refusing to bow to her. 'It's been *my* pleasure, Elena.'

The helicopter shuddered and roared, whipping an icy wind around him as he swung his legs out through the open door and sat on the edge. He looked down at that dark hole, at that enormous, metallic flower; the snow was being whipped off the triangular metal plates and swept over the open cavern to form a whirlpool that obscured the four people for a brief, startling moment.

But he knew they were down there, waiting for him with the Tuaoi Stone, and he glanced once at Elena, at the pistol in her hand, smiled at her and Hans, then rolled onto his belly and inched out to place his feet on the ladder.

'Good riddance!' Elena crowed.

He felt no fear at all. He simply went with the wind. He flew out above the mountain, was blinded by swirling snow, and went down, inch by inch, rung by rung, as he was pummelled from side to side. The wind howled and screamed, a living thing, tearing at him, and he laughed, exultant, defying death, preparing for it; then looked up and saw Elena and Hans smiling victoriously as the latter hacked at the rope ladder with a glittering blade.

The shorn ropes snapped apart, were blown out on the wind, and he fell like a stone through sweeping snow and howling wind, descending for what seemed like an eternity towards widening stone slabs.

It was a brief, tumbling dream.

CHAPTER FORTY-FOUR

To Ingrid, Zweig's fall seemed very quick indeed: one second he was swaying dangerously on the end of a rope ladder, the next he was dropping rapidly with the ropes flapping about him, to land on his feet on the floor beside the Tuaoi Stone. His knees buckled and he collapsed, rolling over a few times, then came to a halt close to St Germain's feet as the helicopter roared even louder and started its ascent, someone hanging out and waving their hand in what seemed like a mock farewell.

Even as Zweig looked up, perhaps hurt, certainly dazed, the bass humming sound began again and the steel plates of the dome began moving in towards one another, prior to closing. Zweig stared at St Germain, then higher at the closing dome, not attempting to conceal his amazement at what he was seeing. The dome eventually closed, the triangular plates joining together; and Zweig looked all around him, obviously getting his senses back, then sighed and climbed painfully to his feet.

As her father stared around him in amazement, then fixed unnaturally bright eyes on the crystal pyramid in its protective case, Ingrid felt herself trembling with fear and revulsion, reminded on the instant of how this man, who should have nurtured her, had almost destroyed her. She then thought of her mother, of how Zweig had murdered her, and a terrible grief and rage threatened to shatter her.

Unable to stand the sight of him, she had to look away, and mercifully found herself facing Jerry, who was smiling encouragingly. Feeling better, she forced her gaze back on Zweig, who completely ignored her.

'Which one of you is St Germain?' he asked.

'I am,' St Germain replied, his voice as calm as a limpid pool.

'And who are *you*?' Zweig asked, glancing at Mephisto, then flushing as that gentleman's unnatural, seductive charm fell relentlessly over him.

'My name is irrelevant,' Mephisto replied.

'You wouldn't, by any chance, be a certain Christian Grabbe, who kindly invited some of my men to the Waldorf Astoria in order to sell them the Tuaoi Stone – then, in some magical manner, caused havoc and death?'

Mephisto smiled at that. 'A name is no more than a name,' he said, 'and I personally have more than one.'

'And did we have an unusual meeting in the Herastrau Park in Bucharest?'

'I believe that was me, yes.'

'That meeting had an unusual effect upon me.'

'That was the intention, Herr Zweig. It's nice to know I succeeded.'

Clearly rendered uncomfortable by Mephisto's mesmeric gaze, Zweig studied the small, crystal pyramid in its transparent casing.

'And that's the Tuaoi Stone?' he asked, as if making a statement.

'Yes,' St Germain said. 'That's what you've been searching for.'

Walking fearlessly to the pedestal, Zwieg placed his right hand on the transparent covering, then gasped and jerked it away as if his fingers had been scorched.

'*Scheisse!*' he gasped. 'What happened?'

'You can only touch the casing if I decree it,' St Germain said sombrely. 'And naturally it can only be opened by the command of the sacred stone's present keeper, this being myself.'

As if unable to accept what had already happened to him, Zweig once more placed his outstretched fingers on the transparent casing – and again had to jerk his hand away. Flexing his stinging fingers and blowing upon them, he shook his head and grinned dangerously, as if at a private joke.

'Most effective,' he said, glancing around the great hall, his smile freezing into a look of controlled rage when he finally saw Jerry. 'Ah, so! My young American friend – with my daughter, of course. How pleasant that we're all together again. We can have a real party.'

'The only party I'd like to attend with you,' Jerry retorted, 'is a lynching party – with you in the noose.'

'What an admirable American redneck you are. You should be on *my* side.' And with that, he turned to Ingrid for the first time. 'You stole my money and ran away, you bitch. I cannot forgive you for that, so prepare to be punished.'

'I won't ever let you punish me again. I'm no longer afraid of you.'

'Really? You're not afraid? Well, we'll see about that. The game isn't over yet, *meine Fräulein*, and you're first on my hit-list.'

'You're in no position to make threats,' Jerry said. 'And you don't have your goddamned army with you. Here you're just one guy, Zweig.'

'I also have a score to settle with *you*,' Zweig responded. 'So don't think I've come here to shake your hand and give you a medal. You're in very hot water, my young friend – and I *don't* need my men here.'

'Just what the hell do you think you can do?'

'I *don't* think. I *act*.'

When he turned away from Jerry, his grin one of

contempt, Ingrid was reminded that as long as she could remember he had either humiliated her (which at least was a form of recognition) or brutally ignored her. His lack of feeling for her seemed singularly unnatural, his urge to destroy her morally, as he had destroyed her mother physically, was something she couldn't comprehend, no matter how hard she tried.

Yet she also felt guilty because of her lack of feeling for him – and wondered again that her instinctive need for a father-figure hadn't managed to quell the fear and revulsion she felt in his presence. She felt no yearning for him at all, and indeed only wanted to be rid of him . . . and that in itself was enough to make her feel guilty.

She didn't want to accept that she had no love for this brute; that she simply wanted him out of her life, once and for all.

Ignoring her again, Zweig stared at the glittering Tuaoi Stone with an insatiable, unholy lust and said, 'I've been obsessed with this for years, wondering if it really existed, and in the end, I simply had to have it, whatever the cost. You practically invited me here, so what *is* the cost?'

St Germain's smile was like ice and fire combined, his grey eyes radiating the light of a distant, alien sun.

'For you,' he said, 'there *is* no cost – quite simply, because you cannot buy it. The Tuaoi Stone is not for sale, not for barter, not for hire; it is not for those who wish to advance themselves in any material manner. It is true, as you have heard, that the stone has enormous powers, but those powers cannot be called upon, except for the good. To you, the Tuaoi Stone would be worthless, no more than an artefact, only worth the cost of its crystal, but otherwise dead. Only the pure at heart can make use of the sacred stone; only those who have explored the Secret Knowledge and know how to

use it. The Secret Knowledge is founded on numbers –
the lost language of ancient man – and unless you can
speak in that tongue, you cannot command the Tuaoi
Stone. Your journey to this place has been fruitless,
since the stone will not work for you.'

'I repeat: you practically invited me here,' Zweig
said. 'Why did you do that?'

'Because you are obsessed with obtaining the Tuaoi
Stone.'

'Since I can do nothing with it, why should that
worry you?'

'You can do nothing with it if it's in your possession,
but your obsession is such that you will not rest until
you have obtained it – and that, Herr Zweig, is
dangerous, if only in the sense that we who live by the
sacred stone would be deprived of it.'

'I still want it,' Zweig said.

'I know that,' St Germain replied calmly. 'And that's
why we guided you to us . . . to put an end to it.'

'To put an *end* to it?'

'Yes. It all ends for you here and now.'

Ingrid wasn't surprised to see that familiar flush of
rage brighten her father's unusually pale cheeks, but
she *did* find herself stepping sideways automatically to
get closer to Jerry when her father reached into his
jacket pocket and pulled out a pistol.

'Yes?' St Germain asked sardonically, raising one
silvery eyebrow. 'And what do you intend doing with
that?'

'I intend using it, *Saint* Germain. I want you to open
that case, give me the Tuaoi Stone, then lead me back
down this hellish mountain. If you try refusing, I'll kill
each of you in turn. Now open the case.'

As Zweig, while keeping his gaze on St Germain,
aimed the pistol threateningly at her, Ingrid felt all the
hurt and indignity of her life welling up inside her,

forcing tears to her eyes. She tried to stop them, not wanting to please him more, but the pain of this final, absolute degradation was more than she could hope to control. She felt the tears roll down her cheeks, bit her lower lip and choked back her pain. Someone touched her and she twitched, then realized it was Jerry, saw his outraged face, then felt his arm sliding around her, to pull her close to him.

A father? She had never had a father – and now had to accept that fact. She accepted it, feeling drained, deprived of the will to live, and could only take comfort from Jerry when he affectionately squeezed her.

'The power of the crystal,' St Germain said as calmly as ever, 'only resides in the hands of those who protect it. For your own good, I would beg you not to force me to open the case.'

Zweig's reply to this was to cock the pistol and aim it more precisely at Ingrid who hugged Jerry and fought her pain with her hatred.

'I don't think that even a sonofabitch like you,' Jerry said as his breath brushed her hair, 'could shoot his own daughter in cold blood.'

'Ask me about her mother,' Zweig sneered. 'I could do it to my wife, so I can to my daughter.'

Even as the final shards of her broken hopes were tumbling about her, as she heard her own sobbing breaking helplessly from her, Ingrid saw through her tears that St Germain was shaking his head.

'No,' he said, 'Ingrid *isn't* your daughter.'

The words resounded through her like the pealing of bells. It sounded too good to be true, too miraculous to be real, but she saw St Germain's smile, quietly mocking, triumphant, then noticed the deepening flush on her father's face, his icy eyes growing larger.

'*Scheisse!*' he snapped. 'What is this you're –?'

'Ingrid is *not* your daughter,' St Germain explained

516

quietly. 'She is in fact the illegitimate daughter of another man – a German Jew, with whom your second wife, Ingrid's mother, had an affair in Argentina, shortly after you began mistreating her. Naturally, when your wife became pregnant with that man's child, she was terrified of telling you – more so because the man was a Jewish refugee from Nazi Germany, and she knew how you would respond to *that* news. So, when she had Ingrid, she led you to believe that the child was your daughter – and once you had murdered that unfortunate woman in Cologne, faking her death as suicide – because she knew you had killed her parents and you feared she might reveal that fact – there was no way for you to find out the truth. So, Herr Zweig, Ingrid is *not* your daughter – and ironically you have spent a great deal of your anti-Semitic life at least paying for the *upkeep* of a Jew, if not actually loving one. Ingrid's mother, even though in her grave, has had her revenge – and justice prevails.'

While the bells pealed even louder inside Ingrid's head, her father turned purple with rage.

'*Quatsch!*' he hissed, waving the pistol like a club. 'I don't believe a word of this! And even if it *was* true, how would *you* know about it?'

St Germain smiled at Mephisto, then turned back to Zweig. 'Why do you think we guided Ingrid here with Jerry? We could just as easily have lost her and drawn him here alone.' Without waiting for a reply, he stared steadily at Ingrid, his eyes filled with an odd, wintry affection. 'Your father,' he said, 'was once one of us, but eventually left us for reasons of his own. He was a good man – a just man.'

First exhilarated, then heartbroken, filled with hope, disbelieving, Ingrid felt more unreal every minute, wondering what she was hearing. When she studied St Germain, with his strange, cold smile, she was convinced that he was not what he seemed, that he had not told them everything.

She thought of how she had come here, recalled Observatory Hill, the great pulsating light that had descended over her and Mephisto. She had been terrified, feeling herself disintegrating, then had felt herself vaulting over time and space, through giant moons and spinning stars. She had seen that in her mind, but had otherwise been blind, and her terror had rendered her unconscious until awakening in this place, stretched out on the bed of stone, being watched by Mephisto and St Germain, both wearing long robes.

St Germain had been kind to her, explaining all with infinite patience, but even then – as now – she had been convinced that he was withholding something.

'You used the past tense when discussing my father,' she said. 'Does that mean he's dead?'

'Yes,' St Germain replied in his unemotional manner. 'Unfortunately he died many years ago. However, please rest assured that your father is not this man standing before you, but was in fact Paul Kahn, a German Jew and student of philosophy who suffered incarceration and torture by the Nazis, escaped while being herded with many others to a concentration camp, and made his way over a period of many months to Argentina, where he lived in relative poverty, eventually became a taxi driver and, as a humble man, continued his philosophical and religious studies in secrecy. He met your mother when he was hired by Zweig to drive her where required because she wasn't allowed to travel anywhere alone – and he and your mother, who was desperately unhappy, soon had an affair. Paul Kahn is your true father, Ingrid, though he never laid eyes on you.'

Too moved to speak, too happy for mere words, she

looked at St Germain through tearful eyes, seeing only a blur.

'After poisoning your mother in that hospital in Cologne,' St Germain continued in a precise, unemotional manner, 'Zweig started his many travels, taking you with him. The knowledge that your mother had been systematically poisoned by him only emerged many months after that – by which time you were well away from Cologne and your real father, Paul Kahn, a man of pure heart, had been approached by us, agreed to join us, and came here for his training in the Secret Knowledge. Unfortunately, he did not stay here long. For reasons of his own, he chose to go back down the mountain and resume his life as a normal man, which included going off in search of you. However, soon after leaving us, he was caught in a cholera epidemic, died in a hospital in Calcutta, and was subsequently buried in an unmarked grave outside the city. Yes,' he added, nodding his head emphatically, 'that was your father – not this man standing here.'

First she filled up with grief and felt a terrible sense of loss, but this rapidly gave way to waves of joy, and even serenity. She wiped tears from her eyes, glanced at Jerry, saw his smile, then turned to face Zweig, that monster, not her father, finally understanding why she had felt no guilt when she found him revolting.

He wasn't her real father – he wasn't related to her at all – he was just a brute who had tormented her all her life as the butt of his cruelty. Her real father was a just man, a good man who had wanted to find her; and even if he was dead, at least she knew of his existence and had found a replacement for him in Jerry, who obviously loved her.

She *had* been born out of love . . . and now *had* love . . . and would not let it go.

'Go to hell,' she said defiantly to Zweig, staring steadily at him. 'It's where you belong.'

'You Jewish whore!' Zweig snarled. 'It will be even easier to kill you now.' He levelled the pistol.

Yet even as he did so, St Germain stretched his right hand out over the transparent case of the Tuaoi Stone and, when the distracted Zweig glanced back at him, waved it to and fro slowly.

A faint, unearthly light appeared around the case, then the case itself started opening in small, triangular sections – like a miniature replica of the immense steel dome above – and only stopped when the small, brilliantly gleaming pyramid was fully exposed.

Obviously beside himself, hardly aware of what he was doing, Zweig started automatically towards the legendary Tuaoi Stone, but was stopped in his tracks when a bass humming noise suddenly emanated from the crystal pyramid, which, like its open case, became covered in an unearthly, pulsating light.

'Take the Tuaoi Stone if you wish,' St Germain said. 'The risk is all yours.'

Zweig reached out greedily to grab what he had so desired, but the pyramid glowed even brighter, emitted a louder humming, and seemed to vibrate as if alive – and he jerked his hand away and started sweating, as if terrified.

'You want to possess the power of the crystal,' St Germain said, 'and what you want, you shall have – *if* your conviction is greater than ours. Now prepare to defend yourself.'

At that moment, the magical power of the crystal became visible in the shape of a bolt of electrical energy that shot from its tip in a phosphorescent, hissing arc to form a rainbow between it and St Germain, then exploded around the latter and became a globe of pulsating radiant colours that lit up the gloom.

St German dissolved partially in the brilliance of that light, seemed to shimmer and float as if disembodied, then raised his right hand, in which the veins were clearly visible, and spoke with an unearthly, distant voice.

'You have been called, Jerry Remick, and now you have come. You are one of the last of the just and therein lies your power. This man, Zweig, is evil, without redeeming features, and his presence is a threat to us all and must be removed. You now have the power, Jerry. You must use it for the good. In this instance, to do good, you must destroy the one who wants to destroy all of us. You profess to despise Zweig. Such contempt is well placed. Now turn that contempt into strength, and being a man of pure spirit, of faith, draw the energy of the sacred stone from me and into yourself – then direct it at him.'

Hardly believing what she was witnessing, but feeling a sudden stab of fear, Ingrid choked back a groan when Jerry, as if in a trance, let her go, stepped well away from her, then turned directly into the line of Zweig's wavering pistol.

Zweig was purple-faced and sweating, his eyes enlarged and glacial, and he muttered an oath and took aim at Jerry, preparing to fire. Yet he couldn't seem to do so, but instead started shaking violently, the pistol wobbling up and down as if out of control.

Jerry raised his right hand, spreading his fingers as St Germain had done. A stream of phosphorescent, hissing energy shot into him from St Germain, forming a rainbow between them, then shot in another arc from Jerry's outspread fingers into Zweig, exploding around him and becoming a ball of pulsating white light.

Dazed and disbelieving, convinced she was having a bad dream, Ingrid stopped her own cry of dread by covering her mouth with her hands as she studied the bizarre scene before her.

A sparkling, hissing stream of magical energy was flowing from the tip of the crystal pyramid to the outspread fingers of St Germain, and from him, through the receiving vessel of Jerry, into the loudly bellowing Zweig.

All three men were cocooned in a pulsating, unearthly radiance that seemed to have partially dissolved them, making them shimmer and look grotesquely distorted, fading in and out rapidly – first clearly visible, then silhouetted; sometimes becoming almost transparent, revealing the tapestry of their veins, the geography of blood and bone.

Jerry and St Germain were quivering like bowstrings just released, but Zweig was bellowing and shaking like an epileptic, as if falling apart.

Ingrid looked on, aghast, shocked by what she was witnessing, but took comfort from the possibility that Jerry, whether or not he knew it, was winning the contest.

Then it all changed. Ingrid knew it before she saw it. The light around St Germain started weakening, then blinked out; and his radiance was sucked into Jerry and left him alone.

Jerry looked like a human torch, a man burning to death, quivering in a cocoon of unnatural light, but still holding up his right hand, attacking Zweig with his new power. Then he glanced at St Germain, saw that *he* had returned to normal, was shocked to realize that he was now on his own, then shuddered as if suddenly losing faith and slumped in defeat.

'Have faith!' St Germain cried out.

But it was too late. Obviously drained and exhausted, Jerry fell to his knees as the hissing light streamed out of him and into the glowing Zweig who, with a bellow of triumph, raced across the room, swept St Germain aside with one hand, grabbed the Tuaoi Stone before the case could be closed and then, looking normal once more, backed away across the great hall, keeping them all covered with his pistol.

'It's *mine* now, isn't it?' he asked rhetorically. 'Now *I* have the power!'

'Oh, God!' Jerry gasped.

'You'll never get down the mountain,' St Germain said with icy authority.

'Yes, I will,' Zweig replied. 'It's no problem at all. Did you really think I'd depend on the bastard and bitch who forced me down that rope ladder at gunpoint? No, St Germain, I didn't. I'm not a fool, after all. My wristwatch is a transmitter, a tracking device for my back-up team, and right now two helicopters are on their way here, to rocket blast this place out of existence after taking me off. It doesn't end for *me* here, St Germain. Here it all ends for you. *Auf Wiedersehen.*'

He turned away and rushed out, disappearing through the first exit, his laughter reverberating eerily as his footsteps receded.

Then he was gone, taking the Tuaoi Stone with him, leaving only the silence.

CHAPTER FORTY-FIVE

Jerry was badly shaken by what had happened, still couldn't quite believe it, and thought of the disappearance of Zweig as if recalling a bad dream.

Zweig had defeated him.

Taking a deep breath, gradually getting his strength back, he glanced up at the empty stand that had supported the missing Tuaoi Stone, felt ashamed of himself, then stood up, feeling older than he was, and found himself facing St Germain and the sombre Mephisto.

Shivering, he glanced at Ingrid, saw her wiping tears from her eyes, was appalled at how weak he felt, though knew his strength was returning. Remembering how that phosphorescent stream of energy had travelled from the crystal pyramid through St Germain, into him and on to Zweig – and how, when St Germain had left him alone, he had collapsed into a fear of the power that was coursing through him – he realized that Zweig's faith in his own invincibility had been greater than his own faltering faith in what he could do.

Virtue had been defeated by evil, because virtue was based on the kind of doubt that evil did not acknowledge.

As Ingrid dried her eyes, his heart went out to her, then he noticed that St Germain had changed, had in fact aged dramatically.

'What happened?' he asked, shocked by St Germain's appearance.

St Germain shrugged. 'You *know* what happened, Jerry. You are one of the pure at heart, a just man who can use the Tuaoi Stone, but you lacked faith in yourself, lost your courage when I stopped helping you, and thus were defeated by Zweig, who believes in himself. Now the power of the Tuaoi Stone, which Zweig formerly could not have used, has passed from you to him.'

'Oh, God,' Ingrid murmured.

'And that's the end of it?' Jerry asked. 'Zweig, with all his monstrous ambition, will be the Tuaoi Stone's new keeper and use its magical powers as he sees fit?'

St Germain sighed. 'Not quite,' he said. 'Zweig can still be defeated – but only you, having given him the power, can take it back from him. And *that*, Jerry, will be your final, most crucial test.'

Jerry glanced at Mephisto, saw his thin, seductive smile, looked away and studied St Germain again. He now looked twice his age, yet that wasn't what disturbed him most, what gnawed suspiciously. He didn't know what it was, but sensed that something was wrong, that St Germain had not told the whole truth, and might even have lied to him.

A secret society of *just* men? A secret order for the pure at heart? He couldn't quite accept that as the truth, and wondered why he had doubts.

'I feel drained of all energy,' he said, 'and *you* look even worse than I feel. What happened, St Germain?'

'The Tuaoi Stone can only be used rarely, with great discretion. Its powers must not be called upon too often, nor treated too lightly. What I *started* to do to Zweig – and what you *almost* succeeded in doing – is something that can only be done occasionally, and even then at great cost.'

'You gave your power to me and now are paying the price. And I failed, thus giving Zweig the power *I* could have had.'

'That is correct.'

'And you? What happens to you? This has obviously damaged you.'

'Naturally it has, but my time has come anyway. Being young, *you* will recover quickly, which is all to the good. As for myself, I am too old, *very* old, too old to measure, and that means that the power the stone gives me drains my physical energy. I am ready to pass on, to transcend, but there are things left undone.'

'What things?'

'Things only known to the adepts – and you are not an adept yet. If you choose to stay here, to make up the magic number, you will learn what it is you want to know – but you must defeat Zweig first.'

To be the last of the first 666 was something that Jerry could only consider with a great sense of disbelief. He had learnt the language of numbers, had resolved its teasing riddles, but hadn't yet learned to live with it – and perhaps didn't want to.

He wanted the normal world, steel and glass, smoke and noise . . . and besides, he still had the conviction that something was wrong, that St Germain's picture of a society of just men didn't seem right somehow.

'You want me to challenge Zweig,' he said, 'and regain the power of the Tuaoi Stone, after which I'll become the last of the just men. But how can I be sure you *are* just men, after what I've experienced?'

'Oh?' St Germain queried, raising one eyebrow. 'Just what do you mean by that?'

'I'm thinking, for example, of Helena Barbanell . . . She placed her faith in you, was convinced she would soon join you, and then was put to death by Zweig's men – as indeed was the old Arab in Jerusalem, who was another of your most faithful disciples. Why didn't you use your powers to save them?'

'We must all be tested somehow. What they suffered was for the good. The two you mention kept their faith to the end and passed over to us. They both became adepts and returned to earth, as immortals disguised as mortals, to continue our great work.'

'I don't believe you, St Germain. Something doesn't sit right with this. You say you represent just men, those who are pure at heart, yet in order to protect the Tuaoi Stone you won't stop at murder. If you people are so pure at heart, how can you do such things?'

'It is sometimes necessary to fight evil with evil. We do such things with reluctance, but must protect the Secret Knowledge at any cost, even though it may wound us.'

'And killing enemies wounds you?'

'Yes. It leaves a scar on the pure soul.'

The argument was persuasive, but he still couldn't accept it, and was just about to retort when Ingrid stepped forward.

'Why did my father leave the Order?' she asked. 'Did he disagree with you?'

'I'm sorry,' St German replied, 'but I cannot answer that question. People stay here voluntarily – and most of them *do* stay, at least until they become adepts and can leave as immortals. But occasionally someone will leave before transcending to the higher plane – usually for personal reasons . . . and those reasons can never be discussed except by the few.'

'Since I'm his daughter, I think –'

Before she could finish her sentence, Mephisto stepped forward, stopped again and stared at her, his wintry-grey, almost silvery eyes focused hypnotically on her.

She blinked repeatedly and lowered her gaze.

'We cannot discuss it any further,' Mephisto said softly. 'The personal beliefs of those who stay here are sacrosanct. Be content with the knowledge that *one* of his reasons for leaving was to find you. We can tell you that. We cannot tell you more. This subject is now closed.'

When Jerry saw Ingrid nodding, her head bowed,

cheeks blushing, he was reminded of Mephisto's diabolical charms and felt the stirrings of rage.

'If people stay here on a voluntary basis,' he said,
'does that mean I can leave any time?'

'Yes,' Mephisto replied. 'It is impossible to climb up
to here without our guidance, but easy to go back
down. That is part of our way.'

'But why leave,' St Germain asked, looking weary,
his voice ravaged, 'when immortality and magic can be
yours? The magic number is 666 and you can make up
that number, thus becoming a guardian of the world, a
magical adept. Why walk away from this?'

'Because I don't believe what you're telling me. I
think something's missing. You have limitless power,
you'll allow murder to protect it, and you use that
power to interfere in the affairs of men when you think
it's called for. I don't believe in that, either. I think it's
morally wrong. You're tampering with the natural
course of mankind and I don't think that's good.'

'So you will let Zweig walk away with the Tuaoi
Stone. You think *that* is better?'

'I won't be morally blackmailed, St Germain, and
I'm leaving right now.'

'Please don't.'

'Come on, Ingrid! Let's go!'

He reached out without thinking to take hold of her
hand, but was surprised to see her stepping away from
him and moving closer to the smiling Mephisto. She
was flushed and trembling, refused to meet his gaze,
and instead looked into Mephisto's mesmeric eyes and,
even worse, raised her face as if yearning to be kissed
by those moist, sensual lips.

'Ingrid,' Jerry insisted, his pain too deep for words.
'I repeat: I'm leaving here right now, so are you coming
or not?'

'No,' she said, shocking him even more, 'I'm staying

here. I want to be a replacement for my father, if not for you. Since you refuse to become the last of the 666, then I'll take your place.'

'A place your father rejected.'

'He rejected it in order to find me, so it's my duty to stay here.'

'That's not quite true, Ingrid. You were only *one* of his reasons for leaving. He obviously had other reasons as well – and these two won't reveal them. We still don't know the truth.'

'I don't think they brought me here just to tell me some lies. I believe my father left here to search for me. Nothing else is important.'

Jerry felt like screaming. He was breaking apart inside. He couldn't believe that this woman, once so weak, was now being so strong. And that strength, which in one sense he admired, was now threatening their love.

'You'll stay here without me?' he asked, feeling shameful, a beggar.

'If you stay here,' she replied, 'I'll stay with you. If you leave, go alone.'

'I thought you loved me, Ingrid.'

'I do.'

'If that's true you'll leave this place – this Frankenstein's castle – and return with me to where we both belong – back to the real world.'

'No, Jerry, I can't bring myself to do that. Not even for you. I've got to stay here.'

She looked solemnly at him – as she used to do when they first met – then turned away to smile at Mephisto. He smiled back and took her hand, drew her to him, his eyes glittering.

'You're tired,' he said. 'So tired. So very tired. So tired you can't possibly stay here. So tired that you must sleep. Come. Come with me. Come to bed. You're so tired. Come with me . . .'

He was stepping backwards as he spoke, holding her hand, drawing her to him, and she followed him, unable to resist him or his voice, his hypnotic repetitions, her breasts flattening slightly against his chest when she almost fell against him.

The pain was deep and lacerating, making Jerry almost choke, and he turned away quickly, not able to look at them, and had to wipe the tears from his eyes and take a deep breath.

'Great,' he said. 'Terrific. Let it be. Let it lie. Now how the hell do I get out of this place? I mean, just let me go. Where's the door? *Where's the door?*'

'It's directly in front of you,' St Germain said. 'Just walk out. You'll be free.'

Taking a final look around him, his tears making everything blurred, he finally met St Germain's gaze, was shocked again by his aged appearance, then looked sideways to see Ingrid and Mephisto walking away from him.

His heart started breaking then. He felt as if he was being stabbed. He wanted to call Ingrid back, to tell her he would remain here, but somehow he just couldn't do it, felt sick just to think of it. They were lying – he knew that; he just didn't know why – and so he turned away, shaking with pain and grief, and walked towards the nearest door.

He approached the door reluctantly, waiting to hear her call his name, but when she didn't, he shamefully looked back, not knowing what to expect. He saw what he most feared – Ingrid departing with Mephisto – and then the melancholy smile of St Germain so shockingly aged. The latter was staring directly at him, his gaze steady, almost reproachful, and he shuddered, still wondering what was wrong, then turned away and walked out.

He entered a narrow corridor hewn out of the

natural rock, winding into gloom and increasingly cold as it burrowed out through the mountain. He realized, then, that the mountain was honeycombed with such corridors, that the great hall in which he had been with the others was the centre of a labyrinthine complex of considerable size. He wondered how they had constructed it, remembered the powers of the Tuaoi Stone, accepted that they could do anything they wanted and walked on, his heart sinking.

He was walking away from Ingrid, from all he loved, and that thought was crushing him. He was walking away, even more, from the knowledge that she had chosen to remain here rather than go with him – and that thought was killing him.

He sniffed back his tears, choked up, continued walking, and felt the cold increasing as the gloom gradually turned into darkness. He stopped walking when the darkness suddenly became pitch-black, felt the racing of his heart, a sickening wave of disorientation, then stepped forward and saw a pinprick of light as he rounded the bend. He walked more quickly then, as if clambering from his own coffin, and saw the pinprick become a sunlit opening that let in the freezing cold.

He hurried into the light, into the grip of the icy cold, was slapped by a wind that swept the snow in hissing white streams across him. He was back on the narrow track, above a pirouetting gorge, saw the peaks and ravines of Kanchenjunga forming a tapestry of gleaming ice and black shadows wherever he looked. The sky was powder blue, streaked with silvery lines of sunlight, but the brightness did not prevent the cold from eating into his bones. He had never known such cold. It bit at him like an animal. He winced and huddled into himself and turned right, down the winding track.

But he simply couldn't do it, and stopped, almost weeping. The cold was too harsh, the swirling snow too thick, and he sensed that it had been created deliberately to hamper his flight. The icy wind slapped his face, tugged him towards the cliff's edge, pushed him back into the rocks and forced him onto his knees. He bowed his head in defeat, growing numb, realizing that the pain he was feeling was not caused by this purgatory.

No, not the elements – and not the knowledge that he was trapped. He was in anguish because Ingrid had failed him and gone off with Mephisto. He had expected more of her, had thought her love equal to his, and now was breaking in the knowledge that his love had not been enough for her.

He wanted to go back to her, to have her at any price, but felt the pain eating through his numbness to render him helpless.

'Oh, God, Ingrid,' he murmured, yearning for her, dying for her, then slumped down on his haunches against the rocks to let the snow gently cover him. 'Oh, God, Ingrid, please don't . . .'

'No,' she said. 'Of course not!'

He looked up in surprise, not believing his own ears, and saw her leaning over him, her fur collar turned up, the wind whipping her hair across her face and into her eyes. She smiled and reached towards him, her features blurred by snow, and placed her fingers lightly on his face, then wiped the tears from his cheeks.

'God,' she said, 'you're a very stubborn man. A real puritan, in fact. I love you. I promise! I really love you! Now please trust me and follow me.'

Stunned, disbelieving, exhilarated beyond words, he took hold of her hand, climbed unsurely to his feet, then let her lead him through the swirling snow and back into the mountain, his heart beating like a drum in his chest, his spirit soaring on high.

CHAPTER FORTY-SIX

Ingrid led him back through the dark, narrow tunnel, through the belly of the mountain, and into the great stone chamber dominated by its high, steel-plated dome, where St Germain and Mephisto were standing in the same place, the former no longer smiling – in fact extremely solemn – the latter continuing to age rapidly in some mysterious manner.

The sight of St Germain made Jerry think he was hallucinating. The man now seemed wizened and stooped, and even his silvery hair, once so lustrous, appeared to be thinner. He was resting with one hand on the pedestal that had supported the missing Tuaoi Stone and his breathing was emerging from shivering lips as if from a punctured tyre.

'No,' he said, as if reading Jerry's thoughts, 'your eyes do not deceive you. Now the truth will be told to you.'

He breathed deeply again, as if fighting for air, while Mephisto stepped forward to stop in front of Jerry, his eyes no longer mesmeric but infinitely weary, and said, 'You have just passed another test. Your moral integrity is absolute. You have proved that you would give up anything – even what you most love – rather than compromise your beliefs. Now the truth must be told to you.'

'And Ingrid was part of the test?'

'Yes, Jerry, she was.' Mephisto smiled at her, not seductively, but like a father, then gave his attention to the ailing St Germain and said, 'The young man has proved himself to be a just man, a pure man, so tell him the truth . . . *Doctor Faust*.'

At first startled to hear that name resounding spectrally in his head, Jerry then remembered the riddles laid before him throughout his journey and understood that the ambiguous references to Faust were at last about to be explained. He watched St Germain carefully, saw an old man growing older, his body rapidly becoming more frail beneath his loose-hanging Tibetan *chuba*, his grey eyes protruding above sallow cheeks, his words spilling from trembling lips.

'Everything you have so far learned about the civilizations of prehistory is true,' he said. 'Also true is that before recorded history, not long before the destruction of that civilization about 4,000 BC, a secret society of so-called just men *was* founded to protect and utilize the Tuaoi Stone throughout the ages.'

'Why do you describe them as *so-called* just men?'

'Because evil does not come from without, but from within, and what we have not told you, what shames us, is the tragedy of that inevitable corruption and its hideous consequences.'

St Germain glanced at Mephisto, taking strength from his steady gaze, then sucked more air into his racked lungs and continued his story.

'It would be pointless to describe the original guardians of the Tuaoi Stone, since they existed long before your known history and would mean nothing to you. However, it is a fact that throughout the ages, the secret society disguised itself in many different ways, that in your recorded history its members included such figures as Apollonius of Tyana, Jesus Christ, Buddha, the wise man of the so-called Arthurian legend, Merlin – whose test of a sword to be drawn from the magical stone in which it was set was actually a disguised reference to the Tuaoi Stone – and even

Roger Bacon, the Franciscan philosopher, alchemist and optical and astronomical genius who, before his death in 1292, had described accurately in his writings: spectacles, flying machines, motorized ships, carriages and the processes for making gunpowder.'

'And Christian Rosenkreuz?' Jerry asked.

St Germain sighed and nodded. 'Yes,' he said. 'The original Rosicrucians were actually members of our society, and at that time, Christian Rosenkreuz was their leader. Christian Rosenkreuz, like the Comte de Saint-Germain of the eighteenth century, was but one of the many earthly forms I took . . . but more of that later.'

He let his breath out in a painful gasp, then sucked it in again, appearing to stoop lower every minute, to shrink under his long robe.

'The original secret society was truly one of just men – but even just men are corruptible – and power, no matter how it is gained, inevitably corrupts.'

He nodded as if confirming that this was indeed so, and continued reluctantly.

'The tragic corruption of which I speak began in the sixteenth century when I, in the earthly form of Doctor Faust, the historically noted magician, mesmerist and alchemist, and a German member of the society of the Tuaoi Stone, was approached by a fellow member, the famed Swiss alchemist Paracelsus who, no longer able to tolerate the severe moral restrictions imposed upon all members of the society, wished to use the Secret Knowledge to create immortality for himself – something strictly forbidden to all but the highest adepts. I take it you *do* know about Faust and Paracelsus?'

'Yes,' Jerry said. 'Paracelsus died in 1541 – the same year as Doctor Faust – after laying claim to the creation, through alchemy, of the *homunculus*, widely reported as a tiny man endowed with magical insight and power.'

'Correct,' St Germain responded. 'But the *homunculus*, which many thought was a figment of Paracelsus's imagination, was actually created by him – in the shape of a disembodied spirit which was doomed to spend the rest of its time yearning and searching for a *normal* birth. And thus was born the legend of Faust: the man who sold his soul to the devil in return for earthly wealth and power.'

He sucked desperately for more breath, shuddered violently and almost fell; when Mephisto rushed forward, took hold of his shoulders and steadied him, he seemed to get his strength back, nodded at Mephisto, then continued when the latter had stepped away again, his face gravely concerned.

'The real life Doctor Faust, being myself,' St Germain continued, 'was born in Knittlingen, Germany, in 1480 and died in Staufen, near Freiburg, in 1541. As a magician, an alchemist, and originally an honourable man, I was chosen to join the secret society and spent many years contentedly pursuing my alchemical studies, based on the magical properties of numbers. However, vanity was my weakness, the need for earthly pleasures, and shortly before my death, after being approached by the rebellious Paracelsus, I agreed to let my spiritual, or alchemical, energy be used in a forbidden experiment conducted by Paracelsus. The results of that led to the creation of the *homunculus*, while I, for my sins, was condemned by my brethren to the hell of an immortality in which I would endlessly die and be reborn as other men, with each of my mortal lives being longer than most – therefore truly anguished. And thus, my young friends, the *homunculus* and Faust were both doomed to hell on earth: one, myself, seeking the peace of a proper death, the other, now named Homunculus, seeking a *normal birth*, also through death.'

St Germain raised his ravaged face long enough to give the solemn, almost tragic Mephisto a look of pity and anguished love, then lowered his gaze and spoke as if addressing himself.

'To cover up this extraordinary lapse in the formerly perfect record of the society of the Tuaoi Stone – and to repair the damage done to the otherwise perfect secrecy of the society, which, at that time, went under the name of the Rosicrucians – and to punish those who had caused the problems, Paracelsus was terminated by some members of the society –'

'Is that why his death is recorded as *mysterious* in all known historical records?' Jerry asked.

'Yes. And so, aware of the fact that the most efficient way of keeping a secret is to spread a distorted version of it, the ancient society of just men condemned me, Faust, to the hell of perpetual reincarnation; deliberately spread the historically unproven myths about me being a charlatan and sodomite; and, finally, encouraged one of their members to become the anonymous author of the first *Faustbuch* – which, published in 1587, obscured the reality of the existence of Homunculus by introducing him to the public as the diabolically seductive fictional character, Mephistopheles.'

Here he nodded in the direction of the silent Mephisto, his face revealing his anguish.

'The *Faustbuch* and, even more so, the infamous magic manuals also attributed to Faust, but actually written by the same anonymous member of the society of the Tuaoi Stone, further debased the truth about the real Doctor Faust and were themselves based on the equally clever fabrications of other members of the society, such as Merlin, Albertus Magnus and Roger Bacon, and the various fabrications were repeated with further embellishments throughout the ages in the published works of other members of the society, including those of Christopher Marlowe, the real author of Shakespeare's plays, as well as other notable Faust writers, such as Goethe and Thomas Mann.'

'Christopher Marlowe was the author of Shakespeare's plays?'

'Of course. Shakespeare was just an illiterate rustic who was paid to keep silent.'

'The eighteenth-century Comte de Saint-Germain is quoted as saying that.'

'I repeat myself endlessly.'

Jerry stared at St Germain as if seeing a ghost. He felt ghostlike himself, not quite real, too stunned to be sensible. Ingrid's gaze, which without her spectacles was lovely, made him feel more at ease.

'Christopher Marlowe also died mysteriously,' he said, having suddenly remembered that fact.

'Yes,' St Germain said, 'he did. He was starting to use his power and influence for political purposes, so was punished, like Paracelsus and myself, to the endless search through repeated reincarnation for the release of a proper death. He is one of us now – as are the many others so condemned – so the existing society, as it is here and now, is no longer a society of just men, wise men, but a society of those like myself, Paracelsus and Christopher Marlowe: mortals who have sold their souls to the devil in return for earthly pleasures, and are now suffering the hell of repeated mortality and the search for release in death.'

'And that's why my father left here?' Ingrid asked him.

'Yes,' St Germain confessed. 'He was disgusted with our obvious degeneration and walked out on principle. He truly *was* a just man.'

'Yet you still guard the Tuaoi Stone,' Jerry said, as he noticed the blush of pride on Ingrid's cheeks.

'The true magical adept transcends the material

state and therefore does not require the sacred stone, which is, in its essence, a material object whose magic powers are wrought from kabbalistic geometry. The *living* just men are now scattered across the earth; those who have transcended are spread throughout the universe, beyond time and space. The Tuaoi Stone has been left to punish us with its power – it is the power of the sacred stone, the Lodestone, that reincarnates us again and again. Only when, if ever, we are released from the eternal cycle of our mortality, will the Tuaoi Stone return to its natural state, which is the seed of the universe.'

'So if I'm not here to join a society of just men, magical adepts, what am I really here for?' Jerry asked.

St Germain stared steadily at him, his eyes burning in a ravaged face, then turned that same haunted gaze on Mephisto, who nodded and spoke for the first time.

'Ask me the final question,' he said. 'You must know what it is.'

Studying Mephistopheles, or Homunculus, Jerry saw immense weariness, the veiled anguish of one who had suffered beyond mortal imagining. Yes, he knew what the question was, and asked it without doubt:

'How can Faust, Homunculus, Paracelsus and all the others so punished, find their release through a proper death?'

Mephisto smiled with relief, perhaps even gratitude. 'This can only be brought about,' he said, 'when an absolutely pure man refuses the magical, corrupting powers of the Tuaoi Stone. For that reason, I, Homunculus, taking human shape as the fictional Mephistopheles, must repeatedly descend to the normal world in order to tempt decent men with immortality and limitless power – in the hope of discovering one who is completely immune to such temptation . . . an absolutely pure man. Any man so pure as to be tempted by me in the first place will, if he surrenders to my blandishments, automatically become a member of this society – a society of the damned – and once the number of such men reaches the magical sum of 666 – the number of the beast – then the world of mortal men will be completely destroyed, like previous civilizations, by the beasts that come out of the sea and out of the earth.'

'Fire and flood,' Jerry said.

'Correct,' Mephisto replied. 'However,' he continued, 'if one mortal man has the strength to *resist* my temptations and retain his absolute integrity, his pure soul, then those of us who have been doomed, including myself and Faust, will be forgiven for our sins, released from this purgatory, and returned to the transcendental glory of true immortality – the spiritual afterlife.'

'And you, Jerry,' St Germain said, 'are the one man to do that. You are the first to refuse what we have offered and actually walk out of here. In your innocence, through the purity of your heart, you can save the world from destruction – and release us from hell.'

Before Jerry could respond, Mephisto walked up to him, took hold of his shoulder and shook him. 'Do it, Jerry!' he whispered passionately. 'To save us *and* your own world. Go and face your final test – your confrontation with Zweig's evil – and if you succeed, thus affirming your moral worth, bring the Tuaoi Stone back here and let your purity free us.'

'Free *us*,' St Germain emphasized, 'and, in so doing, save *your* world from destruction by fire and flood.'

'But how can I –?'

'You can *will* the power back. You will only lose it completely if Zweig defeats you. Close your eyes and concentrate. Lean on faith and *will* yourself down to Zweig, where he stands on the mountain path. Do it now, Jerry. *Do it!*'

Jerry felt confused, disbelieving, excited. He glanced at Ingrid and saw her nod of affirmation, felt her faith flowing into him. He reached out for her hand, squeezed her fingers, released her, then bowed his head, closed his eyes and concentrated on Zweig.

At first he saw nothing, just the darkness behind his closed eyes, then he thought of fire and flood, of his world in devastation, and a fierce rage coursed through him, made him burn and vaporize, and he travelled down through himself, to the centre of his being, then flew out of the prison of his body and winged down the mountainside.

He saw Zweig on a winding path, his feet kicking up the snow, the Tuaoi Stone grasped firmly in one hand as, with his other, he shaded his eyes and scanned the sky over the pirouetting depths for his two helicopters.

Jerry found himself standing in the snow of that same track, above Zweig, looking down at him, hearing the sound of the helicopters approaching as Zweig waved his hand at them.

When he called out Zweig's name his voice echoed around the mountains, making Zweig jerk his head back and stare up in surprise.

Jerry saw the face of evil, eyes gleaming malevolently, thought of Ingrid and what she had suffered at the hands of this monster. His rage gave him back his faith, his belief in the power of goodness, and with that came the strength he would need for the battle to come. He felt himself expanding to link the sky and earth, becoming a bridge between time and the curved banks of space. He drew his power from the ether, from the immortal soul within him, and raised his right hand to focus Zweig's gaze and let the battle commence.

'It ends here!' he called out.

CHAPTER FORTY-SEVEN

Zweig held the Tuaoi Stone tightly, looked back over his shoulder, saw the American standing on the track above him and raising his right hand. He could scarcely believe his eyes, didn't know where the American had come from, but assumed that he could only have rushed after him as soon as he'd fled. Now the hated young man was staring down at him.

'It ends here!' he shouted.

Zweig had to smile. What a melodramatic statement! The American's words were echoing from one summit to another, seeming to come from the sunlit grey clouds as well as the shadowed depths – but then Zweig heard the muffled throbbing of his two helicopters which, following the signals of his wristwatch transmitter, were flying like homing pigeons towards him.

He glanced in that direction, trying to see the helicopters, saw only the snow-capped peaks and their frightening, gargoyle shadows, the swathes of glistening snow.

No matter: the helicopters were coming. He could hear them distinctly.

He looked at the track, saw it winding back and upwards, the American standing just where it disappeared around the cliff face, silhouetted against the sky. He looked very small up there, poised over a dizzying drop, the wind beating at his clothing and hair, as if taking bites of him.

'Put the Tuaoi Stone down!' the American called. 'And then get out of here!'

Zweig had to laugh at the arrogance of the young pup. His laughter, echoing spectrally from one frozen peak to another, finally blended with the dying echo of the American's voice.

'You've *really* followed me to get back the Tuaoi Stone?' Zweig shouted back up the slope. 'Here it is, then! Come, get it!'

He raised the crystal pyramid over his head, felt the cold wind at his hand, almost numbing his fingers, then glanced sideways and saw his helicopters emerging out of the grey haze. A wave of triumph coursed through him, lending heat to his freezing face, and he held the Tuaoi Stone tightly, willing its magic into himself, took strength from his growing hatred for all the world, then looked back up the hill.

The American was slithering down through the snow on the narrow track, a frail figure in that vastness of towering cliffs and deep gorges, his face grim, his eyes seeming to gleam dangerously even from this distance.

'You won't leave with the Tuaoi Stone!' he shouted. 'You're wasting your time, Zweig!'

'*You're* finished, you little turd!' Zweig shouted back. 'You, that bitch and the rest of them – the time has come for the lot of you! Goodbye and good riddance!'

Even as his words echoed around the peaks, his helicopters roared nearby, descended over the American, and started whipping the snow up around him like a minor tornado. He threw himself to the ground, was blown towards the edge, wrapped his arms around a rock and clung to it, above that dizzying drop.

Zweig waved at the helicopters, laughing, exultant, watched as one of them flew away from the cliff face and up towards the circle of triangular steel plates that led to St Germain's hideaway.

He saw its missiles thrusting out like giant phalli, and that made him more joyous.

Any minute now, those missiles would put an end to St Germain's retreat and the three pigs inside it.

As the first helicopter ascended towards the steel petals above, the second raced back towards the path to once more whip the snow up around the American and try to blow him over the side. He clung to the rocks as the snow howled around him, let go and slid backwards, started disappearing into that swirling whiteness as if being devoured.

Expecting to hear the American's scream as he plunged over the side of the sheer cliff face, Zweig held his breath, felt mirth bubbling up inside him ... then felt the Tuaoi Stone quivering in his hand, as if coming alive.

'*Mein Gott!*' he exclaimed involuntarily.

He almost dropped the precious object, but soon got his senses back, then looked uphill in time to see the American walking out of the swirling, howling snow with his hand raised on high. He wasn't looking at Zweig, but at the helicopter above him, and his body was quivering in an unnatural manner – like the object in Zweig's hand.

Zweig knew what was happening. The Tuaoi Stone had come alive. The American pig was trying to get back the power that he, Zweig, had stolen from him and the sacred stone. Zweig laughed triumphantly, feeling the power course through him, then looked again at the American's upraised hand, wondering what he was doing.

The helicopter had pulled back, letting the snow settle around him, and the American was now clearly visible where he stood on the track, dangerously close to the edge of the narrow, curving path, above the snow-filled, black-shadowed gorge, his whole body quivering like a bowstring, even as the stone vibrating in Zweig's hand started warming his cold palm.

Then the American clenched his fist. His body rocked as he did so. The helicopter above him also rocked – and started shuddering as if trying to pull away, then rocked more violently as the pilot, obviously desperate to escape, released his missiles in the direction of the American.

Zweig heard the missiles screeching, saw two streams of white smoke, then the cliff face exploded behind the American, obscuring him in spewing snow, melting ice, flying debris and billowing smoke. The sound reverberated above the gorge, debris rained down, smoke swirled, but then the American reappeared magically – standing upright, still quivering like a bowstring, his right hand upraised.

Zweig felt his own power weakening, was shocked, even frightened, then he focused his strength with his hatred and felt the Tuaoi Stone vibrating.

The helicopter roared, moved backward and forward, swayed from side to side like a fat slug, then suddenly exploded.

Zweig felt the shockwave, was in fact bowled over by it, but kept a fierce grip on the Tuaoi Stone as he fell into the snow. He cursed and sat up, spat snow from his mouth, shook his head and fixed his gaze on the steeply winding path as the other helicopter sent its rockets towards St Germain's hideaway.

The ground erupted around the steel plates, spewing earth, rock and snow, the yellow flames and black smoke swirling in a sinuous, deadly dance before the flames sank back and disappeared and the smoke blew away.

The stupid bastards had missed.

Even as the remaining helicopter pulled away to fire

its second round of missiles, Zweig felt the strength flowing out of him and into the Tuaoi Stone, then his hand shook as his power flowed invisibly from there into the American.

He saw that upraised hand, fingers aimed at the helicopter, a phosphorescent stream of energy racing out from the fingers to envelope the retreating machine in a cocoon of brilliant, pulsating light.

Zweig tried to stop it, to take the energy into himself, but he felt himself weakening, saw the helicopter shuddering, cursed aloud when he heard it exploding, then saw it turn into a fiery ball that stained the whiteness with black smoke.

He couldn't understand it. He had assumed that the power was his. He couldn't accept that the wimp could get it back and then turn it against him. He gripped the Tuaoi Stone tighter. It was quivering violently in his hand. It was starting to burn through his skin and yet he still wouldn't let it go.

He was trapped here on the mountain. Now it was between him and the American. He could feel the American draining his strength even as he moved towards him.

Yes, the American was coming down the track, walking awkwardly through the snow, looking in Zweig's general direction, but intent on the Tuaoi Stone. Zweig knew that its power could not be shared, that he must fight to retain it.

He glanced to his left, saw the sheer face of the cliff, glanced right and saw the black-shadowed depths between the vast, snow-capped mountain peaks. He felt minute in that lonely grandeur, isolated from the world, and he accepted that if he couldn't finally conquer that world, he would rather destroy it completely than have his failure remembered.

If his perverse use of the powers of the Tuaoi Stone

could at least serve that purpose, he would willingly risk everything for it, including his own life.

Yes, he would let his hatred for the American, for Ingrid, for life itself, be his motivating force and source of strength. He would let his belief in the power of evil over good be his armour and shield.

He would gamble on that.

He gritted his teeth as the Tuaoi Stone scorched his skin, then *willed* his anger into manifesting itself as a physical force. He saw the American slithering down through the snow, was surprised at how determined he looked, so willed his malice and hatred into a force that would prevent his advance. The Tuaoi Stone shook in his hand and he had to scream to endure the pain, and then he felt his raging energy vaulting forth to envelope the enemy.

The cliff face beside the American split open, spat snow at him as the ground before him broke apart as if in an earthquake. The American jumped back, was surrounded by powdered snow, glanced down at the gap where the path had been solid, at that new, dizzying drop through the bowels of the mountain, then stiffened, as if gathering his strength or courage, and suddenly leaped across to the other side.

He rolled through the snow, climbed to his feet and started advancing again, his body still quivering as he drew power from the Tuaoi Stone in Zweig's hand, his eyes gleaming with a fierce, unnatural light that Zweig couldn't avoid.

The ground in front of Zweig split open, cracking and snapping, and he looked down those dizzying depths, then gasped and stepped back.

He was trying to gather his wits when the mountainside went berserk.

The cliff-face exploded, showering snow and stones around him, blowing him sideways, towards the edge of the path and almost over the side. He screamed without thinking, saw the gorge below spinning, then was picked up in another angry blast and hurled away from that fearsome drop, slammed backwards and fell into the snow.

The sound of the explosions were still echoing, and his ears were still ringing, when the fear that he had lost the Tuaoi Stone seized him and he squeezed his fist tighter. The stone was still in his hand, its heat burning gradually through his palm and causing him agony.

He groaned and bit his lip, tried to block out the pain, then suddenly he noticed that the American was racing downhill and realized that he and that hated, stubborn figure were now locked in mortal combat, engaged in a battle of wills that could only end one way.

The loser would be obliterated; the winner would own the world.

Convinced that virtue lacked the blind will of evil, he summoned up every memory that would add to his hatred and give him the strength he was missing: the contemptible Jews he had tormented as a Hitler Wolfcub; the Russian beasts who had raped him in the ruins of Berlin; all the enemies he had made in Argentina and Paraguay; the government ministers who had turned against him when the going got rough; all the spies and assassins who had worked for him and then betrayed him; his two wives and their relatives, not to mention Kuragin and Hans and that bitch Elena; then Count Saint Germain and Ingrid, who wasn't even his daughter; and finally this stubborn American ... Yes, he thought of them all, from his distant past to his present, and let his hatred for them simmer and boil until it burned like his scorched hand.

Then he felt the Tuaoi Stone quivering more

violently than before – its magical forces raging between himself and the advancing enemy – and looked up and hurled his will at everything he could see, even as the despised American approaching him did exactly the same.

Their conflicting forces sundered the mountainside, making it roar in protest, cracking open to spit earth, rock and snow through a curtain of flame and smoke. Debris showered into the gorge, red-tinged yellow flame shot from the ether and smoke swirled over chaos.

Zweig felt that he was burning. He seemed to be expanding. He breathed deeply and focused on the American. He had the confidence of evil, the will of true malevolence, and he felt the power flowing into him from the Tuaoi Stone as the American's faith wavered.

'Yes!' Zweig growled. '*Yes!*'

His hatred attacked the mountain, scorched the solid rock, melted the snow and turned it into scalding water. The American stumbled and fell, was blown sideways with the debris, rolled close to the edge of the cliff and almost fell over. He rolled back just in time, scrabbling wildly in the snow, somehow managed to get back to his feet and raise his snow-covered head.

He looked terribly young, almost handsome, and had brilliant blue eyes.

'You evil bastard,' he said.

Yet his faith was wavering. Zweig felt it and was exultant. He laughed aloud and hurled his will at the American and the cliff face beside him.

The din was catastrophic. The scorched rock cracked and exploded. The snow was the water that boiled through the flames that emerged from swirling veils of black smoke and made the air hiss.

The path beneath his feet shuddered. The American ran towards him, clearly determined to grab him, but he made the path before him split open to form a dizzying drop.

Jerry cried out as he fell across the shrieking, parting earth. He grabbed hold of one side, his feet remained on the other, and he briefly formed a heaving, twisting bridge across that terrible chasm.

'Oh, Jesus!' he cried out.

Zweig laughed at that, held the Tuaoi Stone tighter, saw the American stretched out across that horrifying drop and watched with pleasure as his feet slid off the far edge and his body fell down.

Jerry Remick was hanging by his fingers from icy soil, above a drop that fell for a thousand metres to a bed of sharp rocks.

He was trying to pull himself up, but his fingers were slipping.

'*Now* call on your virtue!' Zweig bawled as he held up the Tuaoi Stone. 'See how far virtue gets you!'

'Jerry!' someone called. '*Jerry!*'

Looking up, Zweig saw Ingrid.

She hadn't materialized magically out of nowhere like Jerry, but had obviously come down the normal route from St Germain's hideaway, using the very dangerous path that curved around the cliff face. She was struggling down through the snow, clinging fearfully to the rocks, obviously trying to keep away from the sheer drop on one side as she hurried towards that awful chasm where Jerry was struggling.

Zweig grinned and lowered his gaze. He saw Jerry's fingers slipping. Jerry was staring at him, his eyes bright and wild, desperately trying to pull himself up but gradually weakening.

Zweig stepped towards him, stopped just by his hands, glanced only briefly at that dizzying drop below him, then grinned and raised his left foot to press it down on his fingers.

'*Auf Wiedersehen*, my young friend,' he said.

Ingrid slithered to a halt at the other side of the gap, gasped with horror when she saw the fearsome drop beneath Jerry, then leaned over, ignoring the howling wind, and screamed, 'Don't let him do this to you, Jerry! I love you! I *need* you!'

Zweig raised his foot slightly, tormenting her one last time, then slowly pressed his boot on Jerry's right hand.

The pitiful fool cried out. His free hand slipped off the edge. He was hanging over a thousand-metre drop, his legs kicking, while Zweig slowly crushed the fingers of his right hand with his steel-studded boot.

'Think of *me*, Jerry!' Ingrid screamed. 'I *love* you! Have *faith*!'

Zweig laughed and raised his foot. He looked down at bleeding fingers. He stopped laughing when he saw the blazing faith in Jerry's eyes, saw his panic giving way to determination and a magical strength. Jerry swung his dangling hand, grabbing the edge close to his other hand, gritted his teeth and started pulling himself up as the power flowed back into him.

'*Mein Gott!*' Zweig exclaimed, disbelieving, suddenly panicking, his shoulders slumping as the power was drained out of him and flowed into Jerry. Stunned, he stepped forward, intent on stepping on Jerry's hands again, but Jerry's eyes were blazing at him, filled with faith and the power of love, and Zweig was picked up and thrown back like a rag doll to land on the snow-covered rocks.

Stars exploded before his eyes, sharp pains darted through his bones, and he cried out and rolled away from the edge. He still had the Tuaoi Stone which was now red-hot and he screamed and let it fall as he climbed to his feet. He glanced back at Jerry, saw him clambering over the edge, was riveted by the brilliance of his gaze and then felt himself breaking down.

'No!' he bellowed like a wild beast, his voice hideously distorted, that single word echoing around the mountains to come back and mock him. '*No! No! No!*'

Then it all ended for him. His anguish told him that was so. He was picked up again and flung against the face of the cliff, was crushed by exploding earth and sucked into a whirlwind. More of the cliff exploded in smoke and flames, spewing rocks and earth and snow, and he was scalded by hot, geysering water as he fell down again. A section of mountain collapsed upon him, crushing him, choking him, filling his mouth and nostrils with hot ash and scorched stones and dirt. He heard roaring, smelt smoke, was being roasted in hell's fires, but managed to look out – to catch a last glimpse of Earth – and saw Jerry picking up the Tuaoi Stone with a cry of triumph.

Jerry held the Tuaoi Stone above his head and let the sunlight flash off it.

Ingrid's laughter was loud and clear.

Zweig was in hell. He was buried in snow and rocks. He was forced to watch Jerry wave the Tuaoi Stone to and fro, then abruptly disappear as, using the Tuaoi Stone's power, he closed the gap in the path and made his way back to Ingrid.

Zweig heard them both laughing. They were obviously embracing. Then he heard their laughter receding as they walked away from him, obviously thinking him dead.

But he wasn't dead. No, he would never die. He would let his enduring hatred sustain him and return him to strength.

He got out somehow. It took a long time, but he

made it. He pushed the rubble aside, managed to roll onto his belly, then struggled out of what should have been his grave, away from the melting snow and soaked ash and pulverized rock. He looked down at his scorched, torn clothing, at his black, blistered arms, then gritted his teeth against the pain and crawled forward on hands and knees.

He commenced his ungainly crawl back up the mountain, refusing to die.

CHAPTER FORTY-EIGHT

In a daze of disbelief, feeling drained yet exhilarated, Jerry let Ingrid lead him up the treacherous mountain path and back into St Germain's great hall beneath the steel-plated, open dome. He held the Tuaoi Stone in one hand, Ingrid's fingers in the other, and he entered in the glow of her love and his own renewed confidence.

He now believed in himself, in the love that joined him to Ingrid, and knew that as long as he lived he would never forget this day. At last he knew that existence was an infinite mystery, and that love, which could not be its root, could at least give it meaning.

He also knew that the material world was no more than a blindfold, a necessary reduction of a view that could encompass the universe. Everything and anything was possible, needing only the courage of one's convictions, an absolute faith . . . a kind of love, after all.

Yet what he saw, when he entered the great hall, almost made him lose faith again.

St Germain, or Faust, was ageing with dramatic speed. He was gasping desperately for breath, trembling like an epileptic, and leaning on Mephistopheles for support, like an old man with crutches.

When he saw the crystal pyramid in Jerry's hand, he openly wept.

'It is over,' he gasped, his voice breaking. 'At last we are freed!'

Mephistopheles held him as he lurched forward, pulled him back, lent him support, then half walked, half dragged him across the floor and laid him down on the stone bed upon which Jerry had first awakened in this strange place.

St Germain lay there expectantly, breathing harshly, licking parched lips, staring up at the great, steel-plated dome as it closed up again, shutting out the vast sky.

Mephistopheles said nothing, but offered Jerry a sad smile, then took the Tuaoi Stone from him and put it back on the pedestal where it belonged. He then took Jerry's hand and placed it gently on the crystal pyramid, smiled encouragingly and looked down at St Germain, who was obviously dying.

'Who art thou?' St Germain, the decaying Faust, asked of Mephistopheles.

'Part of that power, not understood,' Mephistopheles replied, still pressing Jerry's hand onto the Tuaoi Stone, 'which always wills the Bad, and always works the Good.'

Recognizing those enigmatic words from Goethe's *Prologue to Heaven*, and remembering that Goethe was also a member of the secret society, Jerry looked down as Mephistopheles released his firm grip, then quickly, almost in panic, removed his own hand from the Tuaoi Stone.

He had no sooner done this than a faint, unearthly light emanated from the crystal pyramid, soon became a brilliant, pulsating radiance, then exploded into fiery striations that wavered and dazzled.

Suddenly frightened, Jerry hurried back to Ingrid and took hold of her hand. She smiled nervously at him, then looked up, thus making him do the same, as an odd but strangely familiar sound increased in volume.

It was a bass humming sound, an infrasound, almost physical, and as it filled the chilling silence, making the very air vibrate, Jerry saw the steel plates of the great dome opening up again. They grew further apart, large triangles glinting dully, forming a gigantic, majestic, flower-shaped frame for blue sky and boiling clouds.

The clouds seemed to be unnatural, gathering together as if alive, low enough to cast their shadows on the snow around the moving steel plates. Then the plates disappeared, leaving nothing but that great hole, and at that precise moment, as the infrasound cut out, a higher sound, a sort of unearthly buzzing, came from the Tuaoi Stone.

Glancing at the crystal pyramid, Jerry saw that it had become covered in that strange, unearthly light and was shaking violently, at great speed, as it gave off its piercing sound. He looked at the stone base, saw Mephistopheles kneeling there, tenderly holding the hand of the dying Faust, St Germain, as both of them appeared to dissolve in the spreading white light.

'It is done!' Faust croaked with his dying breath. 'We are finally released!'

'Yes!' Mephistopheles replied. 'We have no more to fear. It is ending right –'

His last words were drowned out by a fierce crackling and snapping as a phosphorescent stream of energy shot up from the Tuaoi Stone's tip in a wavering, vertical line and then exploded in all directions through the clouds, like bolts of unnaturally coloured lightning. The clouds glowed red and yellow, turned to swirling black smoke which, gaining speed, became a whirlpool viewed upside down. The spinning vortex revealed the stars, sucked the streaming darkness in, disappeared to let the stars pour through the hole like a deluge of diamonds.

Jerry's fear dissipated, was transcended by awe, but he tugged Ingrid very close to him as he stared all around him. The cavern walls had disappeared. He saw only the streaming stars. Close by, he saw Mephistopheles still kneeling by the stone bed, holding the hand of the spectre that had once been Faust. Both figures had become unreal, were dissolving in white light, their Tibetan robes melting like honey being poured from a pot, a web of veins and bones clearly visible through the gauze of their shrinking flesh.

The light seemed to be eating at them, burning through them, erasing them, and then it became too bright to face, forcing Jerry to turn away. He saw Ingrid's eyes close up, very big, smooth as mirrors, and was drawn into them – into a sky filled with huge moons and more brilliant stars.

'Have no fear,' he heard Mephistopheles say. 'What you see will not harm you. Let your love be your . . .'

But the voice faded away – or perhaps had never been – and he felt himself falling through a silence filling up with approaching noise. The great moons turned inside out, the stars bled through one another, the darkness rushed at him and away in the same dazzling instant. Then noise: an explosion, a cataclysmic bellowing, the rending of the fabric of time and space, the universe and what lay beyond it folding back on itself. He saw Ingrid and himself, their reflections growing larger, rushing at him, at her, and passing through them and repeating that endlessly.

He was here and she was there. She was here and he was there. He joined her and became her, looking out through her eyes, and saw the light of the empyrean cascading in silvery splendour. He travelled through the empyrean, through the light of the highest heaven, and was her and himself at the same time – male and female, sol and luna, sulphur and mercury – the secret fire of alchemical transformation, the very seed of existence. That fire came from the sacred stone, the crystal tip of a burning pyramid, and its phosphorescent stream of luminous energy rose on high from the depths, joining the stone to the ether, the Earth to the Cosmos.

He felt himself as her in flight, his being curving to meet itself, transcending time and space and experiencing all on the instant: the past, the future, the multiplying dreams of the present, with Zweig dying and living and dying again, while a helicopter, trying to flee the mountains, kept circling endlessly.

Was that Hans and Elena? Was that Hans *or* Elena? They were looking down, aghast, at the mountain peaks and what was happening to them. Then they were swept away, in fire and smoke, streaming light, and he, as she, saw St Germain in Faust's final dissolving.

His skin was melting off the bone, the bone crumbling to dust, then Mephistopheles, holding a handful of dust, bowed lower and wept. His tears turned to blood, his skin flowed like melting wax, and with a sigh that was like a rushing wind he disappeared in a shimmering light.

That light exploded into a fountain that geysered towards the heavens, fanning out to form great wavering loops and spirals, then a web of crisscrossing bright lines that spread out through the cosmos. The joining lines formed great triangles which then multiplied endlessly, each triangle intersecting another to form more of itself, this process repeating itself countless times, until time itself ended.

The triangles webbed the cosmos with mathematical precision, framed the stars and spinning moons in countless pockets where time had no meaning.

He and she as one saw it, were part of it, streaking through it, and were engulfed when the cosmos turned itself inside out and swept them away in a wave of light filled with thunder and crackling. The light soared up and narrowed, became a majestic pyramid, a window to other pyramidal cities stretching across a younger earth under alien stars. Then a sudden rush of time, aeons racing by on the instant, fire and flood sweeping away the mighty cities to leave grim desolation. The smoke swirled and disappeared, the great waves covered the crumbling ruins, then the water was soaked into the earth and the years brought the dust back.

That dust obscured all, obliterated time and space, moved on to show another mighty pyramid on the great plain of Giza, its crystal tip reflecting the sunlight like a lamp flashing on and off.

Then he as she saw them — in the gloomy chambers of the Great Pyramid — that roll call of the greatest adepts, the just men, the pure at heart, all resurrected here where time and space had no meaning, where the centuries bled into one another and became the same moment. Yes, he as she saw them, the last of the just: Pythagoras wrestling with his soul and the infinite mysteries of numbers; Plato helping to lay down the philosophical foundations of Western culture; Jesus Christ being prepared for his noble, anguished calling; Merlin learning the Secret Knowledge to become the prophet of the Holy Grail — and all the others, great and small, known and unknown, who had given of themselves throughout the ages to better mankind ... until the dawn of their corruption, first Paracelsus, then Faust, creating the *homunculus* which became Mephistopheles, the three of them doomed to wander the earth in many disguises.

He and she as one saw them, here and now, then and there, as they saw the crystal tip of the Great Pyramid coming brightly to life, picking them up and sweeping them away through other pathways of time and space.

They were catapaulted, somersaulting, through the vaults of their own minds, across the curved face of the cosmos, and saw exploding galaxies, dying suns, alien worlds, great spacecraft and glowing discs traversing vast silence, heard the voices of history all around where the silence collapsed.

They travelled out and returned, back to time's constant future, past Faust and Mephistopheles, Zweig and Hans and Elena, past a helicopter endlessly circling a forbidden mountain – travelled back through their joined mind and became two again, separating, returning to mortality and the great hall's exploding.

God! Ingrid thought. *What –?*

The fire of life spewed from the Tuaoi Stone, reached the heavens and beyond, making time and space one, joining the past to the future, then spat out its many imprisoned souls by aborting itself. Thus reprieved, it exploded, belching fire and smoke, bellowing, smashing through the rocks, through the mighty walls of the mountain, and obscuring the brilliant light of day in the dust of its dying.

No more, Jerry thought.

No more –

Struggling with the controls of the bucking helicopter, Hans thought he was losing his senses. He had been trying for more than an hour to fly away from the mountain, but the gyro-controls had stopped working, the sky was changing all the time, and no matter which direction he flew in, he always returned to the same place – directly above the great hole into which Zweig had dropped.

Now his fuel was running out, Elena was growing hysterical, and when he looked down, having no choice but to land, he finally did lose his senses.

'Oh, Christ!' Elena wailed, grabbing his elbow. 'What the hell's *that*? Oh, my God, it's –!'

Hans started counting. It was all he could do. He had lost the power of speech and numbers were all he could think of as his whole world turned inside out. He was counting the seconds off, the final seconds of his life, and the numbers were a magical incantation which he thought might protect him.

Perhaps he didn't really speak them. Perhaps he only thought them. He only knew that the numbers were the last words to pass through his mind as Elena grabbed his elbow, the helicopter turned over, and that extraordinary stream of fire, that phosphorescent, weaving thread, shot up from the inky depths of that black hole in the snow and exploded through the clouds all around him as the mountain peaks rushed at him.

Elena shrieked. Swathes of snow filled his vision. He saw the spinning hole erupting, the mountain face spewing rocks, then another face, Zweig's face – yes, Zweig! staring at him – Zweig badly burned and battered, on hands and knees like a mountain goat, trying to crawl up a path in the face of the cliff.

Zweig glanced over his shoulder as the helicopter fell upon him. He started screaming in protest, waved his hands in wild semaphore, seemed to stare directly up at Hans and Elena – but Hans refused to believe it, not wanting to die this way, so kept counting and counting, through his death, through eternity, hearing Elena's final scream, as he would hear it forever, before exploding with her and Zweig and the helicopter, finally finding the release he had always wanted from the hell of his life on earth.

Zweig looked up in a daze. He couldn't believe what was happening to him. He had burned in the fires of hell and escaped – and now *this* had to happen. He turned around on the mountain track, his body drawn to the helicopter, forgetting that his own machines had been blown to hell and now responding instinctively to a sound that suggested escape.

Then he saw *that* helicopter, *those* faces staring

down, thought, *No! It can't be!* and then heard himself screaming and waved his hands in panic and finally pressed his fingers over his eyes, seeing darkness, his existence, the futility of it all; then started counting off the seconds, each one an eternity, giving him time to wonder how that helicopter could crash upon him; also time to think of numbers that kept repeating themselves – one second, two seconds, three seconds, four – and then he looked up again, saw that nothing had changed, once more threw his hands across his disbelieving eyes, heard the roaring, felt the weight, was crushed and consumed at once, then dissolved back into the fires of hell with Elena and Hans.

And died at that moment.

CHAPTER FORTY-NINE

Jerry opened his eyes to the brilliant Himalayan sky, tried to separate himself from the clinging strands of his vivid dream, then in coughing the dust from his throat knew the dream had been real.

Sitting upright very carefully, fully expecting to find broken bones, he first saw that Ingrid had been lying close beside him, then looked around him in amazement at the shattered remains of what had been the great hall. The walls were pulverized rubble and the dust from their remains still drifted around them, falling upon them like shrouds.

Ingrid groaned softly, then opened her eyes, wiped dust from her face, from her clothes, and gazed dreamily at him. She studied him for some time, as if wondering if he was real, then smiled in a languorous, sensual manner and reached up to him.

'Are you all right?'

'Yeah,' he said. 'I'm okay. I feel strange, but I'm okay.'

He touched her forehead with his fingers, wiped some dust away, then slid his hands under her shoulders and helped her sit upright. She nipped his neck with her teeth, sucked his skin, hugged him tightly, then pushed herself slightly away from him and looked all around her.

'My God,' she said, 'what –?'

'It's all gone,' he interjected, anticipating her question. '*All* of it – all gone. St Germain and Mephisto and the Tuaoi Stone and even this monastery – or whatever it was – all of it, all gone. *We* were picked up and sucked into something and then spewed out again. We've been released – just like they have – and now it's time to go home.'

Ingrid looked beyond the ruined walls, at the snow-capped peaks and gorges, at the barren plains of the distant Tibetan Plateau and the green fields of India much further on. They were sitting on the roof of the world – and that world seemed too far away.

'Do you think we can make it back down?' she asked him, her furrowed brow showing grave doubts.

'Yes,' he said, 'I think we can. Mephisto said it was impossible to get up here, but quite easy to get back down. He said that it was part of their way – and their way is our way. So come on. Let's get going.'

'Do you love me?'

'Goddamnit, haven't I proved it?'

She smiled. 'Oh, my hero!'

He stood up first, helped her to her feet, looked around him at the shattered floor, the ruined, dust-shrouded walls, saw a gaping black hole where the Tuaoi Stone's pedestal had stood, a larger, rectangular black hole where the stone bed had been, then found himself shrugging and grinning disbelievingly as he tugged at Ingrid's hand and said, 'Well, it was certainly a real adventure. Let's just say it was that.'

They went across the dusty rubble of the pulverized stone-slab floor, then through a gap in the broken remains of a wall. He realized that he had changed forever, that he understood himself, and that his world, which had once seemed so familiar and attractive, would never again have the same appeal.

Yes, he had changed, had seen the world beyond this one, and had learned that most earthly aspirations were no more substantial than the dust of Faust's remains in Mephistopheles' hand. What was left was his love for

Ingrid, his mind and heart, her love for him, and he knew that when these were combined he could transcend himself.

The just men were out there somewhere. They were scattered like the wind. They were here — and there also — in the past and the future, and they studied the Secret Knowledge, which was the study of the self, and got on in their quiet way with their lives, letting the world look after itself, as was intended by nature.

He, too, could be a just man and live a noble life. He, too, could go into exile and inhabit his secret self.

He led Ingrid out of the ruins, onto the path that ran down the mountain, gazed over the pirouetting depths and then looked straight ahead. A Sherpa's mule, forlorn, unattended, was standing right there in front of him.

'You think St Germain arranged it?' Ingrid asked him.

'Yes,' he said. 'Probably.'

She brushed the auburn hair from her eyes, hazel eyes, clear and loving, winked at him and smiled in a mischievous manner, then took hold of the dangling ropes and swung herself up onto the saddle.

'Hey, kid,' she said, imitating Lauren Bacall, 'do you know how to whistle?'

Irresistibly amused, washed clean by his love for her, he placed a couple of fingers against his lips and whistled inexpertly.

The mule, not offended at all, moved forward and stopped right in front of him, its rheumy eyes fixed upon him.

'Get on behind me,' Ingrid said.

'I can't,' he replied. 'I'm a New York City boy, born and bred, and I've never had any pets.'

She stared at him in disgust, shook her head from side to side, then reached down to him, told him to grip her arm, and, when he had done so, expertly pulled him up behind her.

'Fasten your safety belt,' she said. 'We're both in for a bumpy ride.'

He grinned and embraced her, holding her as his safety belt, then she kicked at the mule, made some dumb clucking sounds, and the mule turned around and started down the mountain path, carrying them both back to a future they could not yet imagine.

'I think I'm going to be sick,' Jerry said. 'I want transport with wheels.'

She replied by letting her laughter peal like bells through the crisp air, across the snow-capped peaks and shadowed gorges, to the ends of the earth.

'You're some kind of man,' she said.

POSTSCRIPT
Associated Press Release, 20 August 1988

'The major international academic controversy of a few months ago, which erupted when Gerald Remick, notorious son of the highly respected Martin Sydney Remick (b. 1925, d. 1986) – D.Litt., LL.D., F.S.A., honorary A.R.I.B.A., noted archeologist, writer and, prior to his untimely death, Professor of Archaeological Studies in the Antiquities Department of Harvard University – published his inflammatory book, *The Secret Language of Numbers*, in which, among other wild assertions, he claimed to have proved that Shakespeare was in fact Christopher Marlowe and that the latter, in the company of many other great historical figures, was a member of a secret "magical" society, has now reached its rather piquant finale.

'Already expelled from Harvard for what the University officially described as his "adamant refusal to conform to traditional norms of behavior", the disgraced son of the famous academic has now outraged the academic establishment – not only because of what one learned critic has insisted was the "grossly malicious and unfounded historical distortions" contained in his book on the so-called "secret" lives of some of history's greatest men, but also because his scandalous assertions about Shakespeare have been made by one not academically qualified in this particularly complex field.

'The controversial Hack of Academe recently fled the United States with his new wife, one Ingrid Zweig, daughter of the equally eccentric and astoundingly wealthy international businessman and Neo-Nazi, Wilhelm Zweig, whose whereabouts have been unknown for the past eighteen months.

'The disgraced Gerald aka "Jerry the Drop-Out" Remick and his German wife are reported to be living presently with their child on an island in the South Pacific, privately owned by the father of the latter. According to unverified reports, the couple are living very simply, like the natives, while involving themselves in various ecological and spiritual experiments which they hope will benefit not only the island's inhabitants but also, at some future date, the whole of mankind.

'The distinguished mother of Mr Remick was unavailable for comment.'